The Rusted Tea Box

A Novel

Estee Perchik Sery

The Rusted Tea Box
First Edition
Copyright © 2025 Estee Perchik Sery
San Diego, CA

All rights reserved. No part of this book may be used or reproduced in any manner whatsoever, including Internet usage, without written permission from the author.

This story is a work of fiction. References to real people, events, establishments, organizations, or locales are intended only to provide a sense of authenticity and are used fictitiously. All other characters, and all incidents and dialogue, are drawn from the author's imagination and are not to be used as real.

ISBN: 978-1-958105-12-2
Library of Congress Number: 2024920668

Photography of Ellen Silver Coppola by Leetal Elmaleh

CYK Publishing

Cover design by CC Covers

Book formatted by Christa Yelich-Koth
www.CYKauthor.com

Praise for The Rusted Tea Box

"The Rusted Tea Box is an epic story spanning nearly seventy-five years, a moving and sensitive portrait of a family torn apart by war but reunited by fate. Highly recommended."-- Tammy Greenwood, author of **The Still Point, Keeping Lucy,** and **Two Rivers**

"Estee Perchik Sery tells the story of two sisters who escape the Holocaust. The author writes with compassion about their sister-bond and their journey to freedom in a voice I find deeply moving." -- Mai-Lon Gittlesohn, poet, author of **Chop Suey and Apple Pie**

Readers like you:
"I was on the edge of my seat!" - ERIN (San Diego)

"Estee Perchik Sery masterfully blends rich character development with evocative storytelling to craft a heart wrenching tale of resilience, survival, and discovery. The intricate clues woven through the fabric of the story build up to a glorious finale." - ANNETTE (Jerusalem)

"A must read. The Rusted Tea Box is a unique historical fiction [...] I felt the pain as well as the resilience of the two sisters, and was intrigued to follow the twists and turns they have endured throughout their lives. The novel felt authentic, well researched, yet creative." - YAEL (Johannesburg)

"Marvelous. This book is an exhilarating and engaging experience. Sery's unique narrative approach, shifting between the first-person perspectives of various characters, immerses the reader in their inner thoughts. The vivid emotions, reflections, and sensations leap off the pages. With numerous unexpected twists and turns, it also skillfully resolves the lingering questions in your mind."
- EYAL (Los Angeles)

Books by Estee Perchik Sery

The Scent of Heat
The Rusted Tea Box

To Gil and Natalie, I love you to the moon and back

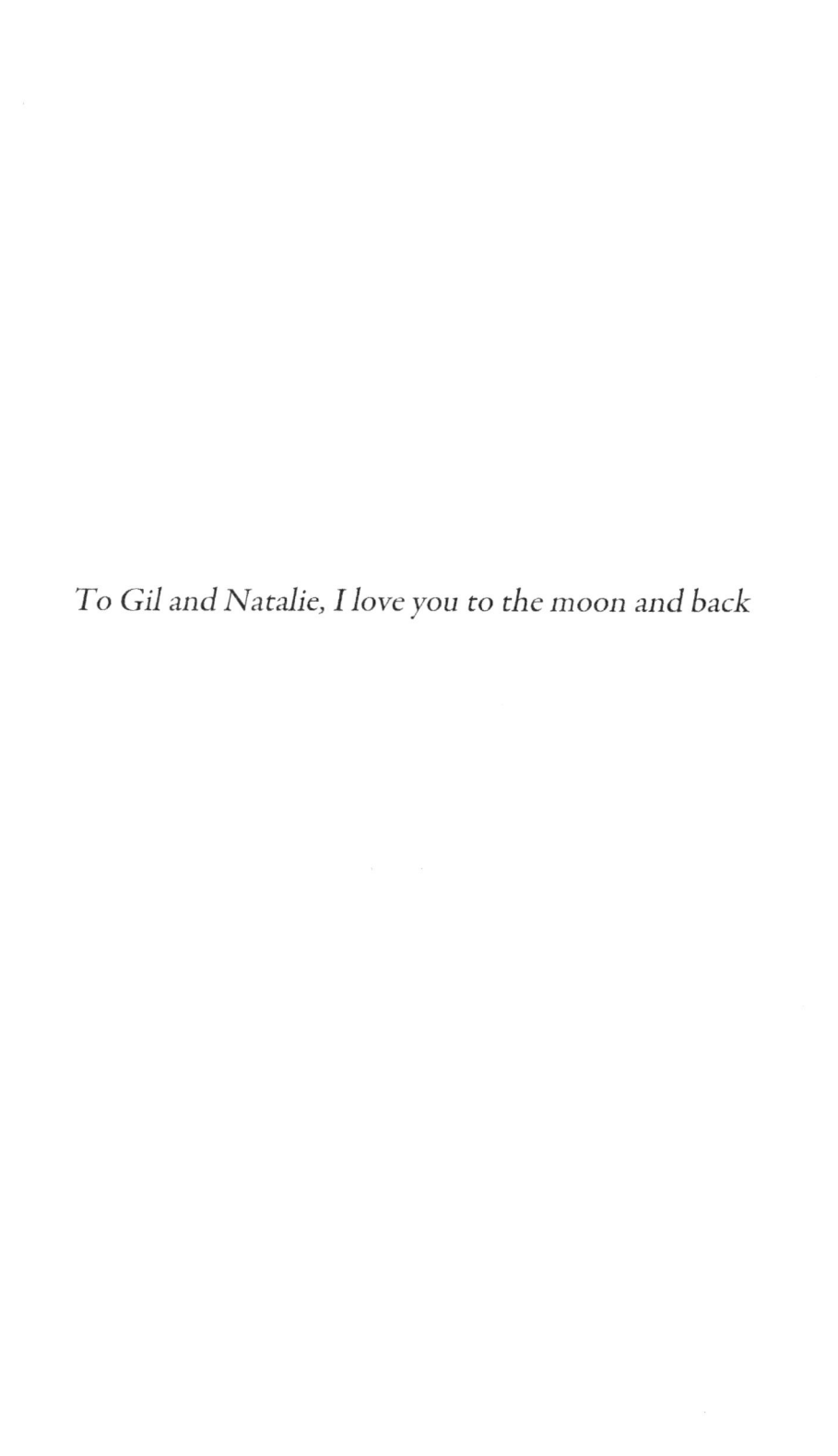

Part One

Chapter One

Vienna, November 1938

ELSIE

MY eyes popped open. Night sounds always scared me: the house creaking, a dog barking far away, a horse and wagon passing on the street below, or men yelling curses. The slightest sound woke me up, but I usually found and hugged my Waldorf doll and dozed off again.

But tonight's noises were different. A scream. Then another. "Mahme," I whispered into my pillow. I started shaking. It was so dark. "Mahme?" I turned on my side, pulling my knees up to my chest, stretching my nightdress down to my feet and pressing my fists to my mouth. I was a big girl, almost seven.

I couldn't call my mother in the middle of the night. But who was screaming outside in the street? Now I could hear men's voices, women's voices, more screams. People talking so loud, yelling at each other. Fighting.

I looked over at my little sister, five-year-old Raizele. When I had a bad dream, I'd usually crawl into her bed, but it was so dark in our bedroom now that I could barely make out the shape of her body. She was sitting up in her bed, rubbing her eyes.

"Raizele?" I whispered, my throat dry. I could feel my heart going boom-boom fast. "Was ist das?" I asked, as if she would know. When I heard another sharp scream, I sat up too. More loud and angry voices came from outside my window, up on the second floor of our apartment. So close. It must have been even closer to my grandparents, Bubbe and Zayde, who lived below us, on the first floor. "Mahme," I called my mother softly, afraid to wake her, but wanting her with us. Raizele started crying, so I got out of bed to get into hers and hug her, which I often did. She looked so scared. I was the big sister; I had to look out for her. Mahme always told me this, and I didn't mind; it made me feel responsible. I was older. Two years and two days older. The floor was ice cold under my feet, so I threw myself into her warm bed. We clung together and listened. When she started to ask me a question, I put my finger on her mouth to keep her quiet. My heart banged all the way into my ears; boom-boom, boom-boom. Somebody else screamed. There was so much noise outside. I was scared the angry people would bash the wall and come in.

Suddenly over the noises I heard a loud crack. What was

that? Was it the window by my bed? Was it glass breaking?

"Mahme," I yelled now. I didn't want my window to break. I didn't want glass pieces all over my bed. I remembered the wet and slippery water glass I once accidentally dropped on the kitchen floor, remembered watching it break into a million pieces. Mahme had picked me up, taken me out to the living room, and gone back to clean up the mess I'd made. She didn't yell at me, even though I felt so bad about what I did. She never yelled. But she didn't like us to wake her up in the middle of the night. Another time, Raizele had wet her bed and started crying. When I'd gone to tell Mahme, she became irritable and angry, so I'd taken my little sister into my bed. In the morning, when changing Raizele's sheet, Mahme said she was sorry she'd gotten mad at me, but she was a deep sleeper and got a fright when woken up suddenly in the middle of the night.

I looked across the room to the window by my bed, but the curtains didn't move. Good. My window was not broken. Suddenly I smelled smoke. What was burning? It was disgusting and made me gag, a bitter taste coming to my mouth. Where was Mahme? Deep sleeping? And Tahte? Didn't they hear the screaming? Raizele and I were shivering, and when I looked at her, her eyes and nose were runny, and she rubbed the snot across her face until some of her blond curls got stuck together. She was breathing quickly, gulping air. Poor Raizele.

"Mahme!" I yelled louder. I didn't care if she got mad; Raizele needed Mahme.

My mother burst through the door. She stood there for a moment, her shape all dark with blinding light behind her, and then she plopped on Raizele's bed, scooping me and my sister towards her. I clung to her shivering body. Was she scared too? I'd never seen Mahme shivering like that. Never. She smelled funny too. I didn't like the smell that came from her mouth, but down her neck she smelled of my father, my Tahte's cologne. I was so glad she was here.

"Was passiert jetzt, Mahme?" I asked her. *What's happening?* Mahme started rocking my sister and me and humming a lullaby. When I looked up, I noticed her lips and her chin trembling, but her beautiful deep blue eyes, like Raizele's, were closed. Her long blond curls were a mess. The screaming outside continued and I heard more glass breaking. Why were people breaking windows?

Suddenly I heard our creaky front door open. I sat up straight. Were the screaming people coming into our apartment? I clung to Mahme. Then I had a thought. "Is Tahte going outside?" I asked her. Mahme stopped humming. She was listening too. I heard quick footsteps and my grandparents' voices; Bubbe and Zayde spoke in loud whispers. I couldn't make out what they were saying. What were Bubbe and Zayde doing here in the middle of the night? I stared at Mahme; she didn't move. Then I heard something being dragged across the room. Oy, it was scraping the wooden floor, something Mahme never allowed us to do. Was Tahte moving furniture around? Why?

"Mahme..." I started, looking at her face.

She got up suddenly and stood like she wasn't sure what to do. Then she turned and ran out of the room. "Mahme..." I called after her, but she was gone.

As I curled up with Raizele again, I heard something

thrown at our window.

"Mahme!" I screamed. "Tahte!" I was so scared; my chest was going up and down fast, and it felt like I couldn't catch my breath. They both came in running, followed by Zayde.

"Sha, Shtil," Mahme whispered, as if the people outside could hear me scream with all the noise they were making. "Be still, stay in bed, it's safe, we have double-pane glass windows; they won't break." Mahme sounded brave and sure; I stared at her in surprise. Wasn't she scared anymore, or was she pretending? Like when we played and I went "Boo!" Mahme pretended to be scared. Now maybe she was the opposite, pretending not to be scared.

"Must be some drunkards," Zayde said. He always used fancy words, even if I didn't know what they meant, but his voice was shaky, so I knew it was something bad.

"The police will take care of them," Tahte added, nodding.

"Go back to sleep, moje dwie perly." Mahme sometimes called us "my two pearls" in Polish. It was the only Polish Raizele and I knew, and I was proud I understood another language. I loved being called a pearl; shiny, bright, and smooth. Mahme left our room after kissing us both on our heads. Tahte and Zayde followed her.

I held on to my little sister and closed my eyes tightly, but I couldn't stop shivering. My chest felt like a mouse was running inside, trying to escape. Like the little white mouse my kindergarten teacher had in a small cage. I always felt so sorry for him. Other children made fun of him and tried to feed him, but he eventually ran away. I kept my eyes closed and pushed my face into Raizele's hair—her curls smelled so good, they tickled my nose—and I tried to breathe slower, but the noise outside didn't stop. Why weren't the police arresting those drunkards? What was burning? I heard no sirens from fire trucks or ambulances, and I was scared to get close to the window and peek outside. I lay there, curled up under my sister's feather duvet, my eyes shut tightly, my face hot, yet my feet as cold as ice. Shivering. And listening.

Mahme, Tahte, and Zayde were all back in the living room. I thought I could hear someone crying. I was surprised. Was it Bubbe? I'd never seen a grown-up cry, but I could hear them all talking at once, Tahte's voice higher than usual. I imagined Mahme and Zayde sitting on the red velvet sofa by the dark low table. Was Bubbe sitting in her favorite red velvet armchair? Tahte liked sitting on the piano bench, leaning his back on the baby grand, where I usually sat with Fräulein Bauer, my piano teacher. Above the piano was a beautiful painting of the frozen Danube with tiny people skating. I did my best to concentrate on how we skated last year, trying to ignore the smell of burning that made me swallow hard what wanted to come up. I needed a drink of water but was scared to move out of Raizele's bed.

I woke up in Raizele's bed. At first, I wasn't sure whether I'd had a bad dream and had crawled in with her. Then I smelled smoke and remembered. Raizele was sleeping, all curled up with her back to me, facing the wall, so I slowly moved out of her bed and went out of our room. I noticed that the large, big, red armchair was by the front door, blocking it. I wondered why. Mahme and Tahte were sitting at the kitchen table, drinking coffee. I wasn't allowed to drink it. I didn't care. Zayde gave me a taste once. It was bitter, and I swore I would never ever drink coffee in my life. I didn't know how they could drink it; I wished I could have hot chocolate just then.

"Guten Morgen," I said, looking from one to the other. Mahme stared into her cup as if she had lost something inside, and Tahte picked me up and put me on his lap, which he didn't do often.

"Guten Morgen, mein Liebling," Tahte said, kissing my cheek. His mustache tickled me. "We're staying home today. No school for you."

"Warum?" I asked. *Why?* Then I remembered. "Didn't the police arrest all the drunk people? It is quiet now, nobody is screaming."

"Richtig," Tahte said, agreeing with me. "I don't know who was arrested, but the streets are still full of broken glass. We can't walk on the sidewalk."

"Aber, Tahte," I said, "I *have* to go to school. If I miss it, my teacher will be angry with me." My teacher wasn't as nice to me this year as she was last year, in first grade. I wasn't called on when I knew the answer and raised my forearm, elbow on my desk and forefinger up, just as we'd been taught. I loved knowing the answer and was proud to say it, but I felt that the teacher didn't like me anymore and didn't want to hear me, because she kept ignoring me. I thought I'd done something wrong, but I didn't know what and felt sad and hurt. Wouldn't she punish me if I didn't come to school?

"Not today, mein Kind," Mahme said. "Come, I'll make you something to eat." She slowly got up and wiped her face. I hadn't known she'd been crying. Mahme crying? I felt scared.

Tahte put me down, stood up, then placed me on his chair. It was nice and warm. I heard him go to the front door. He moved the red armchair, Bubbe's favorite, back to its place, dragging it across the floor. I stared at Mahme, but she said nothing to him; I was surprised. She didn't even look angry; she was just pale. Why didn't she mention her scratched parquet floor? How come she didn't care anymore? Did we have no more rules at home or at school? I had so many questions.

We stayed home that day, and the next. I was scared, but Raizele and I had fun playing together. I liked playing school best. I was always the teacher, and Raizele had to do what I told her. Sometimes she'd say: "Don't tell me what to do, you're not my mother." But I was her teacher. She had to do whatever I told her, like we did at school. But she was too little and hadn't been to school yet. So, I'd say: "Alright, you be the teacher now." She loved that.

On Saturday, when I got ready to go with Tahte to synagogue, Mahme helped me put on my white-and-pink Shabbat dress, my long white socks, and my shiny, black patent-leather shoes. As I was waiting in the entrance hall, wanting to put on my white rabbit-fur coat because it was November and cold—the soft fur I liked patting because it was so soft, like a whole pack of rabbits surrounded me—there was a loud knock on the front door.

Tahte unlocked it, and in stormed Zayde in a huff and a puff, speaking to Mahme and Tahte rapidly in Polish. I didn't understand Polish but knew that my family spoke it because they came from a place called Poland. We spoke German, we were Austrian, as my teacher was always reminding us. Sometimes we spoke Yiddish, but only at home; I never spoke Yiddish to anyone outside our home.

I studied their faces. Zayde's was red with anger, his blue eyes narrow, his forehead squeezed, his lips pressed thin when he wasn't talking. Mahme's face was white with fear, her eyes bulging, and Tahte was pacing and waving his arms and mumbling something I didn't understand, his hair wild. Zayde interrupted him, almost yelling, making my heart race; Zayde had never yelled at Tahte before. I knew that something very bad must have happened. Raizele suddenly started crying and Mahme picked her up.

Tahte turned to me. "We can't go to shul, Elsie. The streets are dirty, and as I suspected, nobody has cleaned the broken glass yet."

"Still?" I asked, disappointed. Why hadn't anybody cleaned it for two whole days? I hated missing a Bar Mitzvah celebration at the synagogue, where the boy's family would throw candy at him after the ceremony. All the kids would then get on their hands and knees and crawl around collecting the wrapped candy from the floor. I especially liked the yellow lemony ones. It was so much fun. Couldn't we walk carefully around the broken glass?

But I couldn't ask all those questions. Well-brought-up girls didn't ask questions.

"We can't go, because we don't have a synagogue to go to," Zayde said in a funny scratchy voice. He glanced at Tahte and whispered, "Our synagogue was burned." But I heard him, even though Tahte gave him a serious look and said, "Shhhhh."

Zayde put both his hands on his head as if he was scared it would fall off, and sat down heavily on the piano stool. I'd never seen my grandfather like that before. He looked sad and old. Who had burned our synagogue? Why? Hadn't anybody called the fire trucks?

Tahte shook his head and started pacing again, glaring at Zayde and frowning as if he hadn't wanted him to say out loud what he'd just said.

We weren't going. I slammed my coat on the floor, ran to my room, kicked off my shoes, took off my socks and dress, and tossed them all on the floor. I flung myself on my bed and started hitting my pillow. Mahme came into the room, picked up my dress, and hung it up without saying a word to me.

Raizele stood by my bed and asked, "Why are you crying?"

"Because our synagogue got burned. Because we can't go and get candy anymore," I yelled. "Go away, Rose." I called her by her official name when I was angry.

Mahme looked at me, still saying nothing, and walked out.

"Want to play school?" my little sister asked. She knew it was my favorite game.

I was still mad, but I didn't want to lie on my bed any longer, so I got up and put on another dress, a plain one, and started playing with Raizele. It was her turn to start, but she let me be the teacher this time.

I didn't go to school on Monday either, although Mahme and Tahte left for work. Bubbe, looking a little pale, the kerchief crooked on her head, as if she had hurried to put it on, came to watch over me and Raizele. Zayde wasn't feeling well, Bubbe told us, so he didn't come upstairs.

Bubbe didn't sit on the thick navy carpet and play with us like Mahme always did. Instead, she sat quietly on her favorite armchair in the living room, wringing her hands and looking at her slippers, or maybe just staring at the carpet. I wasn't sure. Why was she moving her hands constantly? It made my stomach feel funny. She was whispering in Yiddish, her lips moving, her chin shaking. Was she praying? She looked small in the big chair, as if swallowed in.

"Shver tsu zayn a yid." *It's hard to be a Jew*, she murmured in Yiddish.

"What?" I asked. "Why, Bubbe?"

"I don't know, Elsie," Bubbe admitted. "My father used to say it all the time in Poland. A Jew always suffers."

I saw Raizele staring at her, her deep blue eyes wide and frightened. "Jew?" she asked. "Hard to be Jew?"

"What does it mean, 'to be a Jew'?" I asked, confused. "Why is it hard? We light candles on Friday night and go to shul on Saturday. It's not hard."

"They hate us," Bubbe muttered, straightening, and tightening her kerchief as if to protect her head. I wasn't sure if she was angry or frightened. I didn't like the way she looked and the way she talked, muttering. It scared me.

"They"? I didn't know who "they" were. Or why "they" hated us. What did we do to them? I sat on the carpet by Bubbe's feet, thinking if I knew any "they." I wondered if my teacher, who had never called on me, was a "they." I squeezed my forehead hard to think.

Chapter Two

Vienna, November 1938

ELSIE

EVERYTHING was so nice before. When my parents went to the opera, Mahme would put on a long white or silver dress, with her fur shawl on top. She wore her glittering pearls, pinning up her long blond curls and putting on lipstick. Sometimes she'd put some on my and Raizele's lips; we loved it and giggled, but I didn't like the taste. Tahte would part his wet hair in the middle and comb it to the sides, then smear something smelly and shiny in it. He'd comb his long, thick mustache that dropped down the sides of his mouth. Then he would spray himself with cologne. When he aimed the bottle at us, we'd run out yelling and giggling. Then we'd come back to say goodbye. With his round spectacles and a long coat over his white shirt and bow tie, he looked so handsome and smelled so good when he bent down to kiss my cheek good night.

When they went out dancing, Mahme wore special dancing shoes and a floral dress which came just below her knees and looked like a bell when she twirled. I couldn't wait to grow up and be just like her, although everyone said I had Tahte's coloring—auburn hair that was cut just below my ears, and hazel eyes.

Whenever our parents went out, Bubbe and Zayde would stay with us. My favorite thing to do with Bubbe was bake cookies, because I could use the cookie cutter. I loved pressing it into the soft dough, making stars and circles and moons. Bubbe would let me and Raizele pinch sugar and sprinkle it on the dough, but my sister would lick her fingers and not be able to sprinkle because they were wet. Bubbe and I used to laugh at her when she tried. Those golden cookies with a cup of hot tea were Zayde's favorite. Zayde was always serious. He loved reading. Newspapers, magazines, letters, but mainly books. He'd told me that back in Warsaw—that's the capital of Poland—he used to be a banker before he retired, and that they'd all moved to Vienna long before I was born. Zayde taught me to read Yiddish from right to left when I was almost five, even before I went to school and learned to read German.

Last winter, Tahte closed his dental clinic for a whole week. It was between Christmas and New Year's Day, and we had no school. Mahme took a week's vacation from the accounting office where she was a Buchhalterin—a *bookkeeper*.

It sounded like she was literally keeping books, but she explained to me that she worked with numbers and did calculations. It sounded very complicated. So, on our vacation, my parents took me and Raizele ice-skating on the frozen Danube. Raizele's long blond curls blew in the wind while she skated and held on to Mahme's hand, her cheeks red and her big, deep blue eyes sparkling with fear and delight. I held Tahte's hand, and we skated faster and faster, laughing. Tahte was my hero, our protector.

Now, nobody was laughing anymore, not since that awful night of shouting, burning, and window breaking. There was no more music, no more dancing, no more dressing up. Everybody was sad. The corners of my mother's mouth were constantly drooping, and so were her eyes. I noticed a new deep crease between her eyebrows, which made her look old and angry. I hated it. When I sat on her lap, I tried to erase the deep crease with my finger, but it kept coming back. Her beautiful eyes were constantly red now, as if she'd been crying all night.

I wasn't allowed to go to school, and Fräulein Bauer stopped coming on Tuesday afternoons for piano lessons. She'd been coming to our house every single Tuesday for the past two years. I loved her. Mahme had told me that she was sick. But was she really? I refused to sit at the baby grand alone. "If Fräulein Bauer isn't coming, I'm not playing," I said, going to my room with angry tears in my eyes. Mahme didn't force me. She seemed to give up easily these days.

"Can I go outside and play with the neighbors' children?" I asked Bubbe one day when Mahme was at work. I knew Mahme wouldn't allow me, but maybe Bubbe would.

"Nein, mein Kind. It's too cold" was her reply. And that was it. I was bored and angry. I missed school. How long would we be staying inside? Raizele cried a lot lately, and I found myself shaking at times for no reason at all.

The first day Mahme didn't go to work I was happy. I thought she would sit on the rug and play with us. She kept the shutters closed and the drapes drawn, and Raizele and I weren't allowed to even peek outside. It was awful. Once I tried to look outside, in between the shutters, just to see how high the snow really was, and Mahme snapped at me. I quickly moved away from the window. I hated staying in the stinking apartment all the time. Sometimes Mahme would let us cook with her. Raizele was in charge of washing the carrots and parsnips, and I had to peel them. It was hard work because the peeler wasn't sharp. Mahme peeled and cut the onions in half for the soup, then added the meat. I liked to be with Mahme and Raizele but still missed my friends. Were they also at home cooking with their mothers?

Mahme tried to keep us busy with dominoes and pick-up sticks, and at first it was nice. She had brought sheets of paper from her office before she stopped working, and we had colored pencils from school. She made up a game for us. It was a drawing game: We sat in a circle on the carpet, and each one had to draw an animal and hand it to the person on their right, who guessed what it was. I drew a dog and handed it to Mahme. She guessed correctly. Mahme drew a horse and handed it to Raizele, who also guessed correctly. Raizele drew two circles, a large one and a small one touching. The large circle had a long tail, and the smaller one had two ears and whiskers. She handed it to me.

"It's a cat," I announced.

"What is it now?" she asked. She took the paper back, erased the long tail and the whiskers, and drew a small circle where the tail was, and made the ears longer.

"It's a bunny," I said.

"Clever girl," Mahme said, but I wasn't sure to whom. I loved Raizele, but sometimes I got jealous when Mahme hugged and kissed Raizele, because she was the baby, so I would push in between them and we'd all laugh.

We both leaned on Mahme as she read us a story, but it was hard to "concentrate." I learned that word from Zayde when he taught me to read Yiddish. He always said that I had to concentrate, so I would squeeze my forehead to make my head work better.

Tahte went out to work at his dental clinic and to buy food. Lately he didn't bring meat anymore; I didn't know why. The soup tasted different; Mahme added rice to the soup now.

One day, when Tahte returned from shopping, I noticed that he'd been perspiring because he kept wiping his forehead.

"Are you sick, Tahte?" I asked.

He looked at me with small eyes. "No," he said. His voice sounded higher than usual and nasal, as if he had a cold and couldn't breathe properly. I knew he wasn't telling the truth, so I turned and went quietly to my room; his lying to me hurt so much. My Tahte wasn't smiling anymore, and it scared me; I knew he was sick.

The next day he returned with one eye closed and swollen like a ball, and blood dripping from a cut by his mouth.

"Tahte! What happened to you?" I yelled.

"Tahte bumped into a cabinet at the clinic," Mahme said quickly while cleaning his face with a wet rag, but I didn't believe her; she was lying too. I had a bad feeling in my stomach and wanted to throw up. I climbed and sat on my Tahte's lap and looked into his one good eye, bursting to ask who'd done it, who hit him, but I didn't dare. I kept thinking of the screaming people from that horrible night.

"My clinic is burned," he confessed, looking at me with one eye. "The windows are broken and only one wall is standing."

I opened my eyes wide in surprise, but my mouth stayed shut; I didn't know what to say. I felt helpless. He hugged me, and I banged my forehead on his chest and scratched my thighs with my nails until I got red marks. Why? I wanted to scream. My cheeks felt wet, and I tasted salt in my mouth.

That evening, Bubbe and Zayde moved in with us. Raizele was put in my bed with me—which we loved—and Bubbe and Zayde had to sleep in her bed. I wondered how they could fit in it. The truth was that I loved them living with us. I didn't even mind Zayde's snoring. Raizele and I giggled when we heard him until we fell asleep; everybody was home together.

I didn't think that Tahte enjoyed staying at home all the time; his nose was runny, and he was grumpy. He stopped shaving and didn't care about his mus-tache anymore. He didn't smile or talk much, and he had no patience to play with us or read to us. He mostly stayed in bed and read the newspaper. Raizele and I had to play quietly and try not to disturb or anger him. He was so different, as if he were a stranger. I missed my old Tahte, my protector. What was happening to him? What was to happen to me?

One day, when Mahme was out buying food—she didn't get milk anymore—Tahte suddenly got up, got dressed, and went outside, only to return a few minutes later with a bleeding mouth and a cut on the side of his forehead by his left eye. His jacket was torn by the shoulder, and his glasses were broken and lay crooked on his nose. He looked terrible. Bubbe sat him down on a chair in the kitchen and cleaned his cuts with shaking hands. Then he went to lie down again, fully clothed.

I lay on my bed, feeling sad and mad. My Tahte had become a stranger. I made a fist, wanting to hit somebody, but my nails hurt me. I didn't know who hit my father every time he walked out the front door. As if someone was standing out there just waiting for him to come out, and paff! Hit him right in the face.

I decided to ask my grandfather. Maybe Zayde would tell me what was going on. I wiped my eyes and went back to the living room but saw Zayde pacing the apartment up and down, his hands behind his back. He mumbled angrily, like he was cursing, and spit came spraying out of his mouth.

Then Zayde stopped pacing, stared at me, hugged me tightly, and went to the bedroom to bring my sister. He sat us at the kitchen table and gave us picture books to look at, then walked out. He just left us there. We stared after him. I didn't understand why he'd left us alone in the kitchen with those baby books. Were we supposed to wait there for Mahme? Why was everybody acting so strange, so crazy? Raizele was shivering in her seat.

"Come sit on me," I said. "I'll read to you. Which book would you like?"

"Can we lie on the carpet and read?" she asked, her lips trembling. So I put her down, and we went to the living room, where we lay on our stomachs on the carpet, our heads close, and I read to her until my eyes felt heavy.

We must have fallen asleep because we woke up when Mahme came home. I ran to her when I heard the front door open, wanting to hug her, but stopped. As she took her coat off, I noticed some bruises on her left wrist. I could see red finger marks, as if somebody had grabbed her. She quickly pulled her sleeve down to hide it. Before I had a chance to ask her what had happened, there were loud knocks on the door.

Mahme's face turned white. Her big eyes got bigger, and I recognized the fear as she stared down into my eyes and held my gaze for a moment. My heart started that boom-boom again, and my throat went dry. When she opened the door, two men in uniform walked in with a stretcher. I walked backwards and pulled Raizele with me, staring at them. They had caps on, shiny buttons on their green jackets, and red-and-white armbands on their sleeves.

"Dokter Jakub Stein?" one of the men asked loudly. That was Tahte's name.

Zayde and Bubbe came to the door, and I heard Bubbe gasp before she hid her face in her hands. Raizele and I huddled behind them, and I peeked. Without a word, Mahme showed them to her bedroom, where Tahte lay in bed.

I started shivering when the two men returned with Tahte on the stretcher and headed for the front door. Tahte's eyes were closed as he lay on his back, his mouth and forehead swollen. I could barely recognize him with his long-disheveled hair, unshaven cheeks, and wild mustache. I was scared of the two men. They took him out, and Mahme closed the door quietly behind them. She stood for a moment, facing the door, then placed her forehead on it before turning slowly to face us.

She walked to the red velvet sofa, sat down heavily, and stretched her arms toward me and Raizele. We came from behind Bubbe and Zayde and stood by her knees.

"Moje dwie perły," she said in a strange voice that scared me. "Tahte is going to the hospital. He has broken ribs and ... and you saw his face." Her voice was trembling now. "The doctor needs to look at him and give him medication to help him heal." Something in the way she spoke wasn't right, so I studied her face, searching her eyes; maybe I could see something there, but she quickly turned her head away, and I missed it. Then she hugged us both, and I heard her sigh heavily. I didn't like it. I wanted my Tahte back.

Mahme looked so sad that I didn't dare ask how long Tahte would be in the hospital and when would we see him again.

Not asking questions was the worst, and I had so many: Why was Tahte hit? Who did it? If I went to school would "they" hit me too?

But my mouth stayed shut.

Chapter Three

Vienna, January 1939

ELSIE

THE only thing that made Raizele and me happy after that awful day was that Mahme switched beds with Bubbe and Zayde. She gave them her big double bed and moved into our bedroom, sleeping in Raizele's bed. I loved having her close, yet I missed my Tahte. The loving, caring, storytelling, and fast-skating father I adored. I tried not to cry at night, not wanting to wake Raizele or Mahme, hoping Tahte would be back soon. I waited every day for him to come back, and every day I was disappointed.

One evening Mahme came home with a man in a black

suit and a black hat. He carried a big, square, black box. I recognized him from my last birthday party; he was the photographer. He sat us down on the red velvet sofa in the living room, right below the large painting of a farmhouse that I didn't like; it was all painted in gray and brown, and only one tree was green. Yuk.

Mahme sat on the sofa between Raizele and me. The photographer took out the huge camera from the black box and attached it to three steel legs. He stood behind it, his legs wide and his knees bent, and spread a large, black sheet over his head and the top of the camera. I tried hard not to laugh. A bright light came on, and a click was heard. Raizele jumped. I tried not to blink at the sudden light. Then the man sat us each alone in turn, told us not to smile, and took our photos. First, he took mine and then Raizele's; Mahme's was last. When he spoke with Mahme, I heard him whisper the word "Dachau"—I didn't know what it meant—but it was later repeated at home between Mahme and her parents. Dachau. What was it?

About a week later, Mahme came back with our pictures. They were small photographs of our heads only. She explained that we'd need them for the visas. I didn't know what a visa was, and Mahme didn't explain. I didn't dare ask but guessed it was a good thing because her eyes were bright when she said it. She also showed us a photograph of the three of us together: Raizele and me with Mahme in the middle, sitting on the sofa, smiling. I saw her hold three copies of the same photo, and I wondered why we needed so many.

I think it was two weeks later that Mahme told us that she'd managed to get Raizele and me on the list. I looked at her face, not understanding what the list was, but believing it was also a good thing, because Mahme smiled, or tried to smile. Something in her smile was different; her mouth smiled but her eyes were sad. I wasn't sure what was wrong. She kissed our heads, and I thought I saw tears brimming in her beautiful dark blue eyes.

"What's the list, Mahme?" I couldn't hold back. I thought that if she was happy, she wouldn't be angry that I was asking a question.

"To go on vacation by train," she replied.

"Train? We're going on a train?" Raizele asked, and Mahme patted her head and said, "We have to wait our turn; the list is long."

"Where are we going on vacation?" I asked.

"To England."

"England?" Raizele asked. "What's England?"

But Mahme's mood changed, and she didn't seem happy any longer. She kept quiet.

"Is Tahte coming on vacation to England too?" I dared ask in a whisper.

Mahme was mumbling something about him still being held in the hospital.

"Is the hospital's name Dachau?" I asked bravely. I'd heard that word so many times by now in connection with Tahte, that I dared ask. I missed him so much.

But instead of a reply, Mahme quickly turned around and left the room.

When she returned to the living room—she'd gone to the kitchen for a glass of water—her face was white and sad. My stomach hurt, and I wanted to cry. Did I make her sad with my questions?

That night, I tossed and turned while Raizele kicked me constantly. I kept thinking of the vacation we were taking soon. I was excited to leave the darkened apartment and go on holiday by train. Just to go outside would be a treat. To put on a coat and a scarf and gloves and go play in the snow. I couldn't imagine the streets anymore. Were they all white, covered in thick snow? I'd been trapped at home for so long. It was boring staying in day after day, not going to school, not playing outside.

Mahme was the only one shopping now. Bubbe and Zayde hadn't left the apartment in weeks and weeks. Bubbe's cooking was delicious, her chicken soup and knaidlach were the best, but the kitchen made the whole apartment smell of onions and soup because we didn't open the windows. It made me want to vomit.

The next morning, I cheerfully asked Bubbe and Zayde, "Isn't it great that we're all going on vacation to England by train?"

But they stared at me, unsmiling. What was wrong with everybody? I couldn't understand why everyone was so sad about going away on vacation. Was it because we were leaving Tahte behind?

"Let's play school," Raizele suddenly said, and went to Mahme's room to get one of her hats. "I'm going to be the teacher," she announced, the hat on her hand.

"You have to take the hat off," I said angrily.

"Why?"

"Because Frau Snyder doesn't teach with her hat on," I snapped.

"But I want it on," Raizele begged, ready to cry.

"I don't care, it's not appropriate," I said, and pulled off the hat. Some curls got caught in my hand, and I pulled her hair together with the hat. Raizele screamed and Mahme came in running. By that time, Raizele and I were hitting each other, crying and yelling, and Mahme had to separate us.

I stormed out and went to my room to lie on my bed. I hated everybody. Then Mahme called me for breakfast, and I didn't want to come, but she called again, angrily. I joined them all in the kitchen, but I sat with my arms crossed, refusing to talk.

It was January already—I knew because we had a little celebration on New Year's Eve with Bubbe's cookies and tea—and the apartment got colder. Mahme said that the landlord had turned off the central heating. Luckily, I had Raizele in my bed, who was a ball of fire. Mahme would join us in our bed sometimes in the middle of the night, shivering. I could hear her teeth knocking. I jumped once when my leg was touched by her foot; it was as cold as ice. I remembered falling on the snow once, when we were ice-skating, and my hand staying too long on the ice, and my fingers changing color. At night I could hear my grandfather cough in the other room as if he were choking.

One evening, after a dinner of watery soup with some greens floating, I saw Mahme packing two knapsacks which I hadn't seen before. I got excited and thought she'd soon be packing her own suitcase. Yes, we were really going on vacation. We were going on a train to England. I was so excited that I couldn't sleep. Mahme got into our bed and sang us our favorite lullaby and rubbed my back. I must have fallen asleep, because suddenly Mahme called my name and woke me up, but she wasn't in our bed anymore. I was confused and didn't understand what was happening. It was still night and very, very cold. I strained my eyes. I could make out Mahme's shape moving in the room in the dark. When she stood by our bed, I saw that she was fully dressed. She didn't turn the lights on. "You must get up, moje dwie perły," I heard her say. "It's time to go."

Before I had the chance to ask, "Go where?" Bubbe and Zayde walked into our room. They were dressed too. Raizele woke up then, and Bubbe handed us cups of warm chocolate drink. Zayde sat by Raizele on the bed, holding her cup for her to drink and blowing on it to cool it off. My sister played with his graying beard while waiting for her drink to cool down. I held my warm cup in both hands and blew on my own drink. Were we really going on vacation now?

When we were done drinking, we washed our faces and brushed our teeth, and Mahme dressed us in many layers. Bubbe kept handing her more and more clothes. It was uncomfortable having so many layers on. On top of everything, Mahme put a new coat on each of us, but mine was too big. It was red.

Raizele's was blue. When had they been made? We hadn't gone to the tailor for measurements like we had every year.

When we were ready, Zayde went downstairs to call for a taxi, and we all rode to the train station. It was exciting but scary to be outside. The air was freezing, the wind biting my face, and my chest ached. Looking outside the taxi window, I saw the clouds separating, and there was some light trying to stream in. The streets were empty of people and cars, and some streetlamps were shattered. When we passed the elegant stores that we used to shop at, I saw that they had no glass windows and the mannequins were naked. Stars of David had been painted in either white or black paint on shop doors. The paint had dripped and dried onto the sidewalks. I hadn't seen those before. Why had they done it?

I sat back and felt like something horrible was happening outside. My chest felt tight. For a second, I realized that I didn't see any suitcases besides the two new knapsacks. Maybe they were placed in the trunk of the taxi? I guessed they had been.

When we arrived at the railway station and got out of the taxi, Mahme put Raizele's knapsack on her little back and said, "Don't lose it, my little sunshine." Bubbe handed Raizele her stuffed animal and my sister hugged it tightly. I reached out and grabbed my little doll from Bubbe as Mahme placed a larger knapsack on my back and said, "Look after your sister, my darling child."

Why was I supposed to look after my sister? Wasn't Mahme coming with us? And Bubbe and Zayde? Without a word they turned and hugged me so tightly, I thought I'd break. When they let go, they walked back and stood by the waiting taxi. This was very confusing. I didn't understand.

Mahme took my hand and Raizele's and walked us into the station hall. Raizele hugged her stuffed animal in her other arm, and I held my doll's little hand, letting her dangle at my thigh. I kept looking back at Bubbe and Zayde until I almost tripped, and Mahme urged me forward. Were they not coming with us on vacation? Were they waiting for Tahte to come out from the hospital? From Dachau? I could hear my heart pounding in my ears again. Where was Mahme's suitcase? She was holding my hand and Raizele's. Did we leave it by mistake in the trunk? I wanted to remind her, but I was stiff and uncomfortable from all the layers of clothing. I felt so itchy. I heard the shrill of trains coming and going, the whistles and the clacking of wheels on tracks and screeching brakes against metal—I smelled it, too, like smoke and rubber.

We entered a very big hall. The lights were so strong that my eyes hurt. I saw hundreds of children and their parents, some standing and hugging, all talking. There was so much noise. Some children were laughing, glad, maybe, that they were going on vacation; others slept on the long tables and benches. Maybe they had come from far away and had to wait a long time for their train. Everybody wore coats, gloves, hats, and scarves. A mishmash of people.

Mahme stood in a line, holding our hands tightly; my fingers hurt through my mitten. A very serious-looking woman with curly brown hair and small eyes checked our names on a large sheet of paper—"the list," I guessed—and hung cardboards with numbers around my and Raizele's necks. The same numbers were glued onto our knapsacks. Mahme didn't get one. The very serious-looking woman nodded to a younger woman who stood by her side. The younger woman nodded back, smiled, and bent down to face us. She had big brown eyes and pink cheeks.

"Good morning, my name is Bea." She looked up and nodded at Mahme. Mahme nodded back. They all understood each other just by nodding.

Mahme bent down, hugged us both, one in each arm, and wet my whole face with tears and kisses. "You're both going on a train ride. It will be fun. I'll be coming later," she said. "Take care of your sister, Elsie. Please remember that I love you both very much, moje dwie perły."

And she let go.

"No!" I yelled. "You said you were coming with us!" I threw my arms around her middle, hugging it tightly, still holding my doll.

Mahme pressed me hard to her body with both her hands, then straightened up, undid my arms from her waist, and started walking with us and with Bea toward the train. Bea took my hand and Raizele's. A man in black uniform and black boots approached us. He had a long club attached to his thigh and was slowly pulling it out. Bea quickly picked up Raizele, took my hand, and walked very fast towards the platform. My sister kicked and screamed while I was dragged, looking back at Mahme. Salty tears ran down my face when Mahme stopped walking as the man in the black uniform watched her and motioned her away.

It was then that I realized that she really wasn't coming with us. I didn't want to go without her. I wanted to let out a long scream so Mahme would come back for me, but only a weak shriek escaped my throat. I didn't recognize my own voice.

It was like a bad dream. I wanted to run back to Mahme, yet when I looked back, something in her eyes stopped me. She made a slight movement, as if trying to follow us to the rail tracks, but the man in black uniform yelled in German, "Halt. Geh zurück." *Stop. Go back.*

Mahme let out a small cry and quickly put her gloved hand over her mouth.

"Mahme—" I managed to whisper when Bea yanked my hand and pulled me. I felt heavy, like moving underwater, like I was in the pool and there was pressure in my ears.

All of a sudden, Raizele threw the stuffed animal down on the ground, pulled her hand out of Bea's hand, and ran back to hug Mahme's legs. The man in the black uniform lifted his club. Bea let go of my hand and rushed to pull Raizele away.

I glanced at Mahme, who hadn't moved or even bent down toward Raizele. She stood with one hand on her mouth and the other on her chest with great fear in her big eyes. The policeman took a step closer to her, the club in his right hand and its tip banging into his left palm. Was he going to hit her if she moved another step?

Bea pulled both of us up the stairs of the train with Raizele kicking and screaming. What would Raizele do without her stuffed animal? With or without it, we had to keep moving.

It was clear to me that Mahme didn't love me anymore. Why was she sending us away? She had promised she'd come with us. Did she pick up Raizele's stuffed animal?

Chapter Four

By Train and By Ferry, 1939

ELSIE

BEA picked Raizele up and hurried down the aisle, looking for seats. There were so many children on the train; almost every seat was taken. There were adults, too, like Bea, all talking. There was so much noise. Some children were excited and laughing; others were crying. At last Bea found three empty seats and sat herself between my sister and me. When the train suddenly started moving, I felt scared. We'd never been on a train before. I'd only seen pictures of trains in books. Raizele began screaming again, so Bea picked her up and put her on her lap, holding her tight with both arms, but Raizele kicked and screamed until she slid off Bea's lap. Bea got up, but I could tell she was overwhelmed. I didn't know what to do. Then I remembered my mother saying, "Take care of your sister," so I called Raizele to come climb on my lap—she was too heavy for me to pick up—and I tried singing one of Mahme's lullabies. I noticed Bea taking care of other children, and I wondered who she was and how many of us she was looking after.

Raizele and I hugged, and she cried until we both fell asleep.

I woke up to music. My seat was moving under me, and I wasn't sure where I was. Then I remembered. The train. My heart went boom-boom fast in my chest as I remembered. Raizele was on the seat next to me, sleeping with her head down and her chin almost touching her chest. Bea was back in her seat next to her, sleeping too. I stretched my neck to see where the music was coming from, and two rows in front of me, I saw an older girl playing the recorder. I sat back and closed my eyes. The music was nice and calmed me down for a minute. When it stopped, I opened my eyes again and looked around. Behind me, I saw a baby in a basket on the lap of an older girl like Bea. I stared at the sleeping baby, thinking of its mother; where was she? What if the baby woke up and started crying? Babies needed their mothers. I needed my mother.

Something was coming up in me, from my stomach to my chest, a strange kind of heat that I had never felt before, or maybe once, when I couldn't go to the synagogue because it was burned. I wanted to punch something or someone. I clenched my fists and dug my nails into the palms of my hands. My lips pressed together. Where was my mother? How could she send me and Raizele away with a stranger? Who was Bea? I didn't know her. Was she going on vacation with us?

Mahme had lied. I thought you weren't supposed to lie. Bubbe and Zayde had lied, too, although they had never spoken of the vacation. It wasn't fair. Children were not supposed to lie, but grown-ups could? I hated them all for lying and for sending us away. Mahme didn't love us anymore. She had said we were going on vacation, but she didn't come with us. She lied. Then she said she'd be coming later, but would she? I wasn't sure.

The baby woke up and started crying. Raizele lifted her head and opened her eyes with a fright. The baby wouldn't stop crying, no matter what the young woman did.

Bea, who sat next to Raizele, turned to her, and asked in German, "Wie heisst du?" *What's your name?*

Raizele didn't hear, because she placed her little hands over her ears, closed her eyes tightly, and crunched her face; her lips were quivering, and their corners turned down, as if she were going to cry too. I also didn't like the baby crying.

Bea smiled at me and asked, "And yours?"

"Elspeth." I wiped my face with my fingers, not wanting her to notice my tears; I wasn't a baby. "But everybody calls me Elsie," I replied politely. "My sister's name is Rose." I didn't tell her what my sister's nickname was. Strangers didn't need to know everything.

I was hungry, so I asked Bea for my knapsack, which rested in a metal basket above my head. When she gave it to me, I put my hand in, and my fingers touched something cold. I peeked inside and saw a round tin tea box. Mahme must have given us some tea leaves, but I didn't have hot water to make tea. I dug in and found two sandwiches and one apple. Raizele opened her eyes and looked at me. I gave her one of my sandwiches and asked Bea for Raizele's knapsack. I found two sandwiches and an apple in her knapsack, too, and also saw a tea box there. I gave both knapsacks back to Bea. I ate and my stomach felt better. Raizele wouldn't eat; she kept blocking her ears. I asked Bea to put the food back in my knapsack for later.

It was day and night, and day and night, a few times. We were on the train forever. How far was England? Mahme would be waiting for us there. For sure. Maybe she wasn't a liar? I hoped not. I missed her.

I felt the train slowing down. The clicking of the wheels on the rails sounded different. It slowed even more when suddenly two men in black uniform burst into our compartment. I could hardly breathe when I saw them. They were dressed the same as the man who had stood by Mahme with the club in his hand. Were they policemen? My heart was beating boom-boom, and it felt like my teeth were knocking. They each had a red armband with a white circle and a strange black cross on their sleeves. They yelled in German to open our suitcases.

I didn't know what to do, because I didn't have a suitcase, only our knapsacks, so Bea picked them up from the floor and placed them on Raizele's and my knees. I opened mine to show them, but they only peeked inside, not even touching it with their clubs, and moved on. Other children had their clothes tossed out of their suitcases with the clubs and scattered all over the seats and the floor. Many children started crying. I didn't know what the men were looking for. A girl in another row had a thin gold chain pulled and torn from her neck while she shrieked in horror. She started crying, rubbing the back of her neck. I heard her say that the gold Mogen Dovid was a gift from her grandparents for her Bat Mitzvah.

When the horrible men left, most of the children were on their hands and knees, looking for their clothes and putting them back in their suitcases, tears streaming down their faces. Some older children helped the little ones. We were lucky our things hadn't been thrown out of our knapsacks.

Bea went to sit next to the girl who had the necklace taken. She hugged her and helped her repack her small suitcase. I felt sorry for the girl who lost her grandparents' present.

The train, which had been slowing down, came to a complete stop. I looked out through my window and saw a woman running alongside the train. She came to my window, pointing inside our coach and screaming in German, "Das ist das Baby von meine Schwester!" *This is my sister's baby.* The girl who had been looking after the baby rose and passed the basket with the crying baby through the window to the screaming woman.

I didn't know what was happening, but I knew I didn't like it. I took a deep breath and smelled hot chocolate. For a moment I thought of Bubbe and Zayde, the last time we'd been together. Was I dreaming?

Three smiling ladies appeared in our coach and handed us hot drinks. I was hungry again, and the warm, sweet chocolate was delicious. The women also gave us big chocolate bars and cookies. We didn't understand the language they spoke, and I wondered who they were. They smiled and patted our heads, repeating the words "Niederlande. Holland." I didn't know what it meant.

They took us off the train; everybody was hugging their suitcases and other belongings. I was glad to stand up after sitting for so many days. Bea put our knapsacks on our backs. She picked up Raizele and took my hand, and together we walked to a boat on the water. It was still dark, the morning slowly beginning. I had never been on a boat before, and it looked scary as it rocked up and down, side to side.

Bea helped me first, then put Raizele down on a bench in the boat, turned around, and disappeared. I didn't see where she went, and got worried. Raizele asked for Mahme, so I gave her more cookies. I wanted to give her my doll, but I must have left it behind on the train. I was so tired, and the moving boat was making me shaky. Some children were crying.

I smelled hot oil—like when Mahme was frying—and I heard the humming motor as we rocked up and down. I held tightly to the cold and wet railing behind our bench, feeling sick. All the cookies and hot chocolate wanted to come up. Raizele didn't stop crying for Mahme, and she started vomiting.

I didn't know what to do. A lady gave her warm water to drink, but Raizele threw that up as well, and it got all over her coat.

I fell asleep, hugging my little sister on the bench. When I woke up, the sun was up and so was Raizele. She looked at me with her big dark blue eyes and asked, "Where is Mahme?" I had to lie to her and say, "We'll see her soon. She'll be waiting for us in England." I looked away, not believing my own words. But maybe she really would?

Some clouds floated by. I couldn't see Bea anywhere. Maybe she wasn't on the boat at all? Maybe she had gotten off before we sailed. Who would take care of us now? Bea was the last one to see my mother, to know we had a mother. Now she was gone too. The children from the train were on the boat, but the adults were different people. They also spoke a different language, like the ladies who gave us the chocolates.

When the boat arrived at the shore, there were people there who spoke a different language again. I didn't understand what they were saying. They smiled at us and helped us get off the boat. I was so tired. I wanted this horrible vacation to end already. I wanted to go home. All I wanted was to sleep, to lie down in my warm bed under my feather duvet, hugging Mahme.

Was this England? Harwich. I heard people say Harwich. Again, and again. What was Harwich?

I was looking for my mother but couldn't see her anywhere. Was she waiting for us here? I was holding on tight to my little sister, the only familiar thing I still had. I couldn't lose her.

Chapter Five

Harwich, 1939

ELSIE

I STILL held Raizele's hand tightly when we were put onto a bus. I had to help her get on the high steps; she was only five, and Mahme had said I had to look after her.

The bus stopped, and I saw a sign I could read: "Liverpool Station." I could read the words, but I didn't understand them. It didn't say England. Would Mahme be waiting for us here? I couldn't understand what people were saying, and it made me feel lost and scared. Children were crying everywhere. Everything was strange. My stomach ached, and I held back from vomiting again; I was dirty and just wanted to go home. My mouth was dry and my eyes stung. We were all dirty and smelly and I was tired of wearing all those layers of clothing Mahme had dressed me in.

We got off the bus and entered an enormous building with a huge hall. It reminded me of the train station in Vienna. Were we going on another train? There were so many people—millions—and so much noise, and so many languages. But nobody spoke German. I didn't understand what was going on. The room smelled of wet wool, of vomit, and of chocolate. I needed the toilet badly and was scared I was going to wet my pants. Raizele kept mumbling, "Mahme … Mahme … Where is Mahme?" She was looking up at people's faces, her eyes wild, and I thought she was going to get sick again; her cheeks were red and smeared with melted chocolate and vomit.

A woman approached us with a smile. It wasn't Bea. She explained in Yiddish that she and the other teenage girls she pointed at were from a "Jewish movement." I didn't know what it meant, but they smiled kindly and spoke Yiddish, so it felt alright. They divided us into groups and put all the small children to one side. Raizele and I stood in line with this woman and waited. She had short red hair and brown eyes and wore a golden Star of David. At the head of the line, I saw a large table and a man with a hat and a mustache seated behind it. Children were taken to him one by one from the line, and the cards on their chests and suitcases were examined.

When it was our turn and we got to the table, I got scared. The man with the hat and the mustache stared at his papers, glanced at the numbers on our chests, peeked at my face and Raizele's, and looked at his papers again and shook his head. He glanced around as if searching for somebody and said something in English to our helper, the young woman with the short red hair. She bit her bottom lip, her face became red, and she put her hand on her mouth. What was wrong? She moved her weight from leg to leg.

The man with the hat and the mustache motioned with his hand to a man and a woman standing to one side, calling them over. They were both very thin and very tall. The man had a long black coat and a large black hat, and the woman had a small brown hat. They came to the table quickly, bent down, and spoke to him in English. I didn't understand what they said, but they kept looking at us and back at him. The woman pointed at my sister. The man with the hat and the mustache pointed at me. He showed them his papers. They peeked at his papers, at me, back at the man, and shook their heads. The woman said something to her husband, who shrugged, then nodded. Then the woman said something to the man with the hat and the mustache, and he gave her a paper to write on. She did, then handed it back to him, turned to us, smiled, bent down a lot, and said, "Hello."

Her brown hat almost fell off, and I could see she had long blond curls just like Mahme and Raizele, but she had brown eyes, not deep blue like theirs. She had very white skin, pink cheeks, and red lips. When she smiled at my sister, she had crooked teeth. She looked at Raizele and put both her hands out to her, and my sister dropped my hand and hugged the woman as if she knew her.

"Nein," I shouted. I was so surprised. "Komm zurück!" *Come back.* But the woman picked Raizele up, and my sister clung to her, putting her cheek on the woman's shoulder and closing her eyes. I couldn't believe it. I just couldn't believe my eyes. Did she think it was Mahme? "Raizele! Geh runter! *Come down.* "Komm zurück!"

At that moment, I saw a shorter couple rush over. They spoke loud and very fast to the man in the hat and the mustache. They showed him some papers, and I saw the tall couple look at the papers, too, and the tall woman wrote something down. Then the two couples shook hands, and before I knew what was happening, the tall couple walked out with my sister, the man holding her knapsack. Raizele didn't even lift her head from the woman's shoulder. Maybe she fell asleep because of the long and tiring journey? The tall man turned back to me as if trying to say something. I started to run after them, but my shoulders were held back tightly by the woman who was supposed to help us. She didn't let me run after my sister, so I screamed, "Rose ... Rose ... Meine Schwester ... Raizele ..."

But they were gone.

I fell to the ground and started hitting it with my fists and kicking it with my toes. "Nein, nein," I yelled. "Meine Schwester, meine kleine Schwester ..." I was sobbing for the longest time.

In between my tears I suddenly saw two pairs of shoes right by my face. Brown shoes and black shoes. The woman with the brown shoes bent down and tried to pick me up. "Come, my child," she said in Yiddish. I leaned on my elbows and looked up. Still speaking Yiddish, she helped me get up. "We are your family. Please get up." I felt heavy with the big coat and all the clothes that I was still wearing. I picked up my knapsack and stood holding it with both hands, my head hanging down, looking down at my toes. It felt like the room was turning round and round and I was going to fall. The woman held me close to her body, both her hands on my back, and the man, the one with the black shoes, bent down and looked at my face. I recognized them as the short couple that had come running in and showing their papers to the man with the hat and the mustache who sat behind the big table. "Raizele is fine," the man said in Yiddish. "She is going to live with the Quaker couple, and you're going to live with us. It's okay, don't cry, she's okay."

This was very confusing. Why was Raizele going with Quake... Quaker... I didn't know what that word meant, and I was going with them? Where was Mahme? Wasn't she supposed to wait for us?

"Mahme . . ." I stuttered. "Meine Mahme is nisht du?" *Is my mother not here?*

The man and the woman looked at each other and didn't reply.

"Ich been Isaac Nussboim," the man introduced himself, and continued in Yiddish, "and my wife is Judith. We have a daughter, Rebecca, who is about your age. Maybe a little bit older. Come, let's go home."

I could do nothing. The man held my knapsack in one hand and took my hand in the other. The woman put her hand around my shoulders, and we walked out of the big, crowded train station. I could barely walk, so the man gave the woman my knapsack and picked me up. I didn't know him and didn't like it so I fought him, kicking and screaming. He put me down and took my hand again. The card with the number had been taken off my chest, but my backpack still had it. We ran down some stairs to an underground train as if we were being chased, and once on the train, they let go of my hands and sat me down between them, sitting close to me as if I were going to escape. Where would I go? I didn't know anyone in England. The smell in the train was worse than the boat, or even the bus. It smelled like morning breath. Yuk. Isaac and Judith—I remembered their names—tried to speak English to me, but I didn't understand a word. Why couldn't they just speak Yiddish? Maybe they were like me, who didn't speak Yiddish at school, in public. It was warm in the train and I was hot with all my clothes on.

I sat with my hands on my knees and felt that my dirty tights were wet. Had I peed a little bit in my panties? I hadn't meant to. My stomach ached, and I almost vomited. I was scared and lonely; I wanted Mahme. I wanted a hot bath and clean clothes. I wanted to be home with Bubbe and Zayde and have chicken soup with knaidlach. I wanted my baby sister . . . I was hungry and exhausted.

The man kept tapping my arm and smiling at me, and the woman tried again to take my hand in hers, but I pulled it back and shook my head. They were strangers, but didn't they say they were family? How? And how come Mahme never told me about them?

We got off the train and walked up the stairs to a gray street and gray sky. I could barely walk from stomach pain. The man gestured to the street, at the buildings, and said, "Dus ist London." I didn't care; I wanted Mahme.

We arrived at an apartment building and walked in. We had to walk up two flights of stairs, which was hard. The man was holding my knapsack, and I held the rails. Their apartment was dark but warm, and the smell of chicken soup surprised me. I wasn't sure if it was real or just my imagination. I had cramps again.

The man and the woman took their coats off and showed me where to hang mine, which was very dirty. I felt ashamed.

"Toilet?" the woman asked, and pointed to a narrow door. I was relieved. It was so good sitting on a clean toilet and letting it all out. I wanted to stay there forever. But I had to wash my hands—I'd lost my mittens somewhere; I didn't know where—and my hands were cold and dirty. I washed my face, too, but not very well; I left some dirt on the towel. When I came out, the woman, Judith, took me to a bedroom. I saw two beds.

"Is Raizele coming here now?" I asked in Yiddish, my voice shaking.

"Oh. No. This is for you and Rebecca, our daughter. She'll be coming home from school soon."

"Where is Raizele, my little sister?"

"Let's go and eat, and we'll tell you," she said.

The kitchen was small and had a square table with four chairs. Judith turned on the gas under a pot and pointed at a chair for me to sit on. The man, Isaac, came and sat down too.

"Elsie," the man started. How did he know my name? "Your mother is my cousin; we grew up together in Poland. Our mothers are sisters. Your Bubbe is my auntie." I felt dizzy and confused. *My* Bubbe was his auntie? It sounded so strange. "My parents and I came to England when I was fourteen, after my Bar Mitzvah." He stared at me, maybe to see if I understood it all.

But it was hard to concentrate with the smell of the soup filling the kitchen. I glanced at the pot, and Judith got up. She took a plate from the cupboard above the sink, and when she took the cover of the pot off, I felt my mouth fill with saliva. Judith placed a plate with two matzah balls and thin, thin noodles floating in yellow soup next to some golden fat coins. A piece of carrot sank to the bottom. I took the spoon she gave me, and almost burned my tongue with the first sip. Mmmm, it was delicious. I looked up at her; she was smiling. The steam from the soup got into my eyes, and my nose started dripping. Judith handed me a napkin, and I wiped my nose. I forgot about Mahme, forgot about Raizele, about the train and the boat. Only me and the soup.

I heard the front door open, and somebody walked in.

"Hello, Mommy," a girl called out. When she walked into the kitchen and saw me, she stopped. "Oh. Hello," she said. "That must be the orphan."

"Rivka," the man snapped at her. "This is your second cousin, Elsie. Elsie Stein. Say 'hello' nicely."

"Hello nicely."

And that was how I met horrible Rebecca.

Chapter Six

London, 1939

ELSIE

NINE-YEAR-OLD Rebecca was called Rivka, her Hebrew name, by her parents. She stood there staring at me, checking me out. Her father said something to her in English—something about wash and something about hands; it sounded similar to German—but she shrugged and joined us at the table, not a word to me. Not even a smile.

I looked up at Judith—who served her daughter a plate of soup—and asked, "Is Raizele coming soon?"

"Who's Raizele? Another orphan?" Rebecca asked with a full mouth.

"Mind your manners, dear," her mother reprimanded her gently. I wasn't sure if it was because of her talking with her mouth full or because she called us orphans. We weren't orphans. We had a mother and a father, even if he was in a hospital in Dachau, and my mother was coming for us soon. She'd promised.

So I asked Judith again. "Where is Raizele? I must have my sister back. Is she coming soon?"

"Look, Elsie," Isaac said. "Your mother sent us a letter telling us what was happening in Vienna. She asked us to take you and your sister in." He looked at his wife, who was sitting now, having some soup too. She didn't look back at him. "But we couldn't afford it. The government made us prove that we have fifty pounds for each child." He coughed a bit. "We took a loan from the bank, but even so, we could only take one child. We chose you because you're closer in age to Rivka, and we thought it would be a good match." He smiled at his daughter, but she didn't respond. He continued, "Your sister was taken in by a Quaker couple; you saw them at the station."

What was "Quakers"? I remembered the long, black coat and the black hat the man wore. What did "Quaker" mean?

As if Isaac read my mind, he said, "Quakers are Christians who only want to do good. The couple is very young, they just married and have no children yet. She's a teacher and he's a court clerk. They wanted to sponsor a very young child and also had to take a loan from the bank. So, you see, it worked perfectly well." He smiled as if everything was alright. But it wasn't.

"I want to be with my sister," I insisted. "Can I go to stay with her?"

Isaac moved in his seat, and I was afraid he'd get mad at me; he pressed his lips together and hit his thighs hard with his hands and left them there.

I looked at Judith.

"Look, Elsie," she said, throwing a look at her husband. "Raizele is in good hands. So are you. We're going to treat you like a daughter." Now she threw a quick look at Rebecca before returning to me. "One day you and your sister may meet again. In the meantime, you'll learn English, maybe go to school, make friends." She sounded excited. "You're safe here, and that's the main point of you being sent here." She stood up. "Now you can go to Rivka's room, and she'll help you put your things away."

I got up, as did Rebecca, and obediently followed her to her room. I understood with a heavy heart that the second bed wasn't for Raizele and never would be. They said I was safe. Raizele was in good hands. That meant safe too. I suddenly understood that Mahme and Tahte were not safe. I remembered the bruises and the torn sleeve. I was so scared for them.

Rebecca pointed to a chest of drawers in her room. She had emptied the bottom drawer for me. I set down the meager clothes Mahme had packed for me in the drawer together with the knapsack and the round tin tea box. Those were all my possessions.

Rebecca's mother filled the tub for me, and at long last I took all the layers of clothing off. The two dresses closer to my body were clean, as were the two sweaters. The brown dress I wore on top for four days and nights was filthy, and it was hard to peel off my dirty, wet tights and underwear. I left those in a pile on the floor.

When I got myself in the warm water, I wanted to stay there forever; I had not washed in days. I got into my nightgown and straight into the bed Rebecca had pointed at, and immediately fell asleep.

I didn't know how long I slept, but when I woke up, it was the next morning, Rebecca was gone. The room was cold and damp, and I pulled the covers up to my chin. I missed Raizele's warm body. I missed Mahme and Tahte. I wanted to hear Bubbe's and Zayde's voices. My world had melted. Nothing familiar and loving remained. I wanted to go home. I wanted this vacation to end already. I even missed Frau Snyder and her stern look.

A sudden knock on the door jolted me. The door opened and Rebecca's mother walked in. Judith—I suddenly remembered—had straight, deep brown hair down to her chin, and brown eyes. I hadn't noticed it yesterday, but her smiling, kind eyes offered me some comfort. I smelled a light scent of perfume coming from her as she sat down on my bed and started talking in Yiddish.

"Good morning, Elsie. I hope you slept well," she said warmly.

I nodded, my chin touching the covers.

"You know that my name is Judith, but I think you should call me 'Auntie.' Can you say 'Auntie'? It will be your first English word." She looked at me expectantly.

"Auntie," I whispered, tasting my first English word. "Auntie."

"You can call my husband 'Uncle.' Can you say 'Uncle'? That would be two words in English." She sounded excited.

"Uncle," I said. That was easy; I knew "Onkel," the word in German, although I didn't have an uncle to call him that. "When can I see my sister?" That was the only thing I wanted, as I had no more hope of seeing Mahme soon.

"Look, Elsie—" Auntie became impatient and shifted her bottom on my bed. "Raizele will stay with Ann and Paul James, the Quakers, for a while, and you'll go to school here. You're in second grade, right? I'll speak to the principal at Rebecca's school, and although Rebecca is in fourth grade, you can both still walk to school together. It's not far, just two blocks away." She stood up. "Do you have a book to read? Uncle is at work and Rebecca is at school. I'm going to school now to speak to the principal. You can stay in bed longer, if you like, or you can wash and dress, and I'll make you breakfast before I go. What would you like to do?"

I was still hungry, so I took the covers off and headed to the bathroom. The pile of dirty clothes was gone. I wasn't sure if Auntie had thrown them away or washed them. I'd have to wait and see. Auntie made me scrambled egg and toast, and we drank tea together. Then she went out, and I got back into bed, dress and all, and fell asleep.

The next day I was sent to school. It was so scary. On the way, Rebecca walked in front of me, and I had to walk fast, afraid to lose sight of her and get lost. When we got to school, which really wasn't far, all the children stared at me. I followed Rebecca, and we arrived at the secretary's office.

"Go in. They'll tell you where to go," Rebecca said. "I'll see you on the way back home later." And she was gone.

I think that the secretary expected me because she asked, "Your name?" And pretending to understand, because "name" in English and "name" in German sounded similar, I said, "Elsie Stein." Yes. This was my first English conversation.

She smiled, stood up, and walked me to a full classroom where she said something fast in English to a woman who stood by the blackboard. This was my new teacher. She said, "Hello, Elsie," and another word that I didn't understand, although it sounded a bit like "willkommen."

She then pointed to an empty double desk at the back of the room, and I went to sit there while all the children turned to watch me, giggling and whispering. I felt so lonely. I didn't understand a word the teacher was saying to them, but her tone was mad. Then she smiled and said something with the word "hello" and then my name. The children turned to me, and some boys yelled, "Hello, Elsie," until the teacher shushed them. Some girls turned around and waved at me. One of the girls got up and said something to the teacher, who nodded. She then came to sit next to me at my desk. She pointed to her chest and said, "Dorothy, Dorothy Sommers." Then, she opened her book, and as the teacher read, Dorothy followed the words with her finger so I would know where they were reading. I loved Dorothy instantly.

The whole day I concentrated very hard until I had a headache. Why did the English have to speak so fast? How was I to learn to speak like that? But the teacher kept smiling at me, and that made me feel better. At recess I followed the children out to the schoolyard, where the boys ran and shoved each other, yelling. Dorothy motioned with her hand for me to follow her, and I did. We sat on a bench, and I took out the sandwich Auntie had prepared for me. But I was sad. Dorothy was so sweet, but I couldn't speak to her. I put half of my sandwich back in the bag Auntie gave me; I wasn't hungry anymore.

I could read German, and as the alphabet was similar, although not exactly the same, I caught on quickly. At home, I read out loud from a book the teacher had given me, and Auntie kept correcting me. Rebecca kept giggling. She shrugged when I asked her to correct my writing, and said, "I have my own homework, you know?"

I was careful at school not to utter a word in German, because once, when a boy did say something in German, the other boys called him a Nazi and chased him all around the schoolyard until one of the teachers rescued him. I didn't know the boy and was too shy to speak to him. He was also older. I was scared I was to be called that, too, because of my accent. All the kids around me were happy. They all had parents and brothers and sisters. I had none of that and didn't want to call attention to myself.

Five months passed. By the end of second grade, I could speak, read, and write English like a British girl, but with an accent, and I'd made one friend in Dorothy Sommers. I was never invited to her house, and she didn't come to the Nussboims', but we spent recess together. I usually walked back home alone. I thought Rebecca was ashamed of me and didn't want to have anything to do with me. Maybe she was jealous that her parents liked me and I had to sleep in her room? But didn't she want a little sister? I wished my little sister was with me; I missed her so much. She was my only family now, until I would see Mahme and Tahte again.

The Nussboims had a large wall calendar in their kitchen. And as soon as I could figure it out in English, I counted how many days until summer holiday, when I might be able to see my sister again.

Chapter Seven

London, 1939-1940

ELSIE

IT was the first of July 1939. Suddenly I was eight. Overnight. But nobody knew.

No hugs and cheers from Mahme and Tahte, no wet kisses from Raizele, no birthday cake that Bubbe had baked, no new book from Zayde, and no friends and games. An ordinary day. It was a Saturday, and I didn't want to get out of bed. I'd looked at the calendar the day before and hoped that a miracle would happen in the morning. That suddenly I'd wake up at home and everything, everything that had happened had been nothing more than a bad dream. That when I woke up in the morning, eight years old, I'd jump out of bed and wake Raizele up, and ask her urgently, "Have I changed? Look at me, Raizele, do I look any different? I'm eight today!" And she'd giggle and say, "Yes, you look very old," and we'd both laugh and run to Mahme and Tahte's bedroom to see if they were up. Maybe I'd get candy when we went to shul. Maybe . . .

I pulled the covers over my head.

The Nussboims were in the living room, listening to their huge radio. Why were they glued to it every day? The news was in the evening, but they left the radio on when they were home.

"Just in case," Judith replied when I'd asked one day.

Just in case what? Could bad things happen here too?

Two months later, in the first week of September 1939, I started third grade. There was a different feeling at school. Everyone was serious and the boys were horrible. They played at recess with long sticks and yelled, "Boom-boom, I just killed you, you Nazi." I was scared. Why were they doing this? When I asked Dorothy, she said, "Because of the war." I looked at her, not understanding, but was scared to ask. At home, the big radio in the living room was on all the time, and Auntie's and Uncle's serious faces worried me too. In the evening, Uncle sat with a glass of brandy in his hand. I hated the smell.

On the second day of school, the teacher said that war had begun in Europe. She called Europe "the Continent." I didn't understand what a real war was and couldn't imagine it. But I knew that Austria, my home country, was in Europe, the Continent, and war was a bad thing. The teacher declared that England was going to fight the Nazis too. That was good news,

I thought. The Nazis were bad people. I also learned quickly what a war was and understood why the boys at school spent their breaks playing "war," poking each other with pointed sticks.

"Children, we're going to welcome the other third grade class, as their teacher had to go to the army to fight and protect us from the Germans," our teacher—we called her Miss—announced one day. I knew that the other class's teacher was a man. "I need you all to behave nicely and make room for them," Miss added. So now we sat three children at a desk of two. The room was crowded and smelly, so Miss opened the big windows; I'm sure she also didn't like the smell.

Now that my English was better and I read lots of books—Rebecca kept ignoring me—I was one of the best students in the class.

"I'm very proud of you," my teacher said to me one day towards the end of the year.

I finished third grade by June 1940, and one week before my ninth birthday—which was on a Monday, the first of July, again—Auntie called me to the kitchen to help her.

As I was peeling the carrots she'd handed me, she lifted her head from the onions she was chopping and said, "I have a big surprise for you, Elsie."

I gasped. I was going back home to Vienna. My heart beat faster. "Am I going back home?" I dared ask.

"Elsie"—she said my name in a way Mahme used to say it when she was mad at me—"there's a war in Vienna. You know that you can't go back." My heart sank. "But you're getting a really big gift."

I didn't want any gifts. I wanted my family, my home, my sister. Uncle and Auntie were gentle and kind; they gave me a home and food and cared for my education, but they were not Mahme and Tahte. They were family but not really. And Rebecca didn't like me. She never wanted to play with me and always looked at me with narrow eyes, never smiling.

I looked at Auntie, waiting for more.

"Your sister is coming here for your birthday," Auntie announced.

"Raizele?" I called out, tears springing into my eyes. I hadn't seen my baby sister in a million years. Auntie kept looking at her busy hands while chopping the carrots I'd just peeled, her cheeks flushed.

Raizele! I was going to see my little sister. I knew she wasn't little anymore; on the third of July she was going to turn seven. Raizele, seven. I couldn't believe it. "Is she really coming here?" I asked carefully, afraid I had misunderstood. But my English was good; could there still be a mistake? "Will she stay?"

"I don't think she'll stay," Auntie said, putting the chopped onions and chopped carrots in the pot, "but wouldn't it be nice to celebrate both your birthdays together?"

I was so surprised. Last year she didn't even know when my birthday was, and now she knew when Raizele's birthday was?

"Yes. The Quakers, Ann and Paul James. They don't live too far away, about thirty minutes by car. They are bringing her here on Sunday after church, one day before your birthday, so you can celebrate together."

Church? Did she say they were going to church?

"But on Sunday I won't be nine yet," I complained.

"Yes, I know, but they don't want to wait. It seemed urgent for them to bring her."

Urgent? After all these months, now it was urgent. Why? What had happened to Raizele? I looked at Auntie, not understanding, but she didn't explain and continued cooking.

"May I be excused?" I asked, and without waiting for her reply, I went back to my room. To Rebecca's room. She was out, so I could sit on her chair and think. Something must have happened to my sister. Auntie had said, "Urgent." What could be urgent? But soon I was going to see my sister with my own eyes.

That was enough.

That evening, when Uncle came home and after we all had tea together, I sat in the living room with a book. Rebecca was in her room, and Auntie and Uncle were sitting close to the radio, listening to the news. They were talking softly to each other, and I couldn't concentrate on my book. Then I heard Raizele's name mentioned. Auntie was telling Uncle about Ann and Paul James coming on Sunday with Raizele. I pricked up my ears and listened, my eyes on the page, pretending to read.

"Remember we exchanged our name, address, and phone number with the Quakers, Ann and Paul James, so we could keep in touch?" Auntie asked her husband quietly. "Well, Ann rang and asked if the girls could meet."

"Now? After one and a half years?" Uncle asked a bit louder.

"Shhhhh. Yes, there is something wrong with Raizele, and they think that seeing her sister might help."

"What's wrong with her?" Uncle asked.

I also wanted to know and felt my heart beating fast. I kept listening. I turned a page.

"Apparently, she isn't doing too well. She barely eats and her behavior is erratic. They're not sure what's wrong with her. They're trying to love her, but at times her behavior is so strange that they're at a loss."

"How will seeing her sister help?" Uncle whispered, and I sensed that he was staring at me. "Does she know?"

"Yes, I told her. It's her birthday on Monday, and her sister's birthday two days after, so I invited them for Sunday afternoon for tea, to celebrate the girls' birthdays."

"What else did Ann tell you?"

"She said that Raizele was either angry or unresponsive, quiet, closed, and uncooperative." Auntie took a deep breath. "Ann claimed that she'd always been good with children, being a teacher, but she can't understand this one. Some days, Ann complained that Rose—which is what they call her, Rose—would turn obnoxious and forgetful of simple rules, becoming exceedingly difficult to handle. Or she'll sit and stare at Ann and not reply to questions as if she hasn't heard them or doesn't understand, or she'd just stare at the wall."

"This is terrible."

"I know, that's why I agreed for them to meet. Do you think I was right to invite them?"

Uncle was quiet for a moment. Then he said, "Elsie is doing so well. I hope it won't upset her to see her sister like that."

"Yes, but we need to help them. Ann said that sometimes Rose pretends not to know how to pack up her toys and just gets up from the floor after playing and crawls into bed. Instead of brushing her teeth, she just stares at her toothbrush as if seeing it for the first time and not knowing what to do with it."

I couldn't listen anymore. This was too scary for me, and I started shaking. I understood now why it was urgent for her to see me, her only family. I got up from the sofa, startling them, said good night, and went directly to the bathroom to brush my teeth and go to bed. I didn't care anymore about Rebecca; it was her room after all. I was going to see my sister in a few days, and if she couldn't stay here, maybe I could leave with her. But I couldn't sleep. I tossed and turned and the bed creaked until Rebecca yelled, "Stop."

I lay still in bed, thinking of what I'd heard. Raizele being "exceedingly difficult." What did "exceedingly" mean? "Difficult," I understood. Raizele was difficult? How? She was "obnoxious"? She didn't pick up her toys. That couldn't be. Raizele was a good, obedient child. We were both good girls. Mahme had taught us all the good things and how to be good girls.

The next morning Auntie and I were clearing off the breakfast dishes. Because it was school vacation, Rebecca went to a friend's right after she'd finished eating. Her mother didn't even stop her and ask her to help clear the table. But I was happy because I could ask Auntie the question that was burning a hole in my head. "Auntie," I started carefully, as I didn't want her to know that I'd overheard her and Uncle last night. "Why are the Jameses bringing Raizele only now? Why didn't they bring her all this time?"

She stopped, a cup in one hand and a napkin in the other, and looked at me for a second before she replied, "I don't know." She seemed to be looking at the wall, thinking, then added, "Maybe Rose was behaving well. Maybe they had no reason to worry. Besides, you girls weren't very close, were you? She didn't seem to ask for you, and you never asked us to see her."

I almost dropped the plate I was holding. It felt like I had a hammer in my chest.

Was *I* supposed to ask to see my sister? I'd seen her being kidnapped in front of my eyes. *I didn't know that Auntie had the Jameses' name and address all this time.* Was it my fault? Our fault for not asking to see each other? The guilt made me double over. My stomach hurt so much that I did drop the plate and ran to the bathroom. I heard Auntie say something between her teeth that sounded like a curse.

"Raizele," I sobbed as I sat on the toilet. "Raizele, my little Schwester. Why did they do it to us? Why didn't they bring us together if they had each other's address? These are cruel, cruel people, I hate them." I was hitting my bare thighs, my insides turning to water. I then lay on the floor of the bathroom, unable to move. My whole body ached. I was supposed to ask to see her. I didn't know I could. I was the big sister; Mahme told me to look after her, but I'd failed her.

Now I was nervous to see Raizele again; I hadn't done what Mahme had asked of me. I was sad and angry at Raizele for putting her head on the woman's shoulder and not even looking at me. That anger had almost helped me not to miss her every second of every day.

Slowly I stood up. I washed my hands and my face, and as I was drying myself with the towel, I heard a knock on the bathroom door. I opened it, and Auntie stood there.

"I'm sorry," she said in a shaky voice. "I'm sorry for accusing you of not asking to see your sister. You're only a child, and I should have gotten you both together sooner. It was my mistake. You're such a mature little girl that I expected you to ask. I also hoped that you and Rivka would be like sisters, and worried that having Rose here would interfere in your relationship." She took a deep breath. "But I know that you and Rivka aren't friends. The whole thing didn't work out like I'd expected."

I didn't say a word. I was on my way back to Rebecca's room to get my book to read when I suddenly remembered the plate, so I said, "Sorry I smashed the plate." But Auntie had already turned to go back to the kitchen.

Four more days and I'd see my sister. I was nervous and happy all at once. I was nervous because I didn't know what to expect. Had Raizele really changed that much? But I was a child too; how could I help? She needed Mahme. I needed Mahme.

Chapter Eight

London, 1940

ELSIE

RAIZELE and the Jameses arrived promptly at 3:30 p.m. for tea.

I almost didn't recognize her. She was small and so thin and pale, and she looked at me in surprise with her big dark blue eyes. Her eyes were so much bigger now in her small face.

When I called out, "Raizele," she ran into my arms, hugged me, and started crying. I held her tight, trying not to cry along with her—I was almost nine—when I heard the woman, Ann, say, "What a relief. The child can cry. This is not normal, a child her age not crying, is it?"

I wasn't sure whom she was talking to, but I didn't care. I was holding my sister, and I wasn't going to let go. Ever.

Raizele smelled different. I wasn't used to that smell. Her hands were tiny. Her fingers like matchsticks. Her clothes were too big for her. But the blond curls, the soft body, and the little arms around my waist were so familiar. I tried very hard not to cry too.

"She also doesn't eat," I heard the man, Paul, complain. I saw him turn to Uncle when he said, "Maybe she could stay here tonight with her sister—"

"Yes, please," I pleaded with Auntie, holding on to my sister, scared to be separated again. Auntie looked at Uncle, who nodded. Raizele watched them and stopped crying. Then she said something in German to me, which I didn't understand. I hadn't spoken German in months.

"Please speak English," I heard Ann say. "Nobody here in England likes the sound of the enemy's language." Raizele and I fell quiet. Enemy? We were from Vienna, Austria. German was our language; we'd just met after such a long separation, and we weren't allowed to communicate in our language? We didn't have our parents with us to protect us. We didn't—

"You can speak Yiddish." Uncle seemed to understand our struggle. "It's close enough."

"But then we wouldn't understand what they're saying," Ann complained.

Nobody seemed happy. We were supposed to be happy that we met after such a long time, but the truth was that they had kept us apart when they could have brought us together long ago. We couldn't have done it alone.

"Let's have tea," Auntie said, and she stood up to serve.

The whole morning we'd been busy preparing. Auntie had baked a huge chocolate cake. She didn't stop talking about how difficult it was for Uncle to find eggs for the cake, and for her to find flour and butter. With all those difficulties, she still managed to bake this beautiful cake and even little round cookies. I knew that she cared, and it made me feel loved.

Raizele seemed starved. She ate the cake with her fingers, which made me feel so embarrassed. I noticed that first Ann wanted to say something, as she pointed at her and leaned forward to speak, but her husband quickly stopped her. He seemed happy that Raizele ate, no matter how. Mahme wouldn't have been happy to see this, I knew, but Mahme wasn't here. Where was she at that moment? I wondered if she'd even remembered her daughters' birthdays.

After the birthday cake and tea, everybody looked happier. I took Raizele to the room I shared with Rebecca to play. Once we were alone together, it felt as if we hadn't parted. It was so good to have real family right there.

Rebecca stayed with the grown-ups, which was very nice of her; I was surprised, but maybe she wanted to impress our guests, pretending she was generous to let us play alone. Or she was curious to hear their conversation, not really interested in us.

On my bed, there were two parcels. Raizele and I stared at them, then at each other. One was marked "Elsie" and the other, "Rose."

"Oh," I said excitedly. "Let's open these."

We tore the paper and found identical outfits. Light-blue

skirts and yellow shirts with light-blue stripes and little round collars, with short puffy sleeves. They were beautiful. We laughed and quickly changed into them. We looked like twins, only one twin was taller with auburn hair, and one was small and skinny and had long blond curls. Raizele's skirt had to be held by her hand because it almost fell off; she was so skinny.

"Those are for our birthdays," I said. "From Auntie and Uncle. Maybe your foster mother can fix it for you so you can wear it without holding it up."

"It's too big," Raizele complained. She let go of the skirt, and it fell around her ankles, covering her shoes.

"Never mind, it will fit you soon, if you only eat a bit more. I promise I won't wear mine until yours fits you better."

She took the new outfit off and wrapped it clumsily in the brown gift paper. I changed to my old clothes, too, but folded my new ones nicely.

That night Raizele slept with me in my bed, and it was so, so good. Like old times. Like we were back at home, in Vienna, Mahme and Tahte just a wall away from us. Before bed, we bathed together and splashed each other, and Raizele's smell came back. It was delicious.

But the next day she had to go back. They said that this was the agreement. Only one night.

When we said goodbye, Ann promised to bring Rose back, but I wasn't sure if I should believe her. Raizele hugged me very tight and started crying. I held her small, skinny body and looked up at her foster mother. "You promise?" I asked.

"Yes, I promise," she repeated.

I looked at Auntie and Uncle, and they both smiled, and nodded.

During that summer, we met many times and it was wonderful. Ann seemed to be the one to ask for our meetings and sleepovers, and I think it was because she saw that Raizele "improved on the days she was with her sister," I overheard her say that to Auntie once.

No one noticed, but I felt I was improving, too, being with my sister.

And then came September 7, 1940.

Chapter Nine

London Blitz and The Farm, 1940

ELSIE

I WAS so excited to be back at school and see Dorothy again after spending day after summer day with spiteful Rebecca. The only happy days were the ones I spent with my sister. But I'd only been in fourth grade for a few days when on Saturday, the seventh of September, surprising sirens sounded in the quiet night. I didn't know what the noises were at first. I thought I was dreaming. I was petrified and pulled the covers over my head when I heard explosions and the screeching tires of rushing fire trucks. I thought that there must have been a fire burning somewhere because the fire trucks were all out. So much noise. It brought back all the fear I'd experienced at home, in Vienna. Was it happening now in London? Were people breaking shop windows and burning synagogues? Was Uncle going to be hit in the street? Were they going to take him to Dachau? Would Auntie—

Just then Auntie burst into our room and declared in a shaky voice, "The war has reached us here. The Germans are dropping bombs on us. Get up, girls, get dressed, we have to run to a shelter or hide in the Underground. Hurry."

The underground train station wasn't far, but we still had to run in the street, exposed to the sky. Auntie grabbed each one of us by the hands, and we ran together. Uncle ran behind us. People were standing on the top stairs, looking up.

"Get down, you idiots," I heard a man's voice boom. The people on the stairs went down, and we could go down too.

We stayed there for a while, until a different sound was heard.

"Alright, we can go up now, lads. This is a signal that the threat is over," the same man said. He must have been in a war before; he knew what to do.

We walked up the stairs and slowly walked back home.

My heart was beating fast all the time. I was scared a bomb would fall on my head.

After that awful night, the air raids repeated every night. Whenever we heard the warning alarm, Auntie pulled Rebecca and me to hide under the big high bed she shared with Uncle. Uncle wouldn't hide; instead he turned the radio on. One night, a man's voice kept repeating the word "blitz."

I peeked from under the big bed and whispered loudly to

Uncle, "What does 'blitz' mean?" As if I were scared that someone out there might hear me.

He looked at me, then at his daughter, and said, "It's a military attack, when the enemy drops bombs on you. Germany is attacking England."

I wanted to stay under their big bed forever, but when the calm alarm was sounded, we had to get out. Uncle went to work, and we had to wash, dress, and go to school. At school we were given gas masks, which smelled of rubber and made me gag. We each had to keep our masks inside a cardboard box, which we wore on a string around our neck everywhere we went.

One day at school we were told that the Germans were interested in destroying our capital and any city that had a port and that if we could, we had better leave London, because we were in big danger here. The children in class started talking all at once. Some girls cried, and the boys declared that they wanted to become soldiers there and then and go fight the Germans. I was so scared. Leave London? Where would I go?

On my way home from school that day, I saw groups of pupils from another school following teachers, each child holding a small suitcase. I just stood there looking at them, and a flashback came to me: the railway station in Vienna. It seemed so long ago. I didn't want to think of my family, of my mother; it was too painful. I focused on reading books and pleasing Auntie and Miss. I wanted to be a good student.

When I arrived home, I said to Auntie, "We were told at school today that we better leave London. Is that true?" I shivered. "Where would we go?"

"I have no idea," she said, and I saw fear in her eyes. "When Uncle comes home, we'll discuss it." She bit the side of her bottom lip, clasping her hands together, then turning her fingers this way and that. I'd never seen her do that before. Then she hugged herself and rubbed the top of her arms as if she were cold. I looked into her pale face and big eyes and ran to the bathroom to relieve myself. My insides turned to water. As much as I tried not to think of Mahme, the look on Auntie's face reminded me the time Mahme had returned home with bruises on her arms.

Soon Uncle came home and turned the radio on. I wondered why Auntie hadn't done it before he arrived. Was she scared to hear what the broadcaster had to say? I listened with them and heard, again, that women, children, and older people were evacuating to the countryside.

"What is the 'countryside'?" I asked.

But they shooed me away, and I heard the man on the radio say that "the Germans have occupied France and are now holding the west of Europe under their boot. It's clear they have now decided to invade England too."

That night I had nightmares. I saw Mahme and Tahte running from a burning fire but leaving Raizele and me behind. I was standing with my sister, holding her little hand as we watched them run from us. Then I dreamed that Bubbe and Zayde were walking back from the market, loaded with bags full of produce, and a bomb fell on them and made an enormous black hole in the ground where they disappeared. They were gone, the produce scattered on the road. When I woke up, I was shaking.

Next morning, early, the doorbell rang. Rebecca was still asleep, so I sneaked out of bed and stood by the bedroom door, glued to the passage wall, wanting to see who had come so early.

It was Paul James, Rose's foster father. That was what Uncle and Auntie had told me to call him. He was wearing a black hat and a black coat, but under the hat I saw a large forehead, kind brown eyes, and a shy smile. He asked Auntie, who had opened the door in her house gown, if he could speak to Uncle, who was still home, getting ready to go to work. Auntie and Uncle invited Mr. James in, and they all sat in the living room and talked. I was wondering if Raizele was sick again. I hadn't seen her since school started. She should have started school, too, second grade.

They talked quietly, and I couldn't make out what they were saying, but they must have seen me because they called me to join them. I was still in my pajamas, but I went into the living room anyway.

Uncle placed me so I was facing him, grasped the top of my arms which were straight by my sides, looked me in the eye and said, "You are a good girl, Elsie, and you are family. We treated you like a daughter, but the war has reached England, and we all must fend for ourselves."

I had no idea what he meant, but I understood that things were very serious. My heart was beating faster and faster.

He turned and looked at his guest, then back at me, and said, "Paul here, I mean Mr. James, is leaving London with his wife, Ann. They are going to his parents' farm out in the country, where Mr. James grew up. They're taking Rose with them, of course, to be safe, and they want you to join them."

What? I was leaving to be back with my sister. Was my dream coming true?

Then he continued, "We may also have to go someplace, because London is the Germans' target, but I first must make plans with my boss. Auntie and I are not sure yet where we'll be going. We think that you should go with the Jameses, because the Nazis may not bomb farms and empty fields. It's best for you to be with Rose. Please go pack your things. Mr. James is going back to get Mrs. James and Rose, and he'll be back for you shortly."

I looked from him to Auntie and then to Mr. James to make sure this was all true and was happening now. I was leaving after almost two years, when I had finally started feeling that I belonged somewhere. I loved my school and I loved Dorothy, but I was going to be with my little sister. On a farm.

I looked at Mr. James, who nodded and smiled at me. He was young and handsome, and I was sure he loved my sister, because he wanted to protect her, so I liked him. He stood up, and so did Uncle.

"I haven't had breakfast yet," was all I managed to say. I was somewhat sad to leave these two good people who'd treated me like a daughter. They were family, my mother's cousin. My feelings were all mixed up, but I was going to be with my sister and not see Rebecca ever again.

"You go dress and pack, and I will make you breakfast," Auntie said, and got up too. I liked Auntie very much. She never lied to me in all the time I'd stayed with them. Not like my mother.

When I walked back into Rebecca's bedroom, I found her

sitting in her bed, still in pajamas, staring at the wall in front of her, a book turned face down on her blanket.

"So, you are leaving, I heard," she said. "After all we've done for you."

I felt like she had punched my stomach. I was grateful to her parents for giving me a home, but she wasn't my friend. She borrowed the skirt Auntie and Uncle had given me for my birthday without permission. I saw her wearing it one day, and before I could say anything, she put her finger to her lips, indicating for me to keep quiet. She went out, and her mother never noticed. That night I found the skirt on my bed, the button on the belt missing. I had said nothing.

In the almost two years that we had shared a bedroom, she hadn't learned to like me.

I stood for a second now, just staring at her, not sure how to respond. Then I dressed in my new shirt and the skirt she had taken. I had told Auntie I had lost the button, and she had sewn another one on the belt. I never told on Rebecca.

I hoped my sister's skirt had been altered and that she would wear it too. These were the nicest clothes I'd been given since we'd left Vienna. I quickly packed my school backpack and my old knapsack, the one Mahme had sewn for me. My hands shook as I packed the three tops and one dress that Auntie had bought for me while I stayed with them. I checked that I had the tea box, the last gift from Mahme.

I wasn't sure if I was coming back after the farm. I didn't care if I never saw Rebecca again in my life, but I liked Uncle and Auntie a lot. I was sad and glad all at the same time.

I stood by the door and turned back to look at Rebecca.

"Goodbye, Rivka," I said quietly. But she had picked up her book already and was reading.

I had my breakfast in silence while both Uncle and Auntie sipped their tea and stared at their saucers. It was hard for me to swallow, but I knew I had to eat the toast and jam; we were going out to the country, and I didn't know how long the drive would be.

By the door, I hugged Auntie and clung to her. She wasn't my mother, but she behaved like one. She smelled of the strawberry jam she'd just eaten, and she held me so tight, almost choking me. When she let go, I saw a tear roll down her cheek. She quickly wiped it and smiled.

When Uncle hugged me, I said, "Thank you for having me," as if I'd just come for tea, and he chuckled and said, "You're such a brave girl, Elsie. I'm very proud of you."

I wondered why he had said, "Brave." Was it because I had to live with unfriendly Rebecca? Or was it because I was going to live on a farm with strangers? Raizele already knew Ann and Paul James, but I didn't.

Paul James returned in an old car, and I was glad to sit in the back with my little sister. She wasn't wearing the same outfit I had on, and I was disappointed, but I didn't let it spoil my mood, and I took her hand in mine. We were going to be together now, living on a farm, safe from the bombs that fell on London.

Looking out, I saw the horrible mess in the streets: rubble everywhere, smoke from burned and partly destroyed buildings, some completely flattened, and debris being cleared by men with large brooms. There was a policeman holding a barefoot little girl in his arms and walking on broken bricks and glass with his heavy shoes. The stench of smoke slipped through the closed windows. I quickly closed my eyes; I wanted it all to disappear, but instead, images and the smell of smoke reminded me so much of that horrible night in Vienna...

I forced myself to open my eyes when Raizele let go of my hand. She took out a sandwich from a wrapped package and started eating. Ann asked her to give me a sandwich too. I smiled at Ann, who turned around to look at us, and I said, "Thank you." Ann smiled back.

Would she become my foster mother too? A third mother? As if Ann could read my mind, she turned at that moment again and handed me a thermos with tea. I was careful not to spill, and when I did, I quickly wiped it with my hand and hoped she hadn't noticed.

We rode for hours and arrived at the farm in time for high tea. Paul's parents were old but welcoming. They told us to call them Ma and Pa. I'd heard Rose call her foster parents Mother and Father. First it had shocked me, but because those were English words and not German or Yiddish, I got used to it and wondered if I should start calling them that too. I'd decided I wasn't going back to the Nussboims and would never part from my sister. Raizele and I shared the same blood. We had the same parents. We had to stay together. If Uncle and Auntie couldn't keep her, too, I was going to stay with the Jameses.

I loved living on the farm. Being with my sister was wonderful. My new foster parents were kind, but Ma and Pa gave us chores because we were not guests, as they said. Just because we didn't go to the local school didn't mean we were on vacation. Ann, a schoolteacher, was going to take care of our education. She said that the country schools were inundated with children and there was no room for us.

We had to follow a strict schedule: Wake up very early. I didn't have a clock, but it was still dark outside. Rose's job was to collect the eggs from the chicken coop. She had little hands, and it was a perfect job for her, but sometimes she wasn't careful, and she'd drop and break one. Old Ma would then clench her fists and place them on her waist, her lips pressed hard like a dry prune, but she refrained from scolding my sister. Then Rose would be sent to feed the chickens. I was a bit scared of Ma but understood that those eggs were precious, so I tried to help Rose collect them when I could. There was one beautiful white chicken, tall and proud, that Rose liked best and named CooCoo. She would talk to her, and CooCoo would turn her head to one side like she understood.

My chore was to take the goats out of the pen and walk them out to the field to graze with the help of Chips, the dog. Chips was an English Shepherd and I absolutely adored him. I thought that he liked me, too, because he would jump up to lick my face and then roll on his back for me to give him belly rubs. I'd never had a dog before, so this was a new experience. There were four goats, and I was petrified of their horns, so I didn't get too close. The littlest one would always run away, but Chips would chase it back. I would open the gate to let them out, and when it was time to return them back, Chips would run in circles around them, and they'd gallop back as I held the gate open.

"Go wash up, girls, and come to the table," Ma would call.

All of this was before breakfast. For breakfast, Old Ma would serve us thick oatmeal that she told us to sweeten with jam, because there was hardly any sugar to be bought. She made apple and plum jam, which was quite nice with the mixed sweet and tart flavors.

But she also made rhubarb jam and called it strawberry jam, and it was disgusting. Rose and I couldn't eat it. It had no sugar at all and tasted nothing like the rich strawberry jam we'd had at home in Vienna. My stomach would tighten when I thought of the breakfast Mahme used to make us. I'd swallow my tears and notice Ma's stern look when I wiped my nose on my sleeve. It was a new habit.

"Come, Elsie, you first," Mother—meaning Ann—would call after I helped take off everything from the table. Ma didn't have to remind me to say, "Thank you for breakfast," or to help clear the table. I was a well-brought-up child. Auntie had said it all the time.

Mother would sit me down at Pa's big desk table, saying it was better than going to the local school. She'd listen to me read a story, then ask me questions to see if I understood it. If I did, I would have to write a short summary, in my own words, as she said. While Raizele played with an old train that used to belong to Father—Paul—when he was a child, Mother taught me arithmetic and geography. I loved geography best and could draw maps by heart and recite the capital of every single country in Europe.

Then we'd switch. "It's your turn now, Rose," Mother would call.

I'd sit down on the floor to play with the train, but sometimes I just pretended to play. The long train ride from Vienna to Holland—now I knew where Holland was—made me feel sad. I thought often of Mahme, whom we'd left standing on the platform. Where was she now? Back in our apartment? Was Tahte back? I had nobody to ask. I knew that Germany was throwing bombs on London; was Austria in the war too? There was no radio in the living room, and nobody mentioned the war here.

Mother often read with Rose, who had just started second grade when we had to leave London. But my little sister couldn't concentrate. She'd slide off the chair, biting her nails, not reading when Mother started a sentence and asked her to continue, and generally just annoying Mother, who'd say things like, "Please sit still. We can't work like this." Mother would then give up on her, sigh deeply, and say, "Alright, go play. You're not in the mood for studying today."

I was sad because Rose was so different from the little Raizele I'd known. She wouldn't giggle with me when I found something funny, and she barely smiled. She had changed so much in the one and a half years that we hadn't lived together. She'd become lazy and forgetful, and I knew Mahme wouldn't have recognized her.

Mother would sometimes get up, double over as if in pain, and get into bed. She'd stay there for hours, saying she wasn't feeling well and complaining about stomachaches every time I walked in to check on her. She seemed to be in pain most of the time and kept holding her belly. I liked her and didn't know what was wrong, and I was very worried. She was kind and pretty, although strict when teaching.

"Do you know," Old Ma said one cold evening when we sat at the thick wooden table after supper, the wind shrieking outside threatening to blow the house, or at least the roof, away, "we have to turn our beautiful grass fields into plowed earth ready to grow vegetables as the government has requested?" She sighed and looked at her son. "You and I will have to do it, Paul. There's nobody else."

She was a large, strong woman, but Pa walked with a limp. "From the Great War," he'd said to Rose once, when she stood there staring at him walking into the room. He wasn't a strong man, and I wanted to help him, but I didn't know how; I was too shy to offer him help.

Autumn was nice, besides the occasional winds and rain, but when winter came, the ground was frozen, so Father and Ma couldn't work it for a while. Everyone was in a bad mood, but the days were short; the sun set early, and we slept a lot. In the afternoons, I liked lying on my stomach on the rug by the fire and reading. Chips would lie next to me and rest his chin on my bottom. Sometimes Rose would bring a book and ask me to read to her, which I did, although Mother had said that she ought to read by herself.

Mother spent hours and hours in bed. Sometimes a doctor would come, and we were sent to our room. I didn't know what was wrong with her and didn't feel comfortable asking.

When spring came, beautiful flowers popped up, but it still rained a lot. We'd been at the farm for seven months already, and I was wondering when we were going to go to school. I missed the company of other children. The farm was far away from other farms, and for months I didn't see any children at all. Rose had grown taller and filled out, and by now the skirt that Auntie had bought her was too short. Ma was good at sewing, so she let out the hem, and Rose could wear it. I didn't grow that much, so my skirt was fine. I was almost ten and wished my mother could see what grown-up, healthy girls she had. But my memory of her face had started fading, and a cloud of sadness would engulf me every time I thought of her.

Then one evening Father sat Rose and me down and said that our papers had arrived.

What papers? Were we going to be sent away? Or maybe letters from Vienna?

So I asked, "What kind of papers?" My chest hammered.

"The visas," Father said.

This word made my eyes grow as big as saucers and my heart pump even louder. I knew that word; I'd heard it before. It meant a list, a knapsack, a train, and goodbye. Again? Were we going home?

Chapter Ten

The Journey, 1941

ELSIE

"THESE are visas to America," Father announced with much excitement.

America? Who was going to America? I panicked.

"Mother's sister, Margaret Cox, who lives in Boston, Massachusetts, has sponsored us. Visas have been issued for all four of us." He read from a letter: "'Mr. and Mrs. James, and their daughters, Rose and Elspeth, have been approved...'"

What? I looked at him as if he were crazy. Their daughters? To America?

My head was spinning.

I knew America was an ocean away, so it worried me tremendously. "How will my mother find us on the other side of the ocean?" I asked once I had absorbed this information.

"Slow down, Paul," Mother said gently. "This is too much all at once; they are still little."

I wasn't little. In two months, I was going to be ten. But I wished he'd slow down.

"Look," Mother explained. "My sister, Margaret, has a husband and two boys. She's much older than me. She sponsored Father and me, because we're family, and when we told her that we wanted to get you two out of Europe, away from the war, she asked for your names so she could sponsor you too."

"But we're not your daughters," I said firmly, thinking what Mahme and Tahte would say when we got back home after the war ended.

Father looked straight at me. His look was so serious, like he was going to say something awful to me. Was I rude when I said we weren't their daughters?

My stomach turned.

Everybody was quiet for a moment. Then Mother and Father exchanged looks, and he said, "I'm sorry, Elsie, but your parents are most probably dead by now. We've had no word in almost two and a half years. Mother and I are in loco parentis—in place of parents—and you're both our daughters now."

I hadn't thought of my parents as dead before. I refused to think of them as dead now. How could they be dead? They had two little girls to raise; how dare they be dead? I would never forgive them.

But slowly, slowly it seeped in. *We've had no word in almost two and a half years.* Father must have spoken to Uncle, Mahme's cousin. Mahme should have written to him to ask about us, as she'd asked him to take us in and look after us. But maybe no more letters were allowed to be sent out. I had no idea. But dead? Could they be dead? Did Tahte die in Dachau? Did Mahme die in a bombing? Together with Bubbe and Zayde? Did a bomb fall on our house?

My head ached and my eyes burned.

Rebecca had said we were orphans. I hated her when she used that word when we'd met, but now I saw that she was right.

Two days later Pa drove us in Father's car to the nearest train station. I hated it. Coming to the station made me cling to Mother. Father held tight to Raizele in his arms, who screamed in panic. People stared at us, and Father quickened his steps to get on the train, hugging her closer. Once seated, he put Raizele's face between his chin and his neck, and her crying stopped; she fell asleep. In London we had to take another train to the ship. So many trains.

We arrived at the docks. As my last hope, I looked for my mother's face among all the faces on the dock—maybe she'd come and rescue us before we embarked. I was frantic, close to hysteria. It felt like I was abandoning my mother by going over the ocean. I knew she wouldn't find us. I wasn't even ten years old. What could I have done but cry?

It was awful on the big ship, not any better than being on the smaller boat from the Hook of Holland to Harwich, and I didn't feel any safer. For weeks, we rocked and crashed against high waves, and I was sure we'd capsize. Rose was sick all the time, and so was Mother, always in pain and hugging her stomach. Father tried to calm us all down, bringing us buckets to vomit into, warm tea to drink, or wet rags to put on our foreheads. But I was grumpy and moody and cried a lot.

Thankfully, it finally came to an end. It was a relief coming off the ship, away from crowds and cigarette smoke, the smell of vomit and ship oil. We arrived in New York on a foggy day, and Mother's sister, Aunt Margaret—as we were to call her—and her husband, Oliver Cox, waited for us at the immigration hall to take us to Boston. Aunt Margaret was tall and thin like Mother and wore her hair in the same style—loose, long blond curls—but she had light blue eyes. She said she'd prepared a furnished rented apartment for us in Brookline, not far from her house in Beacon Hill, Boston. All those new names and the strange American accent made my head spin. They took us by car. No more trains, thank goodness.

The apartment was small and clean. Mother and Father had one room, and Raizele and I had the other. It felt strange; the smell of America was new.

Aunt Margaret was a good sister and helped Mother, who was constantly in pain. She came to visit every day and took care of us while Father was out looking for a job.

I was terribly worried about Mother, who couldn't do a thing for us, even look for a school. Aunt Margaret did everything, but whatever she did, she did fast, always in a big hurry. She made our beds, cooked our meals, did our laundry, everything quick, quick. Sometimes I got dizzy from watching her rush from room to room, her shoes clicking. It made me nervous and made my heart race.

Unfortunately, Mother really wasn't well. By the time we'd arrived in America, she was seriously ill. I heard the word "cancer" whispered, and because it was whispered, I knew it was bad. She'd spend hours in bed, crying in pain, until Father eventually took her to the doctor, although I heard him repeat the words "medical insurance" again and again. Eventually he took her to the hospital. Aunt Margaret took me and Rose to sleep at her house until Mother got better, but she never did. Four months later she was dead. I felt numb. Rose clung to Aunt Margaret like she'd clung to Mother at the Liverpool train station. She seemed to need a mother, no matter who the mother was.

But I felt lost. First, I had Mahme, then Auntie Judith and then Mother. What now? Who would be our mother now? Who was going to take care of us? I felt like I was on the ship again, rocking from side to side, but the ship was empty, with a huge ocean surrounding me. Only sky and ocean. I was ten—no birthday celebration this year—and I felt all alone in the world.

Father panicked when America joined the war after Pearl Harbor's bombing and wanted to leave America. He said to

Aunt Margaret and Uncle Oliver that he'd decided to go back home to his parents and take "the girls" with him. I felt confused when I heard him. I loved him and wanted very much to be with him and go back to the farm, but I shivered at the thought of being back on a boat, on a train, of returning to London and hearing sirens again, seeing bombs falling down from the sky and debris all over the streets. At least in America it was quiet, the buildings still stood, and there was no debris in the streets. I was confused and scared; what were they going to do with us?

By the end of January, two weeks after Mother had died, Father hugged us each and, with tears streaming down his face, said goodbye and left.

I couldn't sleep that night, wanting him to come back. So many people that had taken care of me had disappeared. Mother was too young to die. Didn't only old people die? She was sweet and kind; why did she have to get sick and die? For the first time in two weeks, I really missed her. Now Father was gone too. Tall and handsome Father was gone. My chest felt tight. I thought it was my fault. Everyone that I liked, or who liked me, disappeared, or died. Would Aunt Margaret die next? Should I not like her? Auntie Nussboim had said that Quakers were kind people doing good things. Is that why Aunt Margaret took us in? Because she was kind, but maybe she didn't really like us? She gave Rose and me a nice large room in her beautiful house. But did she love us? Was she going to take care of us now? After Mahme and Auntie and Mother, was she going to be my new mother?

I tossed and turned the whole night.

In the morning, as Rose and I sat in the kitchen with Aunt Margaret and Uncle Oliver for breakfast, I asked them, "Are you Quakers, like Mother and Father?" then caught myself, "I mean, like Mr. and Mrs. James?" I needed to know. Aunt Margaret didn't wear long dresses like Mother, and Uncle Oliver didn't wear a long, black coat and a wide-brim black hat like Father.

Aunt Margaret smiled and said, "Well, I was. In England. Many years ago." She looked at her husband and continued, "Uncle Oliver is Catholic. So, when I married him, I converted to Catholicism." She sat up straight and became serious. "This is what we'd like to do with you two. We'd like to readopt you, if you will. We'll baptize you, and then we'll have a beautiful family of two older boys and two young girls." She lifted her eyebrows and smiled again.

Were we going to be readopted and become Catholic? What was Catholicism? I didn't really know what being Catholic was. I knew that they were Christians, because I saw a crucifix in the living room and in the bedrooms. But we were Jewish, Raizele and I, not Christians, I knew that.

Chapter Eleven

Boston, 1942

ELSIE

I WAS ten already. I was living through a war, I'd changed countries twice, I'd lost my family, my language, my school, and my friends. I knew I had grown up quickly, but there wasn't anything I could do about that. Still, I didn't want to lose my religion too. It was my identity, my connection to the past, to my parents, to my grandparents. It was the one thing that had been constant in my life.

Maybe my family had left me, but I wasn't going to leave them.

"I'm Jewish. I don't want to be Catholic," I said, my voice

shivering, as I felt scared. I didn't want to be ungrateful, but I felt strongly about being Jewish. I spoke and read Yiddish, which I'd learned from Bubbe and Zayde, and I'd spoken it with the Nussboims in London. I celebrated Shabbat with Mahme and Tahte, when Bubbe donned a head covering before she lit the candles, and Zayde put on his yarmulke and stroked his beard while watching her say the blessing. Tahte and Zayde would take me to synagogue some Saturday mornings for Shabbat services. I liked the candy being thrown at the Bar-Mitzvah boys. I celebrated all the Jewish holidays and liked Purim best because we dressed up and ate hamentashen. I liked being Jewish.

"I want to stay Jewish," I said, my voice getting stronger. "My real parents and grandparents are Jewish, and so are Raizele—I mean Rose—and I. I don't want to become Christian, with all due respect." I looked at my sister. "Do you want to be Catholic?"

I couldn't decide for my sister. Maybe she'd forgotten Vienna and our life there, Mahme and Tahte; she was only five when we left, but she was eight now. Shouldn't an eight-year-old know?

She shrugged.

There was a long silence at the table.

Aunt Margaret said that she understood and respected my choice and promised to find a nice Jewish family to foster me, or even adopt me, but that they were going to adopt Rose.

I stared at my sister, who placed her fingers on Aunt Margaret's hand, and said nothing. I saw how attached my sister had become to her, as if wanting her to be her mother.

Poor Raizele, she seemed to attach herself to anybody who wanted her. All they needed was to have something resembling Mahme. As if she remembered but didn't really remember.

I thought, alright, let Rose be Catholic for a while; things kept changing all the time. We had so many different mothers and fathers. Nothing lasted.

She could be Jewish again if she wanted to.

A few days later, Aunt Margaret told me to dress in nice clothes.

"We're going to a synagogue, Elsie, to meet a rabbi and some people."

"Why?" I asked.

She looked at me, surprised. "I thought you'd be happy to go to a synagogue."

"But it's not Shabbat," I said, confused. "Is it a Jewish holiday?" I'd lost count of the Jewish holidays while living with the Jameses. I didn't celebrate Rosh Hashana or Pesach, or any others.

"Elsie, dear. Trust me. The rabbi is nice, and you're going to like him. Come, let's get ready and go. It will be a nice visit, I promise."

"Isn't Rose coming too?" But Aunt Margaret had left the room.

It was cold outside. It looked like it was going to snow.

The synagogue wasn't far, and when we entered, a smiling man shook hands with Aunt Margaret and nodded at me. He had a yarmulke on his head, but he didn't look like a rabbi. Our rabbi in Vienna had a beard and wore a black yarmulke, and this one had a small, knitted, colorful one. Our rabbi never shook Mahme's hand, nor Bubbe's. This new rabbi showed us to his office, where a couple sat waiting. The man and the woman stood up and shook hands with Aunt Margaret.

"This is Elspeth Stein," Aunt Margaret said.

"Hello, Elspeth." The woman smiled at me. "It's very nice to meet you. My name is Esther Zacks, and this is my husband, Morris."

Morris Zacks stood up and came to shake my hand. His hand was warm and damp. He was short, like Uncle, with a round face and a round belly. His eyes were small and smiling behind his round glasses. He had a bald head with brown hair around the back and small ears. I liked his face; he looked friendly. The woman called Esther Zacks was also short with curly brown hair all around her head and big brown eyes. She had red lipstick on. She wore a navy suit, skirt and jacket, and a white shirt and had a black coat over the arm of her chair.

As I stood in front of her, she put her hand out, palm up, as if asking for something. I didn't know what she wanted, so I put my hand in hers. She closed my hand with her other hand. Her hands were warm, but dry. She smiled and said, "We would love for you to come and stay with us. We have no children of our own, and we want to take care of you."

I liked her. I liked her hands. But I was so tired of new families, new parents, new homes, new beds. I couldn't say all of this to the nice lady, so I asked, "Why? You don't know me." I immediately felt sorry that I was rude.

The woman looked at the man with the yarmulke. He came closer, and Esther dropped her hands. Was she mad that I was rude? I felt the difference in my hands. The one that was in hers was warm and soft; my other hand was cold. I wanted to put it in between her hands and warm it up, too, but I didn't dare. I looked at her open face and smiling brown eyes, and a calmness filled my body. She wasn't mad. I felt like I could trust her.

The rabbi was still smiling. He bent down and said, "Mr. and Mrs. Zacks would like to foster you, they may even adopt you, so you'll have a nice Jewish home to grow up in." He looked at Aunt Margaret, who was standing the whole time. Everyone was smiling; only Aunt Margaret was serious.

Esther leaned forward and said, "We live in Brookline, not far from Beacon Hill, where the Cox family lives. You won't be far from your sister."

Morris added, "We run a bakery and bring home fresh bread every single day, and challah on Fridays. Babka too." He smiled. "Do you like babka?"

I didn't know what babka was, but had no time to think, as Esther said, "You'll go to a school not far from home. It's a five-minute walk, and many children walk together."

I hadn't been to an American school yet. Since we arrived, so many horrible things had happened that nobody thought of sending us to school. Walking to school with other children, having friends, and becoming American sounded very tempting.

"If you come live with us, we'll be a family. No more moving homes or changing families," Esther said. She spoke like she knew how I felt, like she understood what I'd been through. I liked them immediately, hoping they'd want Raizele, too, and would adopt her when she became Jewish again.

They arranged with Aunt Margaret to come that evening to pick me up. I was excited but worried about my sister. Still, I thought I'd try to live with Esther and Morris, and if I liked it, we could come back for her at a later stage. I knew they'd love her, too, because she was much better now than when she'd been in London. I knew she liked Aunt Margaret a lot, so I thought she'd be fine with her for a little while longer, until we came for her. I knew she was safe and nothing bad was going to happen to her.

When Esther and Morris arrived that evening to pick me up, I turned to say goodbye to my sister, hugged her, and told her that soon we'd be together again, just like in England. She stood stiffly and said nothing. She didn't cry and neither did I.

I picked up my old knapsack with the old stuff and the new stuff, and my little suitcase that Ma had given me, and walked to the door. When I turned to wave goodbye, I saw Rose standing, dry-eyed, her little hand in Aunt Margaret's hand, and suddenly my heart sank.

Chapter Twelve

Boston, 1943-1945

ELSIE

I CONSTANTLY begged Mommy and Daddy—that's what my new foster parents had suggested I call them—that when it came time to adopt me, they would adopt Raizele too. They listened and said nothing.

But one evening, they told me that it was impossible; they could only adopt me. Rose had been baptized and renamed Rosalind.

"What?" I yelled. "No, no, no." I almost choked as I screamed until I started coughing. "Mahme named her Rose, and we called her Raizele, she can't be Rosalind. She is not

Rosalind." My stomach ached, and I had to run to the bathroom. My insides turned to water.

When I came out of the bathroom, Mommy was standing there waiting for me. She hugged me and said how sorry she was. Aunt Margaret and Uncle Oliver didn't allow us to meet, and we got a letter stating that they didn't want us to have any contact with them.

Although Mommy and Daddy had her address—they'd picked me up from there—they wouldn't give it to me as much as I begged.

"You can't go there, Elsie dear," Mommy had said. "You can't just appear at their door. We may get arrested."

One Sunday I asked Mommy to take me to a Catholic church to look for my sister. I had no idea how many Catholic churches there were in Boston, but there must have been quite a few, as Mommy looked surprised. "I've never been to a church, Elsie. I wouldn't know where to start."

So, the following Sunday I snuck out early and went by myself and found a church. I stood outside when people came out after services, scanning everybody's faces like a stalker. I did it for several weeks, thinking I was very smart in doing so. I didn't know at the time, but Daddy discovered that I was going out every Sunday morning, and he'd followed me. He stood across the street and watched me, he later told me.

Once, when I walked away to return home, he was suddenly next to me.

"Daddy," I called, "what are you doing here?"

"Me? I'm just looking at people coming out of services. Maybe I can find somebody familiar."

I blushed. He knew. We said nothing to each other until we arrived home. Then he sat me down and explained, "Elsie, I'm warning you. This isn't simple. There's a threatening letter from a lawyer, as you know, and you better be careful." He took a deep breath. "You'll have to wait until she's eighteen and can make her own decisions."

"*Eighteen?* That is a million years away, she's only nine."

"I know, but legally we can do nothing about it. Her parents don't want her to see you, and probably any other Jewish child, because they want her to forget, to immerse herself in her new religion, her new life. It would be too confusing for her to see you. She may remember things they don't want her to remember." He sighed. "Maybe it's for her own good, I don't know. I'm sure they don't mean to hurt her in any way. I do agree that it's cruel to separate you two, but I'm at a loss."

My heart was broken, but I didn't want to get anyone in trouble. Instead, I threw myself into my books and my studies just as I had in London, but I never lost hope that I'd find her one day. I was only eleven, and I couldn't do much at my age.

Things changed when I was finishing eighth grade and getting ready to head to high school in the fall. The school year was coming to an end; it was May of 1945, and I was almost fourteen. I'd gotten used to being bullied and laughed at because of my accent—I had a British accent now, not an

Austrian one—but the teachers were alright. School was quite boring, and I spent hours at the library, devouring books. Boys were boring too. They kept staring at my chest, which was really growing and causing me much embarrassment, but none of the boys interested me. I tried not to blush when Mr. Brown, the English teacher, called on me, because I really, really liked him. Especially his dimple.

Not long after VE Day, the good news arrived: The war in Europe was over. One girl brought cupcakes decorated with red, white, and blue icing, and we celebrated like it was somebody's birthday. We were all very happy.

But I was thinking of my sister. I missed and I didn't miss her, all at once. I felt like I had somehow betrayed her—hadn't Mahme told me to take care of her?—but I felt like she'd betrayed me too. Why didn't she raise hell and demand to see me? It wasn't *me* who didn't want to see *her*. Nevertheless, I decided to take a chance and try to find her.

After school broke up that summer, all confident and adventurous, I opened the phone book. There was a long list of people called Cox in Beacon Hill. I confided in my friend Jillian, and together we made a list of all the names and addresses that were possible, and we started calling and asking for Rosalind Cox. She was almost twelve and might answer the phone herself.

We had to do it when my parents weren't home, which was difficult. Daddy left extremely early. He went to open the bakery and turn on the ovens at 4:00 a.m. Mommy made breakfast for me at 7:00 a.m., and by 7:30 a.m., I'd leave for summer camp and she'd go to the bakery shop. By 3:00 p.m., when I returned home from camp, they were both back home. It was impossible. So Jillian offered that I come to her house one day after camp, with my parents' permission, and make the calls from her house when her mother was out.

But her mother, who checked the detailed phone bill each month, soon caught on and wanted to know who was calling those unfamiliar numbers. We were caught. Jillian's mother spoke to Mommy.

Mommy sat me down and said, "You can't do this, Elsie dear. You can't just call strangers and ask for a child. I understand that you miss your little sister and want to see her, but not before she's eighteen. Do you genuinely think you can find her this way? Let me show you something." She produced a letter.

When I was ten and they adopted me, they knew I wouldn't understand the language, but now at fourteen, I looked at the letter from the Coxes' lawyers. It stated that Rosalind Cox, formerly known as Rose Stein or Rose James, had been legally adopted by Margaret and Oliver Cox of Beacon Hill, Boston, Massachusetts, and had willingly cut off all ties with her birth family. She was a devout Catholic with no familial connections to people of other faiths. Anyone trying to contact her without her adoptive parents' consent would have to face serious consequences.

Willingly.

I looked at Mommy and asked, "Willingly? Did she really want to not see me anymore?"

I was in shock. The letter was dated four years ago, and I was only just seeing it now. Black on white. Rosalind Cox.

Catholic. *No familial connections to people of other faiths.*

Mommy said, "She was very young; she needed a mother, as you did." She smiled at me with tears in her eyes. "It was wartime, and many children were misplaced, changing families, changing names, changing countries." She hugged me. "You weren't the only ones, but you were the lucky ones. You were wanted. We wanted you and the Coxes wanted Rose. Remember that always."

That night I lay in bed and imagined Raizele wearing a small gold cross, the same size as the Star of David that I was wearing. She wasn't Rose Stein anymore but Rosalind Cox.

I could picture it but would never accept it, and all I could think about were ways to search for her that wouldn't get any one of us in trouble.

Chapter Thirteen

Boston, 1948-1949

ELSIE

MY adoptive parents were loving, fair, and honest. We were Zionists, supportive of the "children of Israel" returning to Zion, our homeland. I was proud to be a Jew.

Every year I was sent to Young Judaea summer camp, supported by Hadassah. Mommy was an active member of Hadassah—an American women's Zionist organization—which supported the newly founded State of Israel. She admired Henrietta Szold, the founder of the organization, and, four years prior, had gone with a group of women to what the British named Mandatory Palestine to see where in Jerusalem

Ms. Szold had been buried. I wanted to go there myself and couldn't wait until I was eighteen and independent to make my own choices.

At seventeen I was getting taller, but not by much. I still liked my auburn hair cut chin-length, and at times Mommy allowed me to put on very light, almost transparent pink lipstick, as well as some Vaseline on my eyelids to make them shine. It made me feel so grown up. I remembered Mahme getting ready to go to the opera and could almost smell the scent of the cream Tahte had put on his hair to smooth it. My chest would tighten when I thought of them.

In the summer after my junior year in high school, I went to Camp Tel Yehudah, which was Young Judaea's teen leadership camp. There I joined a small group of three girls and two boys who planned to go to Israel to help our brothers and sisters rebuild the Jewish land. We made a pact to go together for one year, to stay together at a kibbutz and support each other. We'd been taught that being a Zionist in America wasn't enough; we had to go and experience the land. After one year, we would have an honest chat and disclose our personal decision regarding whether to stay or come back home. I was so excited to go and be independent, I could barely wait.

But after Israel's independence was declared in May 1948, the war continued, and our parents didn't approve of the trip.

In July 1949 three wonderful things happened:

One, a treaty was signed between Israel and her neighbors. Mommy and Daddy were as hopeful about the new state as I was. I was allowed to go for one year only; I agreed. I wanted to "taste" life in Israel, then return home to work or study a profession.

Two, I graduated from high school.

And three, I turned eighteen. I was an independent adult. The world was open to me with hopes and opportunities. I could make my own decisions now, at long last.

One girl from our camp dropped out—so much for the pact—and we became a group of five: Mable, Dawn, Jon, Saul, and me.

On a windy day in December 1949, shortly after Thanksgiving, we made our way to New York Port. On the ship, I was sick most of the time; bad memories washed over me until we got to Le Havre, France. Sometimes I was panic-stricken. Saul was always next to me to either hold my forehead on deck when I threw up over the railings or to hand me a glass of warm water. I hadn't told him, or the rest of the group, about my awful journey to America as a small child. I didn't want to share with them any details, not wanting them to pity me. They all knew that I was adopted, but nothing else.

From Le Havre in France, we had to take a train to Paris. Entering the train station, I shivered. Somebody must have bought our tickets to Paris, and onward from Paris to Marseilles, but I had no idea who. I stood in the station hall, looking at faces, thinking maybe I'd find my mother. Was I crazy? I felt like I was crazy. But I couldn't tell anyone, could I? I couldn't tell my friends that eleven years ago I'd lost my mother in a train station with a Nazi policeman standing by her with a club in his hand. That she must be dead by now. That the Nazis must have killed her. They would never understand. I was nauseated, and taking those three steps to get into the coach, I tripped.

Saul, who was next to me again, grabbed my arm and helped me up. "Are you okay?" he asked, concern in his voice. When I looked at him, he cried out, "Oh, my God, why are your cheeks wet? Are you hurt badly?"

I was hurting. Badly. So I said, "Yes, I must have twisted my ankle badly. It hurts, ouch."

He sat opposite me and held my foot on his knee. Sweet Saul. He was so different from me; so stable, so content. Born and raised in Boston to Bostonian parents, he went to Boston Latin Academy and aspired to become a doctor. I wasn't sure which university he was planning to attend after taking a year off to volunteer in Israel, but he was serious and kind, and I was sure he'd fulfill his dreams.

When we changed trains in Paris, I limped more than I needed to so he'd think my pain was physical.

Because it was impossible for my foot to occupy an empty seat, Saul sat opposite me and insisted, again, that I lift my leg. He placed my heel on his knee. I closed my eyes and saw Mahme waving at me. My heart beat rapidly. I thought of her often, but never did I feel so overwhelmed. Could it be because I was on a train again? Did my sister also have flashbacks of Mahme? Of our childhood? Did she also despise trains? Did she even remember me? Or our parents? I longed to see her, to speak with her, to ask her a million questions. Two more years.

In Marseilles we embarked on a ship going to Haifa, Israel. Ships and trains, trains and ships. I was exhausted mentally and physically. By the time we arrived in Haifa, I swore I wasn't going to take another train or ship in my life again. I was going to stay in Israel, and if my parents wanted me back, they'd have to come get me. I was staying, if for no other reason than the level of anxiety and emotional pain another journey would bring about for me.

Chapter Fourteen

Israel, 1950

ELSIE

WE were received warmly by our group leader, a thirty-something, extremely tanned, and good-looking kibbutznik by the name of Yigal—whom I liked instantly—and were shown to two adjacent huts: one for the boys and one for the girls. Each hut had a bedroom with three beds and a small bathroom which contained a toilet, a small basin, and a simple shower, no curtain. No kitchen. No table. One chair.

We were told to shower, dress in the plainest clothes we had—no fancy American garb—and meet him in the communal dining hall right across from the henhouses, which we'd find by the smell.

Sitting in the large dining room with about eighty people staring at us was a little embarrassing, but mainly exhilarating; I was in Israel. Many people stopped at our table to shake our hands, to thank us and say toda raba, but only a few of them spoke English. They were mainly from Poland and Russia. The women were dressed similarly to the men. Clean khaki pants and any color shirt. All clean and pressed. We knew that the clothes were all washed together, that people rotated in their jobs to iron, cook, wash dishes, do laundry, work the fields, milk the cows, and take care of the children. There was one nurse and one vet. We were prepared.

The next morning, at 5:00 a.m., there was a knock on our door.

"Boker tov," we heard Yigal call. "Good morning. Rise and shine." I loved his British accent, which made me feel homesick in a strange way. I used to have that accent too.

The two guys, Jon and Saul, were assigned to the cowshed. "We'll teach you how to milk the cows," Yigal said, and chuckled. "And you girls are going to be divided. I need two in the children's hut and one in the kitchen. Who wants to do what?"

We started haggling and Yigal stopped us. "No fighting. Today you do one job, tomorrow you'll do another. It doesn't really matter. You're volunteers." That was a good reminder.

"I'll go to the kitchen," I said. I was a good volunteer.

"Good choice," he said, chuckling again. Was he making fun of me? But I liked him.

When I met Mable and Dawn for breakfast at 7:00 a.m.,

they told me that they had to change diapers for an hour. I laughed and understood why Yigal had said to me, "Good choice." He was on my side, after all. Good.

After breakfast we were assigned to the ironing room, which was great. It was December and rain was expected, and the room was steamy and warm. The boys were sent to the carpentry shop to sweep and clean, and poor Jon had an asthma attack from the dust. The nurse attended to him, and with his inhaler and medication, he soon recovered.

"No more dust for you, friend," Yigal said to him. "You're lucky it's going to rain tonight; it will put the dust to rest."

In the evening, after dinner, we were exhausted. It was still early, even though the sun had set, and we didn't feel like going to sleep at 8:00 p.m., although we knew that we'd be woken up at 5:00 a.m. again.

"Let's take a walk around," Saul said to me as we walked out of the dining hall. I smiled, and he saw it as permission to take my hand. I didn't resist. He was sweet and kind, and a pleasure to talk to. I winked at Mable and Dawn, and when they turned to walk back to our hut, I yelled, "Go visit Jon!" They both waved with their backs to us.

The smell of the eucalyptus trees was medicinal, and lying under the tall trees, I filled my lungs with fresh, scented air. I felt content, my back on the earth of my ancestors' land and my eyes scanning the stars above. I was eighteen and could choose what to do with my life.

I turned to watch Saul, and he turned to me. We kissed gently for a while. I enjoyed it but felt no passion. We necked a bit, and when he stopped and whispered hoarsely, "We better go back," I agreed.

He got up, then helped me up, and when he hugged me, I felt that he would have loved to stay, but he didn't push. I was glad. I wasn't ready. I didn't even know what I wasn't ready for. I liked Saul, but he was still a boy, somewhat clumsy and hesitant. I had no idea what to do and expected him to lead, but I was scared at the same time. It was so confusing; I was glad we stopped. We dusted soil and dry leaves from our clothes and leaned on each other as we walked back, almost sleepwalking.

At night, in my bed, I would fantasize kissing Yigal instead, and in the mornings, when he came to assign us our jobs, I'd blush, scared that he could read my mind.

Two weeks later, when Saul and I took another walk around the kibbutz grounds, he was prepared. Behind the children's hut, he'd hidden two blankets. When I realized that he was ready to go on, I got scared and wasn't sure if I was.

I'd heard Dawn and Mable giggle about two young kibbutzniks whom they had spent part of some nights with, but they never included me in their whispers. I was quite surprised; I hadn't noticed them absent at night. They were both in their beds in the morning. Had they sneaked back unnoticed while I was asleep?

I felt like it was my turn. If everyone was doing it, I wanted it, too; I was so curious.

When Saul had kissed me for the first time, it was sweet, but I didn't get excited. The truth was that I was actually disappointed, but tonight, Saul had a way to persuade me. He seemed more sure of himself. His kissing was more passionate. I liked it; I felt tingling when he kissed my neck, and my hair there stood up, and I went along. I liked him caressing my body, but I was also nervous; I wasn't sure what came next. I wished Dawn and Mable had told me what they did so I'd be prepared when my pants came down.

I almost yelled out when he penetrated me. He quickly pulled out, and I felt the warmth spread on my tummy. Saul was prepared again. He pulled a small towel from between the two blankets and let me wipe myself. He lay on top of me, the towel between us, and kissed me again and again. I pressed my legs together to try and get rid of the burning sensation. It didn't help. I was disappointed. Was that all? All the girls' giggles were about this pain? All the romance novels I'd read had prepared me for something more exciting, more dramatic. All the tragedies, the suicides, the betrayals were all because of sex. I felt let down.

The following day I got my period. Saul and I exchanged shy looks, and when he asked me to join him for a walk again, I felt awkward. I had to tell him I had my period, but didn't know how.

"I can't this week," I quickly whispered when we left the dining hall, just before Jon and the girls joined us. He nodded. I was glad he got it.

First, I was relieved, but somehow wanted to try again, which was confusing. I couldn't explain; maybe it was curiosity. Maybe there was more to it. I wished I could ask Dawn, but I was too shy to admit I had done it with Saul. But I knew I didn't want to do it again with him.

Every morning when Yigal woke us up and gave us instructions, he'd check me out. I could feel his eyes linger on me. What was he looking for? In the beginning I felt uncomfortable, but he didn't do it in a rude way. He'd look me up and down, and then, as if catching himself, he'd look away. I hadn't noticed him looking that way at Dawn or Mable. He reminded me of Mr. Green, my PE teacher, who would sometimes look at me that way.

I found myself waiting for the mornings to come. Yigal's stares that lingered on my face excited me. I wondered what sex would be like with him.

Friday night dinners were more festive than any other dinner. Some of the women of the kibbutz would light Shabbat candles and say the blessing. Then some men would make kiddush on the wine and bread and break the challa with their hands, passing pieces of the sweetened bread around the table. The kibbutz wasn't orthodox; most people were socialists, but some claimed that they liked remembering their families, whom they'd left in Europe, by following the traditions of their parents. The ones who didn't want to participate in the blessings just sat and watched. I thought of Shabbat with my family in Vienna, and fading memories would surface. I wasn't sure what to call the emotions I felt during those Shabbat dinners. Sadness? Yearning? I tried not to think of my family; it was too overwhelming. I knew that many other people in the kibbutz had also lost loved ones in the Holocaust—we'd been told in the movement, before we left—but nobody talked about it.

As spring approached and it got warmer—we've been in Israel four months already—on Saturday nights we'd sit outside on the ground in a huge circle, singing songs in Hebrew accompanied by Ziggi's accordion playing. I found myself feeling happy, like I belonged.

The only problem was Saul. He tried to ask me to go on walks, and I kept putting him off. I felt guilty about not wanting to sleep with him again, but I didn't know how to tell him. So I would find excuses not to go out to the fields at night, like I had a cramp in my leg, a stomachache, or I was just tired from a long workday. I knew he wasn't fooled; he understood, but we didn't verbalize our needs.

I found myself attracted more and more to Yigal, craving his lingering stares. He was older, in his thirties maybe, and gorgeous. When I looked at Yigal, at his mane of light hair that was almost burned at the edges, his mischievous, constantly smiling eyes, and his strong square jaw, I got a pinch at the pit of my stomach. His full lips made me lick my own. I was longing to touch them, kiss them. When he showed us how to pull out weeds, I could see his arm muscles contract, and I longed to touch them too.

Saul persisted and tried to lure me again and again, but I rejected him repeatedly. That one time with him had taught me a lot, but I wasn't attracted to him and didn't want to sleep with him.

On Thursday, May 4, 1950, the whole country celebrated Erev Lag BaOmer. People lit bonfires, and children carefully added wood and dry branches to the bottom of the flame, together with large potatoes to be baked in the open fire.

In the kibbutz that night, members formed a large circle around the fire, sitting on the ground with folded legs and singing. Ziggi played some Romanian melodies, Russian songs, and Polish polkas. I found myself sitting between Saul and Yigal and wasn't sure if the heat came from the flame or from within me. I felt loved, connected, and excited.

At one point all the people got up to dance the hora. Circle around a circle was formed, and we sang loudly, danced widely, and perspired profusely. I had Saul's arm over one shoulder and Yigal's around my other as I held both their waists when we danced in a circle, singing and laughing. I felt intoxicated from the energy around me.

I saw the children use small branches to pull the potatoes out and almost burn their little fingers, then put them in their mouths to cool. We were all laughing.

As it got late and the fire died down, shadows started moving away, and the crowd thinned out. When I turned to leave, my arm was grabbed by a strong, warm hand, and I was pulled towards the trees. I looked up. Yigal. Away from the crowd, he pinned my back to a eucalyptus tree and kissed me so passionately that I lost my breath. He moved his head back and stared down into my eyes, as if asking permission, then continued to kiss me, pressing his body hard against mine. I felt as if I were floating. I held his head in both of my hands and kissed him back, hard. My heart raced, and I felt that I was wet. I was embarrassed but Yigal was wild, and I had no time to think. All I knew was that I wanted him, oh, how I wanted him. My body burned under his caressing hands moving from my breasts to my waist to the stubborn button of my pants. He put me down, and it was exquisite to feel him inside of me. I moaned and cried out with ecstasy. His passion was contagious. So different from my first time with Saul. I wanted him. I craved him. I devoured him. And he, me.

In the morning, as I woke up, I decided I was going to stay in Israel and live with Yigal. But when he came to assign our jobs, he seemed to ignore me. I smiled warmly, and as I walked towards him, he turned and walked away. I was confused and hurt. I couldn't understand what had come over him. I wanted to call after him but noticed Saul watching me.

That day I was assigned to work in the large laundry room, sweating and laboring over stinking clothes of strangers, my head pounding. I was terribly upset. I was so ashamed of what I'd done that I couldn't face him in the dining room, so I didn't go there for lunch. When the woman in charge of the laundry room wanted to know what was wrong, she asked me, "Mah karah?" I just shrugged. She was kind enough to leave me alone. After work, when I got back to the room and the girls asked what was wrong, why didn't I come for lunch, I said I was getting my period and had terrible cramps.

The following morning, another kibbutznik came to assign us our jobs. He told us that Yigal had taken the pickup truck and driven to Tel Aviv to bring his wife back. Apparently, she'd been there awhile, taking care of her sick mother.

At first, I couldn't believe what I was hearing, but as it sank in, my stomach began to ache. His wife? I wanted nothing more than to disappear, but I couldn't avoid the work I'd been assigned: laundry, again. As I arrived in the laundry room, I told the new woman in charge that I had a stomachache and ran to the communal showers and toilets. My insides turned to water. I sat there and cried until she came looking for me.

"Are you alright?" she shouted from outside.

"I have diarrhea," I moaned. "It could be a bug." But I knew my body; that was the way it reacted to shock.

She left, and I got out, washed my hands and my face, and I was glad they did not have mirrors above the row of sinks.

"Oy. You look terrible, Elsie," the woman said as I walked back into the steaming laundry room. "I think you're getting sick. You're as white as the sheets we're washing. Go to bed, maidale, go rest, I can manage."

Two weeks later, my period didn't come.

Three weeks later, I was vomiting in the mornings.

Chapter Fifteen

Israel, 1950

ELSIE

IN those three weeks I felt lonely and miserable. Saul wouldn't talk to me since Lag BaOmer—I wondered what he'd seen—and Mable and Dawn were annoyed that I needed the bathroom so often. I had no support from them; they stuck together those last five months, and only Jon was kind and wanted to know how he could help.

"If you're sick, why don't you go see the nurse?" he asked me.

I was scared to go. I was afraid to hear what she had to say. I hoped that in one week my period would come; maybe I had miscalculated or just skipped a month. It had happened to me once, when I was thirteen. I had gotten my period only twice, and in the third month, it didn't come, but Mommy said not to worry, the body was adjusting. She had been right; a month later it came back, and since then I'd been regular. Could this be the same?

When the period didn't come a week later, I went to see the nurse. Maybe she'd put my mind at rest. She gave me a small glass and asked me to urinate into it. I had to make sure I didn't spill any when I handed it to her. She put a piece of paper over it and thanked me. "Come back in five days, and I'll tell you if you're pregnant," she said casually.

Pregnant.

The one word my brain refused to spell out. My head was spinning. I could be pregnant. "What does my urine have to do with it?" I asked the nurse.

"Oh, you don't know. The laboratory injects it into a rabbit . . . but don't worry. Come back and we'll discuss it."

Those were the longest five days of my life. I vomited each morning but continued working as assigned, not wanting to think of the possibility of a baby growing inside my small belly.

It was strange, but Yigal was replaced by Oded. No explanation was given to us why our group leader had left, but when Saul asked Oded one morning, his answer was "Yigal was sent to repair the tractors. Our mechanic was injured and was sent to the hospital. I'll be your group leader now, and maybe in a month or two, Yigal will be back."

A month or two? But of course I thought it was all because of me.

The only place I did see Yigal was the dining room. While he ignored me, I was yearning to speak to him. But I didn't know what to say. First, I had to wait a few more days. And then what? Ask him why he had slept with me if he had a wife? I knew by now he didn't love me. Some married men cheated on their wives, I knew that. I wasn't that naïve. But I felt used, cheap, betrayed. He had eyed me for a long time, and like a stupid girl, I had fallen into his trap. I had thought I was sexy, attractive to an older, experienced man. What was I going to say to him?

I returned to the nurse, and she first congratulated me, but when she saw the tears in my eyes, she said, "Oh, you're not happy. Does your boyfriend not know?"

In a kibbutz almost everybody knew everything about anything. She must have seen me with Saul, thinking he was my boyfriend.

"It's alright, deary. I know that you're not from here. If you want, you can have an abortion. The kibbutz will take care of it." She said this casually, as if she were offering me an apple.

"Oh. I . . . eh . . . let me think . . . eh . . . thank you." I ran out of there.

Pregnant. It was confirmed. With one word from me, it could end. But I didn't have the guts. I didn't have a friend I could confide in and who could support me emotionally. I couldn't tell my parents. They'd be ashamed, outraged, disappointed in me. I couldn't return home with a belly. I wasn't married; I was too young. About to turn nineteen.

I went back to bed and told everybody to leave me alone, I was sick.

For a whole week I pretended to be sick, staying in bed, sleeping a lot, and thinking. I couldn't have a baby. For most of my life I'd been scared that if I had children, I'd be running the risk of having to part with them. What if there was a war? No, I would not inflict that pain on a child, sending them away if need be. No. Never.

Yet here I was. With child. What would I do now?

I would part with this child before I knew them, before they knew me. That was the only answer.

I wrote to Auntie Judith Nussboim and asked her if I could come and visit them in London. I received a quick reply; she'd be more than happy to see me. Unfortunately, Uncle had died two years before, but Rebecca, who still lived with her and was studying to become a nurse, would be delighted to see me, too.

I was utterly surprised. Rebecca, a nurse. I didn't think she had an ounce of compassion in her, but who knew? People changed, as I knew well, or perhaps we hadn't really known each other in the first place. I shook my head. Horrible Rebecca, a nurse. Go figure. Maybe she wasn't that horrible after all. Maybe she could help me.

Now I needed to find a way to get to them. I sat down and wrote to my parents.

July 5, 1950

Dear Mommy and Daddy,

I hope my letter finds you both well. Thank you for the beautiful card for my birthday, and the generous gift. I'm not doing too well over here. I'm sorry to disappoint you, but this letter isn't as happy as the ones I've sent you before. I would like to leave Israel now, before the end of the year as I'd planned. You taught me not to quit, but I have to. I'm sorry. Kibbutz life is not for me and I'm miserable. It's extremely hot and humid right now, and I just can't see myself ever living on a kibbutz.

I'm disappointed in myself, and I'm so sorry. I'd still like to finish out my year abroad, and I was hoping to get your permission to go to England to visit the Nussboims. What do you think? They were very good to me, right? Would you agree that a nice, long visit might be appropriate? As I'd like to return home via England, I could just leave here earlier and stay there longer. I really want to see them again and hope you'll both agree with this decision.

I'm not looking forward to being aboard a ship again, so do you both think that I could fly instead? EL AL started flying to London via Rome only a few months ago. Daddy, I hope that this detour isn't going to cost you too much money.

Oh, remember Jon? He is leaving, too, and returning home. His asthma is getting worse in the dust here. The winds from the Sahara Desert are affecting him badly. Thank you for understanding, you're both great parents.

Your loving daughter,
Elsie

Chapter Sixteen

London, 1950

ELSIE

MY first flight was amazing. The air hostess was kind and showed me how to fasten my seat belt. My stomach was still flat, but my breasts and waist had filled out some, which made me feel uncomfortable; not all my skirts would close, and while sitting on the plane, I had to unfasten my belt. The woman next to me slept all the way to Rome but read a book on our way to London. She smiled at me occasionally, like when we bumped hands over the armrest. I tried to nap, but it wasn't easy; people were talking, and the shaking of the plane nauseated me toward the end of the flight. I almost panicked when we were about to land; it was scary, but also exhilarating.

We landed in Heathrow, and I took the Tube to Auntie's home. It was August, hot and muggy, and it felt strange to be in the Underground again. I remembered my first trip with Uncle and Auntie in January 1939. I couldn't stop thinking of little Elsie, who knew nothing of what was to come. My heart felt heavy and I began to sweat, my head spinning with memories. Twelve years had passed since my first Tube ride, yet in some ways it felt like yesterday. The British accent in the Underground made me feel weird: somewhat homesick for the two years I'd lived there, but also evocative of the fear and alienation I'd had in those years. How could one differentiate between all the emotions one feels in one moment? Good and bad all at once. Nausea overtook me, and as I got off, I vomited at the bottom of the stairs. People stared at me. I felt horrible but couldn't help myself. I wiped my mouth with my handkerchief and walked up the stairs to the street, into the fresh air. Auntie didn't live far away from the station; I remembered that.

London was different: cleaner, more orderly. The buildings had been restored, repaired, or rebuilt. I was slightly disoriented; I'd just come from a kibbutz in Israel. A different world. I was terrified of what was coming ahead.

But the hug I received from Auntie melted all my fears. As did the comforting scent of chicken soup—which engulfed me—soup she'd made even though it wasn't yet Shabbat dinner.

Oh, that smell. I felt tears coming into my eyes as I suddenly had a vision of my Bubbe, which I had to push away.

I had to focus on what was coming, I had to be strong, I couldn't crumble. Not now, when a new life depended on my coming decisions.

Auntie and I sat at the old kitchen table and enjoyed her golden chicken soup with thin noodles. I swallowed hard and told her about my life in America and my experience on the kibbutz, and we were just beginning to talk about Raizele when Rebecca walked in.

She had the habit of walking in when I was eating in her home.

I stood up and stared at her, not sure if she'd like a hug or not. She reminded me so much of her father, but she was much, much taller. How had she gotten so tall with such short parents? She was almost a head taller than me. She still had the same white English skin and cascading red curls as when she was a child, but now they had a sheen to them. I had auburn hair, but it was a different shade, not that vibrant.

Standing there for a minute, we both smiled, checking each other out, and then she reached over for a hug. "You filled out," she announced.

I blushed. I was five months pregnant and my body was different.

Rebecca smiled smugly, as if she knew something, and sat down at the kitchen table, staring at me. I wasn't sure how to tell them. I was planning to maybe wait until tomorrow, but Rebecca's eyes were demanding, awaiting a confession. She wouldn't stop staring even when Auntie got up and brought her a bowl of soup. I had to spill it out, and almost out of bread, I said, "Well... I'm pregnant." It was hard to utter these words out loud. I wasn't sure I could trust them, but I had no other choice. I had to trust them. My parents had no contact with the Nussboims, so I knew I was safe.

Auntie opened her eyes wide, and Rebecca nodded, not looking surprised.

"I want to give birth here in London and put the baby up for adoption." I said this all in one breath before I could change my own mind.

Rebecca looked into my eyes and said, "You're in luck." She put her hand on mine, another surprising gesture. "I work with a gynecologist. He's the best." She blushed, and I wondered why; did she have a crush on him? Then she added, "I'm going to become a midwife, you know. I can help you."

Before I could absorb her words, Auntie asked, breathless, as if she couldn't hold it in any longer, "Who is the father?"

"A married man from the kibbutz." My voice shook. I wasn't sure if I had to defend myself, to tell them that I didn't know he was married, but I didn't feel comfortable enough to tell them everything. I hadn't seen them in so many years; I suddenly got cold feet.

"Married." Auntie put her hand on her mouth. "Does he know?"

"No."

"Do your parents know?"

"No, they don't, and . . . I don't want them to know. Only the two of you. Nobody else. Please. Promise me."

They both nodded.

"How far are you?" Auntie whispered.

"About five months." I looked down at my hands.

"Too late to regret it now." Auntie surprised me by her words as she patted my hand. "You can stay here as long as you need." Her kind eyes gave me much confidence. I loved that sweet woman who'd treated me like her own child all those years ago, and now too.

Rebecca said, "I can help you, too, Elsie. I can arrange a visit to the doctor to make sure everything is in order with the baby. I can tell him you're my sister who lives in America, and he wouldn't charge you. In the meantime, you can look for odd jobs that don't require a work permit, like being an au pair, and in a few months, if all goes well, you can have the baby in the hospital, and I can arrange a private adoption."

I looked at her, surprised. I didn't know what a private adoption was.

"An adoption agency isn't always necessary," Rebecca explained. "I can arrange a private placement with a good couple, maybe even a Jewish family." She gave her mother a quick look. "The doctor knows many prospective adoptive parents who can't have children of their own. It's done all the time," Rebecca said with confidence.

And there I was. Fortunate and utterly surprised to receive much-needed help from the last person in the world I would have expected to lend me a hand. I would have had to struggle and not know where to turn had Rebecca not offered to help me. Who would have thought . . .

"You have to tell her," Rebecca said to her mother.

I looked from one to the other. The relief I felt turned to anxiety at her sudden change of tone. "Tell me what?" My heartbeat accelerated. I felt like everything was too good to be true, working out so beautifully, but something bad was about to happen.

"Show her," Rebecca demanded.

Auntie got up and left the kitchen. The silence between me and Rebecca was thick as we waited. Auntie returned with a white envelope with a red cross painted on it. My body knew before I was told; my heart was throbbing in my throat. Red Cross could only mean one thing.

Auntie said, "My late Isaac wrote to the Red Cross when the war ended. He wanted to know what had happened to his relatives, including your parents and grandparents."

My head was throbbing. Mahme. Tahte. Twelve years. I put my face in my hands to cool the heat that had spread on my cheeks.

But Auntie stood there, waiting, the envelope hanging in the air. I lifted my head, then looked at her and took the envelope from her trembling hand. Or maybe it was my hand that shook? I took the letter out and read aloud the first line. "'We deeply regret to inform you that . . .'" My hand went limp, and the letter fell to the floor. It was final. Confirmed. Black on white.

Rebecca picked the letter up and read it out loud, her voice emotionless.

"'In November 1941, Deborah Stein and her parents, Avrum and Rochel Lewkowicz, were deported from Vienna to the Lodz Ghetto with 5,483 other Jews. From there they were deported to Theresienstadt and from there to Auschwitz. It is recorded that they died there. We also regret to inform you that Dr. Jakub Stein was sent to Dachau in December 1938 due to a nervous breakdown and hanged himself there.'"

I stared at Rebecca, not really seeing her. I didn't want to comprehend her words, but I had to; I owed it to my parents. I felt crushed. I saw my father's swollen face when he was taken away, not looking at us. As if ashamed, ashamed that he couldn't protect us. Was that why he'd hanged himself? How? I would never know. What had happened to my beautiful Mahme? She and her parents had been deported at the same time that my sister and I had left England for the United States. I felt as if I'd known it even then. I'd felt it, when I was looking for her on the dock . . . just before we'd gotten on the big ship to leave England . . . I'd looked for her at the port . . . but I'd known then she wouldn't find us.

How did she die? Had she been shot? Sent to the gas chambers? Mahme . . . Mahme . . . Did you hold your own mahme's hand in the showers? Did you think of your two little girls, the ones you loved so much but had to let go to save them?

My heart was shattered. I'd known for years that it was likely they'd been killed by the Nazis, but seeing it written out was brutal.

I knew only one person in the whole wide world who remembered them like I did, but she was out of my reach. In a few months she'd be eighteen. I'd been waiting for that day forever, but now I realized that in my condition I would probably not be able to face her. How could I show myself in my situation? She'd judge me for being promiscuous, be ashamed of me, loathe me, reject me. I didn't know much about Catholicism, but I knew they believed that getting pregnant out of wedlock was a sin. A horrible sin. I had no way of knowing how her Catholic upbringing would have impacted her, but in that moment, with the clarity of the loss of my entire family written down in front of me, I knew that I could not stand to lose anybody else. Even if I could find her and persuade her to meet with me, she wouldn't want me. I couldn't bear the thought of what her rejection would do to me. I swallowed my dreams and tried to focus on the present. I'd have to think about her later . . .

Chapter Seventeen

London, 1951

ELSIE

I WAS thrashing around in the wet hospital bed, soaking in my blood, as I heard his first cry.

"It's a boy," someone said. And then ... nothing. As if my baby had been kidnapped. Where was he? I wasn't allowed to see him, let alone hold him. Or say goodbye.

"Better that way," somebody had said, "you have to forget him."

But he was my own flesh and blood. I wanted to hold and press him to me, to feel his skin on mine. I stretched both my arms up to the ceiling, like a mad woman, fingers spread to receive him. Nothing.

"No, Elsie, I'm sorry, it's not possible." I recognized Rebecca's voice. "It's not healthy for you or for the baby." Decisive statement. Sharp. Cold hospital rule.

He'd been taken out of the room, and I couldn't stand it. I started screaming—I screamed and screamed until I felt a needle in my arm.

In the morning, the bed was clean. I put both my palms down by my sides on the sheet. Dry. No water. I thought I was swimming a minute ago. In the ocean. Swimming home. Or was it a dream?

"You lost a lot of blood, but everything is alright now." Bright ceiling lights burned my eyes. Rebecca was standing by my bed.

Where was I?

Then I remembered. I put my hand on my abdomen and was surprised to feel a bump. For a second, I thought I still had the baby in me, but then my eyes fell on the big bag of blood dripping into my arm. Blood transfusion.

"Luckily, we have the same blood type, Elsie, imagine. We're sisters, right?" Rebecca winked and smiled a crooked smile, then took my hand in hers. Her fingers were cold, but I'd grown used to her strange warmth in the last few months I'd lived with her. "I donated almost two pints for you, my dear, so you're going to be strong and healthy like me, you'll see." She sounded proud. "I'm going home to rest now; it was a long night. Everything has been taken care of, I promise, so just go back to sleep, and I'll see you tomorrow. When you're strong and ready, I'll be taking you home. Ta-ta." And she was gone.

I wanted my baby to have a good home and a good life, to be healthy and joyful, loved and cared for. I had it all planned in my head, and I knew that I was doing the right thing; better to give him up now, before I knew him. Rebecca had promised that he'd be sent to a loving home and be raised by good Jewish people. I trusted her. I had to.

I remembered that one night, before we went to sleep, I'd asked Rebecca, "Why did you hate me so much when we were small? From the very beginning."

She first looked at her hands, then at me, and said, "I'm sorry. I'm so, so sorry. It wasn't personal. I was awful. I know. I was an only child, you see, a spoiled and selfish little girl who hadn't been told anything before you arrived. Nobody had prepared me, asked my opinion, or explained anything about a refugee—I thought you were an orphan—who needed a home. You were a family member, a second cousin." She took a deep breath. "One day this sweet little girl, polite and well mannered, appeared in my house, in my room, and I wasn't the center of my parents' attention anymore. They doted over you. I was just a spoiled little kid, Elsie, bitterly jealous and angry. I'm sorry. I will make it up to you. Promise."

On the flight back home, extreme sadness engulfed me, but I kept persuading myself that I'd done the right thing. That

I'd made the best decision for the baby. I gave him life. But I couldn't give him a good life all by myself, an unwed mother, with an absentee father. I couldn't have returned to my adoptive parents with a baby. I couldn't have faced them, seen the disappointment on their faces, the accusation in their eyes, after all that they'd done for me. I couldn't lay shame on them, humiliate them before their community, their neighbors, their customers.

But I hadn't expected the yearning that I was feeling. Something was missing, and I didn't know how to fill the void. I missed him, I missed the kicks and the first cry. I even missed the labor pains.

I would never forget this child. I couldn't. I didn't want to. I only hoped he'd understand one day and forgive me. Just like I'd forgiven my birth mother for saving me by letting me go.

So many goodbyes, so many losses.

I knew that I wasn't going to tell anybody about him. No one needed to know. Ever.

But what about Rosalind? Could I keep this a secret from her for the rest of my life?

I wanted nothing more than to be able to find her, to reconnect, but at the same time I feared that I wouldn't be able to keep this secret from her, and if I confessed, she'd hate me, reject me.

Part Two

Chapter Eighteen

Boston, 1952-1960

MARTIN ROY

HER dark blue eyes, almost purple, captivated me the instant my eyes met hers. I couldn't look away. Neither could she. We were in church on Easter Sunday, and I fell for her. Rosalind Cox was nineteen—almost twenty, I learned later—an undergraduate student at Emmanuel College while I was busy finishing graduate school at Harvard University and starting my doctoral studies in political science. I was very involved with international colleagues and occupied beyond comfort, but she became my priority.

Soon after her graduation, we were married. I was thrilled,

but I had no idea what I was getting myself into.

I hadn't known much about her, but I thought that what I'd known was enough. She was Catholic, like me, of course, although she had been adopted when she was a little child. She had wonderful, loving parents; she was smart and interesting to talk to, and I was madly in love with the tall, young beauty with long blond curls and luscious lips. At first, married life was bliss.

But things changed after our first son was born late at night, on October 8, 1960. After I'd been pacing the polished floor of the waiting room, I heard piercing screaming. Pumped with sudden adrenaline, I jumped and ran to the nurses' station. "Who's screaming like that? Is that my wife?" I asked in panic. It sounded like a tortured animal and went on and on for a long time. These noises were unbearable, and I feared they were coming from Rosalind. I knew that childbirth was painful, only I had thought that women were given sedation for the pain.

I was grateful when it stopped.

I sat back in my chair and had almost fallen asleep when I heard, "Congratulations, Mr. Roy, you have a beautiful, healthy baby boy." Rosalind's doctor materialized before me, and I jumped up, somewhat groggy. He shook my hand. "Baby is doing just fine, although your wife had a hard time, I'm afraid. We've given her something to calm her down."

"Is that the usual procedure?" I asked. His remarks about Rosalind worried me. The smell in the hospital was nauseating all of a sudden.

"I'm afraid it's not." The doctor rubbed his bald head, then took his glasses off, retrieved a handkerchief from his pocket, and began to polish the lenses. "But I'm sure she'll be fine after a couple of hours' sleep." He put his glasses back on his nose, patted my shoulder, and said, "You should go home and rest too. You look exhausted." Then he left.

The hair on the back of my neck stood up, and a shiver ran down my arms. My stomach flipped, indicating that things were not alright with Rosalind. I went to the nurses' station. They said that she was asleep and I shouldn't disturb her, but asked if I would want to see the baby. Of course I did.

The row of babies was overwhelming. "This one," mouthed the nurse behind the glass as she pointed at a head full of brown hair. Oh, my goodness. Unbelievable. This was my own child, this bundle wrapped like a mummy. I stared at the closed eyes and long eyelashes, the tiny nose, and the sweet, small mouth. My baby. My son. I could hardly tear myself from the glass window, wondering if I should go to my parents first to tell them of their new grandson or go home and collapse on my bed. I felt like I needed a cigarette.

I found the pay phone and called. Mom answered. "It's a boy!" I said. "Thanks, Mom, yes, he's fine, six pounds, three ounces. Yes, he's quite alright and . . . so is Rosalind. I'm going home to sleep and will see them both in the morning. Talk tomorrow, good night."

I found a box of Dunhill in my car's glove compartment and inhaled a long drag before turning the car engine on. The cigarette kept me awake all the way home.

A son. I had a son. We had a son. I was almost singing in my head.

I returned the following morning, but my wife was gone.

Gone.

The sheriff's car was parked right outside the hospital. When I tried to enter the hospital, I was stopped abruptly by a policeman who asked me for my name, then asked if my wife had returned home.

"What do you mean?" I panicked. This was the second time my stomach had flipped in less than twelve hours. "I'm coming from the house to see my wife and my baby, and you're asking me if she's home? This is uncanny. Are you telling me that she's not here?" Sweat dripped down my back. I felt like I was watching someone else, not me.

"Please calm down, Mr. Roy. We'll find her, she couldn't have gone too far in the cold, still wearing the hospital gown..." Inside, everybody was running around frantic, looking for her.

I couldn't believe it. My wife, my Rosalind, where could she be? I hoped she wasn't hurt.

Shivering, I pulled my coat tightly around me, thinking of her out there, in the cold. It was only October, but the mornings were chilly. I was ready to run out and look for her when another cop walked in through the hospital doors, holding on to a barefooted woman in a hospital gown, her long hair disheveled and hiding part of her face, with another unkempt woman in tow. "She kept calling me Mommy... Mahme... or something like that, the poor soul," said the toothless, elderly woman in filthy clothes. "She tried to hug me, crying and mumbling..."

I approached them. "Rosalind?" I asked gently, not believing my eyes. I focused on the face of the woman held by the second policeman, watching from the corner of my eye as the first policeman gently escorted the elderly woman out the door.

I barely recognize my wife. A nurse glided a wheelchair right under her. She sat her down and they entered the elevator. I followed behind. Rosalind didn't look at me. I moved the hair off her face and looked into her beautiful blue eyes, but they were empty. No recognition.

The nurse asked me to sit in the waiting room while they washed Rosalind and called her doctor. I couldn't sit; I paced nervously, my fists in my pockets. I needed a cigarette but had none on me. My head pounding, I ordered myself to relax. I sat down. Then I remembered.

"Can I see my baby?" I asked at the nurses' station.

"Babies are going to be fed right now." The heavyset nurse yawned and didn't even lift her head from her ledger. Nobody was interested in me. Babies were crying in the nursery. I was sure my son was crying too. I had seen him all bundled up for barely a minute last night; I wondered if I'd recognize him among all the babies in the nursery. My baby. My son. More babies joined the crying as feeding time approached.

I heard a sharp scream. Could it be Rosalind?

The nurses' station was empty. I took a chance and walked swiftly to the room I'd seen Rosalind being wheeled into. She thrashed under the sheet and blanket, which were tightly fitted, and screamed again, her hands covering her ears. I stood there not knowing if I could touch her, hug her, or—

"Mrs. Roy!" A nurse came running. "Mrs. Roy, you have to stop screaming, the pain can't be that bad, the baby's out already."

But Rosalind wouldn't stop. I had to help the nurse hold her down. I hugged her, whispering, "It's alright, Rosalind, it's alright, darling. Calm down, my love, please stop screaming, everything is alright." Her hair was wet, her face pale, her eyes wild. I wasn't sure she could hear me while blocking her ears.

Another nurse rushed in with a syringe. "Doctor called back, thank God. He couldn't come... delivering another baby ... but he said to give her this. It will help."

When I was sent outside, back to the waiting room, I found my parents waiting, frowns on their faces. They sat next to Rosalind's adoptive parents, Margaret and Oliver Cox.

I fell onto an empty chair. "I don't think I can do this," I said, choking with emotion as I put my head in my hands. "Rosalind is hysterical. She can't take care of a baby the way she is now." Then I mumbled, "I don't know what's going to happen." I got up and started pacing, feeling my mother's eyes following me as she bit the skin around her nails.

"You'll hire a nanny," Margaret said confidently. "Many parents do. Rosalind will recuperate; it's just the shock of the birth."

I stopped pacing and gazed at my mother-in-law, then sat down, lifted my chin, and leaned my head back on the wall to steady myself. My mouth was dry, my heart racing. I knew I needed help. A nanny, yes. Neither Margaret nor my mother offered to help Rosalind, which surprised me.

"Hey, congratulations, man," my father-in-law said, who stood up and shook my hand.

My parents came over and hugged me. Then Margaret did. I felt better.

Of course, they all wanted to see the baby. So I took them to the nursery, and we stood together behind the large glass window, trying to read the names on the bassinets.

There, "Baby Roy." Big smiles appeared on everyone's faces. I felt proud. I had a son.

On my way home I stopped at the drugstore for cigarettes. I was desperately worried; I didn't know what was wrong with Rosalind. I hoped it wasn't serious. Sucking on a Dunhill revived me. So much better than the Luckys I'd smoked in college. But my head still felt heavy.

Three days later, I took Rosalind and the baby home. In the hospital, Rosalind was sedated, but at home I worried she'd have another screaming attack. Fortunately her mother waited for us with a nanny. God bless Margaret.

"He cries," Rosalind complained almost in disgust as a visible shiver ran along her skinny frame, and she handed him over to the nanny. "I can't do it."

"He cries because you won't hold him long enough," the nanny said firmly, but Rosalind turned her back on her and walked out of the nursery.

I didn't think it was appropriate for the hired nanny to reprimand my wife, so I called the doctor for a new recommendation. I spoke to his nurse, who was most obliging.

"My wife is in pain," I explained. "Mental pain—emotional—not physical. We need a nanny with compassion."

After she gave me several names and phone numbers, I asked to speak to the doctor, if he was available, to ask him about Rosalind's emotional state.

"This is quite normal, it happens," both the gynecologist—and next, the pediatrician— said to me. "Not often, but it happens. Give it time. Some women are overwhelmed after giving birth. It's hormonal. Soon enough, she'll calm down and bond with her baby."

But until that happened, I didn't know what to do with her sadness, her refusal to eat, and with her weight loss. She looked breakable. The baby was beautiful and thriving, and I was delighted, yet Rosalind's behavior was worrying.

As time went on, she developed strategies; such as keeping dozens of pacifiers placed all over the house. She placed one in David's mouth each time he started crying, like a plug. At times, she'd cradle him with one arm and hold her finger firmly over the pacifier so he couldn't spit it out. Other times, I had to take the baby from her when I sensed that they were both distraught. David's face would get scrunched and red, and Rosalind's eyes would open in terror, as if something awful was about to happen. His crying truly upset her; her shaking would start, and I was petrified she'd snap. When I asked her what was so scary about a baby crying, she'd look at me with those beautiful eyes and say in a quivering, almost apologetic voice, "I don't know, I really don't know. It gives me the creeps, I can't stand to hear a baby cry, I don't know why." Tears would appear in her eyes, and I could see her suffering. It was very disturbing to us both.

One night, when Rosalind and I eventually had fallen asleep, I woke up, hearing her repeatedly murmur in her sleep, "Baby ... baby crying ... in train . . . crying ... where is his Mahme ... Mahme ... " She was throwing her head violently from side to side. I had to wake her from that dream and hold her tightly. The strangest thing was that she had been mumbling in both English and another language. I thought it might be German. I worked with academics from other countries, and it sounded like German. I wondered where she knew German from. But this couldn't be. She'd been adopted from England. Perhaps she'd picked up a German word or two there. But then I persuaded myself that I was imagining things so late at night.

Once, after she'd calmed down and was asleep again, I covered her with our blanket, got into my slippers, and went downstairs to the kitchen. I couldn't sleep. Standing by the open window with my Dunhill calmed me, but I knew my wife needed help, and I didn't know how to help her. She was the love of my life and my biggest worry.

"Dr. Stargaze," I said on the phone to our family doctor the next day, "Rosalind isn't improving. I think she needs to see a psychiatrist."

"I understand," Dr. Stargaze said, agreeing after he heard my observations. "I'll get my nurse to call you with a name and number."

The psychiatrist, Dr. Volt, explained that some women experienced trauma from childbirth, but that with time and medication, the anxiety would go away. He gave Rosalind tranquilizers, which seemed to calm her but also made her eyes look glassy.

Some nights I was astounded when she'd crawl out of bed and creep out to the baby's nursery. I'd wait a minute, then follow and find her in her rocking chair, holding David in her lap, staring at his sleeping face with utter adoration. When he was asleep and quiet, her love for him poured out easily as she crooned a lullaby.

I had to keep away, because once I came too close and she jumped and stopped singing.

When David was about eighteen months old, Rosalind, who read him books every single night, introduced him to flash cards with words. I thought it was fascinating, teaching a baby to read, but I didn't interfere. She had tremendous patience to read him her favorites, like *The Peep of Day* series. I didn't know how much he understood, but David loved sitting on her lap in his room, both rocking on her chair while Rosalind read to him. As long as he wasn't crying, she was happy. They were both happy. So was I.

When he was almost two, and Rosalind was pregnant again, I once saw her bribe him with a lollipop when his face crumpled and he was about to cry. He stopped immediately and started licking the candy. Another time I heard her say, "Here, David, take the cookie, but don't cry. Would you rather have a Popsicle? Here, please don't cry."

I didn't like this behavior but figured as long as she stayed calm, I would let it go. I knew Rosalind was young and inexperienced, a new mother, nervous and worried, but she loved David intensely. Almost possessively. David always got what he wanted by just opening his mouth and threatening to cry, his deep blue eyes, like hers, searching her face for a reaction. He was smart and a fast learner.

I was worried he'd grow up selfish and manipulative, but I was too afraid of her moods to intervene in her parenting.

Chapter Nineteen

Boston, 1962

MARTIN

WHEN Lawrence was born in 1962, we thought we were prepared.

Dr. Volt added another medication, and that kept Rosalind calm, although groggy and sometimes lethargic. Lawrence was a large baby, irritable and cranky. He didn't cry; he yelled. So I bought Rosalind a pair of Koss SP/3X headphones, which she'd plug into the kitchen radio so that she could listen to music and shows while Nancy, our new nanny, took care of the boys.

In my early thirties, I was an associate professor, and my

workload was immense. Some days I met the most interesting people and taught smart kids, but with a newborn baby and little sleep, I needed a few minutes to myself. I usually found those in my car, on the way home.

After a typical long day at work, I'd light a cigarette as soon as I parked the car by the house, and take a ten-minute stroll on our street before walking in. Stalling. I knew I was taking away time from my family—which made me feel guilty—when I just stood outside our gate to air my clothes before entering and facing them, not wanting to put my wife or the boys off with the smell. I knew smoking wasn't a good habit, but it was hard to quit. Besides, sometimes I really needed it. Walking in, I'd usually see Nancy handing Lawrence to Rosalind in the middle of his feed, making sure the bottle stayed in his mouth. Rosalind would either hand him to me or put Lawrence down in his crib and prop the bottle with a rolled-up hand towel.

She never held him a minute too long. But she never let him cry, either.

I persuaded myself that not letting the boys cry could be a good thing. What did I know? As a young father, I was inexperienced, too, yet I had a nagging feeling that there was something wrong, that the boys needed protection. But from whom?

I knew Rosalind read to David and Lawrence during the day; that was their favorite quiet time—and hers—but bedtime was reserved for me.

David would lie under his light-blue covers, and I would lie on top of his bed with Lawrence on my chest, snoring softly, my head next to David's on his pillow. While I was reading,

David liked to place his finger on mine and follow along. When his hand dropped, I knew that he'd fallen asleep. He could read by the time he was four, my clever boy.

Lawrence, who had his mother's blond curls, refused to let us cut his hair, and he looked like a beautiful little girl, but when he turned four and was teased at his nursery school, he relented. Always had a mind of his own, that one.

By the time our third boy, Andrew, came along, Rosalind had been stabilized by the pills and the many injections—the doctors had been prepared for his birth—and no drama had occurred.

Andrew was only several weeks old when, on a Sunday morning while Rosalind was feeding him, David and Lawrence were playing in the backyard, climbing trees, laughing and running around shouting. Suddenly Lawrence came in huffing and yelling. "Daddy, Daddy, David fell from the tree!"

I ran out, following Lawrence to where David lay on the ground by the old tree trunk.

Thank goodness he was breathing.

"What happened?" I asked as I lifted him up in my arms.

My four-year-old firstborn was pale, sighing loudly in pain, but not a tear was seen. He held his right arm with his left hand, and I noticed that his right wrist was hanging at an odd angle.

"He fell off the tree, Daddy!" Lawrence cried out. "Is he dead already?"

"No, my boy, he is not dead. But I better take him to the hospital; I think he broke his wrist." I stood up with David in my arms. "You go inside, Lawrence, and tell Mother that David will be fine, but we need the doctor to look at him. Will you, please? It was a good thing that you called us. Thank you, big boy."

Two-year-old Lawrence proudly ran back inside, screaming, "Mother! Mother!" as I took David to my car and laid him on the back seat. Then I rushed inside to grab my car keys and yelled to Rosalind that we were on our way to the hospital.

The x-rays confirmed my suspicion, and a technician put David's arm in a cast.

I didn't realize this at the time, but this would be the first of many breaks leading me to wonder whether he was accident-prone. I was grateful he hadn't broken his neck, this time, but as he continued to endure injuries, I began to worry not just about Rosalind, but about him too.

Chapter Twenty

Los Angeles, 1982

DAVID

MOST of the Southern Californians smiled a lot, and the ones I'd met—who were willing to discuss politics—were friendly and liberal. With my Bostonian friends back home, it wasn't as easy to talk politics. The women here were friendlier too. Almost every waitress in Los Angeles, at least in the French-chef-run restaurants, had the same hairstyle. I presumed those ladies had been chasing a dream, coming to the City of Angels in the hope of joining Charlie's Angels on the silver screen, but instead had just ended up serving fine-dining cuisine to us mortal beings while waiting for their big break. It was noticeable that they weren't trained in hotel schools—the service fell quite short—but their looks and smiles made up for their lack of professionalism.

I hadn't appreciated the difference in culture as a freshman, when I arrived here to study at Occidental College, but now, four years later, I did.

At eighteen I couldn't wait to get away from home and test my independence. I was proud to have been accepted to Occidental College, and I was delighted to move to Los Angeles.

"California?" Mother spat the word as if she couldn't wait to get rid of it. "That's almost Mexico."

Dad, a professor at Harvard, got it. "Let him spread his wings," he said, trying to convince her. "He's still so young. Let him experience something else, versatile landscape, different climate, multicultural communities. It will do him good."

My mother gave him a distraught look but stopped arguing. He was the academic in the family, and we knew she'd lose the argument where schools were concerned.

But shortly before I left home for Occidental, Mother tried to warn me. "Listen here, my dear boy," she said. "You're moving to another planet." Putting her hand on her chest as if to calm her ailing heart was a familiar gesture. "You mustn't forget your roots. You're coming from a good Catholic family, a civilized home, and a respected community. Watch whom you befriend."

"Mother," I said, somewhat belittled and taken aback, "don't you trust me? Whom do you think I'm going to befriend? Criminals? Drug addicts? Why do you call California 'another planet'?"

"Because God knows that they're different from us over there."

"They? Who are 'they'?"

She was silent for a moment, as if trying to find the words. "You know. Mexicans, Blacks, Chinese, Jews." She stopped and looked at me. "They're all mixed and they're liberals."

"So what? Father is a liberal. There are plenty of different flowers in your garden too." Not wanting to fight right before leaving, I tried to soften her by referring to her favorite hobby. As much as I wanted to go away, I knew I'd miss home. Miss her.

"Yes. But my flowers don't mix." Mother took a deep breath. "And leave your father out of it. He's like that for his work."

I didn't reply. I knew she disliked "others." People who weren't exactly like her: white, Catholic, and married. What made her like that? I couldn't understand.

I loved her very much; she was my mother. Nobody was perfect and neither was she. But I had to leave.

When I first arrived in Los Angeles with my father, I was taken by the simplicity of the Spanish colonial architecture with its lower structures, so different from New England's Federal-style buildings. Los Angeles had been built horizontally, while Boston stood vertically. In my fantasy mind they formed a cross, connected in the center. I could look at the cities' differences, in character and in culture, as they sat at opposing edges of the continent, yet I chose to think of them as complementary, because I was looking for unity instead of separation. Like the center of the cross, many religions were tied together; they shared a belief in a power beyond.

I surprised myself with that thought, as I wasn't a religious person like Mother. Sometimes I tended to get philosophical, very much like my dad, the political science professor.

"Let's go get you your high school graduation present" was the first thing Dad said the morning after we arrived.

I was ready. I'd never owned a car before, so I was extremely proud to get a 1970 Chevrolet Chevelle SS blue convertible. With no subway and the city so spread out, a car in Los Angeles was a must. I wanted a red one, of course, but Dad said, "Do you really want every police car to notice you?" It was settled.

What I liked most in the two years at Occidental were the sunny beaches. And the girls.

However, come December, I missed the cold and the snow, the fireplace and the scent of pine. I couldn't wait to return home for Christmas; I missed my whole family after three months away.

In my second year, I wanted to take Sara home with me for Christmas. She was my new girlfriend. Beautiful and smart, a brilliant student; we enjoyed studying together. I was going to invite her to Boston and even pay for her airline ticket, but I knew she was a Protestant, and I feared my mother's disapproval. I didn't know how to tell my mother Sara wasn't

Catholic.

Still, I made the call. After some opening greetings, I said, "Mother, I have a friend whom I'd like to invite home for a few days. She's from Chicago and hasn't been to Boston before. I just wanted to know if it was okay with you and Dad."

"I'm glad you've settled down so quickly in your second year," Mother said. "How long have you known this friend? Three months, since school began?" She paused. "Will she come with us to Christmas Mass? Don't her parents want her to go with them?" That was my mother's main concern.

I became agitated.

"I don't know about Mass, Mother, I didn't ask. I'll call you back."

Now I was worried. What if Sara didn't want to go to Mass? After all, she wasn't Catholic. When I did ask her that evening, she raised an eyebrow in surprise and said, "I'm sorry, hon. I wish I could come with you to Boston, but just this morning, when I spoke to Mom, she demanded I come home for Christmas." She stretched over the table in the diner and kissed my cheek. "She said you're welcome to join me, after I told her you'd invited me first. What do you think? Chicago is beautiful Christmastime. Oh, please. Please, please, please come to Chicago with me." Her second kiss was on my lips, which made it hard to resist.

I had to speak to Mother again and was dreading it. The idea of going to Chicago—where I'd never been to—was very exciting, but that would be the very first Christmas I wouldn't be home.

I called Mother and said that I was planning on going to

Chicago with Sara and experience Christmas with her family.

There was a long silence. I knew I was hurting her, but I really wanted to go.

"David." She paused. I could hear her breathe. "You're making a grave choice by not coming to Mass."

She knew. Hurting her broke my heart.

"Only this time, Mother. I've never missed Christmas Mass before, you know that."

"Look, my dear boy," she replied. I heard muffled anger in her voice. "You sleep in the bed you make. But I think that your non-Catholic friend can go to her own family, and you can come home."

I felt my body tense with teenage anger, and sweat beaded on my upper lip and hairline. I wouldn't let my mother dictate how I should act and whom I should date. I was nineteen already.

"Have a merry Christmas, Mother. I'm really sorry I'm going to skip coming home this year."

I heard a click.

I was sorry to do this to her and felt horribly guilty. But not guilty enough to change my mind.

I joined Sara and her family in Chicago. They were warm and hospitable, and her father, a pediatrician, was most interested in my father's work as a political scientist.

Alas, into springtime, Sara's interest in me slowly waned, and I couldn't work out why.

When I confronted her one day before class, she smiled nervously and said, "I'm so sorry, David. I really like you, but my old boyfriend from freshman year and I reconnected... and

I . . . and I feel that I made a mistake by breaking up with him." She looked down at her desk, then at me, and added, "I'm sorry. I really am, I should have been honest and told you before. I just didn't know how."

It was the first time I was dumped. It didn't feel good. She left me standing there before I could even respond. I felt my eyes stinging. Tears? No. Not me.

As a junior I transferred to UC Davis the following year. The atmosphere in Davis was very different, and it took me awhile to adjust. Davis was a small town and I missed the city life, although the parks and greenery captivated me. I enjoyed the teachers, and an idea of what I wanted for graduate school started forming.

At UC Davis I met Dalia, an Israeli international student. She was smart, and interesting, and I liked her a lot. To be honest, I was also fascinated with her. Coming from a completely different background—a beautiful Yemenite Jew who'd grown up in Israel—she was like no one I'd ever met.

"My parents had left Yemen in 1950 on Operation Magic Carpet," she told me one Sunday morning as we were strolling. "They came with nothing to Israel, which back then was a newly established country, only two years old. My mother was pregnant with my sister and almost gave birth on the way—"

"Wait, what was Operation Magic Carpet?"

"Just before the State of Israel had been established, but there were talks already. Jews were in danger in Arab countries; they'd been attacked and homes were burned. American and British planes helped Israel in 1949 and 1950 to get out almost fifty thousand Jews from Yemen, Aden, and Saudi Arabia. My parents were among the last ones. Maybe because they were young and the elderly went first. I don't know."

"But your mother was pregnant." I couldn't imagine the fear and chaos.

"Yes." Dalia sat on a bench. "Forget it. It's too sad, and they're all fine now. Safe in the land of our ancestors. Where are we having breakfast?"

I was amazed at the bravery of her parents and proud that American pilots were involved in the rescue. What an amazing story. I felt like I was being exposed to the people of the Bible. She knew a lot about the Old Testament, and our discussions moved from religion to culture. My father would have loved her.

That December, Dalia flew back home to Israel for winter vacation. Of course, I couldn't fly with her and was glad I avoided my mother asking in alarm, "A Jewish girlfriend this time?" So I was spared the embarrassment; Mother wouldn't have approved of my friendship with "that kind of person," anyhow. So I flew home alone but didn't have much fun. Andy, a freshman at Boston University, was busy with his new girlfriend, Teresa; Dad was entertaining colleagues from England; and Larry didn't come home from San Francisco—he was a junior at UCSF and loved it there—so all I did was help Mother with food shopping. It was freezing, and I missed the Southern California sun.

As soon as Dalia returned, she was changed; she avoided getting physical again. She gave me an elegiac look that broke my heart. I knew, but I had to hear it.

"What happened in Israel? Why are you so different?" I asked.

"I'm sorry, David. When I was asked by my family—I have seven brothers and a sister and a million relatives—about school and American friends, I mentioned your name. There are a million Jews called David, so nobody said anything." She looked down at her hands. "But one of my brothers asked what your last name was, and I said Roy. There is a Hebrew name Royi, so he asked, 'Why are they called Roy and not Royi?' and I didn't think." She looked up, her brown eyes sad. "'Because they aren't Jewish,' I said. My father got up and slapped my face." Dalia put her face in her hands. I hugged her shoulder, but she moved away. I was stung.

Lying in bed that night, I thought of Dalia's father and my mother.

I hated religions and vowed that I would never let religion get in the way of my relationships again.

It was May 1982. Dad and Andy flew to California for my graduation from UC Davis. Larry flew down from San Fracisco.

Mother didn't fly. Being claustrophobic, she didn't even take trains, or the T in Boston. She would only go by car, with her window down, where she could control it. I understood this but was disappointed. No wonder I chose to study early childhood development when I was accepted to UCLA for grad school. I had to know where people's phobias came from, what caused them to hate people from other countries and cultures, hate what they called "others." Why was my mother avoiding people from other religions and obsessed with her own? Was hate learned?

I read some of Francis Galton's discussions about nature versus nurture. I was hooked. I wanted to study the new research of trauma in early childhood. I knew Mother was adopted as a young child—she was seven or eight, formative years—and her adoptive parents, Granny Margaret and Gramps Oliver, were loving and tolerant people. But what had happened to her before? In England during the war, things must have been hard for her.

She never spoke of it, and we weren't allowed to ask about her time in England or even about her adoption. It had never been discussed. Forbidden. Like a terminal illness. We weren't even sure if she remembered. But I was positive that a deep and unforgettable trauma sat in her subconscious and had been bothering her all her life.

I wondered if I was going to learn something I wasn't going to like. Or that Mother would be livid if I discovered something she would have preferred I hadn't.

I was also wondering why the psychiatrist she'd been seeing hadn't helped her much.

Chapter Twenty-One

Los Angeles, 1993

AVA-MAY

I WAS about to meet the associate professor, Dr. David Roy. I was excited and nervous. I'd heard he was young for a professor, in his early thirties, but he was smart and knowledgeable, yet kind and friendly. That was what I needed.

I panted frantically as I ran, looking for the right auditorium. I had to get there before his session ended. The buzz in the corridors was loud, but the minute I found the right hall and entered, closing the door cautiously behind me, the humming died instantly.

Nobody paid attention to me, as the students inside the hall were focused on the speaker, so I ducked and discreetly found a seat in the last row, among the one hundred or so attentive bodies. I joined them in listening to the lecturer. I peeked at my watch; I still had fifteen minutes until our scheduled introductory appointment. Sitting through these few minutes offered me a way to get a feel for the man. I was nervous about meeting him. He stood tall in a camel sports jacket, with a head full of deep brown hair, which he repeatedly ran his fingers through while talking.

This wasn't my class: these students were freshmen. I was in graduate school; our meeting would be about mentoring me with my thesis.

Once the lecture was over, ten or so female students gathered around him to ask questions. I noticed two guys waiting at the end of the line, but they eventually gave up and left.

I walked down toward the front of the auditorium but stayed far away, leaning on the wall by the window, observing.

Some of the young women blushed as they reached him and spoke nervously, while others were impatient, shifting from leg to leg or checking their watches.

Although I was four years older, I remembered my occasional crushes on my professors. One of the students, with a loose top, dropped her pen near the professor and bent down to pick it up, maybe hoping he'd look down her blouse. I was familiar with the trick and tried not to laugh out loud, but I couldn't suppress the sound that escaped my lips, which made Prof. Roy look my way.

I quickly covered my mouth with my hand and squinted at him apologetically. He frowned, and I approached him, extending my hand and saying, "Hi, I'm Ava-May. I'm sorry, I didn't mean to interrupt. We have an appointment today." The crowd gave a collective sigh and shuffled out of the hall.

"Oh, yes. Hello," he said as he shook my hand and glanced at his watch. "Ms. Carmel?"

"Yes."

"Nice biblical name. Jewish?" he asked. "Never mind." He quickly waved his hand apologetically. "Sorry, didn't mean to pry. I have a fascination with last names and their origins." He smiled. "Would you rather we sit here and talk or go to my office? There's more room here, more air, not so many books and dust." He chuckled. "And I believe the auditorium isn't being used for the next few hours."

"Sure, more room and air always work for me," I said, looking into his deep blue eyes. I'd never seen such a color; they were slightly purple.

We sat in the first row, and I opened my writing pad, but before I even told him what I was planning to work on, he asked, "What made you interested in early childhood education?"

"Well," I replied anxiously, trying to calm down and gain some time to think, as I wasn't prepared for the question, "for my undergraduate, I majored in psychology and sociology and minored in American literature. As I was studying, I became interested in education, especially the preliminary stages."

"Anything personal? We're usually interested in subjects that are close to home."

I wasn't prepared to talk about my family. Not yet. So I said, "When studying psychology, I learned how we learn. Skills and habits are paramount. So I decided to research more about it; I have many questions." I spoke generally, avoiding anything personal.

"Why don't you write down your questions? A freewrite on

the issues you are pursuing. Why is this important to you? Type out your answers to those questions and bring it next time."

I got excited; I liked the way he guided me. We were on the same page, and my enthusiasm rose. I was interested in his input about my grandparents' experience. They had escaped Poland in 1933 and settled in Israel, had to learn a new language, adjust to a new culture, and new climate. I wondered about their strength of character and the skills they had developed early in life to help them adjust. I wondered what my mother had learned from them that gave her the strength to start a life in a different county as well. But my questions had to be general, not about them. I wanted to impress the professor and hoped that my questions would be intellectually sound.

The next time we met was in his office, which was crowded with books. I brought a small tape recorder with me in case he'd give me permission to record our session, which he did.

As we sat down, I handed him my three pages and scanned his face. He flicked his hair from his eyes, held his chin with his index finger and thumb, and read intently.

I watched him read. His lips were full, and the hand holding his chin featured long fingers and beautiful nails.

When he lifted his head and caught me staring at him, I felt blood rush to my face. I lowered my eyes.

"Hm. Very interesting," he murmured, staring back at the

paper. "You write well." He looked at me. "What prompted those questions?"

I answered honestly, "An article in the newspaper—"

He raised his eyebrows questioningly.

"About the war in Bosnia," I continued nervously. "How long will the war last? What will happen to the children? Their schooling? Their future education? The—"

"Yes!" he said enthusiastically. "I have a genius psychologist and educator to recommend to you—if you haven't studied him yet—Reuven Feuerstein. His work and research focus on human learning, children's brain capacity, and what's possible. I suggest you begin with his book, *Instrumental Enrichment*."

I hadn't heard of the book but was excited about reading it.

He continued, "You'll learn how children who have survived the Holocaust and missed three or four years of schooling had to integrate—with a huge deficit in their education—with peers their own age and keep up. We'll go over it together." He smiled. "I believe that academically you have potential."

I smiled back, encouraged and proud.

However, the following week was more challenging. "Your essay isn't what I expected," Prof. Roy said, shaking his head. "You've summarized the Feuerstein research, and I can see you understand it well, which makes me glad, but I need more of you in it." He looked up; his deep blue eyes were clear and bright. "Your own questions are missing. Sometimes the questions are more important than the answers. I need you to dig deeper and ask what's missing, what can make it clearer, what can we learn from it?"

He was right. I'd been holding back. I had to be more

forthcoming, brave, and creative in my research to come up with all the questions that swirled in my head. I had to demonstrate my thirst for knowledge.

Together we sat and discussed my essay, and Prof. Roy talked to me as if I were his equal, not a mere student. He was respectful and his explanations weren't patronizing. And he was extremely intelligent.

I worked hard to prove that I was worthy of his attention, his time.

Slowly, like a crawling snail, as the year went by and I shared my research essays with him, an attraction built up in me; I admired him. His helpful, wise comments and quiet voice filled me with confidence, but I also felt something else. Sweat was my indicator, either dripping secretly down my back, or my palms getting clammy. He never seemed to notice but he would frown when I blushed. That was his one reaction to my nervousness. I realized it made him uncomfortable, because he kept his distance, while I stupidly craved a little touch: a hand on my shoulder for reassurance, a touching of my arm for encouragement. But nothing. I had to remind myself that he was my teacher, mentor, professor. By law, I guessed, he dared not touch me. He was kind and warm but would not do anything out of bounds of a professional relationship. Still, I would count the hours before our meetings in anticipation, adrenaline pumping in my veins. I knew that these meetings would be ending soon. Toward the end of our second year working together, my nights were full of romantic dreams. One morning, before our meeting, I woke up humming the Boyz II Men's song "End of the Road." I was positive I'd gone crazy. Was the title of the song a premonition? I was graduating and getting my master's after working extremely hard those years, and I knew that come April, we were going to meet for the last time. Would this be the end of the road for us?

At our last meeting I was already sweating.

"I want to tell you something, Ava-May," he said, catching me by surprise. "By the way, you may call me David now." He smiled broadly. We sat next to each other on the same side of his desk this time, so he swiveled his chair to face me. My heart leaped into my throat, and my mouth dried completely, as if I'd swallowed sandpaper. The fingers of his right hand brushed his hair away from his forehead in an apparent nervous movement. His deep blue eyes fixated on me, and I waited.

"I'm leaving Los Angeles," he said. "I'm moving south to San Diego."

"When?" I managed to utter.

"At the end of the year. In December, most probably. I'm taking a sabbatical." He raised his hand and almost placed it on mine. It was hovering two inches above, hesitating a split second in the air, and instinctively I turned my palm up as an invitation. David stared at my turned hand, but instead of touching me, he put his fingers through his hair again. He hesitated for only a second, but I saw it unfold in slow motion. He shook his head as if he had made up his mind. Then he rolled his chair back, stood up, and extended his hand. "I'll see you at your graduation. It was truly a pleasure and a privilege working with you. You'll make an excellent teacher, and your students will be fortunate to have you."

Tears filled my eyes and disappointment gnawed at my bones as I stood up to shake his hand. He took my hand in both of his firm, warm hands, and my knees almost buckled, the touch I'd been hungry for. His skin was sweaty, or was the sweat mine? The heat and the moisture sent an electric current from my fingers to my neck.

I had waited so long for him to touch me, but now I was left wondering whether I would ever see him again.

Chapter Twenty-Two

Los Angeles, 1993-1995

DAVID

SHE made my pulse race. The agony of restraining myself, as her professor, was excruciating—but it was more than that. I was in awe of her passion and dedication toward our profession; her quick understanding and ability to compare different points of view in education. Her arguments, reasoning, and conclusions. We exchanged books constantly, and I also found myself interested in her political views.

"I'm so glad I voted this time," Ava-May had told me shortly after we met in 1993. "When I turned eighteen and didn't vote for Dukakis, I imagined that America had failed because of me." Ava-

May laughed. "Don't all teenagers think that the world revolves around them? That their choice counts?"

"Our choices do count. It was your duty to vote then, be part of our democracy, and I'm glad you voted this time too." All of a sudden, the significant age difference between us loomed at me, but as our sessions progressed, it became blurred: we were equals. Although I was guiding her in her studies, we became less formal and let other subjects besides her thesis infiltrate the tail end of our sessions.

"Did you watch *Schindler's List*?" she asked me after the movie had won multiple Oscars.

"Yes," I replied. "I also read *Schindler's Ark* by Thomas Keneally some time ago. The movie was excellent too."

That was when Ava-May told me that her mother was the daughter of Jewish refugees, her amazing World War II personal survivors who'd managed to escape Hitler just in time and settle in what was then called British Mandate Palestine. She admired her grandparents' resilience and courage.

I knew she wasn't religious—she'd mentioned she drove on Saturdays—but she spoke proudly of her Jewish heritage and the land of Israel, where her mother had been born.

"Of all the Jewish holidays, I enjoy Israel's Independence Day best." She laughed. "I was born on that day, you know, May fourteenth, when Israel turned twenty-two."

"Nice," I commented, and quickly figured out her exact age. "Have you been to Israel?"

"Of course." Her smile was wide. "My parents and I used to go every summer until I graduated from high school. I prefer to travel with friends now."

During the summer break of 1994, I missed her. It was unusual for me, missing a student. Although Ava-May was one of many, she was different. I realized that I was anxious for fall to arrive and bring her back again. I counted the months until her graduation on one hand and was sad that we'd have to part in May. I had my own plans for the future, but as time passed, I was more desperate than hopeful. I had to act if I wanted to change those plans.

I liked her a lot. More than liked; I was wildly attracted to her warm eyes, her broad smile. I dreamed of her. I'd picture her beautiful brown eyes before I closed mine at night, and wished I could literally see them first thing in the morning, her silky hair brushing my face. She was the woman I wanted to take to bed, have breakfast with, share ideas with, tell what I thought of a particular author, go on long hikes with, travel with, and—I wanted to date her. But would she be interested in me?

I knew I was getting ahead of myself. Ava-May might not even want me, and there I was, fantasizing about having children with her. But sometimes she'd give me a look with those sweet brown eyes of hers, as if she wanted to ask me something. Something personal. It felt intimate, I could feel it. That gave me hope, but I didn't want to delude myself.

I committed to waiting until after her graduation. I couldn't ask her on a date when she was my student, although the tension between us these past few months had been palpable; the air was charged. Sometimes I had to force myself to hold back from laying a hand on her shoulder or touching her hand.

Here I was, shaving and patting my face with aftershave, smiling and checking between my teeth, combing my hair and wondering if I was due for a haircut, and dreaming that Ava-May was beside me, looking at herself in the mirror and then smiling at me. I remembered that when I'd asked her the origin of her name, she had laughed. "My mother chose it. Ava Gardner was her favorite actress," Ava-May had recited, rolling her eyes, "and I was born in May." She gave an embarrassed smile. "Yes, I've been saying this for many years, many times."

"Do you have siblings?" I'd asked once, at the end of one of our sessions.

"Nope. My mother told me that she'd had an abortion ten years before I was born. She was in her twenties then, so I missed out on having siblings."

"An abortion? Interesting. When my youngest brother, Andy, was in college, he'd gotten his girlfriend Teresa pregnant." I wanted to open up to her, too, to be honest. "My mother, a devout Catholic, wouldn't allow an abortion for Teresa and made them get married. Now they have a second daughter, Susan. Veronica is nine and Susan is almost two."

Ava-May was friendly and easy to talk to. Academically, there was much we could do together, helping students and teachers alike. We had the same understandings and ambitions; we thought alike and sometimes could even finish each other's sentence, but I also wanted to talk to her about mundane things, about family and hobbies, not just academics. I could picture us together, talking into the wee hours of the morning, our heads on the same pillow.

I hadn't felt like that towards a student before and wondered what she would have thought had she known my intentions. But I would never dare to overstep my boundaries as her teacher, and sometimes I berated myself for how I felt.

Chapter Twenty-Three

Los Angeles, 1995

AVA-MAY

A DAY after graduation, David called and asked if I'd meet him for coffee.

One day after.

"Now it's legitimate for us to meet outside of school." He sounded nervous. "For a date. Would you like to?" I could just imagine him pushing his hair back.

Would I? My pulse increased. A date? Hadn't I dreamed of this very moment many a time? I could barely mutter, "Sure. When?" My voice squeaked, although I tried to sound casual. I could barely believe it. I hadn't been sure that David Roy—my brilliant professor, who'd been the subject of my dreams while we worked together—would really, really be interested in me. But he was.

The following day we met at Starbucks. David wore jeans and a T-shirt, no jacket. A younger version of himself. There went my pulse again. After ordering our drinks, we sat at a small round table in the corner. I could unashamedly scan his face now.

"I've been thinking of the future," David said, running his fingers through his hair. He needed a haircut badly; his hair kept falling over his right eye. "About leaving town." He stared at my limp hand resting on the table, took it gently in both his hands, and raised his eyebrow, as if asking, "May I?"

I nodded as a shiver ran down my spine with his touch; at long last. I held his fingers tightly, feeling the longing I'd held for so long pour out through my skin into his. I gazed into his deep blue eyes.

"I have to talk to you, privately," he said in a husky voice.

Holding his warm fingers and inhaling what was left of his aftershave and slight sweat, all of a sudden, I needed to talk to him privately too. After almost two years, I knew exactly what I wanted at that moment. So I let go of his hands, jotted my address on the napkin, and handed it to him as I got up, taking my paper cup with me.

Peeking at the napkin, he said, "I'll follow."

I left.

I had a rule: no sex on first dates. But I didn't consider this a first date. I'd known the man for two years, I adored him, I knew his mind, and I was craving his touch.

I wasn't disappointed. David's lovemaking was everything I'd dreamed of. Slow and tender, then passionate and explosive. I hadn't had a boyfriend who came close. Maybe being older had an advantage; he must have had more experience. But I felt somewhat desperate; he was leaving at the end of the year.

A few nights later, when we were lying in my bed, I asked, "We only have six months?"

Almost six months later, we sat in my apartment after having a light dinner, which David had cooked. He'd been spending the weekdays in San Diego, preparing to move there permanently by the end of this month, and returning every weekend to spend time with me.

He sat now on my navy couch in the living room as I lay with my legs over the armrest, my head in his lap, looking up at him.

"Maybe you should sit up, honey," he said, tucking some strands of hair behind my ear. "I think we need to talk."

I sat up and crossed my arms over my chest defensively, instinctively. Not sure why. Was he breaking up with me? I feared that moment would arrive.

"Don't look so alarmed." David tried to smile. "We saw this coming, didn't we?"

"Saw what coming?" I needed him to spell it out. I placed my hands on my knees and pressed hard. I'd rather concentrate on physical pain.

He obliged. "Your family, your parents. We need to tell them and hope they'll accept me."

I was stunned. I released my knees. He wasn't breaking up with me; he was planning our future. Or was he? I was still not sure I was following.

"But you're leaving..." I muttered.

"I don't want to," he said. "I don't want to leave without you."

Smiling, his eyes shiny, he took both my hands in his and asked, "Should we make it official?" He kneeled on the carpet between the coffee table and my knees, looked into my eyes, and asked, "Ava-May Carmel, my soulmate, I love you. Will you marry me?"

I let go of his hands and held his face in my warm palms, kneeling, too, and looking into his eyes, my salty tears reaching the corners of my smiling mouth. My heart shattered to shreds; I wanted him so much, but I couldn't answer him.

At my graduation, I'd introduced him to my parents as my professor, and of course I'd avoided disclosing my feelings toward him. Since my graduation, I hadn't told them that we'd been dating; I was too scared of their reaction. But now that David had proposed, I had to tell them. So the following Sunday night, while having pizza and salad at my parents', I said, "I want to bring my boyfriend for Shabbat dinner next week. Is that alright?"

Dad just nodded, but Mom looked at me and said, "Boyfriend? I didn't know you were dating seriously."

"Well," I had to look her in the eye, as scared as I was, "yes. We've been dating for six months now, but I've known him for two years."

Dad looked up from his pizza. "Two years? How could you keep a secret like that?"

"We couldn't date then, because . . . he was . . . my professor."

They both stopped eating, looked at each other, then at me.

"Are you sure it's not a fling?" Mom said. "An infatuation of an older, wiser teacher? Didn't you have a crush on a high school teacher once, in junior year?"

"Mom, stop. No. It's not an infatuation. Can I bring him on Friday so you can properly meet him?"

"He's not Jewish, is he?" Dad asked, and took another bite. He asked it so casually that I got the feeling it might not be a big issue with him. But Mom—she frowned and said nothing.

I knew that it was important to my parents that I should fall in love and eventually marry a Jewish man. Although it mattered less to me, I didn't want to disappoint them. I was hoping that they would like him so much that they wouldn't care.

"Well?" I asked, looking at Mom nervously and avoiding Dad's question.

"I think, yes. Bring him Friday for Shabbat dinner," Dad said, looking at Mom.

Silence.

How was I going to tell them that my Catholic boyfriend had just proposed to me? I usually talked to my mother about my boyfriends, but this relationship was different.

Mom's refusal to answer worried me when I left their house.

Chapter Twenty-Four

Los Angeles, 1995

AVA-MAY

I LOVED the kids I worked with, and I knew they liked me too. In the mornings they'd leave their parents happily and run to hug me. I was fortunate enough to have been hired during the summer, straight after graduation, to start working at the kindergarten. Sometimes, when the day was over, little Danny would need some extra attention. He'd ask if he could read to me. "Only five minutes," he'd plead, so I had to stay a bit longer, sit down, and listen to him read. He was a marvel. So much drive in this little person, so much will to please.

"This is amazing, Dan-Dan." I would smile at him as I ruffled his hair. "I knew you could do it."

He'd shut the book, press it to his chest, and run outside to his waiting mother, who'd know he'd be late.

After three months, just after Thanksgiving, two out of the five kindergarteners with special needs were ready to join mainstream learning despite their difficulties. Had they been diagnosed incorrectly? I was too fresh out of school to argue with their tester, but after months of dedicated work with a special ed teacher, their difficulties were manageable and they demonstrated significant improvement in their skills.

I was extremely pleased; school was fulfilling, but on Friday of Shabbat dinner at my parents', I couldn't stay at the school longer. I wanted things to go well at dinner and needed to get my parents some flowers. Traffic in LA on a Friday afternoon was usually chaotic. David was coming with me, and a formal introduction was to be had. I was nervous, and a cold current went through my body at the thought of them not approving of him.

Honestly, I was petrified.

My mom, Ariella Paz-Carmel, was a teacher at a Hebrew day school. She loved spending every Friday afternoon in the kitchen preparing Shabbat dinner. I could envision her standing by the counter and chopping vegetables for what she called an Israeli salad as my dad, Max Carmel, a public defender, walked in from the office, kissed her on the top of her head—he was more than a head taller—asking, "What's for dinner, honey?" and Mom replying with her usual chuckle, "Don't you know I don't give out menus?" It was their daily love ritual, which I'd cherished since I was little.

Now, I was standing outside their front door, my hands sweating and my head pounding from nerves as I held tightly to the yellow roses, my mom's favorite. David stood by me with a bottle of red wine nestled inside his elbow, his other hand on my back for support. Could he feel my heartbeats through his hand? Was his heart racing too? I had invited several boyfriends for Shabbat dinner at my parents' before, that wasn't unusual, but they all had been Jewish. Would my parents treat David any differently? Was it foolish of me to choose Shabbat dinner for the introduction? Too late.

Dad opened the door, and I took a deep breath and smiled at him.

My parents smiled politely, shook David's hand, and kissed me. Then Dad beckoned us toward the dining room sideboard. My mother loved oak. The sideboard had four doors, and it contained our floral Shabbat dinner set and a plain white Passover dinner set, glasses for guests, and champagne flutes. On the wall above it was my favorite original: a Hasid dancing in the street, the edges of his prayer shawl blowing in the wind. It was a happy image that always made me smile.

We stood ceremonially in a crescent by the two candles and the challah, between the sideboard and the large dining table with ten heavy chairs upholstered in a light-brown material, the same fabric as the couch in the adjacent living room. The table was set for four with the floral plates at one end of it, cozy and intimate.

Dad passed everyone a small kiddush cup filled with sweet wine, and handed a small, knitted yarmulke to David, then put one on his own head. David nodded and followed suit.

Mom lit two candles and said the blessing; Dad said the blessing on the wine, and I broke a piece of the challah after saying the blessing on the bread. A weekly ritual.

When Dad took his yarmulke off, David did the same and handed it back. I was proud of him. So far, so good. The little religious ritual was over, yet I worried. David wasn't observant and neither was I, but traditions ran deep in my family. How would it work if we married? Would we have Shabbat dinners with challah and wine and blessings on the candles? What would we do on Christmas? Why was religion such an issue?

"Ava-May." I heard my mother's voice penetrating my thoughts.

"Oh, yes, sorry," I said, and sat down, feeling embarrassed. Had she called me twice?

David was seated next to me, and I was glad to notice that he enjoyed every morsel of Mom's noodle kugel with mushrooms and cream. He concentrated on his food until Dad spoke.

"So, you were my daughter's professor, but now you're done teaching and are moving to San Diego, I understand," Dad said after straightening up in his chair and dabbing his lips with the white napkin. "Why there?"

"I'm going to live in Encinitas, actually, north of San Diego and not too far from UCSD. The fact is that I'm not at all done teaching." David glanced at me sideways, then put down his fork and knife on the white tablecloth. "On the contrary, I'll be continuing teaching early childhood education as a full professor, not as an associate." He picked up his silverware and leaned it on the plate. "But I've taken a sabbatical to se into my new place."

Dad raised his eyebrows. "Why did you choose Encinitas? Why not be closer to the university? Like La Jolla, or Del Mar?" Dad knew the area well, as he'd lived in San Diego as a student.

"That's a long story. My grandfather bought a piece of land in Encinitas many years ago, when he came from Canada, and rented it out to a farmer. The farmer's son died recently, and my father offered it to me and my brothers. I have two younger brothers, and I had to buy their shares."

"And they parted with it easily?" Mom asked.

I started to relax.

David smiled. "I'm still paying them; they're not interested in Southern California, so I am very fortunate they've agreed to let it go." He smiled at me. "I want to renovate the old house."

"Where do your brothers live?" Mom asked.

"Larry is a physician assistant in a hospital in Oahu, Hawaii, and Andy, the youngest, is a lawyer in Boston, close to my parents."

"And are they both married?" My mother asked to my surprise. I felt my body tense. Why was she going there? What did she want to know?

David shot me a quick look, then said, "Larry is a bachelor, and Andy is married and the father of two girls."

"Your parents are lucky that at least one son stayed close by," Dad commented. Was he hinting that the two older sons had moved far away, just like I'd been wondering? It made me uncomfortable. Maybe it made David uncomfortable too. It sounded like my parents were grilling him. I had to think fast, but Mom started talking.

"I can hear that you're not from California," Mom stated, and smiled. "I detect a slight accent because I have one too."

David chuckled. "Yes. I'm from Boston. My father is French Canadian and has a slight accent and so does my British mother."

"We're all immigrants," Mom remarked, and stood up. "Excuse me, please, I'll be right back."

I followed her to the kitchen to help. She turned to look at me, saying nothing, but raising her eyebrows in a question, tilting her head.

I wanted to ask what, but didn't. She was a smart lady, and I felt she had an opinion I didn't want to hear.

She handed me a large plate of roasted chicken and green beans, which I almost dropped. She stayed behind to toss the salad, and I walked out of the kitchen and placed the dish in front of Dad, who proceeded to carve the bird.

I sat down heavily. Oh, boy. As much as I loved my mother's cooking, this time my throat constricted from nerves. Dinner passed in an awkward blur.

"Oh, my goodness, I'm so full." Dad put his hand on his belly when we were done eating. "Everything was delicious, sweetheart." He patted Mom's hand.

"No room for dessert?" Mom asked as she got up and went to the kitchen to retrieve the ice cream from the freezer. Dad collected some dirty dishes and followed her. I heard them whispering in the kitchen.

David took my hand and put his lips to the tips of my

fingers, kissed them lightly, and asked quietly, "Why don't you come down with me tomorrow to see the place in Encinitas? I have an appointment to meet with the architect." He cocked his head. "Please come with me to discuss what changes we want to make to the house."

My cheeks burned. I hadn't replied to his proposal yet. I stared into his eyes and wanted to stroke his smooth face, but Dad returned and sat down. I collected my hand, and the little food I'd eaten turned in my stomach.

"Is your father still working in Boston, David?" Dad asked.

"My father is retired, a professor emeritus now, after teaching political science at Harvard for years. He's crazy for the game of bridge now." David smiled warmly. "An outgoing individual who likes speaking to strangers and finds it fascinating."

"And your mother?" Mom asked. "Oh, yes, you mentioned she was from England."

My pulse increased; David didn't like talking about his mother.

"My mother is a homemaker. Always has been." His smile slowly faded, and he squirmed in his seat. Then he mimicked a British accent. "She is a true English lady. Keeps to herself most of the time, loves working in her garden, and stays busy with her biweekly bridge club and a fortnightly book club."

My mother smiled a weird smile.

Silence fell across the table, and an uneasy mood settled heavily over us. I could hardly breathe. The conversation was going nowhere. I needed to say something but didn't know what.

"Why don't we move to the living room?" Dad said as he pushed his chair back.

But David stood up, saying he had a busy weekend ahead and thought he should be leaving.

Dad nodded.

Mom's eyes bored into mine, so I quickly turned to look at David, who had turned to face my parents, shaking their hands and saying, "Thank you very much for the delicious meal and your gracious hospitality." He kissed Mom's cheek, whispering that her cooking was superb. She blushed.

I kissed my parents, and we left.

The whole drive home I wondered whether he had passed the test. I desperately wanted to go with him to see the house, but something was holding me back. I'd never considered marrying someone who wasn't Jewish, and I just wasn't sure how to navigate my parents' expectations and my own heart. I loved him and wanted him, but I loved and respected my parents too.

Chapter Twenty-Five

Los Angeles, 1995

AVA-MAY

DAVID and I didn't exchange a word the entire ride. We were both nervous, and the space between us was thick with tension.

"I think I need to go back," I said, breaking the silence with a voice I barely recognized. My chest felt tight, and my head throbbed in anticipation. I was dreading the conversation, worried that my parents would hate what I wanted.

To my relief David said, "My thought exactly." His eyes were on me.

I stared back at him. At least we were on the same page. Were we acting like stupid little kids, petrified of our parents' reaction to what we were about to do?

Or was it only me? I was sure it was only me.

I called Mom and Dad as soon as we walked into my apartment. While I waited for them to pick up, I imagined them in their bedroom, Mom already changed into her nightgown and now creaming her face, while Dad—

"Hello?"

"Daddy," I said, like I was surprised to hear his voice.

"Hello, stranger, long time no see," Dad said. "What's going on, sweetie. You okay?"

"Yes, I'm fine, Dad. Please wait. Don't go to sleep yet. Mom too. I'm coming back to talk. I need to talk to you guys. I'm on my way right now. Be there in twenty. See you soon. Bye."

"You what? Why—" Dad's voice sounded far away as I returned the receiver and stood still for a moment.

"Good luck, my love," David said as I grabbed my purse. Then, "Hey, wait. I'm coming with you." He got up and walked towards the door.

"What? Why?"

"It's late. And you shouldn't do this alone. I'll drive you and wait in the car in case you need me."

Mom and Dad greeted me at the door.

"Hi," I said, walking in, swallowing hard; my mouth was dry. I felt a smile sneaking onto my face in spite of my nerves and the seriousness of the matter. Mom and Dad appeared comical. Mom still had her earrings and lipstick on, although she had changed into her nightgown, and Dad had his pajama top on inside out, as if he'd been in a rush to change. My cute mommy and daddy. Was I going to shatter their trust in me? Their one and only child?

"Everything alright?" Dad asked.

"Yes, but let's sit down." I walked toward the light-brown living room couch, sensing that they still stood by the door, staring at me. I turned my head and stared back. I was so scared they'd say I was ruining my life, wasting my time with a non-Jewish boyfriend, that he was very nice but...

My father made the first move and followed me into the living room, saying, "He didn't dump you, did he, now?" He sounded agitated as he sat on the couch across from me.

I was confused. Dad didn't want David to dump me.

"No, Daddy, he didn't. He had actually proposed—"

"He what? Now? He proposed now, tonight?" My mother rushed in and stood by my father.

"No. Not tonight."

"So when? Before you both came here?" Dad, who had been leaning forward, elbows on his thighs and fingers locked together, sat up. The corners of his lips were turned down in disappointment, as if he'd been left out of something important. "Why didn't you both say something while you were here tonight? I don't understand." He shook his head.

"We didn't say anything because . . . because I haven't given him my answer yet," I said, staring up at Mom, who was still standing, her hands on her hips now, waiting. "He had proposed before I invited him for dinner to meet you guys, but—but—"

"But what?" Mom stepped closer, a cloud over her face,

her eyebrows arched.

"I wanted you both to meet him first," I explained. "I didn't want to tell you anything about him before your first meeting. I didn't think it was fair to drop any info down on you like that. I wanted you to meet him, speak to him, get a sense of how you feel, but I need to tell you something important about him." I lifted both my hands in a protective gesture. "Mom, please . . . won't you please sit down? You're making me nervous." Her hovering over me made me feel closed in, threatened.

"Sure," she said softly, and she took a seat close to Dad on the couch, then turned her eager face to me, waiting.

"David isn't Jewish...you know that."

They didn't move.

"He's Catholic."

There, I'd said it. Out loud.

"I knew it," Mom murmured, looking at Dad and shaking her head.

Dad, the public defender, turned to her. "You suspected it, Ariella. You didn't know."

I wanted to be strong, assertive, but my eyes filled with tears as my chest filled with pain; I knew I was hurting them. "But David is not a practicing Catholic, like I'm not a practicing Jew."

Mom stood up again. "What do you mean you're not a practicing Jew? Just because you don't keep kosher and drive on Shabbat—"

"Let it go, Ariella. We know what she means." Dad only used Mom's name when he was dead serious, and now he'd used it twice. Not a good sign.

"You've known this man for two and a half years, you worked with him and have been dating, but you didn't know that he was Catholic?" Mom took a seat on the arm of Dad's couch, facing me, her cheeks flushed. "When did you find out?"

"I didn't know right away; I didn't think of it or care," I said honestly. "At the beginning his religion didn't enter my mind, and I didn't inquire." Angry tears rolled down my cheek. Anger was better than pain, and it gave me energy. So I swiftly wiped my face with my fingers, sat up straighter, and said defensively, "It just happened, Mom. I fell in love and didn't think anything would ever come of it. You don't plan to fall in love, do you?"

I looked at my mom, then at Dad, and back down at my hands. I didn't know what else to say. I was tossed from shame to pride, as if I'd done something awful and had to confess, but at the same time, the deed made me happy. Wasn't that crazy? Confusion and sadness engulfed me; why did it have to be like that? Why was the world so screwed up? Why did religions have to tear people apart? Did I have to justify why I was in love? I knew it was ridiculous. I didn't have to do it, but I needed to give my parents time to digest the news.

"David has so many wonderful qualities, Mom, Dad. He's a good man. He's kind and smart, I love him and he loves me." My confidence rose. "He's so intelligent, actually brilliant in our field." My excitement and my energy were lifting; I was talking about the man I loved and admired. "He's a leader, a great teacher, and we both love our profession." I paused to catch my breath. "We want to get married next summer . . . but

I need your blessing..."

"But he's Christian..." Dad moaned as if in physical pain. The big humanitarian, the honest man and liberal father I adored, the son of persecuted Jews—a people who kept their nation together, our nation together, no matter where we were in the world—was being hurt by his own daughter. When I was a kid, he always reminded me that although for two thousand years the Jewish people had no country of their own, the nation stuck together through religion and culture and survived all the attempts to destroy them.

"He's Catholic!" Mom cried out. "How can we give you our blessing? How do you think we feel to have our one and only child give up her heritage, her people, her history?"

"I'm not giving up anything, Mom. We'll work things out, you'll see."

Mom stared at me, her eyes piercing into mine. "What do you mean you'll work things out?" She sounded mad, but I knew she was in pain too. "Culture, religion, background, history are not 'things' you can dismiss. You have a heavy responsibility on your shoulders. You should be proud of being born Jewish. So many generations before you, before us, have fought and died to overcome the attempts of annihilation. Your own grandparents, from both sides, had luckily escaped persecution—"

"I am proud—"

"And does David know that his children will be Jews by Jewish law, having a Jewish mother?" Mom was on a roll.

"Yes, of course he does," I said, trying to get a word in. "And of course I'm proud of being Jewish. I didn't say yes immediately to his proposal, because I wanted you both to meet him first, but I'm going to accept his proposal. David and I respect each other and honor one another's upbringing, and yes, our children will be Jewish," I added, hoping to pacify them. "He's thirty-seven, and he claims that I'm the only one for him, the one he's been waiting for all those years. No other woman he's ever met or dated was so right for him." I took a deep breath, my confidence rising. "And he's the one for me."

"Doesn't he mind that his children will have a Jewish upbringing?" Dad asked.

"Look. We three are liberal and modern, and so is David, no matter what his family is. He's not Orthodox and neither are we. He doesn't follow the doctrine of Catholicism. Only his mother and youngest brother do. His father and middle brother don't practice either, like him." I paused and took another breath, hoping I was convincing them. "He's spiritual, he likes meditating by the ocean, we both do, but he doesn't practice a formal religion. He says that he wants to raise our children to be decent people, respectful, ones who do good, and we'll do it, Dad. We've discussed that if we marry, we'll work everything out, it will be fine."

It was late and I was exhausted. My shoulders sagged. This was too much; I was looking too far ahead, talking about children. I turned back to Mom. "We'll instill the right values in our children just like you both did with me, Mom. He's decent and honest, and you both taught me to respect that above all."

"Yes, but . . ." my mother said quietly, and sat down again.

"What do you know about his family?" Dad asked.

"As he told you, he has two younger brothers, his father is a retired professor who was born in Montreal, Canada, and his mother is from England," I said. "She's adopted."

"Oh. Who was her birth mother?" my father asked. "An unmarried English girl?"

"Who knows?" I shrugged. "It was wartime. I have no more details." I stood up. "You've only just met David, but I'm sure you'll learn to love him once you get over the shock of his family's religion."

"It's not only religion," Mom said, and stood up too. "It's a whole different culture. We come from completely different worlds. We were persecuted, gassed, murdered in the name of our religion, no matter if we were religious or not. Yet we built a country to safeguard our future, we stuck together, we persevered. This is who we are. Does he know that? Does he understand our responsibility?"

I ached for her. I saw anguish on her face, her eyes narrowed and red, her skin pale and her mouth droopy. Was I betraying her?

"He does, Mom," I said quietly, and I hugged her. I was too tired to defend David or my decision to marry him any longer. "I love you. I'm sorry if this hurts you. It wasn't an easy decision for me to marry a Catholic man, but I'm going to," I said to her shoulder as she held me tight. I wanted to let go and hug my dad, but Mom held me a minute longer. I gently held her by her elbows, searched her face, and noticed her mouth trying to smile, while her eyes didn't.

Dad hugged me and kissed my cheek.

"It's late; I need to go now. We're going down to San

Diego early tomorrow morning."

I walked to the door, knowing that I'd let them down, but I knew it was my life's journey, and I had to take it.

By the door, I turned and said, "I wanted you both to know what's happening in my life and hope you'll understand and give us your blessing."

"What are David's parents' names?" Dad asked suddenly as I opened the front door. I felt they were scared to let me go, as if I was going to vanish right then and there.

"Martin and Rosalind Roy," I said, holding on to the door handle.

"Rosalind," Mom repeated quietly, as if not sure if she'd just made a friend or a foe.

I walked out, and as I was halfway to my car, Mom cried out, "Does his mother, Rosalind, know that he wants to marry a Jewish girl? Does she realize she'll have Jewish grandchildren?" But I pretended not to hear her as I closed the car door behind me.

The truth was that I didn't know the answer.

When I got into the car, I sat quietly for a moment. David looked at me, put his hand on my hands resting in my lap, and asked, "Are you okay?"

I looked at my David and said, "I love you. And so do they. Let's get married."

Chapter Twenty-Six

Boston, 1996

MARTIN

THE phone rang in the almost empty house.

I was in the kitchen about to pour afternoon coffee into two mugs. I took the extinguished pipe out of my mouth, placed it on the counter, picked up the receiver from its wall cradle, and said, "Hello?"

"Dad? How are you?" It was David.

"Hello, my boy," I said excitedly, looking at my watch. It was only noon in California. I was delighted but somewhat alarmed. Lately David had been calling me only on my small Motorola mobile phone, never on the home phone. "I'm fine, thank you. What's going on with you? Do you want to speak to your mother?"

David not calling the house and speaking to his mother this past year had been disturbing to me and disappointing to her. He hadn't even come home last Christmas, saying that he was busy moving to Encinitas and couldn't leave. I knew that he was changing jobs and taking a sabbatical to fix the house and get settled, but I sensed there must have been something else he wasn't telling us. Didn't building contractors usually break for Christmas week?

"I'm in the old house, Dad, as you know," David said, "and I have great news." He paused for a second, then, "I'm getting married."

Boom.

I staggered to the kitchen table and sat down. "What? You're getting married? When? To whom?" He had caught me by surprise. I was dumbfounded. Since he left for college, he'd never brought a girlfriend home. Nor a boyfriend, for that matter—I would have accepted either. I'd worked with young students for decades and wasn't blind. I also hated the thought of David and Lawrence still being bachelors. They were in their thirties, for heaven's sake. They'd both left Boston so many years ago, but David usually came back for Christmas. Besides that one time when he went to Chicago, many years ago, and devastated his mother. I quickly had to return to the present. "Are congratulations in order?" I asked cautiously, before giving him a chance to reply. I wanted to call out to Rosalind. Where was she? She'd be so happy to hear.

"Of course, Dad." David chuckled. "And you can say

mazel tov too."

Boom.

I was glad I was seated.

"What?" I needed a moment. "Really? Is she Jewish?"

"Yup."

"That's ... that's really big news ... Congratulations ... and ... mazel tov," I stammered, not sure what to think. David was marrying a Jewish woman. I hoped he knew what he was facing. I looked around. Where was my pipe?

We didn't have any Jewish friends, although I had many Jewish colleagues. I didn't really mind; I could accept it. It was his choice, after all. He was thirty-seven, and I was glad he'd found a partner he wanted to spend his life with, but ... Rosalind?

My thoughts chased each other at a hundred miles an hour. I knew that it wouldn't be easy; he'd been groomed by his mother. He had admitted to me once that as a child he always worried that God was watching him constantly, "like Mother had said," and it scared him. I admit, I hadn't interfered in her religious guidance of the boys, and maybe I should have. But marrying a woman of another faith? What was to happen now—adrenaline flooded my body—and how would Rosalind react? David's children would be Jewish. Our grandchildren. I knew that much. I'd seldom heard of a Jewish woman not raising her children according to her faith; the non-Jewish husbands usually went along, and I knew David would go along too.

But Rosalind? She had a dislike of everything Jewish, which upset me no end. When a colleague would invite us for

Rosh Hashana meal or a lavish breaking of the fast after Yom Kippur, she'd refuse to go and become agitated and moody. "It's not our holiday," she'd said.

Three years ago, when the Holocaust Memorial Museum opened in Washington, D.C., a mixed group of local and visiting professors organized a visit, but Rosalind refused to join us.

"You go. These are your friends," she'd said. I knew that anything to do with the war upset her, so I had joined them without her.

"Can I speak to Mother, please?" David's voice broke through my thoughts, though it sounded far away.

I had to shake off the fog. Rosalind. Where was she? I wished I had some cigarettes in the house, although I quit when David and Lawrence were in high school, not wanting to set a bad example, so I had diverted to smoking a pipe, more distinguished. Alas, Rosalind didn't like the smell, so now I only smoked in the car. Didn't I bring the pipe into the kitchen early this morning to clean it . . . ?

"Wait, let me find her," I said, and called out to Rosalind, who walked into the kitchen wearing a blue dress, which made her eyes profound.

"What? Who's on the phone?" she asked.

"Here, sit down and speak to your son David. He has some news."

Rosalind sat down and took the receiver into her hand. "Hello, David. How are you?"

I couldn't hear what he was saying, but seeing my wife's face turning white was alarming. Rosalind had a heart condition, and the doctor, when checking her last and adjusting her medication, told her to take things easy and not get too excited.

She listened intently, then asked, "Why on the beach, David? Why in California? Why can't you both come here and marry in our church?"

Again, I couldn't hear his reply, but I knew what was coming.

"Jewish?" Rosalind asked, and handed me the phone. She looked at me with big eyes, got up, and left the kitchen.

"David," I said into the receiver, not sure if to follow her. "What did you say to her?"

"I said that the wedding would take place in Del Mar, on the beach, in August," David's voice came back, but he seemed in a rush. "We can't marry in a church, Dad. You understand that." He paused. "I'll call you back soon with more details. Hope you and Mother can make it." Neither of us mentioned it, but of course we both knew his mother would not get onto a plane. "And Andrew and his family too." Another pause. Then, "I love her, Dad, and you're going to love her too. Just get Mother on board, please." He waited. I heard the pleading in his voice, but I could give him no assurances. Finally he said, "Bye, Dad. I love you," and hung up.

"I love you too . . ." I said to the empty receiver.

I went upstairs to our bedroom and found Rosalind sitting on our bed, a box of pills in hand. I stared at my wife. I didn't fully understand why, but I knew she was shattered to the core.

David, our firstborn, the boy she loved so much, the man she missed so much, was getting further away from her. How would she ever accept him marrying a Jewish woman?

Whatever crazy beliefs were planted in her head had been deeply engraved. I couldn't erase them, no matter how illogical they were and how hard I tried to reason with her. Her phobias, like all phobias, were incomprehensible, and all the nightmares and dreams she suffered from—without ever sharing details about them—were hers alone.

She'd been taking medication for depression and arrythmia, but seeing her with a bottle of pills in her hand worried me.

She stared at me. I sat by her, then took the pill bottle from her hand. These were for her heart. I stared deeply into my wife's beautiful eyes and tried to read her mind. We had our challenges, and her bigotry certainly bothered me, but she was my wife and I loved her.

Each blue pool brimmed with water, and she whispered in a quivering voice, "They don't want to get married in our church."

Was that the only thing that worried her? Didn't she care—or comprehend—that David was marrying a Jew? I knew how important it was for him that she support his marriage, so I sat next to her, determined to figure things out, not only for David. But for all of us.

Chapter Twenty-Seven

Del Mar, California, 1996

AVA-MAY

WE stood under the chuppah, in Seagrove Park in Del Mar, a Jewish Angelena and a Catholic Bostonian, with seventy invited guests—almost all from LA—seated on white folding chairs.

The deep blue of the ocean filled me with reverence and ancient yearning. The purple horizon, far, far away, where the sky touched the waters, was the color of the rims of David's irises. His shirt was a shade lighter, and his suit and tie were the color of sand.

My delicate, white-with-a-tinge-of-lilac, chiffon, backless

dress seemed like it had cascaded right from the soft clouds above us. My white sandals, looking like they came from the surf's foam, sank into the green grass. The scent of the freshly cut turf—bright and sharp—filled my chest and mixed gently with the perfume of white star jasmine and the faint salty ocean air. My lungs were brimming.

True, it wasn't how I'd envisioned my wedding to be when I was a little girl. I always thought I'd be wearing a pure white, puffy wedding gown with little satin bows at the waist, like a Disney princess, with pink heels, pink lipstick, and pink nail polish. I'd grown up in LA, after all.

But I was happy now that my sleek brown hair was cut in a bob, right side rounding my face to my chin, and left side tucked behind my ear, exposing a shiny, little pearl earring. A thin veil fell softly over my face, almost reaching my chest, and my lipstick was deep rose. I smiled, my heart swelling.

Standing between Mom and Dad, I faced my beloved. His tall father, Martin, was to his right, and his two younger brothers, whom he adored, stood just behind them, erect and tense. Four handsome men.

I tried to catch David's eye, searching for a hint of sadness for his mother not being here, but I saw no cloudiness in them. They were as bright and clear as the ocean when he smiled right back at me. He lifted my veil, exposing my face to make sure it was me. I giggled. An old biblical tradition.

"Do you, David Roy, take this woman to be your lawfully wedded wife?" asked Roger, David's friend, who was officiating the wedding under the canopy.

"I do," David replied, his voice strong, his hand reaching

out to take mine.

Tears sprang to my eyes.

"Do you, Ava-May Carmel, take this man to be your awfully bedded husband—I mean, your lawfully wedded husband?"

"I do, yes, I do," I said, maybe too enthusiastically, my cheeks blushing as the guests laughed.

David took the smaller ring from the satin pillow Larry had offered him, and put it on my finger. I took the same, yet larger ring and placed it on his finger. Were my hands damp from nerves or the slight August humidity?

"By the authority vested in me by the State of California, I now pronounce you husband and wife!" Roger exclaimed.

My father bent down and put a glass wrapped in cloth before David's foot. David stomped on it hard, breaking the glass, and our friends and family jumped off their seats, clapping their hands and bursting out in shouts of "Mazel tov!" and "Congratulations!"

I was in David's arms, registering his now-cool hands on my bare back and his soft, warm lips on mine. My David. My husband. My soulmate. I was in heaven. Life was good, and I could have just melted with delight into the grass had he not held me so tightly.

The three string players, their backs to the shimmering blue ocean, started playing the happy melody of "To Life" from *Fiddler on the Roof*.

Martin hugged his eldest son and held him for a long moment before planting a kiss on his cheek and looking into his face with damp eyes. I didn't hear what he whispered. He let go and turned to me, and I got a whiff of his slight tobacco scent mixed with Old Spice aftershave.

"Mazel tov, my dear. My apologies on behalf of my wife," he said again as he kissed me on both cheeks. He had already said these words to me when he arrived at the San Diego airport, although at that time, he added that his wife couldn't fly.

David had told me that his mother was claustrophobic and didn't fly or take the train.

But until that moment, I was still hoping that Rosalind would make the effort and overcome her fears. That she'd be well enough to come to her son's wedding.

David had said that she was disappointed that we weren't marrying in Boston, in their church. Me, I had thought, getting married in a Catholic church? I hadn't asked David to marry me in a synagogue. Now I thought that maybe we should have gone to Boston; they had beaches there too. But wasn't this venue magnificent? I looked around and saw Martin giving my dad a firm handshake and pulling him gently, bringing him closer, hugging his shoulder. Now he was kissing Mom's cheek. Sweet, sweet man. It made me happy to see this friendly and engaging man being so warm to my parents. Although he'd lived in Boston for over fifty years now, he hadn't lost his slight French Canadian accent, which had instantly charmed my Israeli-accent-bearing Mom.

Suntanned Larry—who'd just been called Lawrence by his father—hugged my waist, picked me up, and swung me around. I laughed, somewhat embarrassed. He had long blond hair all tied in plaits and might have been slightly tipsy, but I enjoyed the energy of this fun-loving new brother-in-law. When he put me down and my friends clapped, I noticed his youngest brother, Andy, frowning with disapproval, then turning his back on us and walking away to rejoin his family. I knew that Andy was a practicing Catholic, and this wedding on the beach wasn't his idea of a serious ceremony, but he'd come anyway. And he'd brought his whole family with him. I knew he loved David dearly, so it wasn't a major surprise.

Andy now stood by his wife, Teresa—who was also tall and slim with straight brown hair and thick bangs—wearing a long black skirt and sleeveless, black-and-white chiffon top, and holding their three-year-old daughter, Susan, on her hip. Stunning Veronica, their ten-year-old daughter in a violet dress, was tall for her age. She held her head tilted slightly to one side, where soft, long blond curls streamed down and surrounded her face. Her piercing deep blue eyes were the same color as both her uncles'.

I approached them and put my arms out to take little Susan from her mother, who was happy to be relieved. Susan wore a sage green dress and little silver sandals, and when I gently tickled her torso, she giggled and tossed her head, shaking a mop of auburn hair as her shiny hazel eyes squeezed tight with laughter. Her contagious laugh spread like music and made me laugh too.

I thanked them all for the effort they'd made in coming from Boston, and told them how sorry I was that their mother wasn't well enough to fly. Susan played gently with my earrings as Andrew and Teresa nodded and smiled, accepting my thanks in silence. Then I noticed Teresa sneak a lingering look at her husband. I had a feeling there was something they weren't telling.

I put Susan down carefully, touched Veronica's shoulder fondly, and excused myself to go and greet other guests.

I walked away thinking, What was that look? What were they hiding?

I remembered David telling me that their mother wouldn't get visibly angry with them when they'd misbehaved as young kids. Her power was in her glare: she'd barely blink, and her intense stare would pin them in their tracks. Then she'd raise her index finger to the ceiling and say, "God can see you. He knows what's in your head and in your heart. Watch out, you can't hide from him." Only after they'd broken down and gone for confession and later begged her for forgiveness would she nod, accepting their apology. I found it horrifying. What a way to discipline children.

Fortunately for her, Andrew, the youngest, followed her rules to a tee. He and his young family were as religious as Rosalind was, and joined her at church every Sunday. Today was an exception. I'd heard that Martin stopped going a while ago.

That family had secrets, I thought as I walked across the lawn to join my new husband. But which family didn't? Now that I was part of this family, their secrets would have to be mine too. But Rosalind, not coming to the wedding held no secret at all. She had heart problems and wasn't well. She was claustrophobic and just didn't fly. So I'd been told, and that was that.

Now I wondered if I'd been told everything. But it was my wedding day, so I let it go and went to greet my friends.

Chapter Twenty-Eight

Boston, 1996

ROSALIND

MY David. My darling boy. My precious son betrayed me. Betraying God. Betraying the Church. Right now. Right now as he was marrying her. *No. No.* I shook my head from side to side on my pillow. *No.* How could he do this to me, to our family, to the community?

To his soul.

It had been two whole days since they'd all abandoned me, Martin and Andrew, and yes, his family too. Not caring about me. Doing nothing to stop this madness. I'd prayed constantly since I'd received this news, but I could find no comfort at all.

Oh, dear Jesus. Make me feel your presence. My pain and suffering are so great, and who knows suffering better than you do? Take the suffering from me, please. I'm losing my son.

I couldn't comprehend how David could have done this to me. To us. Marrying that girl. Why her? She wasn't one of us. Those people weren't like us. They were different. I was different; I accepted the Lord.

I placed a wet rag over my throbbing forehead.

I tried watching CNN to get my mind off these thoughts, but neither the images nor the words penetrated my foggy mind. I doubled up on my nerve medication, but it didn't calm me down one bit. It only caused more confusion and sleepiness. Sleep was bad; it brought dreams, and the dreams wouldn't let me rest. Sirens shrieked in my ears, the smell of fire in my nostrils. But where was the fire? I saw images of burning buildings. Debris in the streets. I kept shaking my head to dismiss it all. I heard babies cry. My bed was moving. Floating. Was the boat going to capsize? I was trapped. I had no air. I stirred and woke up, my white sheets all tumbled. I shuddered. My nightgown was drenched with sweat.

I almost stumbled on my white carpet when I got up to go to the bathroom. My dreams exhausted me. Why did those images keep popping up?

I needed the bathroom badly after all the tea I drank. Irene, the woman who stayed with me while Martin was away, brought me tea all the time. "You need to stay hydrated," she kept saying. She might come back again. I better fix my sheets; she'd see, she'd wonder, she might be mad that I had messed my sheets like that.

I staggered back to bed, my brain hammering, *Da-vid, Da-vid, Da-vid.*

My beloved firstborn. My beautiful baby who learned not to cry to keep his mommy happy. I'd been so delighted then. My poor little boy who broke his right arm when he was eight and had to write with his left hand. That was the second time he'd broken it. I'd sat with him patiently and helped him every time he lost his grip on his pencil. The doctor said it should have healed fully, but I believed there was a vulnerability there, where it had been previously injured.

My darling son who broke his leg when he rode his bicycle one summer and had to hop on crutches, his cast so heavy that I wanted to pick him up. But he was thirteen then.

His shocking news several months ago had upset me so much that it had almost sent me back to Mass General Hospital, where they knew me very well at cardiology.

Oh, Lord, oh Virgin Mary, why was I suffering so much? This brought me so much pain. Didn't he love his mother anymore? I'd been sure his infatuation with *that* girl would pass. I prayed and prayed he'd come to his senses and realize that it all had been a fantasy, a horrible mistake.

But as the months dragged on, I sensed with all my being that he was going to go through with *that* wedding after all.

And there it was: He was marrying *that* girl.

He would go to hell, as would his children, if he had them. They would suffer for all eternity. I shuddered to think of it.

My tears flowed incessantly. I prayed that he wouldn't give his children nicknames; nicknames were bad. Small children with nicknames were in danger. I was in danger. My boys had been given proper names, Christian names, no distortions. Did his bride have a nickname? A Jewish nickname? She might be in danger. Or dangerous. My heart thought to explode; sweat rolled down my back. I needed another tranquilizer, or a better distraction.

I turned to the TV. On screen, a couple kissed, happy. Oh, no. David. *That girl* had trapped him just like that woman in the movie. He was handsome, well educated, established in his profession, from a highly respected Catholic family. What did she want with him? He was out of her league. I would not let her trap me like she had trapped him.

I had to beg the Blessed Virgin Mary. My rosary. My only consolation was prayer. Like our Lord Jesus Christ, who prayed several times a day.

Every morning and every night I'd take the rosary beads—which were hanging on the bedpost by my head—kneel by my bed, and say my prayers. Twice a day. I was good. I would start with three Hail Marys: one for my son who'd lost his way, one for the rest of my family, and one for the community. I'd recite all the rosary prayers, praying and begging and bargaining to erase the spell on our family. On me. In the past, prayer had dismissed thoughts and memories and brought me peace and comfort.

But my prayers felt unanswered now. I tossed again. The humiliation of rejection was so strong, so familiar that I almost choked. Being unloved and rejected was such a familiar ache; it cut my gut like a knife. I wondered when I felt rejected for the first time. I must have been little. I didn't remember an incident, but I remembered the feeling. My heart beat so fast; I felt it on both sides of my throat and in my temples. I had to take another pill.

I closed my eyes and wished to die. I stayed almost alone in my home, but it was better than witnessing my son throwing his earthly life away and going to hell.

My bottom lip almost bled from my biting it. Tears dropped into my ears. I couldn't take another Ranolazine, could I? Not until tonight. My head spun.

I tried to think of something else.

Lawrence. I missed Lawrence. Had he flown from Hawaii to California too? He hadn't returned to Boston to visit, even though I'd repeatedly offered to send him a ticket. How long had it been since he'd left? Ten years? Fifteen? I had not laid eyes on him for so long; I'd lost count. Did I drive him away? My beautiful boy. He'd sent only one photo . . . Yes. Photos. Photos would take my mind off thinking. Maybe my own wedding photos. Yes. They were proof I'd done the right thing: I married a good Catholic boy. That was the way things ought to be done. The right way. We stuck by our own.

I got up slowly, stiff from lying in bed, and smoothed my full-length, ivory satin nightgown. Shuffling barefoot into my large, windowless dressing room, I had to hold on to the wall because my head was spinning. I took a deep breath. Mar-tin thought the dressing room was oversized, but I needed it; I needed big spaces. No closed rooms like boxes, no planes or trains or boats. Too restricting. I had to be sure I could get out. In small spaces I would retrieve whatever I needed and walk out as quickly as possible. I didn't know why, and I didn't like to think about it.

There they were. The photo albums stood at attention on the shelf in the dressing room, like soldiers in a row, ready for inspection. I swiftly grabbed the large, white satin album to carry back to my bed when my toes hit something cold under the bottom shelf, and a surprise shiver ran down my back—

A knock on the door.

I was startled for a second but then remembered. Irene.

"Come in," I said.

The door opened slowly, and a tray was followed by a sturdy middle-aged woman.

"Here is your supper, Mrs. R. I made fish and chips especially for you, deary." Irene's Irish accent vibrated in the room.

"Fish and chips?" I asked. Was that what I'd smelled? It didn't look burned.

"Yes, ma'am," Irene said cheerfully. "Your favorite. If I don't know how to make these to perfection, ma'am, nobody does." She set the tray on the nightstand and left.

As I sat in bed and ate, I remembered my conversation with Martin just before he left for the airport.

"I'm sorry you won't try and fly with me to the wedding," my husband had surprised me by saying.

I stared at him, feeling the tightness in my chest resume. "Are you serious?" I asked. I didn't want him to go. I thought we should present a united front, but he hadn't been listening to me. We'd been arguing about it for weeks, but this was the first time he indicated that I should actually be going too.

"Our David is getting married—"

"Yes, to *that* girl."

"Stop it, Rosalind." Martin got up angrily, his food untouched.

"*That* girl is Jewish. She'll have Jewish babies." Tears choked my throat. "They'll go to hell. And I don't know why, but Jewish babies always cry." My anger rose; it scared me.

Martin looked irritated. "They don't cry any more than other babies. Even our Catholic babies cried, until you made them stop." He was red in the face and clenched his fists. "And stop calling her 'that girl,' her name is Ava-May."

I put my face in my hands; Martin seldom scolded me. I wasn't a child; I was sixty-one, but I couldn't get over my fear. I felt awful.

"I'm leaving now, dear. I'll be back on Wednesday. Get a hold of yourself." He kissed the top of my head and went upstairs to take his suitcase.

I had been glued to my chair, my tongue stuck to the roof of my mouth. I wished he understood me, but there were things I couldn't explain even to myself.

This memory made me stop eating; I'd lost my appetite. I wanted Irene to return. Should I ring the bell? I enjoyed her company and being mothered by her. Or anybody. Out of the blue, the scent of chicken soup engulfed me. From nowhere. I panicked. Was Irene cooking? I wasn't sure where it came from, but I opened my eyes in horror and saw Irene staring at me. I didn't recognize her for a moment, expecting her to be wearing a kerchief over her hair. Had I rung for her?

"Please eat. The food will be getting cold soon, y'know." And with that, Irene turned to leave the room again, but hesitated. "Or would you rather I bring you a cup of chicken soup—"

"No!" I cried out, and quickly put my hand on my mouth. "Sorry. Sorry." I hadn't meant to yell at her. My tone must have scared her, as Irene stared at me strangely before leaving my room, shaking her head.

I fell back on my pillows, exhausted. My legs ached, and the nerve on my upper left cheek began to twitch. I was wired on the one hand and somewhat weak on the other. I slowly sat up, lightheaded. Low blood sugar? Too much caffeine. I wanted to ring Irene for tea, but I knew I'd better eat more first.

Reluctantly, I brought the plate closer and nibbled on a thick French fry. It was lukewarm and greasy by now. I spat it out; I liked my fries piping hot. No, Irene would see this and hate me, so I hid it in a Kleenex and tasted the fish. Not bad. How I wished it were a bit burned and wrapped in newspaper, like Mommy used to make—hot and tasty.

How I wanted my mother now.

I pushed the tray aside and got up. I hugged the photo album tightly, missing Mommy.

I opened my wedding album to look for a photo of her. There she was. Right behind me, as I was seated in front of the mirror. I had just gotten into my wedding dress and adjusted my little pillbox hat on. We both faced the mirror, my mother standing and towering over, smiling proudly. The photographer had done an incredible job; one couldn't even see his reflection in the mirror.

I dabbed my eyes with a tissue. Crying too much wasn't good for me; I was getting puffy cushions underneath my eyes. I remembered the warm look in Mommy's eyes when she'd say, as she often did, "I always wanted a little girl, one little girl, and there you were." That always made me feel so special. She wanted me.

I found a picture of me and Daddy walking me down the aisle. My handsome, tall Daddy, who read me *Winnie-the-Pooh* just before I fell asleep, who bought me a brand new car when I turned sixteen, ignoring Mommy's objections ("You're spoiling her rotten"), and who said, to my delight, "Yes, if that's what she wants," to Martin when he'd asked him for my hand.

I shut the album closed and lay back, closing my eyes. Suddenly I saw Daddy lying on a stretcher, covering his face with his hands, carried by two men in uniform.

I opened my eyes. What was that? When was Daddy on a stretcher?

No, he wasn't. I didn't remember that he was. But the image was real, familiar; it had flashed before my eyes.

I hated those sudden images that kept popping up so often. Hated them.

I crawled out of bed. I took the prayer cards that I'd kept in a small silver box on the nightstand, and knelt by my bed. There lay the "In Memoriam" cards from my parents' and my two older brothers' funerals. There were the holy cards from my three sons' baptisms and confirmations.

I concentrated on the prayer card that I had chosen for my firstborn son until I couldn't see anymore. I shut my eyes and placed the prayer card over my thumping chest and called for the Lord to save him. Then I prayed for myself:

Please, my beloved Jesus Christ, save me from my suffering. Save me from exposure. I'm one with you. I'm sorry for my sins with all my heart. Mary, Mother of God, have mercy on me. I've been devoted to you all my life. Hail, holy Queen, Mother of Mercy, hail, our life, our sweetness, and our hope. My hope.

Please forgive my son, his transgressions.

Chapter Twenty-Nine

Encinitas, California, 1996

DAVID

I LOVED my wife of three months dearly, but I loved my mother too. I might not have liked some of Mother's actions or her attitude towards people who weren't like her, but she was still my mother. It was hard to criticize her, even if just in my mind, because I felt her vulnerability so keenly.

I adored her when she'd sat with me and taught me to write with my left hand when I'd broken my right arm. Every time I lost the grip on my pencil, she'd pick it up, then pick up my left hand, kiss it, and say, "You can do it," as if my hand had a will of its own. Sometimes I'd let go of my pencil on purpose, just for her to repeat this.

I was now a married man, living a continent away from my mother, but still wanted her love and approval. It pained me greatly that she'd missed my wedding, but it worried me that she might not accept Ava-May.

If married life could be perfect, mine was very close. Ava-May was definitely the half that completed me. She understood the pressure of my new workload at a new university in a new city, and I supported her in adjusting to her new school.

However, a heavy weight sat on my chest concerning my mother. Why couldn't she love me back unconditionally and understand and accept my choices like I'd always accepted hers?

The love and regard I had for Ava-May should have been enough for my mother, who'd accepted Teresa, Andy's wife—a pregnant teen—as her daughter-in-law. My wife ought to be accepted too.

"Honey," I said to Ava-May one evening at the beginning of December, as we were sitting together on our new blue couch. "Christmas is coming, and I feel somewhat torn. You and I are not going to celebrate at home, but my family in Boston is. I'm still pissed that my mother didn't make it to our wedding, but maybe we should go back east for Christmas? What do you think?"

Ava-May eyed me suspiciously, her chin tilted sideways, eyebrows knitted in a frown. "Sure. I know your mother is sickly. But honestly, I also wonder whether there was something else that kept her from coming." My wife looked at me intently, judging my facial expression, looking for an unspoken reaction. I knew her by now.

I couldn't spell out my mother's shortcomings, but I wasn't a good liar, either.

So I said, "She couldn't get on a plane, that was established, but she also wanted us to get married in the church, which was out of the question for you, I know. But we can't just cut ties with her."

"Cut ties?" Ava-May asked. "I have no ties with her to be cut."

"Yeah, but I do; she's my mother." I was looking for more excuses and was petrified my wife was going to read my bluff. "Mother hasn't flown or taken a boat or even a train since she was little. I know she arrived by boat from England. Who knows what trauma it caused that she wouldn't be able to be in a closed space again?" Both of us were interested in the research about the impact of trauma on children.

"Oh. You mean she never travels?"

"Only by car. Luckily Dad loves driving, so they've been all over the States. As kids we visited all the national parks and east Canada. But she hasn't been back to Europe or visited any other country. My dad would fly to conferences alone."

"Poor woman. Maybe we should still go."

I was glad her mood lightened, but I suddenly got cold feet. Sometimes, when things seemed too good to be true, new fears gripped me. A scary thought that visiting Mother was a bad idea popped into my head; their meeting could be disastrous; I knew I couldn't tell my wife how my mother felt towards—

The phone rang.

"Hello?" I asked, relieved.

"Hey, bro. What's up?" Larry beamed across the Pacific. "I'm taking a short vacation and flying with some friends to Malaysia for Christmas." Straight to the point; my brother didn't mince words. "Want to join us?"

"Malaysia?" I repeated doubtfully, looking at Ava-May, who shook her head. "Thanks, Larry. I don't think so, not this time, but thank you for thinking of us." I knew my wife wouldn't feel safe visiting a Muslim country. "Would you ever consider coming back home to Boston for Christmas?"

"Nope" was his short reply. "Love to your new wifey. Bye."

Now I wondered whether I should find an excuse to stay away for Christmas too. A feeling of dread overcame me; an image of Ava-May and Mother facing each other, both wearing boxer gloves, and—

"What's wrong, honey? You're suddenly pale."

I stared at my wife. "You know what?" I said slowly. "Larry never goes home for the holidays, and all of a sudden I don't feel like going either."

Ava-May widened her big eyes and looked at me, surprised.

"I have a lot of work to prepare for next semester, and if we go back east, I'd be anxious that I won't be ready." I got up and went to make tea to avoid looking at her. I knew she'd suspect I wasn't being honest with her, and I felt so bad. Standing and waiting for the water to boil gave me time to think. But I didn't even want to think of my mother. It hurt too much. How would she behave if I brought Ava-May to meet her? Would she hurt my wife? Not physically, my mother wasn't violent, but would she say hurtful things to her? I struggled to push down the anger that threatened to well up. Anger at my mother for making me choose between her and my wife.

I returned to the living room with two cups of lemon-ginger tea and said to my wife, "There will be other opportunities to join Larry on a trip, or to go back east for Christmas, another year."

Ava-May shrugged and took her cup. She was too smart to believe a word I was saying, but also knew me well enough not to pursue the subject right now.

I knew a confrontation was coming, but for now, if I could avoid it, I would.

Chapter Thirty

Encinitas, California, 1997

AVA-MAY

LAST year, when David suddenly changed his mind about going home for Christmas, I had a feeling that he was hiding something, but when he spent the whole winter break working, I hadn't had the heart to confront him. Truth was, I was quite relieved that I didn't have to meet the woman who hadn't called even once in three months to congratulate me or welcome me to the family. So when David had called on her birthday in July, he thought it was a good opportunity for us to "meet." Before handing me the receiver, he said to her, "Mother, Ava-May would also like to say hello."

My heart was beating hard; he hadn't prepared me. So I took a deep breath, and said, "Hello, Mrs. Roy. This is Ava-May."

Silence.

"I would like to wish you a happy birthday..."

Silence.

"Mrs. Roy? Are you there?"

Click.

Blood rushed to my face. I wasn't sure if she'd heard my greetings, but my gut sank, and dread spread into every cell of my body. I wasn't sure if she had hung up on me. But if she had, I hated her. How would I ever face this woman? She was so rude. I wanted to hit David, who first stared back at me in shock, then rushed to hug me. We were both silent. I knew he loved his mother, but I felt like I'd done something unforgivable to make her behave like that.

Feeling defeated, I took David's face in my hands and asked, "What did I do to her?"

"You did nothing wrong," he had said quietly. "That's just her."

And now, in December, he wanted to go visit her. "We have to," he'd said. I tried to resist his suggestion.

"I don't think it's a good idea," I said. "She may not even want to see us. See me."

"I can't ignore her just because she's ignoring me."

"Us."

"Yes. Us. Mother has to meet you eventually and accept you." David sounded in pain, desperate, but also mad. "She just has to, there is no other way." He looked at me. "You're my wife, the mother of my child."

I was ten weeks pregnant, and that was the reason he wanted us to go. He must have thought that a grandchild would change everything.

"Look, honey." I patted his cheek. "She's your mother, I get it. You love her and respect her, but she's selfish. And rude—" I quickly put my hand on my mouth. "I'm sorry. I shouldn't have called her names, but her behavior is horrible. What kind of a grandmother would she be to our child?" I put both hands on my still-flat belly protectively.

"I don't know." David was clearly upset; his face was pale, cheeks drawn in. He abruptly got up to leave the living room and make his way upstairs. "But she was a good mother." He mumbled, "She did love me."

Did she really? How good of a mother was Rosalind that two out of her three sons had moved out of state to get away from her? Or was it coincidence? I stared after him, and my heart broke. He genuinely wanted to believe what he'd just said. He missed his mother. He loved her, I knew that much.

My mother-in-law got to me, even from across the continent. Only David and my parents knew that I was pregnant. My child would have two sets of grandparents: one close by and one a flight away. The grandparents in Boston were not going to be actively involved in this child's life. Good.

I wondered if my mother-in-law would even be happy to welcome another grandchild. Would the baby bring us all together? What if it wouldn't? Would it affect my marriage? I was too hormonal. I had to relax. As I continued to think about it, I remembered that my father-in-law was nice enough. It would only be for a few days, and Boston should be pretty that time of year, Christmas lights and all. I hadn't been to Boston before. So what if I went to meet the woman? Could it be that bad? As some point, I'd be too far along to travel, and later I might not want to fly with a baby.

I decided: If she couldn't fly to me, I'd fly to her. I could do that. For David and the baby.

Three weeks later I stared at my ticket: Mrs. Ava-May Carmel-Roy. I was excited to see my name in bold letters on the airline ticket. I had decided to hyphenate my last name just like my first name. David's only comment was "Carmel-Roy sounds good. I don't blame you for not wanting to be another Mrs. Roy. There are two already." He sounded bitter, though.

The flight from the San Diego airport would depart in three hours, and I had almost finished packing my suitcase. The pink cashmere sweater I'd bought for my mother-in-law lay there wrapped in tissue paper and pretty green Christmas paper speckled with snowflakes, right on top of the other gifts; I wanted it handy. My little suitcase contained clothes for three days. We'd be back before the New Year.

David had shut his own overnight bag and rolled it to the entrance hall. He came to zip mine and take it, too, so I wouldn't have to lift it off the bed.

We were ready to go and face the woman. I felt a sense of dread, but visiting was the right thing to do.

Chapter Thirty-One

Boston, 1997

ROSALIND

I HAD to be careful with the scissors. As I cut paper and wrapped the Christmas gifts, my hands jerked nervously. Was it too much medication? Too little? My neurologist didn't like it when I self-medicated, but "use as necessary" meant I could take as much as needed. Right?

Wrapping Christmas gifts was usually my happiest time. I would buy presents well in advance throughout the year, collecting favorites for my sons, for Teresa and the girls, and for my sweet Martin, of course. I liked giving many little gifts and enjoyed watching each and every box being unwrapped on Christmas morning. A thrill with each one. At the end of the holiday season, I'd buy on-sale Christmas wrapping paper for the following year. I also collected boxes in varied sizes so each gift would lie nicely wrapped in tissue paper in the appropriate box. I always enjoyed buying gifts for people I loved. But not this year. I still had two gifts lying on my bed, unwrapped, and my heart was heavy with grief and disappointment.

I shook my head. I just couldn't find the right boxes. I stared at a small, black box with cuff links. A gift Martin had gotten for his retirement from some colleague but hadn't used. Brand new. Good enough for David; they were gold-plated, after all. But it was the tiniest box, and I needed to find a larger one to put it in so it wouldn't get lost under the tree. What else could I use? Somewhere there was the violet cashmere sweater I'd bought for myself the previous winter, on sale, and forgotten to return. It could be for *that* girl.

Nobody would accuse me of not getting gifts for everybody, of not being the gracious hostess.

My anger rose. I had to be careful that nobody noticed. Over the years I'd gotten good at hiding my anger, but this year would present an extra challenge, and it made me extremely anxious.

How dare he bring her into my house? She had no place here. I couldn't help my extreme anxiety after David's call, which caused my migraines and nightmares to return and my heart to play tricks on me. He had plainly declared that he was coming home for Christmas with his *wife*. His Jewish wife. He didn't ask, didn't propose; he just stated the fact.

I tossed and turned in my bed that night. I could barely sleep, and when I did, I dreamed of rubble. Streets filled with scattered debris, ash, smoke and fire, sirens bleeding, and babies crying. Again. Where were the babies hiding? In the rubble? I tossed and turned constantly. Why was I thinking of babies again?

I stared at the wrapped gifts scattered across my bed. Looking without seeing. My recurring dreams exhausted me and stayed at the edge of my consciousness all day. I felt light-headed, foggy, dying for some peace, so I lay back and closed my eyes.

Suddenly I felt my bed move. I felt as if I were in a large box with wide windows, rolling on wheels. Outside one of the windows, I saw an image emerge through the fog. I looked back and saw a woman in a coat and a hat, receding and slowly fading away, waving with a gloved hand, her mouth wide open as if she were yelling out, but no sound came. I hated these nightmares.

I opened my eyes, heart racing; was my bed really moving? Shutting my eyes again, I saw an image of a beautiful white chicken drifting by. I put my hand out ... almost touching, petting ... whispering CooCoo ... CooCoo ... I thought I was going crazy. What was happening to me? I was on my bed, among all the boxes, when all of a sudden, an image of a girl with auburn hair and hazel eyes appeared before me. The same girl who'd visited me often in my dreams and reminded me of Susan, Andrew's little girl. Who was she? What was her name? Did I know her?

I tried to make the images disappear, although the image of the girl had brought me some peace and tranquility I couldn't understand.

Mommy had told me once when I was little that when I

came from England, there was an auburn-haired girl with me. Who was she? My friend? Mommy said she didn't know. Was the girl the one who took care of me on my way to America? It was all very confusing, and I couldn't understand why these memories kept popping up, but so unclear and muddled.

Sometimes I had what felt like memories of a farm. I could vividly smell wet dirt. A dog. Chickens. A pretty white chicken. I felt little, warm eggs in my hands. I had to be careful. What was it? Old people. Two of them. Was that real or was I hallucinating? But the auburn-haired girl felt real, like I knew her—I could feel her, smell her, almost touch her. Who was she? That kind and sweet girl loved me. What was her name? I could almost remember, if I reached my hand, I could almost touch her . . . just at my fingertips . . .

A box fell off my bed, and I opened my eyes with a jolt. I had to make these images go away. I never told anyone of these nightmares, not even my psychiatrist. I just wanted pills from him, tranquilizers. He didn't have to know about my nightmares, only that I was a nervous person who couldn't sleep. I insisted that I had no memories before Mommy and Daddy.

But I did remember some things. Or was I making those up? Thinking of those images and remembering—remembering what?—frustrated me and made my heart race again, which wasn't good in my condition. My poor heart. I ran my hand over my forehead—as if to erase the images—and sat up. Gifts. I had to find boxes and get those gifts wrapped already, even if my hands were shaking from nerves. I was going to meet that girl. I was going to be polite and gracious for my David. He'd be proud of me. Oh, Lord Jesus, please help me.

Chapter Thirty-Two

Boston, 1997

AVA-MAY

WE arrived late that night—the day before Christmas Eve—and took a cab from Logan Airport to Beacon Hill. Martin was still awake and waiting for us, apologizing on behalf of Rosalind, who had gone to bed early. David didn't respond, and I followed his cue, although I felt it was a bad omen. Wasn't she eager to see her son? Wasn't she curious to meet his wife?

Martin apologizing for Rosalind seemed to be a habit.

In whispers, we declined his offer of a drink. Martin nodded and seemed relieved. Was he also anxious?

We walked quietly upstairs, and David cautiously opened

the door to his old bedroom so as not to wake his mother next door. We were all walking on eggshells.

※

The next morning David descended the stairs, holding on to my hand. We were both dressed in jeans and buttoned-up, long-sleeved white shirts. Like twins. "Good morning, Dad. Mother."

Approaching Martin and Rosalind, we halted at a distance. They stood by the coffee machine, but Rosalind quickly turned to face us, fastening her back to her husband's front as if she needed support. She wore a cream morning gown and cream slippers. They were both tall, about the same height, and I couldn't see Martin's face behind her long blond curls, which were very much like Veronica's, Andrew's daughter. Martin held her close by her shoulders, and I noticed that he was still in his pajamas too.

I stared at her. Her face was serious, her eyes narrowed. I couldn't see their color.

"Good morning," Martin said. "You're up early. Here, coffee is ready, and here is your mother. I need to go change." And in one swift motion, he dislodged himself from behind Rosalind and walked quickly to the stairs. Rosalind opened her eyes wide and stared right at me. I shuddered; I'd never thought eyes could look that mad. But the color was the same as David's. I also noticed extreme sadness in the droopy corners of her mouth, her lips pressed together to a thin line. Her chin quivered, and a twitch appeared by her upper left cheek. Her whole face was contorted as the three of us stood facing each other in awkward silence.

There was no room for escape, and there was barely air to breathe.

I sensed Martin standing by the bottom stair, probably watching; I didn't hear him walk upstairs.

David let go of my hand and approached his mother, opening his arms. "Mother."

Rosalind didn't move her body, only shut her eyes for a moment. Two tears escaped while her son hugged her. Slowly, hesitantly, like a controlled marionette, she lifted both her arms and placed her hands oh so gently on David's back. Then I watched how she pressed her fingers to his shirt. He held her and rested his cheek on hers; she was almost as tall.

Knowing how much he'd missed her, I was overcome by emotion, and tears sprang into my eyes, too, as the kitchen door that led to the backyard burst open in a flash, and Veronica, now eleven years old, followed by Susan, now four, rushed in. Without taking the scene in, Susan ran to her grandma, waving her arms as if swimming, pushed David forcefully aside, and clung to Rosalind's legs fiercely.

David almost tumbled as he stepped aside, surprised, yet smiling, and I saw that Rosalind's eyebrows were momentarily knitted, but she recovered quickly, looked down, and smiled through her tears, placing her spread fingers on Susan's back like she'd just done to David's.

Andrew and Teresa followed their daughters. "Hello,

California people," Andrew greeted us. He hugged David warmly and lightly kissed my cheek.

The moment was gone.

I quickly wiped my cheeks with my fingers, and as I opened my arms to hug Teresa, David grabbed my wrist, as if not wanting to lose the momentum, and pulled me back toward his mother. "Mother, this is Ava-May, my wife," he announced. Teresa took a step back.

A hush fell over the kitchen, as the intruders just realized that they had interrupted something. Even Susan let go and stood aside silently, watching us with her large hazel eyes.

Her grandfather, still in pajamas, must have descended the one stair he had been standing on and come to stand close behind me and David, because I could feel his presence. The three of us faced Rosalind. For a second, I wasn't sure what I was expected to do, so I took a step forward and extended my hand. "I'm so glad to meet you at last, Mrs. Roy."

Rosalind stood unmoving and stared at my extended hand in silence, like it was an uncommon gesture that she hadn't seen before.

Martin cleared his throat behind me.

Rosalind, without lifting her head, gave me a limp hand and said quietly, her voice quivering, "It's nice to make your acquaintance."

I let go of her dry, cold fingers and moved closer to hug her stiff body while her arms dangled by her sides.

After a second, I let go and said, "We were so upset you were sick and couldn't make it to our wedding, so I'm honored now that you've allowed us to spend the holidays with you in your beautiful home." Was I babbling nervously? I took a step back and almost stepped on David's toes. I stood in the middle, David beside me on the one side and his father on the other. Now I was confident; I felt strong, secure, and protected, the three of us facing Rosalind, who for a moment seemed like the one who needed a way out. I knew I had done nothing wrong. Why did she make me feel like I had? Why did she have such sadness all over her face?

"Come on, Grandma." Little Susan grabbed Rosalind's hand and, with her other hand, reached out to catch mine. "Let's go have muffins. Mommy bought so, so many." She pulled us both to the dining room, where Teresa and Andrew started setting the table for breakfast.

"Maybe I should go and change now," Martin said, and he walked upstairs.

"Welcome to Boston, Ava-May," Teresa said, turning to me when Susan let go of my hand. "I hope it'll snow tomorrow. Christmas without snow is no fun."

"Snow, snow, snow. I want snow. Please," chirped little Susan, putting both her hands in prayer position.

David pulled a chair out for his mother, who sat down. He poured some coffee for me and for himself, and we shared a muffin, still standing, although I could barely swallow.

"Why don't you both take your seats?" Andrew said as he and Teresa sat down.

David finished the last of his coffee, took my mug from me—although I wasn't done—placed both on the table, and said, "Thank you for the muffins, Teresa and Andy—er, Andrew." He grabbed my hand. "But I'm taking Ava-May out to show her a bit of Boston before the holiday traffic gets too heavy." Susan's disappointed face made him add, "Just for an hour or so, sweetie, there won't be another chance, we'll be back soon."

I was stunned. What was the rush? Did he want to escape the very place that used to be home?

At that moment, Martin came down all dressed and, seeing us still standing, asked, "What's going on?"

"You're staying home, right, Dad?" David asked.

Martin nodded; his eyes narrowed.

"May I have the keys to your car, please?"

Martin raised his eyebrows. "Where are you going?"

"Just to show Ava-May around before the holiday traffic starts," David repeated.

Martin opened a kitchen drawer and handed his car keys to David, wordlessly.

David ran upstairs to get our coats, scarves, hats, and gloves while I waited awkwardly downstairs, feeling everybody's eyes on me, biting my lip and watching the staircase for David to come and save me. We quickly pulled on our cold-weather gear while the family watched silently.

At the door, David yelled, "Tonight, we'll have a big surprise for you." He tried hard to sound cheerful.

Out of the corner of my eye, I saw Rosalind lower her head.

Martin's car had a sweet smell of tobacco. I wondered if his pipe was somewhere in there.

While waiting for the engine to warm up, David ran his fingers through his hair continuously.

I sat with my hands in my lap, staring ahead, but finally couldn't hold it any longer, anger welling up. "What came over you? Don't you think it was rude of us to run off like that?" I turned to look at him. "I wasn't prepared, and neither were Andy and his family, who had come with fresh muffins, and your father was—"

"Sorry," David said, and he rubbed his face vigorously with both hands, as if to erase something. "I just had to get out of there."

He started driving and I kept talking. "Wasn't the whole point of coming here to be with your family? It was your idea."

He drove in silence and I felt like crying.

David parked outside a coffee shop.

"That's how you're going to show me Boston?" We were not on the same page.

He ignored my questions and nervously got out of the car, came around to open my door, took my hand, and together, still in silence, we walked in.

"Two large hot chocolates with whipped cream. In mugs, please." David gave the order as I found the last two vacant seats at a small table in the crowded coffee shop, feeling furious at him and sad for his mother, waiting for an explanation.

David paid and came to sit by me, waiting for his name to be called.

He took my hands in his over the table, gently pulled off my gloves, and blew hot breath onto my almost frozen fingers. "Your fingers are so cold, but it must be very cold in your bones too." How he knew me.

But I was still mad. "I think it was rude and unnecessary

to leave abruptly. We could have stayed and patched things up. Coming all the way from California and then running out like that just doesn't make sense." I couldn't understand what had possessed him.

His eyes moved nervously from my held fingers to my face and back to my fingers. "I'm sorry, love, but I had to run out before I exploded and yelled at her. I so wanted to shake my mother by her shoulders. I'm sorry, but that's the way she is—cold, detached, distanced. It's one of the reasons I must live far away. Why is a son's wife never good enough for his mother, especially—"

"Honey, you're babbling. Tell me what's really on your mind. What does it have to do with me?"

"You're too good for her." David shook his head, let my hands go, and then held his head with both hands and elbows on the table. I could see he was extremely upset. "She was the rude one, and you're afraid that we were?" he said angrily, lifting his head and putting his arms down. "Okay, maybe we were, to Teresa," he added reluctantly. "I'll apologize to her, but I didn't expect them to come that early, to interrupt, just as I was introducing you to Mother. It was so unfortunate. I wish we had more private time with Mother, away from Andy's family."

"Yes, you're right, honey. Andy and his family did interrupt, but your mother was distant even when I tried to hug her. Like she didn't want me to touch her. Something deep is going on there. Like she's afraid of me, like I'm contagious. I don't know. I have a strange feeling—I'm not sure what it is, and I'm truly trying not to take it personally, but the woman is suffering. It's written all over her face. There's some deep pain in there, and I have no idea what it is, but it's important you know what's going on. Maybe she misses you and she's hurt that you left, maybe she feels that I'm the one keeping you in California, away from her."

"I think I know what it is."

"You do? You think there's something wrong with her heart? Is she afraid of dying?"

"No, I think that something in her childhood screwed her up. Very early childhood." He didn't make eye contact with me, which was odd. It didn't make sense. We hadn't discussed his mother's early childhood in detail before, not her adoption, not any of that.

"What do you mean?"

"My grandparents were wonderful people. I wonder who screwed her up before they'd adopted her—"

"David!" called the barista. "Two large hot chocolates with whipped cream."

David got up and brought our drinks to the table.

I stood up and hurried to bring napkins and two plastic spoons to scoop off some of the whipped cream.

David sipped his drink and jumped back as if he'd burned his tongue. "Shoot."

I quickly got up and brought him a small glass of ice water. "Here, this may help." As I sat down again, a nagging feeling about his mother wouldn't leave me. "I feel so sorry for your mother, you know."

"I'm amazed you're not taking it personally."

"Should I? What have I done?"

"I really don't know what to say." He shook his head. "Maybe she was abused as a baby during the war. Maybe she saw people being killed. Her early childhood has always been a mystery, but my father said it was taboo, not to be questioned. It upset her deeply, so we never asked."

"You're her firstborn, honey, and you've absorbed all her sadness and insecurities. I guess it was diluted by the time your brothers were born."

"Talking about my brothers"—David pulled his hand out and stood up abruptly— "we'd better get back. I have a surprise for you." He winked at me. "Larry promised me to come this year, knowing we'd be here. He should be in the house already, if his plane wasn't delayed."

I looked up. I didn't really care if Larry was coming or not, as much as I liked him. He might cause more drama, as his mother hadn't seen him in years. "So no Boston? You were going to show me the city."

David went behind me, grabbed my coat, and helped me into it. I felt disappointed, but David was agitated. I took my scarf and gloves and looked out through the large windows behind me. The cars outside now had snow on them, like powdered sugar. How long had we been sitting here? It must have been snowing for a while, but we hadn't noticed.

We started walking towards the doors, but for a moment I stood still and watched what was happening outside through the double doors in awe. I hadn't seen anything so pure and calm, so innocent before. Fluff flying in the air. "Snow." I must have muttered it a bit too loud. Some people in the coffee house smiled at me. My first snow.

Walking to the car in the soft snow was fun. I had boots on, and my feet sank into the new white fluff. I held on to David and laughed.

When we got into Martin's car and started driving south, we realized that the traffic had already gotten heavy. Christmas Eve, of course. David gave me a quick apologetic glance. "Sorry, love, we'll have to come back to show you Boston another time."

"Well, I'm sure I'll come here many more times, and you'll show me around then." I tried to be cheerful. "Let's go home." The white beauty had lifted my spirits.

I knew that as much as David didn't want to face his mother, we had to return. I was somewhat scared to see her again, but placing both hands on my belly, I drew courage from my body, from my baby. It couldn't be that bad. I tried to focus on the beauty and purity all around me rather than my awful thought that maybe coming here was a grave mistake.

Chapter Thirty-Three

Boston, 1997

AVA-MAY

AS we walked in, I noticed a shift in the air. It was very quiet. The girls were gone, their parents gone, and Martin was standing in the entrance hall, holding on to the phone, his face ashen. He returned the receiver to its cradle, shaking his head and the corners of his mouth turned down, which wasn't a good sign. I noticed his eyebrows furrowed as he rubbed his forehead.

"Lawrence was supposed to come, but he missed his flight," he said, and stared sadly at David. "No surprise here. He sounded drunk. Or stoned." He took a deep breath. "Your mother is in the bedroom, so it's a good place for her to be when I tell her." He pressed his lips together in bitterness as he walked heavily up the stairs, shaking his head and leaning on the railing, instantly looking very old.

I ached for my father-in-law. I'd met Larry only once, at our wedding. His sunburned skin, his long, thin, blond braids lying on the back of his dark suit in a strange contrast. I remembered his piercing blue eyes were unusually dark and his pupils wide, and now I could see how much he resembled his mother—same shaped face, high cheekbones, chin. At times during the wedding, Larry had laughed exceptionally loudly, as if he'd had too much to drink. He seemed wild and hard to tame. He'd also made a pass at one of my married friends, whose husband wasn't impressed. Was Larry high or just drunk? I couldn't tell. I hadn't wanted to ask David on our wedding day. Later, I just forgot. Rosalind had three sons, and they were so different from each other.

Larry not coming for Christmas this year, again, was a letdown.

David had seated himself on the high kitchen stool, then shook his head and pursed his lips when I approached and hugged him. He lifted his head and smiled sadly at me. "See? This is my crazy family. Welcome to the clan." A sigh of despair escaped his lips, and I knew that no words of comfort would soothe his disappointment and pain, so I just held him, leaning my body on his, my chin on his temple, and matched the rhythm of my breath to his.

We spent most of the afternoon lounging in the living

room, alternating reading with watching TV. I missed the noise David's nieces had made, and wished they'd be back soon. Martin and Rosalind were upstairs, and the house was very quiet. I couldn't concentrate on my book and felt like I was in the wrong place at the wrong time. Alienated. Something was wrong. Thank goodness for David; resting my eyes on him from time to time, I was anchored again.

We peered up from our books when Susan and Veronica walked in, followed by Teresa and Andrew. I never heard the front door open. They were all dressed formally for Christmas dinner and church, and the girls' faces shone with pride. Thank goodness for grandchildren. It was evening already—I must have napped on the floral couch—and the snow was piling up, uninviting this time.

Martin came downstairs and explained apologetically that Rosalind, who had taken an extra tranquilizer, had been dozing off most of the day. The girls asked if they could go upstairs and wake her up now, and Martin smiled and nodded.

"I guess we need to get dinner ready before we go to Midnight Mass," Teresa said, opening the refrigerator and taking out food.

I jumped up from the floral couch to help her in the kitchen but wasn't sure what to do, so I was standing there waiting when the sounds that came from upstairs suggested that the girls had woken Rosalind.

The men joined Teresa and me in the kitchen, with Martin taking out wine and placing the bottles on the dining table.

"Would you two like to set the table?" Teresa's eyes moved

from David to me and back to David. "Rosalind and I cooked like crazy the last couple of days, so all we need to do is heat up the food and dress the salads."

We worked in silence. I was fascinated by the efficiency they all displayed, which contrasted with the noise and chaos in my mother's kitchen when preparing for holiday meals. If a stranger had just walked in, the idyllic scene would have been quite deceptive: a happy, united, tranquil family preparing the table for dinner.

When the table was set and the food laid out, Rosalind started coming down the stairs, holding on to Susan's hand and the banister, following Veronica. Rosalind was dressed in church clothes: a multilayered, blue-and-gray, long-sleeved dress reaching down to her calves, and gray, leather, low-heeled pumps. Her curls were piled up and pinned, showing off two gray pearl earrings and immaculate makeup. She looked beautiful and elegant; the rest must have done her good.

"Thanks for helping Grandma get ready, sweet girls," Andrew said, and he smiled at the three as they came down.

Martin checked out his wife. "The sleep did you good, dear. You look stunning. Come sit, and I'll pour you some sherry."

"I guess we need to go upstairs and change, honey," David said to me, looking me up and down. I hadn't realized that we were still in our jeans.

Rosalind didn't even glance at David and me as she passed us at the bottom of the stairs.

When we came back downstairs dressed casually—but not

in jeans—they were all seated at the table waiting.

We took the last two empty seats, and Rosalind, who sat in between her husband and her youngest son, took their hands in hers, preparing to bless the food we were about to eat. When she was done, Martin stood up, wineglass raised in his hand.

"I'd like to propose a toast." He turned to face David and me. "I'm glad you both made the trip from California to be with us. Thank you. And I'd like to especially welcome you, Ava-May, to our home and family, and hope that this will be the first of many visits." He lifted his glass higher. "Merry Christmas, everybody."

We all lifted our glasses, and I pretended to take a sip.

Rosalind's hand shook as she sat her glass down, and I saw a small red drop spill onto the white tablecloth. The stain slowly spread thread after thread like blood. She tried to hide it with her napkin.

Dinner passed cordially enough with the girls chattering happily, telling stories about school, as Martin kept encouraging them.

After dinner, David stood up and raised his glass. "Mother and Dad, Teresa and Andrew, Veronica and Susan," he said ceremonially, looking at each person in turn, "Ava-May and I are going to stay in the house tonight and not go to Midnight Mass." He eyed his mother directly. "But we want to tell you some incredibly good news before you leave for church. Next April, we're going to become parents. Yes. You'll have a third grandchild," he said proudly, raising his glass toward his parents, a wide smile on his face.

"Congratulations!" Martin cheered, getting out of his seat

to give his son a bear hug and a kiss on his cheek before he hugged my shoulders lightly.

But Rosalind, staring straight at me with her big, wide dark blue eyes, turned as white as the wall.

"Congratulations," Andrew said, raising his glass. He looked at David with glistening eyes.

Martin was almost back by his seat when Rosalind murmured, "I suddenly have such a headache." She struggled to stand up, her legs unsteady. "Maybe too much wine. Too much food. I need to lie down a bit."

"What about Midnight Mass?" Teresa, who had been quiet until now, asked anxiously.

"It's still early," Martin said as he turned to Rosalind. "I'll take Mother up for a little while."

David sat back down, looking deflated, pale, tired, and sadder than I'd ever seen him. I could understand if the woman was sick, but couldn't she at least offer a word of congratulations to her son?

Andrew and Teresa stared at him. Veronica asked to be excused from the table and went to read in the living room. Susan followed; her eyes droopy.

"We'll call you when we're ready to leave," Teresa called after them.

I looked at my watch. It was only nine thirty.

"Mother's behavior is bizarre lately," Andrew complained, as just the four of us remained seated. "No wonder Larry doesn't want to come visit."

David sighed. "It's not only lately, Andy." They used their nicknames only when alone; they were forbidden in their mother's presence. "She's always been unkind to people who were different from her." David's voice was heavy with emotion, as if he were about to cry.

"Yeah, but she's been worse since... since your wedding..." Andy caught himself and stopped.

"I believe you," David snapped angrily. "Mother isn't happy about our baby, because she doesn't approve of Ava-May. Not because of the person she is, but because my wife is Jewish."

Andy put his head down.

My heart skipped a beat as I stared at David, feeling my cheeks burning. What? His mother had never accepted the fact that her son had married a Jew? Was that it? But I'd never, ever heard it so blatantly and directly from my husband.

I leaned forward to support my head in my hands, elbows on the table, staring at the red stain by Rosalind's seat, feeling it was my blood spreading there.

So there it was: the big secret was out. Now I understood it all: why she had avoided our wedding, why she ignored me, why she hadn't ever talked to me on the phone, why she was so cold to me and hadn't welcomed me to her family and home like Martin had done.

I was disgusted. Anger welled up in me. I felt suddenly frightened too. Shouldn't David have warned me beforehand? I lifted my head and stared at my husband, who all of a sudden seemed like a stranger to me. Had I seriously come between him and his mother? Was something awful about to happen?

I felt confused when David got up and stood behind me, putting his palms on my shoulders. His touch sent a cold shiver down my back, so I shook them off. It seemed as if he barely noticed, but he walked away and started pacing. He stopped before Andrew.

"Why do you think she's ignoring us and not talking to Ava-May like a mother-in-law should? Like a decent human being should? She has hatred streaming in her veins."

I shuddered. I felt so alone, like I didn't know my husband, like he wasn't my soulmate, or even my mate at all. Shouldn't he have told me frankly and to the point that his mother detested Jews? Hated them. How could he have kept such a horrible secret from me? But would it have made a difference? Would I have not married him if I'd known?

Heat welled up inside me from my stomach to my chest and my face, my temples throbbing, but my fingers were ice cold. I felt humiliated, and my body shrank in a tight knot.

Martin came back into the dining room. Had he heard his sons? He had always been kind to me, but I couldn't even turn my head now to look at him.

He sat down next to me. "I'm so sorry, Ava-May," he said, looking at the tablecloth. "I'm getting tired of apologizing for her." He sighed. "We've been married for over forty years." Shaking his head, he added quietly, "And it's only getting worse with age. I'm at a loss."

He must have heard us.

I looked back at him. I was at a loss too. Why hadn't Martin warned me? Somebody?

"When are we going?" Veronica appeared by her mother's side. "Susan fell asleep on the couch, and I'm getting sleepy too."

"You sure you still want to come?" Teresa asked her.

"Yes, if we go now."

"Alright, we should get going," Andrew said, and stood up, relieved he could be excused, I thought. "Soon there'll be no good seats left, people fill up the church quickly." Checking his watch, he added, "Carols begin at ten thirty, and it's almost ten." Looking at his father, "With the storm out there, it'll be a slow drive, we'd better leave. Is Mother ready?"

"Mother and I are not going," Martin said heavily. "She's asleep, and I won't leave her."

"Rosalind isn't coming to Mass?" Teresa sounded shocked.

"I'll take Susan upstairs to bed. You can go," David, still standing, said to Andrew, and got up to go to the living room to pick up his sleeping niece.

I stared after him, thinking: Who was that man?

When Andrew, Teresa, and Veronica were gone, Martin turned to me and took my hand in his, saying, "We had three sons and also wanted a daughter." He smiled a sad smile. "Andrew married Teresa, who became like a daughter to us, very close to Rosalind, very much like her, and then came two more girls." He let go of my hand. "It was like a miracle. Three boys and three girls. When David married you, I was so happy that he had found a woman to love, to share his life with. Then I met you, and I'm very fond of you." He patted my hand. "What else could parents ask for?"

Tears flooded my eyes as Martin continued, "But Rosalind doesn't see it that way. I don't know what she sees. I don't know what's in her head. She won't share, and I've stopped begging her to." His face looked tired. "I do apologize on her behalf, and I know I do it a lot with you. None of this is your fault, I need you to know that." He patted my limp hand again, stood up, and walked to the stairs. "Good night, my dear."

"Good night." I then whispered, "And Merry Christmas."

I sat alone, feeling guilty. Feeling I'd put a wedge between David and his mother. But David should have been frank with me. I'd taken him to meet my parents, and I was lucky they'd accepted him, maybe out of love for me. But Rosalind was a different story. Anger welled up in me. I knew I needed to talk with David, but I didn't even know where to begin.

Chapter Thirty-Four

Boston, 1997

DAVID

WE didn't fight. We didn't yell. We didn't even speak to each other, and that felt worse. My throat felt tight. Ava-May simply took some blankets and a pillow from our bed and walked back downstairs. I realized she was preparing to sleep on the floral couch in the living room, where we'd spent the afternoon reading. I stood, stunned, by the bedroom door, letting her do as she wished, then sat on the bare bed. Should I have told her? Could I have? Would I have lost her forever then? How could a man say to his wife-to-be, "My mother hates you"? I had to pretend that this wasn't the case, especially when her parents were so welcoming to me. I was stupid enough to hope that

Mother would change. Childish, naïve.

Was I going to lose Ava-May forever now?

I descended the stairs quietly. Ava-May sat on the couch, her head in her hands, the pillow by her side, the blankets a heap on the carpet.

"Honey," I whispered. I stood two feet away and looked down at her, my arms limp and my chest aching. I wished I could take back the whole day. The very thought that bringing my wife to meet my mother would be a good idea was a mistake. Wishful thinking.

My chest felt heavy with sadness and regret. I'd hurt the person who was most important in my life, and I didn't know how to remedy it.

"Honey," I tried again. Ava-May put her hands down and looked up at me. I could have screamed when I saw her beautiful, big brown eyes, now narrow slits, looking at me with anger, almost hate. "I'm sorry," I said, and I sat on the couch, not too close, although all I wanted was to take her in my arms. "I know now, I understand, I know I should have told you. But I never had the right words. I didn't know how to justify her, explain her, as I didn't really understand it myself."

Ava-May looked ahead, staring at the wall and saying nothing.

"I love you and respect you," I said. "I truly thought that once she'd met you, she'd come to know you, and she'd change. She'd just fall in love with you, like I did. Stupid. Stupid of me. People don't change. I should have known. But I couldn't tell you, because I didn't want to lose you. Your parents weren't thrilled, but they accepted me. My father accepted you too; he likes you a lot, and he'd never been prejudiced. My mother is entirely different. I couldn't have told you the whole truth. It was selfish of me, I admit. I see it now. I'm so sorry." I put my face in my hands and whispered through my fingers, "I hope I'm not too late." I lifted my head and looked at her, ready to beg. "I love you so much, and I really don't want to lose you." My throat was dry. I feared that Ava-May would change now. After the painful encounter with my mother, she might feel out of place, a stranger to this family.

Silence sat like a cold, dark cloud between us. I was willing to stay like that for eternity so long as she didn't get up and leave me.

She gulped. "I want to leave as soon as the sun comes up. Do airlines fly on Christmas Day?" Her voice was gruff.

"In the morning, we'll go to the airport and sit there until we get on a plane. I promise. Would you like to come upstairs to sleep for a few hours? You'll be more comfortable in bed. I'll sleep down here."

"No, I'm staying here." Ava-May placed the pillow at the end of the couch, hit it a few times, and lay on her side, her back to me. I picked up a blanket and covered her. I understood that she didn't want to sleep upstairs in a room so close to my mother's. I took the other blanket and lay on the carpet by the couch, close to her, as if I could protect her that way. I felt awful for putting her through this ordeal, and guilt spread like venom through my veins.

Chapter Thirty-Five

Boston, 1997

AVA-MAY

I SAT by the plane window and stared out at the clouds. I felt like I was weightless, just like the little floating cloud right below us, which seemed to follow us. I kept both my hands in my lap, not wanting to accidentally bump my elbow against David's. Although my anger from last night had subsided, I was still hurt. David should have trusted me. He should have told me the truth about his mother and let me make up my own mind whether I could live with it or not. He should have warned me and not let me be surprised, when he insisted we fly to Boston.

"What would you like to drink?" The flight attendant's voice pulled me out of my thoughts.

I asked for coffee with sugar and cream, and David, in the middle seat, asked for the same.

He could have taken the aisle seat—the plane was only half full—but chose to sit right by me. I glanced up at him. He sat straight, leaning his head back, his eyes closed, his face pale. I felt a squeeze in my chest. I loved this man. He had so much good in him. But he'd made a huge mistake. Was it all his fault? I asked the little cloud below as I looked out again. I must have ignored some obvious signs: his mother skipping our wedding, not wanting to talk to me when we called for her birthday, never calling me on the phone or sending a card. It was an odd kind of behavior for a well-educated, intelligent woman. And I guessed she was one; otherwise how would a professor husband tolerate her? And David adored her. I gathered that from things he'd told me about her. Like teaching him to write with his left hand. It was a big deal to him.

But she hated me. She hated Jews. And I didn't know why.

Whatever the reason, it wasn't David's fault but—

"Here's your coffee, ma'am."

David took both Styrofoam cups and handed me mine. Our eyes locked. My hand froze in the air. His beautiful eyes were bloodshot. He looked so sad; my heart broke.

"David," I whispered.

"Yes, honey."

"We need to talk."

"Yes. And I'm so sorry. I should have told you, spelled it out. But I didn't know how. I didn't have the right words.

Every time I decided to talk about her, I froze. I felt I was betraying her. And I didn't want to hurt you with words. Instead, I hurt you with deeds, which was worse. I should have cleared the air—or not—with her first, before I took you to meet with her. I should have prepared you. I was an idiot. I'm sorry."

I didn't react immediately. I needed that little speech, an apology.

I thought of my response for a minute. Then I said, "Thank you." After a moment I added, "We love each other, and we're a family. If our family of three is enough for you, it's enough for me too. But one thing we have to promise each other, what we truly owe each other, and that's honesty. No dark secrets and not hoping the other will guess. If in doubt, spell it out."

David smiled. He took my hand and kissed my fingers, and a drop of blood fell.

"David," I called in alarm. "What was that?"

David quickly put his head back and said, "Tissues, please." His nose was bleeding.

I rang for the flight attendant, then quickly looked in my bag for tissues. A second later the attendant was by our side.

"May I have some tissues, please? My husband's nose is bleeding." I tried not to panic, but there was suddenly a lot of blood.

She quickly came with a whole box and tried to comfort me by saying, "It happens. Dry air, pressure, you know. Please keep your head back, sir."

Some passengers stared at us, so I smiled back, not to alarm anyone.

    I was hit with a sudden memory. In one of our first meetings, David had a nosebleed, and it took a while for it to stop. He disappeared into the men's restroom, and on his return, he apologized and mentioned that he got nosebleeds occasionally. It had only happened twice in the five years I'd known him. I wondered if it was from the air pressure of the plane or perhaps the pressure of the situation with the family. After all, we had left the house very early, before his parents were up, not saying goodbye to them. There was no way I could lay eyes on the woman again.

    When we arrived home, David got into bed. I sat beside him, saying, "I love you, honey, but you can't use your nosebleeds as an excuse to interrupt a serious conversation." I kissed him on the lips. I was being playful, but inside I was nervous. The situation with the family was awful, but his nosebleed worried me.

    David smiled. Then he got serious. "There's no use in taking sides, honey. This is not a match. I love my mother, and I tried to reconnect, but my life is here, with you. You are my life. You and the baby." He put his hand on my belly. "If she ever wants to see us, maybe after the baby's born, we'll have to discuss it." He sighed deeply. "But I doubt she will. It's the kind of loss I'll have to accept, maybe even grieve."

    My heart broke for David. His mother's rejection put a stain on our marriage, and I knew he'd mourn the loss of her love, but I was more worried about the baby coming with a grandmother hating it before it was even born.

Chapter Thirty-Six

San Diego, 1998

AVA-MAY

FOUR months later, I held my six-pound, twelve-ounce baby boy in my arms. My chest expanded with unbelievable joy. I kissed the pink cap on top of his little head and smiled from ear to ear, as if I hadn't just labored for almost twelve hours. All forgotten and forgiven.

"Just his luck they ran out of blue baby caps." My mom chuckled. The proud grandmother of twenty-four hours had walked into my room, elated, releasing David to go buy himself something to eat before we were discharged for home. He hadn't slept nor eaten since yesterday, not leaving my side.

About an hour later, the nurse came in. "Mrs. Carmel-Roy, I don't want to alarm you, but we've just treated your husband for a nosebleed. He is fine, no need to worry, but it was hard stopping it. Does he get those often?"

I sat up in bed quickly.

My mother, holding the baby, asked, "Nosebleed?"

To the nurse, I said, "No, not often, but yes, he's had nosebleeds before. Where is he? Is he alright?" I wanted to get out of bed and go to him, but a sharp pain stopped me.

"He's okay," the nurse said, putting her hand up to stop me. "You have stitches, remember? He's sitting down outside my station with his head raised."

"It couldn't have happened in a better place," my mother commented.

"It might be a good idea to have him seen by his doctor," the nurse said, "to rule out any abnormalities."

Abnormalities? I didn't know what to think.

Mom handed the baby back to me and asked the nurse, "How can I help?" but before the nurse had a chance to reply, Mom quickly added, "I can leave my car here, and Dad will bring me back later to pick it up. I can drive you all home in David's car if you're ready to go."

She was trying to be helpful, but the worry in her voice made me more alarmed.

"Relax, everybody," the nurse said. "Mrs. Carmel-Roy, your husband will be fine, and there's nothing you can do at this moment to help him. I first need to release you and your baby. Please just wait a few minutes."

The nurse and my mother left the room. I sat back, leaning

on my pillow, pressing my sleeping newborn to my thumping chest and closing my eyes. I remembered David's last nosebleed. What was happening to him? Was he overtired? Maybe the excitement of watching the birth and not sleeping for over twenty-four hours had been too much for him.

One week after the birth, Martin arrived. He never mentioned our sneaking out of his house on Christmas; it was as if it had never happened. Neither did he say anything about it over the phone in the past four months.

He came especially to participate in the bris—the circumcision—of his first grandson. The baby was held by the first sandak, who was my dad, on a white pillow. After the ceremony, Dad passed on the baby to Martin, a Catholic man, who sat in another armchair and performed the Jewish mitzvah of being a second sandak. He proudly held his baby grandson on the pillow that was placed in his lap. I was overwhelmed by the willingness of this kind man to participate in a ritual not of his religion. He had accepted us as we were, no demands and no conditions. I glanced at David to see his reaction; I saw the emotion on his face, a nervous smile, his fingers going through his hair, but not a tear in his eye. I'd never seen him cry.

Aaron Daniel, named after my mom's Jewish father and Martin's Catholic father, the baby's great-grandfathers, came into the covenant of the Jewish people on the eighth day of his life. Having Martin in our home and celebrating this occasion with us was an honor and a delight. What a man. He brought light and warmth into a room just by being there, smiling, which almost made up for his wife's horrid behavior.

Two weeks later, David came home from visiting a new doctor.

"Nothing to worry about," David announced. "The doc said nosebleeds happen, and if it's seldom, there's no need to worry. When he heard we'd just had our first baby, he laughed and said, 'No wonder you're fatigued. Sleepless nights are the lot of parents with newborn babies.'"

I wasn't convinced. Maybe I should have gone with him to this new doctor and asked more questions; David was pale and drained. He was still working while I had maternity leave and could take naps in between feeds. Since the baby had been born, David had taken to lying down on our light-blue couch in the living room straight after dinner. "I'll do the dishes later, okay, honey?" he'd ask.

I'd stack the dishwasher, saying nothing. This was new.

I concentrated on our child and made plans to return to work the following school year, but I was often tired too. Being a mom was delightful yet exhausting. When Aaron cried at night, I'd moan all the way from my bedroom to his nursery, leaning my hand on the wall, but when I picked him up, nuzzled his neck, and breathed in his baby scent—it was so good. Then I'd sit on my rocking chair—a gift from Martin—to nurse the baby, and I could close my eyes again.

I knew the gift was from Martin alone, although the card in the box with the chair had said, "From Grandmother and Grandfather Roy." We never heard from Grandmother Roy. She hadn't called to congratulate her son for having a baby, and I didn't know if she'd ached or not, yearning to see him. I wondered what Martin had told her about the celebration he'd attended.

It was all very painful, I presumed, but David didn't talk about it. Although we'd promised not to keep secrets from each other, it was easier said than done.

I was lucky Mom came often to help. She'd taken the drive from LA in her stride, listening to books on her way, but I knew that soon—when I'd return to work—we would need a nanny, and wondered how we could afford one.

Chapter Thirty-Seven

San Diego, 2001

DAVID

THREE years passed, and Aaron grew up and delighted us, but my health deteriorated, and I was treated for anemia. The doctor made me take iron supplements and change my diet. I still had occasional nosebleeds and suffered from fatigue, but I also had chronic pain all over my body, which I'd tried to ignore for years. I had been checked for Crohn's disease, colitis, and arthritis, but all were negative, good.

A ray of sunshine appeared when our precious daughter was born in October 2001, one month after the horrible terror attack on the World Trade Center on September 11. It was a rough time to be an American. We were all in shock. My wife couldn't stop crying, and I wished I could join her, but I just didn't cry.

"I know what I'd like to name her," Ava-May announced, leaning back on the hospital pillows as she held our baby girl in her arms, staring admiringly at her face.

"You mean . . . not Ophelia?" I asked, surprised. I knew she wanted to call the baby Ophelia after her maternal grandmother.

"Sure, Ophelia, but I'd like to give her a second name."

So we added Liberty to our daughter's name—Ophelia Liberty.

"It's a teeny-weeny gesture of tikkun olam, of repairing the world," my wife said. "In honor of the babies who had died in utero on 9/11 and never had the chance."

I loved her. Always thinking of others.

One Wednesday evening two months later, after Ava-May had nursed Ophelia and joined me in bed while I read the paper, I said, "I'd like to write a letter to the Catholic church in Boston."

My wife looked at me in surprise. "To the Catholic church? Why?"

"Can I denounce my Catholicism?"

"You're asking me?" She almost laughed.

"I want to defect, or to leave the Church, or whatever." My anger rose.

"What happened?"

"The allegations against the Church for sexual abuse reported by *The Boston Globe* have really impacted me. You know that because of 9/11, this scandal wasn't talked about as it should have."

"Neither you nor your brothers were personally affected, were you?"

"Of course not, I would have told you, wouldn't I?"

"So why now?"

"It's just that being a father makes me think differently. You know, when the *Globe* started investigating and reporting the scandal, I spoke to Dad about it. I told him I wanted to have nothing more to do with the Church."

"What did he say?"

"He said he understood and that it was up to me to do with my religion as I wished. He also tried to talk to Mother about it, but as expected, she got angry and denied any accusations."

"I agree with him," Ava-May said, yawning.

I thought of my mother's answer to Dad. It was typical; but I wished she loved me as much as she loved the Church.

I lay down, spooning my wife, needing a soft body to hold. Our children were asleep in the room next to ours, and I thought of the cousins they didn't know. Granted, Ophelia was still an infant, but wouldn't it have been nice for Aaron to be introduced to Veronica and Susan?

I missed Andy too. We spoke on the phone every few

weeks, but we hadn't seen each other since that catastrophic Christmas. At least my father visited when Ophelia was born.

"The extra bed you have in the guest room, the mattress and duvet are so comfortable," Dad had said, laughing. "I may want to stay longer."

It was easy to love him, as he'd been nonjudgmental and patient.

I approached him during his last visit. "This isn't normal, Dad," I'd said. "Mother can't keep ignoring us. She has a new granddaughter, for heaven's sake, and she has never acknowledged her grandson." I shook my head. I called her every July on her birthday, and she never asked after my wife or my child. "She needs help, Dad, don't you think? You need to take her to a therapist." I'd almost begged. "It's the twenty-first century already. We have psychologists and support groups and—"

"Impossible, son," he said. "I've tried for years. The neurologist who first prescribed her tranquilizers referred her to a psychiatrist." He sighed. "She's an adult. All I hear from her is 'I need just a few little pills to help me relax.'" Dad pinched his lips together and rubbed his chin. "Talk to a psychologist? No, she won't, but maybe the psychiatrist talks to her. I have no idea."

"We can't give up on her." My heart broke for my mother. I knew she was suffering.

Dad had shrugged, helpless too. I wondered how he navigated this marriage. Couldn't have been easy for him.

I hadn't seen Mother in four years and barely spoke with her on the phone. When Ava-May and I would call my parents before Christmas, first she'd speak to Dad, telling him about

Aaron and herself. Then I'd talk to him at length about my students and staff. After we spoke, he'd put Mother on, but we'd always talk for under a minute. Just like when I'd call her for her birthday. Same conversation, always.

She'd say, "Hello, David. I'm fine, I'm sure you are too." And before I could say a word, she'd add, "Thank you for calling." Never asking about my wife or my child or even about myself. I tolerated this for four years, but after Ophelia was born and I had heard not one word of congratulations, I stopped calling.

Chapter Thirty-Eight

Encinitas, California, 2006

DAVID

THE next five years passed in a blur. The children were growing, and much noise and happiness filled the house, but on some days, I could barely keep my head up. I was looking forward to Thanksgiving, like every year, but this year's had been a long and exhausting weekend.

Thank goodness it was over. I was constantly tired and mostly in pain; my whole body ached, although I tried my best not to complain. Occasionally, a sigh would escape my lips, but when my wife would give me a worried look, I would smile in reassurance. However, I wasn't myself. The episodes of chronic pain over the years came and went, but I was going through a particularly difficult bout now.

Ava-May's parents had brought the turkey, the stuffing, the pumpkin pie, and all the sides. I'd bought the ice cream and wine, and Ava-May had tossed the salads and set the table. Having Thanksgiving in our own home was exciting but stressful with two young children, eight-year-old Aaron Daniel and five-year-old Ophelia Liberty.

After Max and Ariella, my in-laws, left, I tucked Aaron in bed and sat by him to read a bedtime story while Ava-May tended to Ophelia. Aaron and I loved those bonding moments. I remembered how Dad and I used to read together before I fell asleep.

I kissed Aaron's forehead as he closed his eyes, and Ava-May came in to kiss him good night. I went and kissed Ophelia good night, holding on to my aching side, and slowly made my way to the living room to sit and wait for Ava-May.

"I'm totally pooped." She plopped down on the now-slightly stained light-blue couch, nestling her head in my lap. Searching my face, she asked, "How are you doing, hon?"

I smiled down at her. "I'm okay, love."

Ava-May wasn't convinced. "You're constantly sighing. What are you actually feeling?"

"When I stood up from Aaron's bed, I got that sharp pain in my back again," I confessed. "Then it traveled to my side." There was no use in hiding it. I was getting worse.

"Shoot." Ava-May sat up.

"Well, tonight it was pretty nasty." As I said it, my nose started bleeding down my face. The drip passed my lips, and within a minute, the front of my shirt was stained with blood.

Ava-May quickly laid me back and lifted my chin as the doctor had instructed her.

The following morning she made an appointment to see another doctor.

It wasn't until the following January that we could get an appointment with the internist Dr. Kent.

"Mr. David Roy?" the nurse called out. "The doctor will see you now."

We rose and followed her.

Dr. Kent rose from behind her desk, walked around it, and first shook Ava-May's hand, then mine, and invited us both to take the two empty seats. The doctor then returned to her desk, sat back in her swivel chair, and stared at her computer.

She was petite—very much like Ava-May and her mother, Ariella—in her fifties, maybe, with short dark hair, and she was holding a pair of glasses that she kept passing from hand to hand. Was she more nervous than me? I felt like my life was in her hands. Like she was the one to finally find what was wrong with me. I had been so frustrated that none of my previous doctors took my symptoms seriously and could give a name to what I was suffering from.

"Mr. Roy," the doctor said, looking at me, "I've been checking the blood work from the two physicians you've seen before me, but I need to send you for some more. I have a suspicion, but I need to make sure before I discuss your assumed diagnosis with the hematologist and maybe consult with another specialist." Dr. Kent stopped and frowned, looking at her hands, maybe realizing what she was doing with her glasses. Then she relaxed her face and gently placed the glasses down on her desk.

"Would you care sharing your suspicion with us?" I asked.

"Well, I need to ask you a few questions first."

"Sure. Go ahead."

"What is your religion, Mr. Roy?"

I peeked at Ava-May, then back at Dr. Kent, and chuckled. "I was born and raised Catholic, why?" It was an odd question coming from a physician.

"My suspicion needs to be verified by your answers and your blood test results. The more accurate we are, the better the diagnosis and the suggested treatment."

"What is your suspicion? And what does religion have to do with it?" Ava-May asked.

"Well, we need more blood tests and some consultations with other specialists, but we may be looking at something quite rare, a genetic disorder."

"What kind of genetic disorder?" I asked. In my mind, I saw my parents before me, frowning. My father was healthy enough for his age, although my mother had a heart condition. But my heart health wasn't in question; it was my nosebleeds, bone aches, and some upper stomach pain.

"Mr. Roy," Dr. Kent proceeded, "you say that you come from a Catholic family. May I ask you the origin of your parents?"

"My father is French Canadian, and my mother was adopted from Britain."

Dr. Kent sat up straighter, raising her eyebrows. "She was? Do you know anything about her birth parents?"

My pulse picked up speed. "We have no records, so we have no clue." My palms were wet. I wiped them on my thighs.

Dr. Kent was quiet for an awfully long time.

I could sense Ava-May looking at me, but I couldn't move my eyes from the doctor's face. "Dr. Kent?" I said quietly, not wanting to disturb her thinking. "Do we need to know more about who my mother's biological parents were and what other illnesses they had? Is that the genetic mystery?"

Dr. Kent looked up at me. "It was during the war, right? Do you know in what year your mother was born?"

"Yes, in 1935. Before World War II started. Why?" An uncomfortable sensation crawled down from my neck to my back. This line of questions felt invasive and irrelevant. It was getting closer to a taboo subject I'd been taught not to touch since childhood.

"Is there a possibility that her birth parents were Jewish?"

I looked at the doctor in surprise. "Jewish? *My* mother? She's a devout Catholic." Anger rose in me, and I didn't even know why. "Her parents were Quakers, and when her mother died, her sister, my mother's aunt, baptized her just before the adoption." Why was I so worked up?

Dr. Kent took a deep breath. "I don't mean to lessen your Catholicism, Mr. Roy, nor your mother's, but if your father is French Canadian and your mother is adopted, but the Quakers weren't her birth parents, perhaps a Jewish couple was—it was wartime. She may have Jewish genes, and we may be closer to a diagnosis." She sounded apologetic. "Do you have her birth certificate? Many children were misplaced during the war."

I couldn't speak. This was an outrageous theory. How could we prove anything? Tremendous fatigue poured into my limbs like heavy oil.

Dr. Kent pressed a button on her phone, then stared back at me. "Mr. Roy, I don't mean to upset you, and you look a bit shocked." She reached out and gently placed her hand on mine. "I need you to please go to the lab for more blood tests. I will need some x-rays too. The sooner we have the results, the sooner we can solve this and determine the exact diagnosis and the right treatment for you. Your extreme fatigue and bone pain can be treated with the right medication once we know what the illness is, and I do have a suspicion." She rang her nurse, who materialized in a flash. "Please direct Mr. Roy to the lab."

Dr. Kent shook our hands goodbye with a trace of a smile, and before we left, I saw her sit back at her desk, glasses on her nose, eyes on the computer screen, her eyebrows knotted.

I gave blood again and had more x-rays taken, and then we rode home. So many questions chased each other in my brain. Had Mother lied to us? Or had someone lied to her?

"I wish Dr. Kent could have given you a diagnosis today. It's been years, and nobody asked you those questions," my wife said.

I've been wondering about that too. "She wouldn't give me a diagnosis just on suspicion; doctors are careful. We need evidence; where can we find evidence?" My chest was tight, and it was hard taking a deep breath. "I can't believe it," I whispered. "I just can't believe it." My head was pounding and my hands were sweating. Could my mother's birth parents be Jewish? This was a shocking thought.

Had my whole life been one big lie?

With a cup of lemon-ginger tea in my hand and peppermint tea in hers, Ava-May and I sat in the living room.

"What if my mother's biological parents were Jewish, and Paul and Ann James adopted her before Granny and Grandpa did?" I asked, looking at Ava-May. "Imagine that. We must find her birth certificate. I never saw one. Who asks their parents to see their birth certificate?" I had to stand up and pace, my insides in turmoil. I stopped abruptly and stared at my wife, remembering. "You know what? I saw a picture of Ann once, years ago. An old passport photo, in black and white. She had a long, thin face and looked nothing like my mother, but she had long, curly hair. Of course I couldn't see the color."

I couldn't stop considering whether my mother had lied to us or been lied to.

I stared out the window, thinking out loud, "My mother looked more like Granny, her adoptive mother, with blond curls and blue eyes."

"Children look like their aunts or uncles sometimes," Ava-

May said quietly.

"Yes . . . yes . . ." I murmured, pacing. "Imagine. Imagine me asking my seventy-two-year-old mother with a heart condition if she was Jewish." I burst out laughing, nervously.

Ava-May looked at me like I'd lost my mind. "It could kill her," she whispered.

I looked at my wife with wild eyes. What if our kids had inherited my genes? My mutated genes, I thought in a panic, a new fear gripping me. I must get a diagnosis quickly. My children, my mother. We were all connected. Could I speak to her?

The thought of asking my mother if she might be Jewish was overwhelming.

But I needed to find out. Not only for myself. But for our children. I had to know.

Chapter Thirty-Nine

La Jolla, California, 2007

DAVID

"GOOD afternoon," Dr. Kent said, smiling and standing up to shake our hands. There were three chairs prepared in front of her desk, and we were invited to sit. "It's good to see you both."

I was nervous; it felt like I was soon going to be sent to the electric chair. How serious was my illness? I was scared it was terminal and I didn't have long to live. Leaving my wife and kids to fend for themselves . . .

"David is in a lot of pain, Doctor," Ava-May said to my surprise. "He isn't a complainer, so he suffers in silence, but it's time to find out what's wrong and get him the right treatment."

After taking a deep breath, she admitted, "We've been waiting so long, and we're both getting very nervous."

"Yes, I agree. Just taking painkillers isn't the answer," the doctor said. "So let's get to the point." She faced me. "I have consulted with several specialists as promised, including a geneticist, and we studied your test results." Dr. Kent bent closer, her forearms leaning on her thighs, her eyes looking up into mine, as if she was going to divulge a secret. "We've come up with a diagnosis and possible treatment, Mr. Roy."

Hallelujah: a diagnosis.

She straightened in her seat. "We have three factors here: your symptoms, your test results, and your possible ancestry. Let's talk about the first two. Your fatigue, your bone pain and frequent breaks, your abdominal pain—the last one being due to an enlarged spleen—your frequent nosebleeds are all consistent with this diagnosis. So are your blood test results, which show anemia and a low platelet count, the latter being what's causing your bruising." After a deep breath, her eyes pierced mine. "Regarding your ancestry. The fact that your father is French Canadian and your mother may be of Jewish descent—and one needs both parents to be carriers of the gene mutation—we believe it means that you have Gaucher disease."

Gaucher disease. I'd heard the name but had never met anyone who had it, to my knowledge.

Dr. Kent stood up and started pacing, poking her index finger in the air, as if lecturing students. It was quite irritating; I wished she'd sit down and look at me. "This is a rare disease," she said. "You've told your family doctor that your two brothers have no symptoms like yours. This is good news." She walked behind her desk. "Let me show you a chart."

Dr. Kent turned her computer screen to face us and pointed at the diagram on the screen. "If a mother and a father both have the disease, *all* their children would be affected, meaning that your brothers would have the disease too. The fact that your parents have no symptoms but one of their children is sick—unfortunately, you—means that they're both just carriers. If your brothers have no symptoms, they may be just carriers too."

There was a moment's silence. It felt like there wasn't enough air in the room.

Ava-May squeezed my hand and asked with alarm, "What about our children?"

The doctor looked at my wife. "You have no symptoms, Mrs. Roy, but you should get tested; one never knows. If you're not a carrier but your husband has the disease, your children are only carriers," she explained patiently, then turned to face me again. "So what does all of this mean?" She walked behind her desk and sat down. "We believe you have type one Gaucher disease. It affects one in eight hundred Ashkenazi Jews and one in forty thousand non-Jews. French Canadians—descendants of Europeans—have a high rate of susceptibility too. We treat it, in your case, intravenously with ERT, enzyme replacement therapy, every two weeks. We also have drugs that can be taken by mouth, but we can discuss that at a later stage. Let's talk about what we need to do to get your treatments started."

My panic had been rising as she spoke.

"Do you have any questions, Mr. Roy?"

My stomach and side hurt again. "Is this condition

curable?"

"It is treatable, but not curable. I'm sorry,"

It wasn't encouraging to hear that, but I wanted to start treatment right away. I also wanted Ava-May to be tested. If this would impact our children, we should know about it sooner rather than later.

Chapter Forty

Encinitas, California, 2007

AVA-MAY

I COULD relax only after we'd put Aaron and Ophelia to bed. David and I sat on our light-blue couch in the living room, in our favorite position, only now I was sitting up and David was stretched out with his head in my lap.

Secretly, I hoped it was all true.

The chance that David's mother might have been born to a Jewish couple, or at least a Jewish mother, which would make her Jewish, therefore David and his brothers, Jewish—and that I had actually married a Jew—was too fantastic, too outrageous, but possible.

In a weird way, this could give me some kind of satisfaction.

Imagine that: what a twist of fate. Straightaway, my parents came to mind; wouldn't they be surprised? Their utter acceptance and love for David had been enough for me, but still...

We were very fortunate that my BGL blood test did not show a low enzyme activity level. No further genetic analysis was required. I was not a carrier.

But we had two urgent problems now: It had been six months since David started treatment every two weeks, but he wasn't really getting better. The treatments were costly—we were still waiting for the insurance to cover it—and less effective than they might have been had we known his mother's genetic information. We urgently needed an answer from her; maybe a change of medication was required, as the price of his current treatment was burning a hole in our pocket.

With his head on my lap and his eyes looking up at me, David asked, "Whom in my family should I tell?"

I was glad he was finally ready to tell them. Maybe his parents could help us financially. David had refused any money from my parents when I offered to ask them.

Hesitantly, I asked, "Maybe tell your dad first?"

"He is a carrier, and he may feel guilty I inherited the gene mutation." David sounded worried.

"Maybe Andy?"

"He's bound to tell Mother, and she'd freak out." He sighed. "But I do think they need to know; they are my parents."

I wanted David to get the information he needed, although I couldn't think of a safe way for him to break it to his parents. Out loud I said, "That leaves Larry."

David was quiet for a moment.

"You know what, honey," he said as he slowly sat up, facing me. "Maybe you're right. Maybe he's the right one. He's a medicine man..."

Medicine man, yes. Larry, the physician assistant, knew more about medicine than we did.

"Are you scared?" Panic started rising within me; I needed him to be there with me, to be strong. "I don't know what's in your head. You have to tell me, please, you have to."

I looked at him; would he cry if he were scared? I was convinced that David had been born tearless. A physical flaw.

"Yes, I am scared," he admitted, and he opened his eyes, which were dull and red, but not wet. "Of the disease and of the expense. The treatment isn't helping much, and that sucks. How important is it to know Mother's heredity? I so don't want to hurt her by asking." He sighed. "She may react badly."

"If it will help to find the right treatment, yes, it is important. Your bones are brittle, your spleen is enlarged, your blood is lacking red cells. You saw the test results."

"My God. That sounds like I am dying," he said. "I just hope we can afford it in the long run."

I couldn't think of the money just then; that would have totally broken me. We'd held off telling his family, hoping for him to get stronger, but things hadn't gone according to plan. He was ready to involve his family now, and Larry was our only bridge.

Do you want to speak to Larry now?" I glanced at my watch. It was only 7:00 p.m. in Hawaii.

David slowly sat up. "I think it's a good idea. Let's start there. Would you get me the phone, please?"

He called Larry and put him on speakerphone.

"Hello?" Larry's voice boomed in our living room. I lowered the volume; the kids were asleep upstairs.

After some brotherly greetings, Larry told us that he was thinking of moving to LA, following his girlfriend, a pediatric nurse.

"This is great news. Listen, Larry, I'm thrilled that you'll be so much closer to us now. My children need an uncle close by. But I have to discuss something personal with you," he said, looking at me.

I smiled and nodded in encouragement.

"Hmm. You and Ava-May are okay, right?"

David chuckled. "Oh, yes, not that personal." He winked at me. "And you're on speakerphone, so she can hear you."

"Hi, Larry," I called.

"Hey there. How you doin'?"

"I'm good. But listen to David, please."

"Okay, what's up?"

"It's about my health," David said.

"Hey, you okay, bro?"

"Well, as a matter of fact, I have some problems, but the main issue is Mother."

"Wait. What? I'm confused."

David took a deep breath and told Larry the results of his tests. "Yes. Type one. Lots of tests. All the years of fatigue and pain have an explanation now. I'm being treated, but the medication is shockingly expensive. I'm not sure how I'm going to—but never mind. I didn't call for that." David was getting very tired and sounded embarrassed; he never discussed money with his brother. "I need to speak to Mother, and I have no idea how."

"Why her? What about Dad? Did you speak to Dad?"

"Not yet. You're the only one who knows so far, aside from Ava-May and her parents."

"It's a genetic disease, David. I'm sure they've told you. Mother may not have the answer, you know, or if she does, she may not tell," Larry said. "You need both parents to be carriers. Did they tell you that?"

"Yes, they did. But Mother, how can I ask her? Would she even know... Larry, I need your help," David said, sighing heavily.

"Let me think. I'll call you back next week." He paused. "I may have a plan, dude."

As David reached for the speakerphone button to disconnect, I heard Larry say quietly, as if talking to himself, "Hey, if you're Jewish, then so am I—" before David disconnected.

I felt a little bit better that David had opened the door to discussing it with his family, but I wasn't sure if any plan coming from Larry could be trusted, if he had a plan. I kissed David lightly on his forehead; he had always been precious to me, but now more than ever.

Chapter Forty-One

Encinitas, California, 2007

DAVID

IT was October already, and Larry was with us in San Diego. He was returning to the mainland, looking for a job in a Los Angeles hospital where his new girlfriend had a contract.

"You look like shit," he greeted me as he walked in.

"Hey, nice to see you, too, bro." I smiled and hugged my younger brother. "You should have seen me before I started treatment. Thank goodness for modern medicine."

"What are you on now?" My brother, the physician assistant, had become all professional.

"I'm on an infusion every two weeks," I said, and shared

the names of the drugs I was on.

Larry whistled softly. "Wow. Those are pricey."

"Yes, the infusions cost over a quarter of a million a year, but the insurance covers it. Then they want to give me pills that cost $850 each, and every month I'll have to shell out $23,800, which I don't have. I'm working only part-time, you know. They may change my medication to something that costs 'only' $311 a pill. It's astonishing what the pharmaceutical industry is making. How can I afford it all?"

Larry grimaced but didn't look shocked.

"We may have to sell the house," I confessed. This had been on my mind, but before now, I had only spoken to Ava-May about this option. It was too depressing.

I didn't tell him that we were taking the kids out of the private school they loved, or that we had sold one car and mine was now leased, but he still seemed upset.

"Whoa," he said. "You can't sell the house now; the market is horrific." He rubbed his chin. "What have you told Dad? Surely, he can help?"

"Nothing about my new expenses. He only knows that I have a 'condition,'—you know he always worried about me breaking a bone—but he's almost eighty, and I don't want to upset him."

"First of all, he's only seventy-six. Second, does Andy know? What does he say?"

"Well, Andy also knows I have a 'condition' but not about the cost, same as Dad," I said.

"Listen, dude, I think that there are several issues here. Your health comes first, and if knowing your ancestry can help with the right treatment, we must know. Also, I'm sure Dad and Mother would only be happy to help you, at least until you get the right treatment and get back on your feet. I think that you need to confront Mother and ask her flat out. It's vital."

"Are you nuts? To ask Mother? She'll have a heart attack, literally."

"Maybe she will and maybe she won't." Larry cocked his head to one side, then added, "Don't you think your own parents should know that their son is sick and needs help?"

"I don't know..." I was agitated. "It's impossible for me to fly, Larry. With the infusions and constant pain and sitting for six hours on the plane—" I stopped. Complaining hadn't gotten me anywhere, and I hated being pitied.

"Listen here. I'm willing to do something for you I wouldn't do for anyone else," Larry said.

"Like what?"

"If you can't go there and you're afraid it would be too much for Mother and Dad to hear it over the phone, I'll fly to Boston and put them on a Skype call with you so you can tell them face-to-face." He shrugged humbly and stared at the floor when he said, "I'll be there for them; it's the least I can do."

There was a moment's silence; emotion overcame me. I knew he hadn't seen Mother in about twenty years.

Still, I wasn't sure how I was going to tell my parents that I had a genetic disease they were responsible for, and possibly ask my mother about her birth parents.

Did she even know?

"They would love to see you, but not to hear my news." I groaned.

"Nor your questions to Mother." He sounded doubtful, and I got worried.

"You have no idea how much this means to me, Larry." I almost choked, hoping he wasn't changing his mind.

"Yes, I do. I'll do it for you, and for Dad and Mother. You're my big brother, and you've always had my back. I love you. It's also good timing before I start my new life back on the mainland." I could see that he wanted to change the subject, as he was getting overcome with emotion. "I may get over some guilt too..."

He relaxed and tried to smile again. "Just give me a few days to be an uncle here with my niece and nephew, enjoy you all, and then I'll be off." He clapped his hands once as if he'd just come to a decision. "I also want you both to meet Lisa. She's the best thing that's ever happened to me in my life, I swear; I've been sober for three years now, thanks to her. She's something else. So, you see, I'm a changed man. All's good that ends good." He stood up.

"I'm delighted, Shakespeare." I smiled and got up to hug him. "All's well that ends well."

"That's what I said." He winked, then frowned. "Hey, you look tired, man. Go rest."

I was relieved and anxious at the same time. Having him with my parents would certainly make it easier on all of us, but I couldn't help worrying about Mother's reaction.

Chapter Forty-Two

Encinitas, California, 2007

DAVID

MY wife and in-laws were busy playing with my kids or having breakfast, as I sat in my home office with the computer off and the door closed. I had asked Ava-May to tend to them all. It was about 9:30 a.m. here, 12:30 p.m. in Boston, and I'd been sitting at my desk since 8:30 a.m. that morning.

I needed some time to be alone and gather my thoughts. I had to think of what to say and what to keep to myself. I didn't want to come on too strong; I didn't want to hurt Mother, but I had to be frank. I needed to know the truth. But did she know it? I felt hot and cold waves going up my body. One moment I felt like I was running a fever, and the next I had cold shivers.

Relax, I commanded myself, not sure if it was a reaction to my treatment; maybe this would have to change too.

It was 9:45 a.m. when I turned my computer on.

Larry called me at 9:50 a.m. to ask if I was ready.

I was.

The computer buzzed. A picture came up. Larry was on Skype.

"Hey, bro. How you doin'?"

I coughed. "I'm good. How are you?" I wiped off the sweat above my lip with a tissue. I took a sip of water.

Larry moved backward, and I saw Dad sitting to his right with a big grin on his face; Mother sat next to Dad. She was her usual self, serious.

"Listen, David," Larry said nervously. "I told Mother and Dad that you wanted to tell them something, so go ahead."

"Hi, Dad. Hello, Mother." I wasn't sure how to start, although I had two pages filled out with notes. "How are you?" I tried to smile.

Mother replied first. "We're fine, thank you."

"Hi, son. Happy Thanksgiving. So good to see you." Dad seemed to genuinely mean it. "Isn't technology wonderful?"

"Er, yes, it is. Happy Thanksgiving to you too. I'm sure it's great for you two to see Larry, eh, Lawrence—"

"Yes, it's wonderful. Mother is ecstatic. After all those years. But Lawrence said that you had something extremely important to tell us, that you couldn't fly and that he had to come especially to help us with this computer thing," Dad said.

"Yes, Dad." I paused. "Isn't it great to see him after all

these years, Mother?" I was trying to stall the conversation.

"Are you sick, David?" Mother had a hunch.

"Yes... I..." I couldn't get it out. I felt like I was going to shatter their lives.

My father frowned, and a cloud of worry passed over his face as he came closer to the computer's camera. "I noticed last time that you'd lost weight, but is it serious? Not cancer..." He opened his eyes wide with fear.

"No, Dad, it's not cancer. It's a genetic illness."

"What do you mean by genetic illness?" Mother inquired. Her voice sounded soft and kind. Like when I was little and she'd read a book to me.

"Did you mean a genetic disorder?" Dad asked. "From me or your mother?"

"Correct, from both of you, but—"

"David, what is it? Were you assessed and diagnosed?" Dad went to the point, but I couldn't say it yet.

"Remember me breaking my arm, my ankle—"

"Of course, David, several times. But every child breaks a bone at some point." Mother sounded dismissive.

"Larry didn't. Andy didn't," I blurted, forgetting she forbade nicknames, sounding like a child.

"You were always accident-prone—" Dad interjected.

"Lawrence and Andrew were more careful—" Mother suggested.

"No, Mother. It wasn't that I wasn't careful. It was a symptom. Like my constant fatigue and stomachaches due to a swollen spleen. The disease can be diagnosed in children or in adults, but I only just found out recently." I was getting tired and felt flustered. "I've been diagnosed with Gaucher disease, which is inherited from both parents who carry a gene mutation—" I ran out of breath.

Both my parents and my brother stared at me, and my throat dried out. No more words would come out. I took another sip of water.

Larry turned to Dad. "Do you know what that is, Dad? It's treatable, but it requires extremely expensive medications." I was grateful. I felt that he wanted them to understand that money was an issue here too.

"Gene mutation . . . from both of us," Dad said thoughtfully, as if to himself, as he settled back into his seat. "This is awful, son. I'm so sorry." He moved closer again, and I saw tears in his eyes, which almost made me choke. "I feel responsible—"

I quickly said, "Don't be silly, Dad." My heart went out to him and to Mother. They must have felt guilty, as if they'd neglected me as a child. That wasn't my point. I so wanted to calm them. Thank goodness Larry was there; they couldn't have handled this alone. "No parent is responsible for passing on their genes to their children. This is unavoidable. I'm fortunate there is treatment, although expensive—" Shoot. I didn't have to repeat that.

"And there's no doubt, you've seen a specialist." Dad had stated the obvious; I guessed he was trying to digest the news. I was pleased he didn't get hooked on my last comment; I felt embarrassed.

"Yes, several, but—"

"You said from both of us," Mother interrupted. "Does it

mean that we're sick too? Both of us?"

"No, Mother, you're not sick, you're only carriers," I said, trying to explain patiently but feeling annoyed at the same time. "You've had no symptoms all your life, but we need to know... We need to find out... just to be a hundred percent sure... We need to verify... what your heritage is."

Silence.

I saw Mother turn to look at Dad, asking him to go to their bedroom to get her heart medication, then back to the camera, and I noticed the blood drained from her face. I had to continue. This was my only chance, having Larry there as support. "It's important to know what your biological roots are, Mother. We know you were adopted, but do you know who your birth parents were? Were they Ann and Paul James? It's important for a precise diagnosis and for future generations, for my children, and—" I was drained yet fired by curiosity and the need to know.

I could hear my mother's shaking voice, whispering to my brother, "What did he say about biological roots?" She suddenly looked even paler. Or was it the computer light?

"My doctors want to know if they're giving me the right treatment for the right diagnosis. Who were your parents, who was your birth mother..." I said, annoyed that I had to repeat myself and feeling exhaustion pour over my aching body like soft, warm water.

Mother stood up abruptly. I saw her torso but couldn't see her face. I could still see Larry sitting at the dining room table, looking up at her, saying, "It might help David's doctors if they know his origins, your origins, Mother. Information about your birth mother." He was trying to help me, bless him, repeating my words to her.

I barely heard Mother's voice when she said, "You know that my first parents were from England—"

"But you were adopted," I snapped, desperate to hear her reply.

"So?" I heard her say. Then she asked Larry to get her some water. Larry got up and left, and she was alone now. I was staring at my mother's midriff as she was standing, and I pressed on.

"You were adopted twice, right?" I mustered all the patience and care I had in me. "Ann, Granny's sister, and Paul James adopted you first. From whom? How did they get you? Please, sit down, Mother, so I can see your face."

Silence.

"Could your birth mother have been Jewish?" I asked in anguish.

Silence again, then—

"Jewish?" Mother spat the word, bending down, trying to find the camera, her face all too close and distorted. I couldn't ask her to sit down again.

"I know it was wartime, Mother." I felt like I was explaining something gently to a child. "Maybe your birth mother gave you to someone to save you, to save your life, because she was Jewish—"

There was silence.

Then I heard her mumble incoherently. "Meine Mahme? . . . ja . . . und Tahte auch . . . Bubbe . . . Zayde . . . ja . . . der Zug . . ." She sounded like she was crying.

Her face disappeared.

"Mother! Mother! Please, someone! Dad! Larry!" I shouted. Where was everybody?

What happened? What was she mumbling? Did she slip off the chair? Oh, no.

I heard her voice call out: "Maaaa mehhhh ... Maaaa mehhhh ... " Mother sounded like a child.

Suddenly I saw Dad holding an orange medicine bottle, mumbling, "It's empty..."

Where was Mother? On the floor? Had she fallen? Larry was now up close; I could see his torso, but both he and Dad slipped right down the screen.

"Dad! Larry!" I shouted. "What's happening?"

The door to my office burst open, and my wife rushed in, followed by Max.

She stood with her father behind me as we all watched my father and my brother lift my mother up—she seemed like a rag doll—then suddenly a hand came close to the camera.

The screen went black.

Chapter Forty-Three

Encinitas, California, 2007

AVA-MAY

DAVID was seated, his eyes glued to the black screen. So were mine.

"David, are you alright?" My father was the first to speak.

Nothing.

"Honey?" I tried to get a reaction, shaking his shoulder gently.

David jumped off his seat, turned, and looked at me wild-eyed, yelling, "She fainted; my mother fainted when I asked her if her birth mother was Jewish. She fainted, or worse..."

"What are you talking about?" My heart broke for him;

his face was contorted with pain.

"You saw her . . . She fell . . . and it's my . . . fault." He fell back onto his seat.

"Well, I saw your father pick her up. She could have just fallen off her chair," my father suggested. "I know she's a bit frail."

David stared up at my father blankly for a second, then turned back to his desk and frantically called his parents' house.

Nobody answered.

He tried Larry's cell phone. When Larry didn't pick up, David left a message. "Larry, Larry, answer your damn phone. Tell me what's going on." His tone sounded panicked and my heart raced. I ached for him and for his mother; I knew he loved her, even with all her craziness. As I hugged him, I heard Dad leave the room.

My parents took our kids to the San Diego Zoo and promised to be back for an early dinner.

"Come with me to the kitchen, honey, don't stay here alone," I suggested.

But David wouldn't budge. "I have some work to do." He turned his computer back on. I understood by his expression that he wanted to be left alone.

My mother had prepared the turkey, so I heated up the oven and put it in. I started on the salads. I knew what the conversation was about, but I hadn't heard the exchange. I didn't know what David had asked, nor how, nor what his mother had replied. But fainting? That was extreme.

A while later, I returned to his study with a cup of tea and a sandwich and asked David if he wanted to tell me how the conversation went. He did. I wasn't surprised. But I assumed that Rosalind must have been shocked and that was why she had probably fainted. There was nothing for us to do now but wait to hear back from them, although I was surprised they hadn't answered the phone.

Thankfully Larry called back, but it was afternoon already. David put him on speakerphone. "Mother is in intensive care. She had a cardiac arrest."

"What?" David yelled.

"Did you call 911?" I asked.

"No, we decided to take her ourselves instead of waiting for the ambulance."

"Why?" I whispered, surprised at that choice.

"Was that a good idea?" David was as surprised.

"I don't know, David," Larry snapped. "Traffic was chaotic and we couldn't wait. Thanksgiving, right? Dad drove while I did CPR, but I couldn't get her to breathe again."

My poor David looked like he was hit in the stomach; all the blood drained from his face, and his hands were limp.

After a long pause, Larry said, "She's not good. She's in a coma, David. She's getting oxygen, and I hope it's not too late. We can do nothing but wait."

Wait, I thought. That was almost all we'd been doing today.

I heard my parents return with the kids.

Larry told us that when Martin had gone to get the heart pills, the bottle was empty.

Apparently, she hadn't been renewing her prescription, or maybe had taken too many. Martin was shocked and furious. He tried to call her doctor, but the office was closed due to the holiday. At the hospital he was asked if she'd been consistent in taking her medications as prescribed, but he couldn't confirm it.

We decided to fly back east.

Two days later, Aaron, nine, and Ophelia, six, couldn't have been more excited to get on the plane for their first flight. We'd told them that their Boston grandmother, Daddy's mom, was sick, and they both wanted to visit her. The six hours passed quickly with books, puzzles, and snacks.

David was extremely quiet on the flight. I could only imagine the heaviness in his heart. I knew how conflicted he felt about his love for his mother and his anger at her not acknowledging me and the kids. The woman was in a coma, but if she did survive, I hoped that perhaps being so close to death she'd welcome us now, ten years after I'd met her for the first time. Maybe that would wake up something in her, the motherly feelings she'd had for David when he was little. The tender moments they'd shared. I didn't usually pray, but I wished, oh, how I wished, that she'd be a changed person now, that she'd recuperate and accept our love and care.

Christmas lights always made me feel festive, and although it was only Thanksgiving weekend, some houses already had lavish decorations on.

But not the Roy family's house.

Chapter Forty-Four

Boston, November 2007

AVA-MAY

WE rang the doorbell, and Martin opened the front door. I could read in his face how bad things were. David was the first to move forward, and I watched the two men hug, glued with grief.

It was bitterly cold, and I shivered but couldn't move. Ophelia and Aaron moved closer and took my hands, staring at the two hugging men, then looked up at me with questioning expressions. I tried to smile reassuringly but could barely move my face in the cold. I let go of Aaron's hand and put a finger to my lips. The children followed my stare and stood quietly, respectfully, watching. I felt them shiver. Although they were excited to see their beloved grandfather, they sensed the seriousness of the situation, and they were unusually quiet.

Martin, who usually hugged and kissed the kids passionately, came closer to me, hugged me lightly, and simply said, "She's gone."

David took the kids inside, and I followed Martin. "I'm so sorry for your loss," I said quietly, feeling foolish. Wasn't there a more personal, warm, and intelligent thing to say at that moment? I couldn't think.

I walked towards my husband, hugged him, and said, "Oh, honey. Oh my darling. I'm so, so sorry. This isn't fair . . . Not like that . . ."

David hugged me tight, then took a step back and said, "The kiddos."

I pointed up, and Martin nodded.

I took the children upstairs to David's old bedroom. We took our coats off, sat on the bed, and I told them that their grandmother, who'd been so sick, was now dead. That we were all very sad they'd never met her before, and that we now needed to be very considerate and extra kind and gentle with Daddy. "He's very sad that his Mommy is gone," I added. "You understand that, right?"

Aaron nodded, and Ophelia hugged my waist. "Gone forever?" She asked quietly.

That was the first time they had experienced a death in the family, but they must have been too scared to ask more questions. I knew it would come up later, and I'd have to be ready. Ready to explain death to young children wasn't simple. I kissed my daughter's face and whispered, "Yes, my sweetie. But I'm here and so is Daddy. And he needs me now. Are you okay to stay with your brother while I go to hug Daddy?" She nodded solemnly.

The kids stayed upstairs and I returned to David.

I noticed that Martin wore a dark suit and a black armband on his sleeve, as if ready to go somewhere, and suddenly I heard Larry's voice coming from the living room. As I entered, I heard him say, "It was my fault. I should have called an ambulance, paramedics have oxygen. Five minutes without oxygen to the brain, no wonder she slipped into a coma." He stood by the fire, leaning on the mantelpiece, wearing a suit and a black armband, too, staring into the flames and nursing a glass of scotch. This was alarming; I thought he was in recovery.

"Stop it right now, Lawrence," Martin said sharply.

Larry muttered something as he swayed slightly. We all stared at him. I was grateful my children weren't present to witness their uncle's behavior.

"The vicar is waiting for us at St. Joseph's Church. He'll explain everything about the wake and the funeral tomorrow."

I stood there thinking: Even if Rosalind was Jewish by birth—and it was only a suspicion—she'd still lived a devout Catholic life and would want a Catholic wake and a Catholic funeral by a Catholic vicar. She was going to be buried as one.

Martin's composure was somewhat unnatural, too erect and poised. As if he had to be in full command and be doing stuff just to keep from thinking. I feared he would crash later, but I knew everyone mourned differently.

David lumbered upstairs with both suitcases. He went to shower and change while I took the kids for a tour of the first floor. We left Martin and Larry in the living room, both staring into the fire.

When Teresa and Susan arrived, my children stood awkwardly by me, both staring at fourteen-year-old Susan, her auburn hair, like Aaron's, her similarly shaped face and the same color eyes, but she was a girl. They could have been siblings by their looks.

David came down the stairs, wearing his dark suit that hung loosely on his thinning body. He kissed me, kissed the kids' heads, and helped Martin support Larry out the door; a black limousine awaited them. The men walked out, followed by Teresa and Susan, who left without glancing back.

I took a deep breath, feeling very out of place in that house.

Ophelia pulled on my hand. I looked down at her and tried to smile. "Come on," I said, and I climbed the stairs with my children, trying to cheer myself and them up. "You know that this is Daddy's old room, right?"

I hadn't been here since that disastrous Christmas of 1997. I shuddered at the thought—

The doorbell rang.

"Please unpack your suitcase. I'm going to see who it is." I ran downstairs.

Veronica was at the door. I was stunned at her beauty and resemblance to Rosalind. Was she twenty-one already?

"Hi, Ava-May. My dad went to the vicar to meet with the others. I didn't want to go, so I asked him to drop me here, although he said that my mom would be mad." She peeled off her gloves and tucked them in her coat pockets, removed her coat, and shook her blond curls out of her beanie, shivering and muttering, "I forgot how cold it can get here, I hate it. California is so different."

"You can say that again." I chuckled, hugging her. "I'm so glad your father dropped you here first." I liked the kid, who I hadn't been surprised, had chosen a California school, Stanford University. So many kids in this family seemed to have chosen to move far away from home to find their own identity.

I held onto the banister and called up to the kids, "Come downstairs, please. Your cousin Veronica is here."

They came down, skipping stairs. They liked Veronica, who'd come once to visit us from Stanford, staying a long weekend and having fun in San Diego.

After hugging her cousins, Veronica turned to me and said quietly, "I don't believe in any of this, you know, religion. I'm more like Grandpa. Nonpracticing. But please don't say anything to my mom and dad. I just came home out of respect for the family because it was expected of me. In two days I'm going back to Palo Alto. I don't like or go to church anymore."

I was surprised by her confession. I thought she'd come out of love for her grandmother. But maybe they'd grown apart once she went away to college, or was this her way of dealing with grief? In any case, I had to focus on David's grief and help him get through the next few days.

Chapter Forty-Five

Boston, December 2007

DAVID

DAD wasn't feeling well. He stayed in his bedroom two days after the wake and the funeral. I sat with him, but he didn't want to talk. We watched TV together in his bedroom.

Larry was either drinking or sleeping. Nobody had the fortitude to talk to him about his drinking. But I was worried about him; he'd been so proud to be sober, and he was clearly out of control now.

Veronica flew back to Stanford, claiming she had work to do over the winter break, ignoring Teresa and Andy's pleadings that Christmas was coming and it was family and church time. I didn't interfere. Fourteen-year-old Susan kept my children busy, and I was thankful.

While Dad rested upstairs, I asked Andy if he would talk with Larry.

He said he already had and he received a promise that Larry would try again to give up his drinking. I felt awful that my little brother, and not I, the eldest, had to speak with Larry and support him to return to his program. He'd been doing so well in Los Angeles, going to AA daily, that it broke my heart to see him this way. I believed he felt incredibly guilty that he couldn't save Mother. I could just imagine his desperation when he gave her CPR while Dad drove like a maniac, and the anguish he felt when he couldn't revive her. Not breathing for several minutes had caused the coma, we were told. But it wasn't only that; she had also not been taking her heart medication. *Why, Mother? Why didn't you take care of yourself?* It was like self-punishment. But Larry wasn't to be blamed. I was. I'd pushed and pushed and asked Mother the most crucial question when she was alone. Alone. The whole idea was for Larry to be there to support them. Ultimately, it was me. I asked. I pushed. She'd muttered words in German, or another language, I had no idea, but that only proved to me that she wasn't British. Was she a child of Germans? Jewish or Christian Germans? It didn't make a difference. She was from central Europe if she spoke German. But I hadn't ever heard her speak that language. How could she have hidden it for so many years? I had no idea what I was going to tell my doctors now, I had no answer, it was all in vain. I remembered Dr. Kent giving us the statistics: one in eight hundred Ashkenazi Jews. She had to have been Jewish; it was the only thing that made sense.

My thoughts were interrupted when Teresa returned from dropping Veronica at the airport.

Andy called Larry to the living room. "We have to discuss what we're going to do with Dad now." Andy seemed so put together that I wondered if faith had really helped him.

"He shouldn't stay alone in this big house with all the memories," I said.

"But it's much too soon to move him anywhere," Andy, the attorney, replied.

"I have to go back to Los Angeles," Larry claimed, fidgeting. "I have to settle down before I start my new job, but I do hate the idea of leaving Dad alone like this." He seemed sober enough to care, but not enthusiastic about staying longer in Boston.

We all sat quietly, thinking.

I wished I could stay longer, but I had to return for my infusion.

Ava-May broke the silence. "I guess it always falls on Andy and Teresa, because they live here. Maybe I can stay a bit longer and help?"

Everyone stared at her. I was astounded; had she thought this through? It was news to me; we hadn't discussed it beforehand. My wife raised her eyebrows at me questioningly.

"You would do that?" Teresa sounded surprised, but hopeful. "I don't think I could touch her things to clear them . . ." She hesitated; tears sprang into her eyes. I knew she loved Mother for welcoming her into the family and accepting her, no matter her transgression. I tried not to let this rankle me; my wife had done nothing wrong to be forgiven for, yet she hadn't been accepted by my mother as Teresa had.

"Well, I guess I could go back with David and the kids and help out for a couple of days," Larry offered.

"That's not a bad idea, sweetheart," I said to my wife, hesitantly, not sure how it would work out with Larry needing AA so desperately. "Are you sure you're okay to stay for a while, honey, and help Teresa and Andy tie up loose ends?" I was grateful for my wife's offer, although we had never separated or slept apart. Then I had an idea. "I can always ask one of your parents to come help me if Larry needs to return to Los Angeles." Larry stared at me suspiciously yet understanding.

"I think so . . ." Ava-May sounded hesitant and scared all of a sudden. "How long do you think I should stay?" my wife asked, her big brown eyes on me.

"You decide, honey. One week? Two the most?" I suggested.

My cellphone rang.

"Hello?" It was Max Carmel.

I handed my phone to Ava-May, who rose, excused herself, and went to the kitchen for privacy, most probably to explain to her father why she was staying behind.

When Ava-May returned and conveyed that her parents would come down to San Diego after Larry left and help me and the kids until she returned, I was relieved. Maybe it was time Larry and I had a serious talk about his drinking.

Now I had to hope that she'd be fine. I knew she loved Dad, but staying with him in the big house where she was hated by its mistress could feel a bit creepy. I was most grateful for her offer, and not surprised, but slightly worried.

Chapter Forty-Six

Boston, December 2007

MARTIN

THE house was quiet. Strangely quiet. They'd all left. The kids were gone; the grandkids were gone. It had been ten days since Rosalind had died. Died. I could barely say the word

Only Ava-May stayed behind. I wondered why. I'd asked Irene to come back and help Ava-May pack some of Rosalind's clothes to take to the church's thrift shop. I had many memories; I didn't need her clothes. I knew that needy people would be happy to get them.

I wanted to return to my bedroom, the one I'd spent fifty-two years in with my bride. I hadn't been able to sleep there since her death. I still couldn't believe she was gone. It felt like she'd just dropped out to go shopping, to her Bible group, or to the book club. Maybe she was outside tending to her roses.

No. She wasn't coming back. We hadn't called an ambulance. Paramedics had oxygen tanks. I could hardly push my way through the heavy traffic. Now she was gone.

Gone.

Ava-May made lunch one day while I sat at the table with a warm cup of tea snuggled between my hands.

"I still feel like I'm dreaming," I said into my mug. "Since I retired, Rosalind and I had been together day and night. Besides my trips to you, of course."

Sadness mixed with anger welled up in me. If only I had fought harder for her to accept Ava-May and David's children. Her Jewish grandchildren. Now it was too late.

Ava-May turned to me and asked, "Did you ever see Rosalind's birth certificate? This is crucial for David's treatment, do you realize?"

I shook my head. "No, I never saw it," I replied sadly, understanding the urgency. "And I don't have the answer. Her very first document was her English parents' adoption papers and then her readoption by Margaret and Oliver after her baptism." I looked up at her. "There must be a way, though. We can't just let it be. Let me think."

"Do you have dates?" Ava-May asked, still standing by the toaster, waiting. "You don't know whom her English parents adopted her from, but do you know when? How old she was?"

"According to her British parents' adoption papers, it was in 1941; she was seven."

"So where was she before? Her first seven years, the most important in a person's development?" Ava-May said in exasperation.

I knew what she meant, but I had no answer. "If I had a last name, I could've looked her up in the Holocaust survivors' archives. But Rose? Just that name gives me nothing. There must have been many by that name."

We sat in silence.

The phone rang. I answered, nodded, said, "Yes, I can, thanks," then put the phone down.

I took a deep breath. "Do you mind? An old friend of mine, a retired professor, just invited me to play bridge now. One of the guys bailed out on them, and they need a fourth."

I felt bad to leave her alone, and Irene would only come tomorrow, but I missed some male company. I was driving myself crazy obsessing over Rosalind.

"That's a great idea. Why don't you go?" Ava-May said, smiling in encouragement. "It will take your mind off things." She paused, then added, "Anything special you'd like me to do while you're away? I've done the laundry, and I made double the quantity of soup last night, so we can eat the same tonight, if it's okay with you."

"Actually, yes. Yes for the dinner and yes for your help." I stared at her. "Would you like to start sorting Rosalind's clothes or wait for tomorrow, when Irene comes?"

But Ava-May didn't reply, she just nodded thoughtfully.

I patted her hand before I got up to get ready. I knew the task before her wasn't going to be easy.

Chapter Forty-Seven

Boston, December 2007

AVA-MAY

I STOOD alone in the cream-colored room; it felt eerie. For the past ten days, since Rosalind's funeral, as far as I knew, nobody had entered the room, nor had it been aired. The smell of Rosalind's Amarige perfume lingered on—I recognized it; my mother had been using it too—and I half expected her to walk out of the bathroom in a white robe any second and inquire what was I doing there.

But Rosalind was dead. Dead and buried. Under a cross.

She might have been a walking time bomb ready to explode at any minute, but the poor woman couldn't hurt my feelings anymore. Nor my family's.

First, I drew the cream curtains aside and opened the windows. Ahhh. The cold December air blew in, and the stale fragrance made its way out.

Folded carboard boxes were leaning on the walls. Martin had moved to Andrew's childhood bedroom. I knew he wanted to return to the room he'd shared with Rosalind, but somehow her clothes had been too much of a reminder. I understood; it felt as if she'd come in any minute and change, or grab a hat, or a purse. It was too painful.

I walked into the dressing room and faced half-empty wardrobe rails, bare shelves, and empty drawers that were half closed. Two ties, both blue, lay on the cream carpet—abandoned—as if somebody had been in a rush to grab things and had missed them before running out as fast as possible.

I entered the bathroom, pushing the door open slowly and peeking. Everything was intact. I stared at the two orphaned toothbrushes for a moment longer and walked out.

I assembled one cardboard box, applied packing tape at the bottom, and put it on top of the white bedspread. I started folding and packing Rosalind's dresses. They were elegant and conservative. All size four. There were five dresses with the price tags still attached. Interesting. Compulsive buyer? Were they intended for return? Had she planned on choosing one for Christmas?

The pantsuits needed another box. There was one suit with a price tag. The delicate blouses would fit in there too. A third box was for sweaters, gloves, and scarves. Oh, five scarves with price tags on, neatly folded in soft tissue paper. She hadn't been a kleptomaniac, had she? Maybe they had been intended as gifts. One familiar soft packet wrapped in green Christmas paper speckled with snowflakes ... hmmm ... ten years. She hadn't even opened my gift. My heart skipped a beat.

Shoes were next. Rosalind's shoes were lined up on special racks. Twenty-four pairs. Three pairs with paper inserts and perfectly clean soles. Brand new.

Right in front of me, on one of the shelves, I saw photo albums. There were three light-blue ones. I picked up the one on the left. It plainly said "DAVID" in large silver letters, a large silver cross below the name. I opened and stared at the young, smiling woman with a head full of curly hair, holding a perfect-looking baby wearing a long, white-lace dress. Oh, David at his baptism. I gasped. I kept looking at the pictures and saw Martin as a young man, two older couples, and many others.

I closed the photo album gently and placed it at the bottom of a newly assembled cardboard box. Martin might want to keep it or give it to David.

I took out the other two blue ones named "LAWRENCE" and "ANDREW" and, without opening, gently laid them on top of David's. Then I saw a large, white satin one: a wedding photo album. As I was about to pull it out, my toes knocked against something. I looked down.

That something must have hit the wall when my shoe touched it under the bottom shelf, and then rolled right back out. I let go of the album, bent down, and picked up a cold, round tin canister. It looked like nothing I'd ever seen before. An ancient tea box? I thought I could see a faded letter *T* in red. Something else was printed on it, but I couldn't make it out, as the writing had faded with time. The box was colorful but also old and rusty looking.

The wedding album found its place in the cardboard box together with the boys' albums before I sat back on the bed and tried to open the canister carefully. It was stuck. I tried to wiggle the round cover gently. It wouldn't budge. I got very curious, so I took it downstairs to the kitchen to find a knife to force the lid open.

A puff of mildew scent hit my face once it opened, and the lid fell onto the kitchen counter. I sneezed. Twice, three times, just like my mother. The box must have remained unopened for decades.

"Bless you."

I jumped in surprise. "Oh. Martin. I didn't know you were back from bridge."

He stared at the tin in my hand. "What's that?"

I felt bad, like an intruder. "I found it in Rosalind's closet as I was packing her clothes and got curious. It was right under the bottom shelf, and it looked so old and interesting. Sorry, maybe I shouldn't have—"

"What is that awful smell?" Martin stood by me and peered into the box as if scared to touch it. "What's inside?"

We sat at the kitchen table. I turned the box upside down to empty its contents onto the table, but something was stuck. I had to put two fingers in very gently to pull it out. Two black-and-white photographs and something wrapped in thin, yellowing tissue paper fell out. Martin picked up one photo and stared at it. I glanced at it too. We stared at each other. Martin was holding an image of a woman with long blond curls sitting on a sofa with two little girls, one on each side. He gasped and whispered, "Veronica and Susan." The blood drained from his face. "Rosalind?" He stared wide-eyed at the photo. "Who is this woman?"

I picked up the other photo gently and asked, "And who is this?"

Martin took the second photo from my hand and stared at a girl who looked just like the older girl in the other photo. "I have no idea," he said. "But doesn't she remind you of... Susan?"

"Yes... and a bit like my Aaron... but it could just be a coincidence."

"Yeah."

I picked up the photo of the three seated figures and turned it over. There was a handwritten inscription on its back, the ink fading: "'Moje dwie perły,'" I read aloud. "'Styczeń 1939.'" I stared at the date again. "1939?" I gaped at Martin.

"That sounds Polish," Martin said, astonished. "1939?"

"Polish," I said.

With shaking hands, Martin took the small packet of tissue paper, which crumbled almost to powder at his touch, and revealed a gold Victorian shell cameo brooch surrounded by small pearls. As he handed it to me, I saw something glisten in the light, mixed with the crumbled tissue paper.

Diamonds.

I gazed at them in astonishment. They were almost lost in the dust of the tissue paper. Six cut diamonds. I carefully separated them from the tissue paper. But as I picked up the brooch, the pin broke. The diamonds must have been wedged at the back of the brooch by the pin.

"Oh, I'm so sorry," I cried out.

"Careful. Don't prick yourself with that rusted pin. This must be like a hundred years old," Martin said in a shaky voice. "Diamonds. It looks like Rosalind had never opened this tin, doesn't it? Imagine she would have found this treasure. I wonder who put it there. Do you think it was given to her by her birth parents? They must have been wealthy." He picked up the tin and studied carefully the writing on it. "The letters are faded. What a pity." He took the brooch, examining it. He put it down on the table and fingered the diamonds. "Do you think these are real?"

I got up and brought a box of white tissues. "Would you like to put the diamonds into a clean tissue until you decide what to do with them?"

"No. I may confuse it with a dirty tissue and throw it away. I have an idea." He got up and opened the cabinet where he kept his pills. He brought an empty orange pill container and put the diamonds inside, then put it back on the shelf in the kitchen cabinet.

Returning to his seat, Martin looked at the brooch and said, "Brooch, I understand. Diamonds, I understand, but Polish or German, I don't. Let me call my friend Marek, he's Polish."

Martin got up to get the phone, and I went to wash my hands and my face and gather my thoughts. It was becoming more and more clear to me that Rosalind could have been Jewish. Her birth parents must have handed her to non-Jewish people to save her and given her valuables to be able to survive.

A shudder went through my body. Poor Rosalind.

After speaking to his friend, Martin had some information.

"I had a hunch it was Polish; 'Styczeń' means 'January' in Polish. Somebody had written 'January 1939' on the photos. Now we need to find out who the people in the photos are."

I looked at the back of the photo again and asked, "Did he tell you what 'moje dwie perły' means?"

"Yes. 'My two pearls.'"

I got excited. "Maybe Rosalind had a sister." I stared at the picture again. "She looks older. 1939. It was wartime—who knows?"

"But Polish. Was Rosalind Polish? I thought I heard her mumble in German . . . some kind of lullaby."

"You did?" I stared at him.

In an instant, he stood up. "They could have been Polish refugees." He said it a bit too loud, like he was getting excited. Looking at the pictures for another minute, he said, "I'm going to bed now, but I have an idea. Let me think about it some more. We'll talk in the morning."

I could hardly sleep that night; so many questions swirled in my head.

Next morning, Martin said to me, "We didn't place an obituary for Rosalind in the newspapers, so we'll do it now, together with the photos."

I stopped chewing my toast, swallowed, and stared at him. I understood where he was going with it. If the girl in the photo was still alive, she might see the obituary and recognize herself.

"In which newspapers?"

"The *Boston Globe*, of course, the *New York Times*, and maybe also in the *Los Angeles Times*," Martin said, getting excited.

"Why the *LA Times*?" I asked, surprised.

"Many people from the East Coast moved to the West Coast. Who knows? Someone might recognize the people in the photographs."

I brought a pen and paper, and we started composing the obituary.

We had a common goal: finding the information we needed to help our David.

A few days later, my suitcase stood by the front door. I had only brought a small one with a few clothes, thinking three weeks ago that I'd only stay a couple of days. I was aching to return home, missing David and my kids. I called a cab to take me to the airport, and as I put the receiver down, the phone rang. I looked at it in surprise, took a step back, and let Martin answer his house phone.

"Hello?" Martin said, and he pressed the speakerphone

button. He peeked at his watch. "The boys" were coming soon to play bridge. I was glad he'd be busy the whole day and not notice my absence.

"May I speak to Mr. Martin Roy?" A woman's voice was heard in the kitchen.

"This is he," Martin said, frowning and staring at me.

"Hello, Mr. Roy. My name is Elsie Wolfe. I have the identical photograph as the one you placed in the paper."

A cab honked once.

Part Three

Chapter Forty-Eight

New York City, December 2007

ELSIE

MY Raizele was gone. Dead. And so was my hope. The hope that I'd held for over six decades that I'd see her again one day. Now it was final. She'd had a heart attack, the obituary said. The regret made my bones ache, my stomach twist, and my skin shrink. The feeling of hopelessness made me want to scream. So I did. Raizele. Meine kleine Schwester.

What did I know about her? Only that she'd had a husband; I'd just spoken to him. I wondered if they had children. Grandchildren. That gave me hope. Heirs. Maybe she had heirs.

My chest tightened; I was on heart medication too.

Oh, how I missed her. How I wanted to hug her, hold her. Beg her to forgive me, to forgive the big sister who was supposed to look after her and hadn't. The last thing Mahme had asked of me. I'd carried that guilt for decades, unable to let go. It was a cruel thing to separate us, two little sisters, and forbid us to meet again.

But I knew it was my fault too.

I should have sought her out and found her and told her about my dishonorable behavior and my illegitimate baby—and come what may. She might have judged me and rejected my love and friendship, but it wouldn't have killed me. And maybe, just maybe, we could have had a relationship. Me being Jewish and her, Catholic. We were still sisters.

My feelings of regret had gnawed at me for sixty-six years, but I had done nothing. I was stupid, stupid, stupid. But I was scared. That was my excuse. I was afraid that my shameful secret would be exposed to my parents. And to my husband, Ronnie. I had wanted a clean slate when I met Ronnie, but my slate was never clean. Shame and guilt had followed me like my shadow.

***

"I can't watch her like that, Morris," Mommy said to Daddy on January 30, 1952, when I was so depressed that I couldn't stop crying. It was my baby's first birthday, and I couldn't tell anyone. I had sent Rebecca several letters that past year and asked her for information: Who had adopted my baby boy? How was he progressing? Had she stayed connected with the family? Was it a private adoption? But nothing. Not a word back from Rebecca.

"Why don't we take her to Colorado to a ski school?" Daddy had suggested. "Michael can run the bakery and the store for one week, and we can have a vacation too." He hadn't insisted I tell him why I was crying. Daddy just let me be and looked for a way to help, no questions asked. Mommy, though, tried.

"What's wrong, Elsie?" she asked. "Did something happen at work?"

I had taken a job at Jordan Marsh & Co. department store for the Christmas rush, but they liked me, so I stayed there in January, too, when people returned unwanted gifts and the store was still busy. So now I felt I could ask for one week vacation to go with my parents to Colorado. Not that I was keen to go; I didn't care either way. I knew what I wanted, but I also knew I couldn't get it. I wanted my baby. I even wanted Yigal. I felt tears dripping on my cheeks, and I didn't bother wiping them. I knew my parents were worried, but I also didn't know how to manage the emotions that were flooding me. I'd made it through the year with sheer force of will, but my baby's first birthday seemed to have unlocked all the grief I'd felt.

At first, I didn't care much about Steamboat Springs Ski School; I just went along. But in spite of myself, I had an enjoyable time.

"I'm pleased to meet you, Miss Zacks." A handsome guy

extended his hand. "My name is Ronnie Wolfe, and I'd be delighted to teach you how to ski. You're from Boston, I believe? So am I, but now I live in Manhattan. I'm a real estate agent, but the market is quiet in January and February, so I come here to teach. It's wonderful to meet you."

Ronnie was an excellent instructor, but more importantly, he seemed to take a genuine interest in me. He didn't mind my sad, quiet moments. With the wind whistling between us on the hills, neither of us had to talk. I felt calm in his presence, no pressure, and it nurtured me.

And so the courtship began. Ronnie would drive up to Boston once a week, usually on Wednesdays, and I'd take the train down to Manhattan some Saturdays. It wasn't easy, this long-distance relationship, but it kept me busy and not thinking of the child I'd given up. I fell in love with Ronnie because of his kindness, his persistence, and his ability to make me laugh. He had a wonderful voice and would sing with the radio in the car. He'd encourage me to join him, and first I was shy, but as time went by, I learned to enjoy it, and when we sang loud, it made me laugh.

The following February, my parents didn't have to join me in Denver. I went to Steamboat Springs with Ronnie.

On July 26, 1953, we got married. I had just turned twenty-two.

The morning before my wedding, Mommy knocked, then walked into my bedroom. She sat on my bed, handed me a small, black box, and said, "Elsie, love, I have something very special for you." The box wasn't wrapped, so I opened the cover. Something familiar glistened. "It's not from us. We'll give you our gift tomorrow. This is from your family, your very first family that sent you away to save your life. Do you remember the tea box you had in your backpack when you came to live with us?" She looked me in the eye, and I suddenly remembered. The tea box. Mahme had put a tea box with pictures and other things in my backpack. I had completely forgotten about it until that moment. Memories flooded my head and my heart raced.

"I kept it for you all of these years," Mommy continued. "You may remember it contained photos and important documents. When you go to your apartment with Ronnie, I'll make sure you have the tea box with all the documents there. But these were also in the box, and I think that these should be worn with pride. I can take you to my jeweler, and he can fit all six of them in a beautiful gold bracelet. A gift from your parents."

I looked at the six beautiful diamonds. Mahme. My Mahme had given them to me so I wouldn't be poor, I wouldn't go hungry. But wonderful people had taken care of me, and I hadn't needed to sell them to survive. How fortunate was I?

I fingered the cut diamonds and said, "Yes. Let's set them in a bracelet so I'll always remember them."

I was fortunate to have fifty-two years of blissful marriage to the kindest, most loving, and considerate man I'd known. The best thing was that when we married, I settled with him in New York City, which I loved. Ronnie was a young, established New York realtor and an extremely successful stockbroker. We were financially comfortable from the start and eventually became more than comfortable; we were able to donate generously to several charities. Ronnie left me very comfortable, my dearest husband, who'd died two years ago and left me lonely and quite desperate for family.

Ronnie and I had no children together. I couldn't conceive and thought of it as punishment for what I'd done … abandoning my baby. My body knew better. Ronnie had accepted my infertility without blame or fuss. He treated me like a precious jewel and said that I was the most important thing in his life and we would concentrate on each other. I was greatly, if secretly, relieved. I wasn't sure what I would have been like as a mother; I might have been always anxious and worried that something awful would happen.

But now, I saw the possibility of having a family. Rosalind had a husband. He sounded polite on the phone but somewhat distant. Maybe they had children. Maybe grandchildren. The thought of Rose having children filled me with complicated emotions. Jealousy, of course, and regret, but also hope; I might find a family, my family.

I was a seventy-six-year-old widow, and alone.

Chapter Forty-Nine

Boston, January 2008

ELSIE

THREE weeks later, I took the train to Boston. It took four hours to get from Penn Station to Beacon Hill. I was to meet Raizele's husband and youngest son, who was a lawyer. She had three sons, I was told when I called again to arrange the meeting.

I was nervous yet excited to meet them.

He walked towards me. Raizele's son. Confirmed. He could have easily been my child. My son. His dark auburn hair, oval face, and a small chin; a replica of my face. An elderly gentleman accompanied him, slightly taller. Must have been Martin. They were both wearing a suit and a tie and an overcoat.

"Mrs. Wolfe?" her son said.

We shook hands. I wanted to hug them. I needed to, but I didn't think they'd appreciate it. The feeling just wasn't there, which disappointed me.

Andrew drove us. I was offered the front passenger seat. We rode in awkward silence.

The house was spacious and painted white inside, and the aroma of coffee filled the entrance hall. Fresh pastries sat invitingly on the coffee table in the large living room, and a fire crackled softly. I was glad my sister had lived well.

"Please make yourself at home," Martin said. "The train ride was long, wasn't it? Do you prefer it to flying? My Rosalind didn't like flying either. She was claustrophobic, you know." He paused. "She avoided trains too."

I nodded. I wasn't surprised. I hated trains and ships, but it didn't keep me from using them. Or planes. I'd traveled excessively with Ronnie, but I couldn't help remembering my horrible first train ride. It wasn't easy to recover from that, and maybe Raizele never had.

After we shared refreshments, Andrew said, "Do you mind telling us about yourself?"

I was ready. "My parents got married December 2, 1929, in Warsaw—I have a copy of their marriage certificate." It had been rolled up and hidden in my tea box, but I hadn't produced it yet. "They immigrated to Austria on December 23 of that year, accompanied by my mother's parents, Rochel and Avrum

Lewkowicz." I looked Andrew in the eyes. "Avrum was a banker in Warsaw, my mother was a bookkeeper, and my father, a dentist. I was born in Vienna on July 1, 1931, and my sister, Rose, was born on July 3, 1933." I felt proud to share that information; I hadn't talked about my family in so many years.

Martin and Andrew exchanged looks. Martin nodded to me as if confirming my information.

I told them about my father's arrest after Kristallnacht, and my sister and I being sent via Kindertransport to England. I reported that information as if talking about somebody else; I didn't want to break down in front of them; we'd just met. But it was difficult, trying to be detached from my own life story.

Martin and Andrew sat quietly and listened. I talked about both adoptions and how Rose and I were separated.

"You said you had your parents' marriage certificate; do you have any other documents?" Andrew seemed to be wanting concrete evidence, and it was annoying. We looked so much alike.

"I do," I said, not specifying which ones.

I felt like I was in an interrogation room, although there was no single chair at a bare table with a light hovering above it. Having them both on the couch, across the coffee table from me, put me in an awkward position. I felt very alone. And uncomfortable. That wasn't the family for which I was hoping. And not the people I wanted to leave my estate to. I was ready to leave, but an idea popped into my head.

"The photo that you placed in the *New York Times*. Where did you find it?" I asked.

Martin seemed puzzled. "I found it in an old tea box," he said. "An old, rusted can, together with a brooch."

"A brooch?" My heartbeat accelerated. "May I see the photographs and the brooch?"

Martin got up, and I could hear him open a drawer in the adjacent room, most probably the kitchen.

He returned and put two photos on the coffee table. The same as the ones he'd put in the paper.

"Was there anything else in that tea box?" I asked. "You mentioned a brooch."

Martin turned pale—which was surprising—took a deep breath as he straightened in his seat, then got up and went to the kitchen again. They wanted proof from me; let them produce theirs.

Andrew excused himself and followed his father. Whispers were heard, but I couldn't make them out. Not with my old ears.

Martin returned with an old, rusted tea box just like mine. My heart was racing; seeing in his hands something my mother had held, my eyes filled with tears. This box was dented, and the paint had peeled and faded at the cover's edges. Martin opened it and took out a gold Victorian shell cameo brooch surrounded by pearls. The welded pin had been broken off.

I gasped. Mahme . . . moje dwie perły . . . my two pearls . . .

Carefully, I took it from Martin's hand, my hand shaking, and said, "Mahme . . . This belonged to Mahme . . ." Tears blurred my vision. "She always wore it on her coat. On the left lapel of her winter coat. I'd noticed it wasn't there when she had said goodbye . . . now I know why . . ." I placed my right hand on my heart and whispered, "My two pearls. She would call us her pearls..." I held the brooch gently in my cupped palm as if it were a fledgling. I looked up at Martin. "May I keep it?"

Martin hesitated. He glanced at Andrew. Andrew put his hand out, wanting me to return the brooch, and said, "I think we better keep it with the photos at the moment."

I slowly put my mother's brooch in his large, white palm, feeling like I was saying goodbye to Mahme again. I felt jealous. Why had Mahme put the brooch in Raizele's tea box and not in mine? But on the other hand, she'd put both our birth certificates in mine, and her marriage certificate. What else had she put there? Diamonds, or was I supposed to share my diamonds with my sister? I could just imagine Mahme's anxiety and shaking hands when she placed all those valuables in our tea boxes. Oh, Mahme, Mahme.

Martin stood up again. "You must meet my other children," he said decisively. "I have two sons in California: one in Los Angeles and one in San Diego. The one in San Diego is married and has two children. I need to call them. And you must meet Teresa, Andrew's wife, and his two daughters." He spoke fast, then turned to Andrew. "Can you please call Teresa and see if she's free to come now?" He was suddenly very excited, which puzzled me.

"Wait, Dad." Andrew stood up too. "May I have a word with you, please?" He tilted his head towards the kitchen.

Something wasn't kosher; they were whispering again.

I looked at my watch. I still had a four-hour train ride home. I'd been in my sister's house for over two hours and felt disappointed. Deflated. I hadn't expected her to walk in suddenly; I also hadn't expected those two men to hug me and declare me immediately part of their family, but I'd expected something . . . some kind of familiarity. After all, they had known my little sister. But she hadn't been a little girl when they knew her. She had been an adult, and I had never known her as an adult. All of that was very confusing. I wanted to leave. I wasn't feeling well.

But Andrew was my nephew, my blood. And I had two more. Plus grandnephews and grandnieces. That thrilled me; a family of my own. Whatever they were discussing now in private, they couldn't take that away from me.

When they returned, I stood up and made my way towards the front door. "I need to get back to the train station; it was very nice meeting you both." Suddenly I felt very tired. "Do you mind calling me a cab?"

"No, no, we'll take you back," Martin said.

And back we went, quiet on the way to the train station until Andrew asked, "You said you had documents; would you send us copies?"

I glanced at his profile. He sounded like he had no intention in seeing me again, so I said, "I will do no such thing. But I will show them to you if you come to New York." I knew I had to keep in touch with them; they were the only family I had.

There was silence in the car.

"You may be interested in my sister's birth certificate," I threw in as bait.

"You have Rosalind's birth certificate?" Martin asked from the back seat, sounding anxious.

"Rose Stein," I said. "That was the name our parents gave her." I turned around to look at him.

Martin lowered his eyes and moved back in his seat. He physically moved away from me, which made me feel rejected. They didn't believe me. They must have thought I was an impostor. But why? Would they believe me if I told them about the money I was thinking of giving them?

After Ronnie died, I donated a lump sum to a particular charity in Israel, an institution that housed and supported unmarried mothers. The rest would go to Raizele's offspring, I decided. After all, they were my only heirs. But I didn't want to buy their love and acceptance.

Then it dawned on me.

They didn't believe me.

Did they need me in their lives as much as I needed them, or was it just my wish, my illusion?

Chapter Fifty

New York City, January 2008

MARTIN

ROSE Stein. A Jewish name. But no proof that it was really Rosalind. I was utterly confused. Elsie Wolfe seemed authentic enough to me, but not to Andrew. As an attorney, he had a sense for people before he saw any evidence. I wasn't sure it was a good thing. Hence my confusion.

I had to think clearly.

Elsie had produced photographs of herself with her mother and sister, my Rosalind, identical to the ones I'd found in the tea box. For me, that was enough. She also knew Rosalind's date of birth and claimed she had her birth certificate.

Then, she had her parents' marriage certificate. Granted, she hadn't brought any documents with her, but if we wanted, she'd produce it all, and she invited us to come to New York. What interest did she have in pretending and lying, in being an impostor?

That was where Andrew's opinion differed from mine—the diamonds. He thought she was after the six diamonds. How would she have known of their existence? Who had placed the diamonds in the tea box?

She said that her family were Polish immigrants in Austria. Her grandfather had been a banker in Warsaw. They could have been wealthy then, but she might need money now.

Andrew wanted proof. So did I.

Andrew, Teresa, and I took the train to Penn Station. We were to meet Elsie in the lobby of the Hilton Garden Inn on West Thirty-Fifth Street. I wondered why she hadn't invited us to her home like we had. I wondered again if she was financially needy.

Entering the hotel, I immediately spotted her next to a tall man in a suit and tie.

"I'm glad you could make it," Elsie said, and shook hands with us. "Please meet Charles Northton, my late husband's attorney and my best friend."

Andrew introduced Teresa. I glanced at him. Elsie had brought a lawyer. Interesting. But Andrew was seasoned himself; he didn't flinch.

Mr. Northton directed us into a small conference room. The whole meeting took a very businesslike turn, something I hadn't expected.

"You look so familiar," Teresa said to Elsie as we sat down. "Have I seen you before?"

Elsie looked surprised.

"She reminds you of Susan, dear," Andrew said quietly to his wife as he sat down next to her.

"Who's Susan?" Elsie asked.

"My younger daughter..." Teresa seemed distressed. "The same hazel eyes, yes." Teresa's voice had a distinct quiver now. "The rounded jaw... I noticed it the minute I first saw you..."

Elsie just sat back and stared at her. Yes, I also saw the resemblance. To Andrew too.

"Charlie is here as a friend," Elsie said. "I brought originals and copies of the birth certificates, but I also need to share with you my surprise."

I noticed Andrew tensing his shoulders.

"My mother gave Rose and me a knapsack each, and among some clothes and food, she placed in each a tin tea box. In mine she placed her marriage certificate to my father and Rose's and my birth certificates. She also put the photographs I've shown you." She took a pause, and I wondered if that was all she'd been given. "I need to know what was in Rose's tea box, besides the photos and the brooch."

I was taken aback. Did she know what was in Rosalind's box? Did she know of the diamonds? Andrew and I had been arguing about whether or not she knew. I tended to believe that she didn't, so why was she asking us now? This was very confusing.

"You were given the most important documents," Andrew said. "But we need to verify that Rose Stein was really

Rosalind Roy."

"All I have is what my mother placed in my knapsack before sending us on Kindertransport," Elsie said, looking at Andrew.

"What is Kindertransport?" Teresa asked.

I was astounded. This wasn't the time or place. Teresa was a good wife and mother but not worldly or well-read, to say the least. I noticed Mr. Northton raising his eyebrows.

"It was a children transport," Elsie said kindly. "Ten thousand Jewish children were sent away on trains by their parents from Europe to England—"

"Alone?" Teresa said.

Elsie nodded.

"Who has ever heard of parents sending their children away alone?" Teresa asked.

"Many," I replied in place of Elsie, and I looked Teresa in the eye, which she quickly averted. "From December 1938 until August 1939, twelve thousand children were rescued from Poland, Germany, Austria, and Czechoslovakia. Ten thousand were Jewish children—"

"You want to tell me that two thousand Christian children were sent away too?" Teresa asked, surprised. "It's ridiculous. What a story."

"My sister and I were among those Jewish children—" Elsie tried to add.

"How old were you?"

"I was seven years—"

"And your sister?"

"Raizele was five."

"Raizele," I whispered.

"That's insane. How could you remember?" Teresa's tone became more aggressive, and Andrew put his hand over hers, which she shook off. "How could parents do such an awful thing?"

"To save us," Elsie said angrily, her cheeks flushed.

I wasn't sure if Teresa was mad at not knowing those historical facts or with the idea that children were sent away by their parents; her motherly instincts were hurt. But she sounded like a Holocaust denier, and I got mad, but before I got up and faced her, I heard Elsie saying, "Our mother tried to save our lives. And she succeeded. We survived, but she did not." Elsie swiftly got up and her chair fell back. "I need the restroom," she muttered, and left the room.

As I bent down to pick up her chair, I met Mr. Northton's eyes.

"This is unacceptable, that exchange," he said to me, then turned to Teresa. "Are you a mother?" And without waiting for a reply, he added, "Can you just imagine the excruciating pain that must have infused every cell of such a mother's body when she let go of her children? Can you imagine the trauma the children suffered the rest of their lives? They thought that after the war they'd all get together again, the children would return home and the parents would be waiting. But those brave parents went up the chimneys, murdered by gas and burned by the Nazis, and the children never saw them again. Only one thousand of the ten thousand Jewish children met their parents again after the war." He was almost shouting in anger, and spittle was sprayed out of his mouth.

Teresa just stood there, her head bent.

Controlling his temper, Mr. Northton asked her quietly, almost in a whisper, "Haven't you learned anything about the Holocaust at school?"

Teresa turned to Andrew, "I'm going to the bathroom."

As she walked out, Elsie returned. The two women stopped abruptly, looked down, and parted quickly.

I took my seat again, as did Mr. Northton.

Elsie looked at us puzzled but said nothing. I was glad she hadn't been here when Mr. Northton reprimanded Teresa. It was a shameful scene. I loved Teresa, but I was also ashamed at the same time. It was awful to have a member of my family not only be so ignorant but also act so rudely.

"Did you and your sister look alike?" Andrew, calm and collected, asked Elsie as she took her seat. I felt like rolling my eyes.

"Not at all," she replied. "As you can see by the pictures."

I couldn't understand Andrew's and Teresa's attitude. Earlier Andrew acknowledged the family resemblance, so why was he asking this now? Was he ashamed of his wife's behavior, as he should be? So I said to Elsie, "You know, Andrew's eldest daughter, Veronica, looks a bit like Rosalind did in her youth. The same big blue eyes and long blond curls. But the younger one, Susan, has your coloring."

Elsie smiled.

Teresa returned and, still standing, turned to Elsie and said, "I'm sorry if anything I said earlier upset anyone." She glanced quickly at Mr. Northton. "It was all so shocking." Then she looked back at Elsie. "My daughter Veronica looks very much like Rosalind." She swallowed hard, then added, "So if Rosalind was Jewish . . ." She stared at her husband, who looked utterly disturbed by the thought, then back at Elsie. "Does that make my daughter Jewish too?" She sounded like she was going to cry. I felt sorry for the woman; she was so uneducated.

Elsie took her time to reply. I had the feeling she enjoyed Teresa's hysteria, even if it came from ignorance.

"Not necessarily," Elsie replied. "By Jewish law, the mother, not the father, needs to be Jewish for the children to be Jewish too." She took a deep breath and added, "So Andrew—"

But Teresa didn't hear and asked, "Like Ava-May's children?" She sounded triumphant, as if off the hook. I could have slapped her; I was so ashamed at her behavior. Andrew seemed to have given up. I had to have a serious talk with him later.

"Who's Ava-May?" both Elsie and Mr. Northton asked.

"David's, my eldest son's wife—" I tried to explain before I was interrupted by Teresa.

"Rosalind wasn't happy about David marrying a Jew, you know," she huffed, "to say the least. She wouldn't even come to the wedding."

We were all dumbfounded by this open display of hostility, especially after her attempt at an apology. I looked at Elsie, who turned white. She must have realized that, just like Teresa, Rosalind had hated Jews. She looked at me for confirmation, but I couldn't bring myself to nod. Instead, I said, "Rosalind had a very difficult time dealing with her emotions. It was complicated."

"This sickens me to the core," Elsie said. "That my own sister could think like that." She turned to face Teresa. "Look what Hitler had done; that's how he'd won, you know. He had managed to turn my sister against her own religion, her own people, her heritage, and her own identity." She had tears in her eyes when she said, "Our grandmother used to say, 'Shver tsu zayn a Yid,' it's hard to be a Jew. And she was right."

My heart went out to her. My head pounded as my emotions swirled. Suddenly I had a flash of insight; I believed the things she was telling us. She had not reached out to us for the wrong reasons, and she surely hadn't expected a scene like we'd just had with Teresa.

Maybe Rosalind's only way of escaping her painful past—the agonizing memory of being sent away, of feeling rejected by her own mother—was by denying her own Jewishness. She was scared to be Jewish. It was easier to be Christian, Catholic, and disassociated from Jews. That way she'd never be rejected again, never be put on a train again, never be sent away. I suddenly missed my Rosalind desperately. To have loved her for all those years and yet never understood what she had been through felt agonizing. If I could only have her for five more minutes to say that I loved her, that I understood.

I looked at Elsie and noticed she was exchanging looks with Mr. Northton. He nodded, and they both stood up. Mr. Northton said, "It was enlightening meeting you all. Thank you for coming to New York." He looked at his watch. "I have a meeting in my office and must drop Mrs. Wolfe at her place first. Maybe we'll meet again."

"Wait," Andrew said, and stood up too. "We wanted to

get the birth certificate of..."

"Rose Stein?" Elsie asked. I thought I heard a tone of sarcasm in her voice. Well, good for her. We had been treating her horribly.

We were all standing in silence, and as I wanted to answer in the affirmative, Elsie added, "It would be nice to meet your other two sons, Mr. Roy. Maybe you can all come again next month. There's a long weekend, Presidents' Day, I think."

I looked at her. I felt that Teresa's animosity had changed her, but I wasn't sure how; I didn't really know the woman. I was torn. Why had she contacted us? She had responded to my announcement in the paper, but I didn't know what she wanted. We needed proof that Rosalind was Jewish for David's sake. I didn't know what Elsie really wanted.

Maybe Andrew was right, and she was after the diamonds after all. Didn't she say, "I need to know what was in Rose's tea box, besides the photos and the brooch." How did she know?

Andrew and Teresa were acting as if they would do anything to prevent Elsie from proving that she was Rosalind's sister.

But David needed the exact opposite. I wasn't sure whose side I was on.

Chapter Fifty-One

New York City, 2008

AVA-MAY

MARTIN called. He told us that he'd met Elsie Wolfe and that he would like us all to come to New York to meet her and "to welcome her to our family." Those had been his exact words, David told me. Martin almost begged us to come, but "please don't discuss it with Andrew or Lawrence before we meet." David, surprised, asked his father, "Why?" But Martin only said, "I'll tell you the details when you and Ava-May arrive." He offered us frequent fliers' miles on American Airlines, and David and I decided to turn it into a mini vacation and fly out on Thursday, St. Valentine's Day. We planned to return

Sunday night, as Monday was Presidents' Day, and we could relax. It was going to be a nice, long weekend.

We were grateful for the miles. We still had to pay for a hotel for three nights. What a luxury. We hadn't had a vacation for ages, and a visit to New York City was always exciting. We needed some excitement and good news in our lives. David's medication was outrageously expensive, and the doctors weren't even sure it was exactly what he needed, but it was our first priority. We'd had to cut down on all luxuries, like the kids' private school and annual vacations, and some necessities, like making do with only one car, and we were considering putting our house on the market. We could barely afford the mortgage, the taxes, water, and electricity of such a big house, as well as the maintenance of the large yard and the pool. We didn't want to bother Martin with our financial concerns, but this trip was an exception. We were going to meet Rosalind's Jewish sister. I wouldn't have missed that for the world, whatever the cost.

My parents drove down from LA to stay with the kids, and I could leave with a content heart.

We settled into Pod 51 in Manhattan—a cheap hotel room wasn't easily found—and waited to hear from Martin. He had taken the train from Boston and was joining us for Valentine Day's dinner. First, he had refused the dinner, saying it was for lovers, but I had persuaded him that I was going to spend the entire day flying with my lover—David had laughed at that—and we'd both be honored if he'd join us for dinner. Martin had accepted on the condition that he was to make the reservations and we would be his guests.

I hadn't argued.

Martin looked good when we met in the restaurant. It'd been two months since I left his house, and a new glitter shone in his eyes. We ordered, and David went straight to the point. "What's with the secrecy, Dad? When are Andy and Larry coming? You said the whole family was coming but not to discuss it beforehand. What's going on?"

Martin took a deep breath. "I need your help. Both of you. I have no idea what Elsie Wolfe's financial situation is. She may be in dire need. Or not at all." He leaned forward. "Andrew and Teresa think that she's after the diamonds."

"What diamonds?" David asked. I followed their exchange curiously, remembering the diamonds in the pill box in the kitchen.

"There were six diamonds in your mother's tea box," Martin said. "I haven't had a chance to have them appraised yet, and they might be valuable. But Andrew and Teresa are adamant that Elsie knows about them and is after them."

"How could she know? And how much could they be worth?"

"I have no idea, if real, maybe a hundred thousand? More? Less? Their grandfather was a banker in Warsaw, I believe, and he must have earned handsomely. They could have sold what wasn't movable and bought diamonds for easy transfer during the war. I assume that they could have had more but maybe had kept the rest for themselves and placed those six for both their daughters."

Or maybe Elsie had another six in her own tea box, I thought.

The food arrived.

We ate in silence; everybody was thinking.

"When we met, Elsie hadn't asked about any diamonds and neither did we mention them," Martin said. "But she said, 'I need to know what was in Rose's tea box, besides the photos and the brooch.'" Martin looked from me to David. "She claimed she had important documents in her own tea box: her parents' marriage certificate and both her and your mother's birth certificates."

"Mother's birth certificate? In a tea box?" David almost yelled it out, caught himself, and lowered his voice. "My doctors need it ASAP."

"Yes, but it's under the name of Rose Stein. How do we know that Rose Stein was really Rosalind?"

Silence again.

"DNA test," I said quietly.

Both men stopped eating and stared at me. Then at each other. "Yes," they said simultaneously.

"The truth is," Martin said, "that I really tend to believe Elsie. I truly believe she was Rosalind's sister, and Mother was Rose Stein. You'll see her; it's uncanny how much she looks like Susan, just as much as Veronica resembles Rosalind. But if Andrew doesn't rely on his eyes and the documents, we're going to get from her on Sunday, he could take a DNA test if he wanted."

Maybe he just didn't want to face the fact that he was Jewish himself.

"Forget Andrew," David said excitedly again. "*I* want to have a DNA test and compare it with hers. Oh, boy. I'll solve the mystery once and for all."

Martin and I shared a dessert. David was too worked up to have another morsel.

Chapter Fifty-Two

New York City, 2008

DAVID

MOTHER could have been Rose Stein. Then Rose James. Then Rosalind Cox before she married my father and became Rosalind Roy. What a way to grow up when your identity kept changing. Owning our name gave us an identity, security; we knew who we were. Mother must have had a torturous first eight years. Thank goodness for Granny and Grandpa for giving her stability. I wondered how much she actually remembered. She must have pushed those memories deep into her subconscious, but as we knew, the subconscious played tricks on us and memories popped up unexpectedly, or when triggered. And Mother had many triggers. Poor soul.

But I might have been ahead of myself, as usual.

It was Friday morning, and California was still asleep when I lay in bed in New York thinking about my mother and waiting for Dr. Kent's office to open. Ava-May and Dad went to MoMA, and I got up to sit and read the *New York Times*. I kept looking at my watch. I wanted to meet Elsie. What would it mean to me if she were Mother's sister? That would mean that I was born Jewish. Was my whole life a lie? Was my upbringing a façade? Mother might have been a baby who was given away to non-Jewish people to save her life. I wondered how Ann, Granny's sister, got hold of her and what she went through for the first eight years of her life. And I also wanted to know where her sister, Elsie, was all that time. Her older sister, I presumed. And why were they separated? I was exhausted from thinking.

It was noon.

I called Dr. Kent in San Diego. I told her that I might have found a relative of my mother's—I couldn't say "sister" yet, some doubt stopped me—and that I wanted to do a DNA test. She got very excited and said that I needed that relative to take a test too. I knew that.

"How long until we'll get results?" I asked.

"About two to three weeks."

Damn. I could do it through her office, but not before Wednesday next week. We made the appointment.

I had two days before meeting Elsie Wolfe for brunch. Dad said that Larry was flying in from Los Angeles tomorrow night, Saturday, and Andy and Teresa would come on Sunday morning by train. Elsie wanted to meet us all around noon in her apartment. She said she'd text Dad her address.

I looked at my plane tickets. Our flight back home was on Sunday at 5:00 p.m.; we had to leave for the airport at 3:00 p.m. Well, that would give us only three hours to get an impression. And I also had to ask her to take a DNA test. Too much pressure.

I took a nap, and when Dad and Ava-May returned, I asked him if it was possible to meet Elsie earlier than Sunday. "Like tomorrow. Without Larry and Andy. Just the three of us," I said. "I have so many questions."

Dad said he'd call right away and ask her.

Dad burst out laughing when he put the phone down.

Elsie had invited the three of us for dinner at her apartment in an hour and given him the address. "Unbelievable. Fifth Avenue," he said, laughing, and grabbed his head. "Across from Central Park."

I didn't get the joke, but in the taxi—we had showered and dressed quickly—Dad told us that he couldn't wait to see Andrew's face when he realized that Elsie wasn't after our diamonds. However, Elsie seemed as anxious to meet us as I was to meet her. I wondered why.

The doorman showed us to the elevator, and the attendant inside it took us to her floor.

A woman who must have been Elsie opened the door. I could definitely see a much older version of Susan and my

Aaron. I was fascinated.

Dad seemed incredibly pleased to see her. He hugged her lightly, kissed both her cheeks, and introduced us. I hugged her too.

"I'm delighted to meet you both. Please come in," Elsie said to Ava-May and me, and motioned us into the dining room. "Sit down, please. Sylvia is helping me, and we can eat right away. I'm so glad you could come at a moment's notice."

"You look well," Dad said, and sat down at the glossy mahogany dining table when a young woman walked in.

"Please meet Sylvia, everybody." Elsie smiled warmly. "She's my London friend Dorothy Sommers's granddaughter. Dorothy Sommers, now Lampert, was my one and only friend when I came as a seven-year-old child from Vienna to London and didn't speak a word of English." Elsie chuckled. "Sylvia goes to NYU and occasionally helps me."

Sylvia smiled and nodded. "Pleasure to meet you all." Her British accent was charming and reminded me of my mother's. I glanced at Dad and wondered if it had stirred anything in him too.

"How did you whip up dinner in only one hour?" my wife asked. I looked at her. Her heart must have been aching from looking at this luxurious apartment and thinking of our own beautiful home we were about to leave. I ached from disappointing her and felt guilty for not being able to give my family all that I wanted to provide them with.

"Well," Elsie said. "I do keep a lot of food in the house. My late husband and I grew up in the war era, so we always overstuffed the refrigerator and the pantry. Just in case." She sounded apologetic as she got up and joined Sylvia on her way to the kitchen. Ava-May wanted to get up, too, but Elsie waved her down.

We talked about food and the foreseeable coming snow, and when we finished eating, Elsie asked us to come to the living room.

We sat at a coffee table, and Sylvia brought a pot of tea and some scones for dessert, excused herself and went to the kitchen. Elsie picked up a large, puffed scone and broke it easily in half, put half back, smeared a spoonful of jam on it and topped it with some thick cream, then laid it on a plate. Sipping her tea, she said, "The best cream I've ever eaten was on the farm during the war."

"The farm?" I asked.

Elsie looked at me with a warm smile. "It's a long story; I'll tell you some day. But please tell me about yourselves. I want to know everything about my sister's children."

"I have some questions, if you don't mind," I said.

"Sure, go ahead."

"When was the last time you saw your sister?"

Elsie's facial expression changed. She took a sip of tea, put her cup down slowly, and stared at the wall ahead as if watching something moving by. Then she looked at me and said, "I was ten when we arrived in America, and Rose was eight. She was baptized and renamed Rosalind and adopted by the Cox family. She was raised Catholic. Esther and Morris Zacks, a Jewish couple, adopted me. After the adoptions went through, we were forbidden to meet in order for us to settle in our new lives and not be confused by our past."

I was shocked. That was so sad. I glanced over at Ava-May. I could just imagine her thoughts. Very young children who were separated from their families might have forgotten their parents. Children sometimes did that for survival. Just to be able to go on.

"Although young children adapt fast for survival's sake, it doesn't mean that they forget," I said. Thinking of Mother, I added, "But they can build resentment and mistrust and sometimes become passive aggressive."

And before I presented my next question to Elsie, my wife asked, "Did you try to reconnect when you were both adults?"

Elsie looked thoughtful, hesitated, then said, "I have no idea if she remembered me and tried to find me. But on my end . . ." She looked at me, at Ava-May and then at Dad, and said in a quivering voice, "I am going to confess to something I have not told a soul in . . . fifty-seven years." Her facial expression changed to fear.

I was surprised. One could hear a pin drop in the room. It seemed like we were all holding our breath.

"I got pregnant when I was in Israel and had an illegitimate son whom I gave up for adoption in London. My cousin was my midwife then. I've written to her since for many years afterwards. Sending letters and birthday cards but hearing nothing back. I wanted to know if she kept in touch with the adoptive parents—she'd promised she'd arrange a private adoption—but she never replied. After thirty years my letters started coming back. She may have moved and hadn't left a forwarding address." Elsie took a deep breath and sat back as if relieved.

For a moment I looked at her, wondering what to say, what anyone could say. We were in a room with a woman who was a stranger and family both, hearing a confession nobody was prepared for, but then Ava-May asked, "Are you okay?" as she leaned forward and placed her hand on Elsie's.

Elsie smiled sadly, her eyes glistening. "I feel relieved." She looked again at each of us. "I was so afraid to find my sister and tell her what I'd done, that she'd judge me and reject me. I know now that this was an idiotic thing to do. But I was nineteen, lonely and rejected by the man who got me pregnant, and I couldn't bear another rejection if my sister would have judged me as a sinner. I didn't seek her out. I'm sorry. I lost them both, my sister and my son."

We all sat silently, absorbing the painful confession, but it wasn't all.

"Neither my adoptive parents nor Ronnie, my husband of fifty-two years, knew of the baby. No one. Only my cousin Rebecca, who was my midwife, and her mother, because I lived with them in London." She looked at her hands. "It might be difficult for you to accept, or even understand, how heavy and damaging keeping a secret is if you haven't experienced it yourself." Elsie looked at me as if asking for forgiveness. My heart ached for her. "I was full of shame and grief. Shame for having sex with a man I barely knew, and grief for losing my baby. I couldn't discuss it with my little sister. By the time she was eighteen and I could seek her out, I was twenty-two and married Ronnie. I vowed not to tell him about the baby, scared he might leave me or make me look for my child. How was I to face my parents then, with this huge secret that I'd kept from them?" Elsie lifted her chin. "So I soldiered on, doing my best to be an excellent wife and the good daughter my parents thought I was."

Now I had even more questions. But this wasn't the right time to ask. The woman shrank in front of my eyes. She wasn't as tall as my mother had been—they looked nothing alike—but they both looked like the girls in the photos from the tea box. I had no doubt that her story was genuine, but I had my own selfish reason to ask, "Could we please see my mother's birth certificate?" And as I said it, I realized that I had admitted my belief in her. So I added, "And I also have another big request."

Elsie straightened up and looked at me.

"I have Gaucher disease. It's a genetic disorder that needs to be treated delicately. I had no idea that I had Jewish origins. But now that I do, I need to make one hundred percent sure, for my medical team. I'm going to have a DNA test and was wondering if you were willing to have one, too, to see if we match. It's a simple blood drawing and saliva collection. Would you do it for me?"

Elsie took my hand in hers and said with a big smile, "Of course, David. I'm your aunt, and aunts adore their nephews." We all laughed.

Yes, we were family. I felt it in my being. But I was wondering how my brothers would feel, as they had no dire need to find their origins.

Chapter Fifty-Three

New York City, 2008

ELSIE

DNA test. Well, would it help me to find my son? There was motivation. I had no idea where he was. Maybe he didn't even live in London. He might not even want to find me. Then a horrible thought crossed my mind: He might not even know that he'd been adopted. Not all parents told their children. But he wasn't a child anymore.

Enough.

I had to stop that train of thought or I'd go crazy. I had to concentrate on Rose's family. They existed, and they were here. It was my only chance of having a family. It felt good telling them about my son. For some reason I didn't feel judged; I even felt compassion. He was delightful, that David. And his wife was sweet too. I had a feeling that even his father was warming up to me, although he'd barely uttered a word all evening. His other son, Andrew, and that cow of a wife he had, was a different story.

And there was one more son to conquer.

I was glad they came for dinner last night. It gave me a chance to meet David and his Jewish wife. Good for them, to overcome prejudice. His mother's prejudice.

But I had to put it all behind me. None of that could help now. I had to prepare for Sunday.

Good old Charlie Northton stayed in town this weekend. He'd promised to be available.

At noon on Sunday my doorman called. My guests were making their way up.

I was ready.

I opened the door and was so glad to see a tall man who reminded me of someone.

Martin introduced the young man to me. "This is my son Lawrence."

"Nice to meet you, ma'am," Lawrence said, extending his right hand, his dark blue eyes sparkling.

"Oh, my. You're . . . you're a grown-up Rose . . . my sister

... oh ... I haven't seen her grown up ... but I can just imagine ... oh, I'm so sorry, I'm being rude." I couldn't contain my excitement. It was amazing. Lawrence had Rose's features and her dark blue eyes, just like David's. My chest contracted, thinking of how I'd missed Raizele's adult years. But there was no time to think or reminisce.

Ava-May, David, and Charlie followed Lawrence and Martin into the apartment.

I didn't see Andrew and Teresa. Nobody apologized on their behalf or explained their absence.

I was glad; they might have been unhappy from what was to come.

I invited them to the dining room. When we were all seated, Charlie, still standing, opened his briefcase and retrieved some folders. He produced five blue plastic folders and positioned them in front of me. I extended one each to Martin, David, and Lawrence, keeping two to myself.

"Welcome, everybody," Charlie said, gazing around the table. "Mrs. Elsie Wolfe, the testatrix, has requested that everyone be present when I read on her behalf what we have drafted together." He glanced at me, and I nodded, so he continued, "She would like to gift her late sister's husband and children, after her death, on certain conditions."

My heart sped up; it felt like it was going a hundred miles per hour. My stomach contracted, and I prayed that I wouldn't have to leave the table running. With years of experience, I had learned to control myself. This was the moment. The moment I was waiting for since I saw Martin's announcement in the paper.

I had met them. I had met my sister's family and liked them. Most of them. I had a feeling that they liked me, too, and would accept me into their family. The DNA testing was for them, not for me. I knew who I was, but I'd oblige. For David's sake. I didn't intend to buy these people's love, but now that I'd found Raizele's family, I wanted to be generous, to gift them what I would have gifted her. I had enough to share. I wanted to try and make a tiny amend to quiet my burning guilt.

Money was a funny thing; it could heal at times, soothe injuries, but now it was the only way I could make up to my sister for my dreadful neglect.

Each folder contained a copy of Rose Stein's birth certificate and our parents' marriage certificate.

"Martin Roy," Charlie said, turning to face Martin, "you're getting a symbolic gift now, an expression of appreciation for opening your heart and your home, and for letting Elsie into your life—"

"Five hundred thousand dollars is a symbolic gift?" Lawrence was the first to open his folder and start reading the first document.

"Well," Charlie said, smiling, "and that is after tax." He nodded firmly and added, "Elsie will explain." He sat down.

"Dear family," I started. "I feel extremely fortunate that not all the money my dear late husband, Ronnie, and I have accumulated will be going to hospitals and refugee camps. We also support the Quakers Organization in England." I looked around the table at the four new members of my family, and my heart warmed. "As the beneficiary of the estate, I'm beyond excited to share some of our resources with my flesh and blood, my beloved sister's children, whose existence had been unknown to me until recently." I felt a lump in my throat and had to cough.

"Martin"—I turned slightly and placed my hand on the table, my fingers pointing in his direction—"you're not a blood relative of mine, but you are the father of my late sister's children. My gift to you will be immediate." I smiled at him and watched his eyebrows raise. I liked him and hoped he'd like me in time.

I turned to David and Lawrence, who sat quietly, staring at me intently. "As my nephews, my dear little sister Raizele's children, I will bequeath you each one million dollars." I paused and looked at their astonished expressions before adding, "Under several conditions." Looking at Charlie, I leaned back.

He rose again and, without looking at any papers, said, "Elsie has to die a natural death before any of you may receive the inheritance from her estate." His face stayed solemn, and he coughed nervously. "In case she dies in an accident by motor vehicle, train, plane, ferry or ship, a full postmortem investigation would have to be conducted first, and five years would pass from the conclusion date to the release of the funds."

"Formalities," I interjected. I looked at their faces and noticed David paling.

Charles took a breath and relaxed somewhat. "However, a loan against the inheritance, or part thereof, may be obtained from her bank at a percentage decided upon at the time of application." Charles sat down.

I noticed David and Ava-May exchange looks. David

blushed and said, "Your generosity is overwhelming. I don't know how to thank you."

Lawrence muttered, "One million dollars. In five years."

I got up and walked out of the room, leaving them in shock.

I opened the refrigerator and got the bottle of champagne out. I opened the drawer and retrieved the bottle opener. I wasn't sure if anyone had noticed the champagne flutes on the sideboard. When I returned to the room, the tension was palpable.

"I have a surprise for you all." I tried to keep a straight face. "Including you, Charlie."

Charlie looked at me, puzzled.

"Would you mind bringing over this tray with glasses?" I pointed with the bottle opener towards the sideboard.

Charlie obliged, and as he placed the tray before me, I placed the cold bottle of Dom Pérignon by the flutes and said to him, "Here is an envelope for you too."

"What? Why?"

"Just a little bonus for you so you won't be mad about changing my will now."

Charlie looked confused. He was at a loss for words, and it made me laugh.

"I've decided that I wanted to see you all use and enjoy the money while I'm still alive." I stared at each one. "Therefore, I'm giving you each a gift of one million dollars right now," I announced, "after tax! You may now open your envelopes. Current checks are there." I turned to Martin. "Would you mind opening the bottle so we can all celebrate?"

Everybody cheered, but Ava-May and David got up to hug me.

"You have no idea what this means to us," David said shakily.

"Yes, I do," I said quietly. "I called my doctor yesterday and asked about Gaucher disease. When I heard the price of the treatment, I changed my will."

David was startled.

Ava-May opened her mouth to say something but stopped. I saw tears in her eyes.

Martin waited his turn, and his hug was long and warm. I liked it.

Lawrence still sat at the table, his head in his hands. I wondered what he was going to do with one million dollars.

I had no idea what anybody's financial situation was, and it didn't concern me. Giving them gifts was unconditional.

But Andrew and Teresa had a surprise coming.

Chapter Fifty-Four

San Diego, 2011

AVA-MAY

MY mom didn't pray. Mom also didn't attend synagogue services but liked to meditate on her own in her garden, always ending her meditation by blessing the universe or jotting in her gratitude journal. A religion of her own; although she started lighting Shabbat candles on Friday nights after she married Dad, claiming that some traditions were valuable, especially when one lived in the Diaspora out of Israel. It was important to her especially when I was born and she had her own little family, she'd claimed. But still, no weekly visits to the synagogue on Shabbat.

Yet this Saturday was different. This Shabbat, she'd attend the synagogue services.

Three years had passed since David had met his aunt, and he'd changed somewhat. He was more relaxed; the treatment he was getting was effective, and he felt much better. He wasn't concerned so much about the cost of his medications, and he could even afford a personal trainer who helped him strengthen his muscles. His optimism had returned, his mood had improved, and he enjoyed his work at UCSD much more. I had my David back, and so did our children.

We also were less worried about finances, due to his aunt's huge gift, and so glad we didn't have to sell the house.

Aaron was preparing for his Bar Mitzvah, and David, embracing his roots, took much interest in those preparations, which bonded father and son even more. For his Bar Mitzvah project, David had suggested Aaron research and learn about Kindertransport.

I agreed and thought it would be important for Aaron to study that part of our history and learn about children whose parents had planned ahead to save them, and the pain of separation they all had endured. Many of his friends had never heard of Kindertransport.

Together, father and son read hundreds of testimonies of Kinder, as the survivors were called. It was not an easy read for a twelve-year-old, and I was very proud of David for taking the time to do this with our son.

One day, David surprised me. "Aaron has a brilliant idea," he said.

I waited for my husband to tell me more as I continued chopping vegetables for a salad.

"He wants to donate the money he'll receive as gifts to the Kindertransport Foundation." David sounded extremely proud.

I stared at him. "He does?" I whispered, a lump in my throat.

"Yes. And I have an idea too." David looked at me, his eyes shining and his smile somewhat secretive.

"And what's your brilliant idea?" I asked, putting down the knife.

"I'm converting."

I stared at him in shock. "To what?"

He was Jewish by birth, Catholic by upbringing; what was he planning?

"I'm converting to Judaism, officially," David said.

I had to think, wondering whether this was necessary. "You don't really have to, you know," I said, returning to my salad. "You're Jewish by birth."

"Yes, I know, but I want it to be official, legal, whatever you call it. I'm going to study Judaism, like any convert, and join Aaron by celebrating my Bar Mitzvah together with his."

"What?" I looked up.

That was a real surprise; never in a million years would I have expected this.

When David hugged me, I fell onto his chest. I kissed him a thousand times until he grabbed my face in both his hands and kissed me passionately back on my mouth.

On his father's next visit, David sat with Martin on the back patio. The sky was blue, and only two or three little white clouds floated by. Through the open kitchen back door, I saw David refilling Martin's glass with iced tea and heard him telling his father about his own Bar Mitzvah. I stayed inside to give them privacy but couldn't help eavesdropping.

My heart was beating fast. Was that the right way to tell a Catholic father that his son was converting to Judaism? I wasn't sure but had no control over it. It was David's decision.

"Look, Dad," I heard David explain while I was drying the dishes. "Mother was Jewish, so I'm Jewish too, right? I practiced Catholicism as a child because Mother made me, and I have no regrets. As an adult, I don't practice; you know that. You don't practice either." He took a deep breath. "Since we've met Aunt Elsie, I feel somewhat different. As if I've arrived at myself. As if the secret of my life has been discovered and resolved. I'm at peace."

David shifted in his seat to face his father. "For the first time in my life, I feel whole. Since the truth has come out, I am content. I feel closer to Mother than I've ever felt. I love her and understand her craziness more than ever, her fears and phobias. After learning about Kindertransport, her extreme suffering has touched my soul, bless her." He sounded emotional. "I wish Mother were here with us, and in a way, I feel she is."

My heart went out to David, so I walked out to the patio and joined them. David stood up to hug me, and I noticed tears in his eyes. David. Tears. I smiled as my own eyes filled up. David said to his father, "Marrying Ava-May was my destiny. I didn't understand nor fully appreciate it until recently." He kissed my cheek.

Martin smiled as David pulled a chair for me, and we both sat down.

David continued, "I would have lived my life differently if you hadn't placed Mother's photos in the paper, which led us to Aunt Elsie." A tear escaped and rolled down his cheek. "The DNA results confirmed everything, right? So you see, you had a hand in it too. You could have just discarded the photos and forgotten about it. But you didn't, and I'm most grateful."

Martin stood up to hug David.

I put my face in my hands and cried; my emotions overflowed.

I was extremely glad and proud of David, but I also knew that a rift could deepen between him and his brothers. Andy still hadn't accepted the fact that his mother was born Jewish. All the proof in the world couldn't change his mind. It was a matter of the heart, not the head.

Elsie shared with David that, because Andrew and Teresa hadn't bothered to come to see her in New York, Charles Northton sent them a letter with documents to state that Veronica and Susan would be getting a handsome gift when they each turn twenty-four.

She also said that she didn't want to give Andrew and

Teresa a gift, but their daughters were still Rose's granddaughters.

Larry was somewhat different. He'd realized that he hated LA, and his relationship with Lisa had gone south, so he'd returned to Oahu. He bought some bungalows last year and opened a fully equipped surfing shop, but drugs and alcohol had taken hold of him again, and he was running the business into the ground. Poor Larry. He must have felt guilty for being the bearer of shocking news to his mother, which had contributed to her death. It must have all been too much for him.

Martin was the only one visiting us, in spite of his advanced age—he'd just turned eighty-two—and he'd decided that the best use of the money he'd gotten from his generous sister-in-law would be to fly often and comfortably in first class to California.

He also mentioned that he had another trip in mind. Maybe to Europe.

Today was the day. After studying together for a year, Aaron's and David's special day had arrived. A double Bar Mitzvah of father and son. Each having an aliyah and a reading from the scroll of Torah before family and congregation.

Ten-year-old Ophi insisted on wearing a violet dress with cream trimming and cream-colored shoes. She looked like a mini model, her brown hair long and shining and her hazel eyes bright with excitement.

My midnight-blue dress and my mother's surf-green pantsuit threw a stunning contrast against the bordo-covered seats of the synagogue. Elsie, who sat in the row behind David and me, between Mom and Martin, glowed in a cream-and-gold dress. She looked regal.

All the men—David, Aaron, Dad, and Martin—wore dark blue suits and ties. I smiled at the uniformity.

But the surprise of the morning—as the synagogue started filling up and the rabbi was chatting casually with the head of the board, both standing on the bimah and waiting for people to settle—was a tall figure by the wide-open double doors, wearing a cream suit, a white shirt, and a dark blue, almost purple tie matching his eyes. His light hair was gathered in a ponytail.

Larry.

David jumped up and rushed to him. I thought I heard a collective gasp from my family as David and Larry hugged, surrounded by the light coming in from the open doors.

I looked at the double doors, still hoping. But just like at my wedding, a family member was missing. Andy had boycotted this celebration, like Rosalind had done fifteen years earlier. I had known to expect it, but still, it stung.

The rabbi cleared his throat. It was time. The cantor joined the rabbi with his acoustic guitar, and the ceremony began.

I was thankful for Conservative Judaism; I could sit with my husband, my son, my father, and other men and women in a mixed crowd. I appreciated sitting in the first row, having my children on either side of me, with David between Aaron and Larry.

Right behind us sat my parents, and next to them, Martin and Elsie.

Martin beamed with pride, but I noticed a sad glimmer in his eyes. He must have been missing Rosalind badly. If only she could have sat between him and Elsie...

I smiled as I thought of the gift he'd given his son and grandson. On the occasion of their celebration, Martin had promised to travel with them both to London, Vienna, and Jerusalem. David had voiced an interest in tracing his mother's voyage, and Martin was interested in visiting Yad Vashem, the Holocaust History Museum in Jerusalem. He had been talking about a trip to Europe for a while, and I was pleased he wasn't going alone.

A thought crossed my mind: Shouldn't they invite Elsie? This would be an important trip for her too.

Ophi and I couldn't go—I was in the midst of preparing for my PhD defense—but I knew that Ophelia's time for a meaningful trip would come one day too.

I peeked back and saw my mother point at an amazing gold bracelet Elsie wore on her wrist. It had beautiful shining diamonds. Mom commented how beautiful it was, and Elsie whispered, "Thank you. I wear it for special celebrations."

I counted. Six diamonds.

Martin glanced over and smiled. I guessed we both realized that Rosalind wasn't the only one to have been given diamonds by her family. I wondered what Martin had done with his.

Mom held a bag of individually wrapped candies in her lap, awaiting the end of the ceremony, when it was customary to throw the candy in the direction of the celebrated young man who had reached Jewish adulthood. I looked back again and saw her take out a piece of candy from the bag in her lap and hand it with a nod to Martin. I was surprised to see Elsie holding a candy bag of her own. She seemed to be staring at something that wasn't there. Maybe something far away in the past. I wondered if she was thinking back on this age-old tradition, maybe remembering something. She looked so serious and so sad, but she smiled at me when she caught my glance.

We were family.

Acknowledgement

'Kindertransport' is not a word we use daily. The transportation of children (kinder) immediately raises questions: Why are the children being transported? From where to where? Where are the parents, the adults, the guardians; the ones responsible for them, the ones who are supposed to protect them?

To learn more about the 1938-1939 Kindertransport, I read a dozen non-fiction books loaded with testimonials, researched the web, and visited Yad Vashem in Jerusalem.

I am most grateful to the following people who helped me bring this fictional story—a blend of hundreds of true stories—into the light.

Thank you to my 'midwives' Marni Freedman and Tracy J Jones, who helped me 'birth' my book with their early guidance and encouragement.

Many thanks to Abigail Holstein, Jennifer Silva Redmond, Jennifer Coburn, and Shannon Green, for their professional feedback.

Much love and gratitude to my first readers, Gil Sery, Hadas Propper, Annette Driesen, Yael Shalem, Sally Pollock, Kerry Ojeda and Pnina Gruer.

Special thanks to Paula Gilbert, Dr. Ruth Gilboa and Danielle Barger, for their professional advice.

Last but not least, I couldn't have done it without my wonderful editor Kathleen Furin, copy editor Chih Wang, formatting and cover designer Christa Yelich-Koth, and 'final eyes' Zan Strumfeld.

Thank you to Ellen Coppola and Leetal Elmaleh for the cover photograph.

Made in the USA
Las Vegas, NV
28 January 2025